COMPETITIVE
GRIEVING

NORA ZELEVANSKY

COMPETITIVE GRIEVING

A NOVEL

BLACK
STONE
PUBLISHING

The characters and events in this book are fictitious.
Any similarity to real persons, living or dead, is coincidental
and not intended by the author.

Printed in the United States of America

First edition: 2021
ISBN 978-1-09-400783-0
Fiction / General

1 3 5 7 9 10 8 6 4 2

CIP data for this book is available
from the Library of Congress

Blackstone Publishing
31 Mistletoe Rd.
Ashland, OR 97520

www.BlackstonePublishing.com

For Nick, with whom I daydreamed in tandem.

"Either he's dead or my watch has stopped."
                              —Groucho Marx

"Afraid of death? Not at all. Be a great relief. Then I wouldn't have to talk to you."
                              —Katharine Hepburn

"I have lost friends, some by death—others by sheer inability to cross the street."
                              —Virginia Woolf

PROLOGUE

What would I tell them about you? The ones who only knew your contours? You, as a paper doll on which to pin pictures?

What would I tell the ones who shared excited whispers over green juices the morning after? Who posted the news online with frowny faces and then moved on with their days?

What was the story I'd want them to know?

Was it of a little kid, spastic and unchecked, bouncing off walls? Was it of a teenage you, first gawky, then too cool?

Was it of us falling against each other during those struggling years? You, sitting next to me wrapped in a comforter, sleep and cigarettes on your breath, telling me you loved me as I shook my head and pronounced it untrue. For sure, it was not the story we'd all like to forget: You, alone. In that strange apartment. The one I never saw.

Would I tell them you were funny? Because you were. To me, one of the funniest people in the world. Would I tell them about your talent? Because it was boundless. But what good is something that loses all value in the dark? Would I tell them that you were adorable? Because you were. Some of the time to me; a lot of the time to others. Would I tell them that you were selfish but sweet? You had a soft spot for kindness in others but didn't require it of yourself.

I would not tell them that you loved me, although I know now that you did. In a way that was at once simple and complicated as hell. Like a sibling. Like a best friend. Like an object. Like an idea. Like a competitor. Like a book that you once loved and still carry from apartment to apartment when you move—formative, but no longer top of mind.

What hole did you leave in the world—aside, of course, from the one in my heart? What would I tell those strangers—even the ones who thought they were your friends?

What was the story of you?

CHAPTER 1

Today 10:46 a.m.

Stewart, about our conversation two nights ago. I may have overreacted. A little. Okay, fine, A LOT. I hate when you call me RESPONSIBLE like it's a synonym for LEPER. It makes me feel like that lame friend you keep around for when you're feeling lame too.

And I can just hear you saying, "You're not lame. You just act like you are." And that makes me mad all over again. ☹ Whatever.

Also, when you say you worry that if you weren't around, I'd become a "cat lady," it's obvious what that implies about my romantic prospects. Would you call a MAN a "cat lady"? #microaggression Why

is everyone always so disparaging of cats anyway?! The felines and I are all offended. 🐱🐱🐱

Wait—do you have a possible movie shooting somewhere far away? Is that what you're hinting at? The tropical resorts and exotic markets where you'll be living your best life, while I'm being subsumed by fur balls? I'm mad, but still—tell me! I want to live vicariously!

I guess that's your point. My vicarious life. Whatever. That doesn't mean you're right. 👇

Are you loving these emojis? I know you hate them. That just makes me want to use MORE. 🙀😣😖😫🙈

ANYWAY. I love you, even though you're a total jerk. ♡ Text me when you can. And by that I mean, get off your lazy ass and text me NOW.

Today 2:13 p.m.

Hey, you're probably shooting MM today, but just let me know you got this, okay? So, I know we're good

and I don't have to feel guilty about calling you an "asshat" behind your back.

Today 5:41 p.m.

Hello? Anyone? Bueller?

Today 7:03 p.m.

. . .

CHAPTER 2

The evening was too good to be true. I should have seen that from the get-go.

The previous night's finale of *The Bachelor* was recorded and queued up, and, by some miracle, I had avoided spoilers. A Postmates delivery girl named Mercedes, in heavy eyeliner and a crop top, had arrived at my building's entrance with enough vegan taco salad and tiramisu cupcakes for eight people (not that I'm vegan—only lactose intolerant. And a sugar addict).

I followed Mercedes' side-eye to my hoodie with the holes in both elbows and my baggy yoga pants that have never seen the inside of an actual yoga studio. I did kind of look like I had given up. *Oh well.*

Shivering against the cool air, I managed a "Thanks so much!"as I shut the door, and jogged upstairs to my apartment. Fall was beginning to descend—my favorite season for its smell of fireplace and artificial pumpkin-spice candles, and for that tug of melancholy that makes you feel engaged with the world.

I'd hurried home earlier than usual today from the coffee shop I treat as an office with visions of an evening spent cocooned on my couch. Now, I shook lavender essential oil into my diffuser, took a deep breath, and settled in to start the show!

As if sensing the imminent appearance of his TV namesake, my cat, Chris Harrison, jumped up beside me and manspread against my favorite woven throw pillow from the Brooklyn Flea (which he thinks is his). I shot him a chiding look, lifted the remote, pointed and . . . *riiiiiiing*!

I glanced down at my phone: "Mom." Always with the timing. We'd catch up later. I pressed Decline.

I raised the remote, pointed and . . . *riiiing*! *Damn!* My best friend Gretchen this time. I shook my head. *Love you, Gretch. But I have a date with reality TV destiny.* Decline.

Just as I was setting it down, the phone startled me with a more authoritative *bong*! *Omg. What the hell is happening?* Against my better judgment, I checked it: a DM from my high school classmate, Morgan. *Oh, hell no.*

I had abstained from social media for twenty-four hours to avoid being spoiled. No way I was going to let dumbass Morgan "Fluffy" Tobler—with her frizzy blond hair and empty eyes—screw this up for me. At least that was the Morgan I knew a decade ago. Last I heard, she was married to a gynecologist in New Jersey. I put my phone on airplane mode, then set it down with a warning glare.

A wave of unease settled over me. Was it a bad sign that I was this excited to be alone on my couch? I mean, I wasn't totally alone, I reasoned: I glanced over at cat Chris Harrison, who was licking his butt.

Ugh! I was letting Stewart get in my head with all that "cat lady" bullshit. Forget him! I would reappropriate the term "cat lady" and make it cool. Like "dog person." *You'd like her. She's awesome. She's a total cat lady.*

I shook my head clear, picked up the remote, and pointed it at the screen.

Brrrrring! My home phone. *Oh, my fucking god!* No one had that number but my mother. I let it ring—once, twice, three, four, five times—until it went to voicemail. Then I pressed "play" before anything else could interrupt me.

The human Chris Harrison—the host, the legend—was standing on a sound stage wearing a signature suit, no doubt from his own collection. He smiled tightly, his lips disappearing. "It's time for the conclusion of the most shocking season in *Bachelor* history. Tonight, we'll watch as our bachelor faces the most important decision of his life—"

"Whether or not to do *Dancing with the Stars*?" I grinned and took a forkful of fake taco meat. *Good one.*

"Will our bachelor find love? Or will his journey end in heartbreak?

Can Bethany F. come to terms with her fear of helicopters? Can Bethany M. recover from the hot tub incident? Or the other hot tub incident? Let's get right to—"

Bluuurg! My downstairs buzzer blared. *Why, God?!* This happened all the time—wrong bell. No way was I heading down three flights of stairs to redirect a confused delivery person.

Bluuuuuuuurg! The buzzer rang longer this time. "Decline!" I shouted out loud.

Back on screen, establishing shots of some all-inclusive Caribbean resort were interspersed with images of the bachelor standing alone, shirtless and pensive, on his hotel balcony, staring out toward the sunset. Perhaps in search of his five brain cells.

"Last week on *The Bachelor*—"

Bang, bang, bang! I nearly jumped out of my skin. Someone was knocking—no, *banging*—on my front door.

For real? How ill-equipped was this delivery guy? If the food looked good, I decided I was claiming it. That's what people get for entering the wrong information on Seamless! Also, I was enjoying the vegan salad and everything, but fried pork dumplings suddenly sounded really good.

Bang, bang, bang . . . bang!

Resigned, I exhaled, rose, and padded across the creaky hardwood floor. Unlocking the deadbolt, I swung the door open, remembering too late that I should have looked through the peephole to make sure I wasn't inviting a serial killer in.

What stood in my doorway was far more statuesque and familiar than I'd expected. And it was not bearing Chinese appetizers. "You're not a delivery man."

"Thanks for the update." As usual, Gretchen was pulling off some black asymmetrical cloak that would have looked on me like a costume for an apocalyptic Renaissance Fair. I told myself it was her extra six inches of height (at five foot ten) that had allowed her to rock "grown-up" clothing, while I still kept it basic in jeans, shearling-lined clogs, and faded T-shirts. Her dark curly hair spiraled out in every direction like a loudspeaker announcement: *I'm here! Take note! You may begin!*

I was suddenly annoyed. "What are you doing here?" It may have sounded more accusatory than intended.

"Hello to you too." Gretchen moved past me into the apartment, letting the front door slam behind her. She shed her wrap, throwing it over the arm of a chair, then turned in my direction and surprised me by taking my hand. Confused, I followed, as she led me over to the sofa to sit. "Hey, honey."

Gretchen never calls me "honey." What was happening? Was this about her work crush flirting with the donut truck girl again? I looked longingly at my taco salad.

"I figured you'd want company."

Really? Why? "Oh, okay. Great," I said. Gretchen stared at me until I added, "That's nice."

She furrowed her brow. "That's it?"

"I think so. Should there be more? I just wasn't expecting you."

"I know. But are you . . . okay?"

"With what?" I shifted under her intense stare. "Am I missing something? Why do I feel like I came into this movie in the middle?"

"Wren, I just wanted to see if you were okay. You wouldn't answer your phone. Or texts. Or FB messages. Or Insta DMs. I was worried!" At that moment, she seemed to notice my dinner spread and the paused TV. "But you look . . . fine."

"I was just trying to watch *The Bachelor* in peace! Can't a person stay off social media for twenty-four hours without—"

"Wait. Off social?" She dropped my hands, bringing a palm to her cheek. "You've been *off* the internet? Completely?"

"Yeah. All day. Digital detox! Analog self-care."

"Shit. I assumed you knew." She closed her eyes, her shoulders drooping. "Oh, Wren. You don't know."

"No! And no spoilers! I feel like he could pick Bethany F., but then Bethany M. has blonder highlights, so—"

"No, Wren." Gretchen was wearing her serious face: the one she wore when she found out her parents were getting divorced junior year of college, the one she wore when she realized we'd run out of Scotch on election night. "You don't understand."

"What? He doesn't like blonds? 'Cause I've thought about this and he does 'cause on the vineyard group date and during the Mexican wrestling date, he—"

"Wren." Gretchen's expression softened, her chin quivered. "Wren, listen. Please."

Something was not okay. Of course, I could see that. Gretchen was not acting normal. But the more I talked, the more time I could buy before she said whatever she was about to say. My throat felt tight; I tugged at the collar of my tee. I couldn't stall anymore. "G, what's wrong? Do I have cancer? Is the show canceled? Not necessarily in that order."

"Wren. It's Stewart."

"What's Stewart? Like, *my* Stewart?" I leaned in. "Wait! Is he the next bachelor? Are they doing one of those C-list celebrity seasons? 'Cause that's really a new level of cheese. But I wouldn't put it passed him. Ooh, do you think I'll get to meet Chris Harrison? Like the *real* one?" I turned to face my cat. "No offense."

Gretchen didn't crack a smile. "No, Wren. I'm sorry. I don't even know how to tell you this." She exhaled. "Stewart—he's dead."

I looked at her for a beat. "Wait, what?"

In that moment, the floor dropped away. Gretchen's face became a mass of fragmented colors. I had no comprehension. I kept waiting for more. *He's dead broke. He's dead tired. He's dead serious. He's dead—*

Pixilated Gretchen held up her phone, her eyes watery. On autopilot, I took it and watched as a *Deadline Hollywood* article loaded. The headline read, ACTOR STEWART BEASLEY DEAD AT AGE 36.

Stewart? Dead? But I just—But he's too—But no. My brain rejected the information. Surely there was some mistake?

Everything paused. Time. Drake blasting from a car speaker outside. My own breath. It all stopped for the world's longest millisecond while I struggled to process this impossibility. One minute ago, Chris Harrison was cleaning his privates. Now Stewart is just . . . gone?

I was blindsided. Wasn't bad news supposed to come in the middle of the night? When you're awakened from a dream—legs twisted in sheets— and can't assimilate reality?

A world without Stewart wasn't conceivable to me. He was like the sidewalk or the color green or wallpaper or bubblegum. He just existed—maybe somewhere faraway, maybe he disappeared for months on end and you forgot to notice—but you knew he was on the planet, somewhere. If you needed him.

"Oh, God. Oh, God. Oh, God." I barely recognized my own voice. How long had I been repeating that refrain? "I need to—" *What? I needed to what? Call Stewart? Let him know?*

Stewart. Gone. Could it be a hoax? At my core, I knew the answer was no. Hadn't I felt oddly worried when he didn't text me back? Was he already dead when I called him an "asshat"?

Oh, God. The shame. I peered up at Gretchen's familiar face—her high cheekbones, full lips, freckles against tan skin. "When? How? Where?"

"They're not releasing official information yet, but your mom called me when she was trying to find you. She talked to Stu's mother. It was an aneurysm. Last night. He just complained of a headache and then—" Gretchen snapped her fingers.

An aneurysm? Something in his brain erupted? That kind of thing happened to people I didn't know—a kid at a nearby elementary school; a coworker's friend's wife. *An aneurysm.* I realized I was feeling almost relieved. What had I thought it would be? Murder? "In LA?"

"I guess? Didn't you say he was staying in the network's temporary housing?"

A nameless, faceless apartment: blank walls, generic Marilyn Monroe and *Casablanca* prints, popcorn ceilings, beige cabinetry, a chipped sink, the dry heat of the Valley.

"Was he with anyone?"

Gretchen shook her head. "It sounds like he was alone."

It was exactly as he would have feared, then. We had talked with horror about the lonely ladies no one finds for weeks, who get eaten by their cats. *Cat ladies.* I was definitely going to have trouble making that cool.

I pictured my mother's condolence call to Stewart's mother, Helen Beasley. The women hadn't been friends in decades. They probably hadn't even spoken since Stewart and I were in middle school together. They weren't fond of each other. But now, with this, past slights were meaningless. I knew I should call my mom, but I didn't want to—not yet. Hearing her "careful" voice would break me. The slow way she'd say my name.

"I'm so sorry, bug," Gretchen was saying. "I know how much you loved him. *Love* him." She wrapped her arms around me and hugged me for a long time then, showing no signs of letting go. Her cashmere sweater smelled safe and knowable, like the Jo Malone perfume she'd worn forever—vanilla and fireplace.

Unexpectedly, I felt Gretchen's shoulders begin to quake in place of my own as she released a quiet sob. I smoothed her hair. We stayed like that for several minutes, me comforting her.

Finally, we parted. Is it weird that, even with my closest people, I sometimes feel awkward in those intimate moments? I didn't quite know where to look. Gretchen wiped stray eyeliner from beneath her eyes and tears from her flushed cheeks.

"Are you okay?"

"Yeah," she said with a shuttering sigh. "You know, I didn't really like him. He was *your* friend."

Against the odds, I laughed. Sharp and loud. "I know."

"It's just, I didn't think he was a very good friend to you. After all those years. The way he moved in and out of your world. The way he always criticized your decisions and soaked up all the light."

"I know."

"And he was pompous!"

"He could be, yeah."

"And he thought he was *so* adorable. And it was like, oh, God forbid Wren make any friends after high school! Like God forbid you connect with anyone other than him—or have a boyfriend! And I know you think we competed for your attention, but he didn't own you, you know?! I mean—"

"G. He's dead. I think you can put the argument to rest too."

Gretchen pressed her lips together. "Right. Sorry."

I lifted my legs up onto the couch and hugged my knees to my chest. "So why the tears for the pompous jerk?"

"'Cause it's still terrible and so, so sad. His poor mother. His poor family. Poor you. It's just a shame and a waste and . . . hey, here's a better question: why no tears from you?"

I blinked my dry eyes, trying to ignore my thumping heart. "I have no idea. Shock?" *'Cause I'm defective?*

"Totally shock," Gretchen nodded. "The shit will really go down later. Don't you worry."

I wondered. I knew from past experience—when my grandfather died, for example—that I tended to go quiet in the face of others' grief. It might have been Gretchen's tears that staunched my own. As my parents sat at his hospital bedside, heads bent and faces damp, I watched from the doorway, hyper-conscious of how artificial the scene felt, half expecting the cast of some medical drama like *Grey's Anatomy* to appear. It felt so scripted; I couldn't connect to the catharsis.

"Everyone does grief differently," my parents assured me, when I confessed to feeling numb. "This is how *you* cope." People always want to let you off the hook when you've suffered a loss.

A loss. My loss.

"Stewart. Gone," I repeated, hoping to make the news penetrate. "A world without Stewart." I rubbed my forehead with my palm like a genie might pop out and impart some wisdom—or a different outcome. "I don't remember life before we met. I can't believe it's true. Just something bursts in his brain, something maybe waiting there since he was born, and that's it? His life is just over? Irreparably? It doesn't make sense."

"It's so hard to believe; he was larger than life. People always say that, but he really was. I guess it's just a lesson to never say no to that third martini . . . and sixth beer. Make the most of your time while you can." Gretchen slumped back against the couch cushions, her eyes finding the TV screen. "Speaking of which, you still watch *The Bachelor*?"

"You know I do." I rolled my eyes. "I named my cat, 'Chris Harrison, so.'"

"Unbelievable. You look so smart."

"Really? You're going to give me shit? Right now?"

Gretchen smirked. We went silent, the normalcy of our banter disorienting.

I exhaled, trying to find my place in the moment. "Stewart. Just gone?

Forever? Sorry. I'll probably need to repeat that eight thousand more times before it begins to sink in."

Gretchen bit her lip as her eyes welled. "Don't apologize. Whatever you need."

I felt empty. Like I needed to do something, to fix things, but there was nothing to do. The heat in the apartment kicked on, banging like a baby with kitchen pans. I toyed with a string hanging from the wrist of my sweatshirt. I thought about Stewart, the way he would shrug and smile self-consciously when he made a good joke. The way his body shook when he laughed. I don't know why.

After a minute or so, Gretchen gestured toward the TV, a frozen frame of the bachelor seated on a volcanic rock, pondering love, life, and the efficacy of spray tans. "So this is the reunion show, right? 'Cause he already picked the brunette from Alabama yesterday?"

I looked at Gretchen. I sighed. "Spoiler alert."

A few feet away, Chris Harrison the cat puked on the rug.

The evening was too good to be true.

CHAPTER 3

Stewart. Gone.

CHAPTER 4

A small funeral was planned for two days later. I doubted Helen Beasley was feeling conciliatory enough to put my parents on the guest list. Old habits die hard—even when a person has too. I understood, but going alone sounded like torture.

Stewart's older sister, Kate, had reached out via email with the details. Like a freak, I got a jolt of excitement when I first saw her name in my inbox, before I remembered that I'm an adult now and she was emailing because my best friend is dead. I had idolized Kate as a kid. Her wavy red hair and red lips reminded me of Ariel from *The Little Mermaid*. That would have been enough to win my undying affection, but also, even before Stewart's father, Ted, started making so much money, Helen had transformed the Beasley's apartment into something out of a catalogue and her daughter's room into what seemed to me like a fantasyland. Kate had a full-on canopy bed, the kind with an excess of lace-trimmed pillows and dust ruffles, a crystal chandelier in the shape of a boat hanging from her ceiling and one of those life-size stuffed horses from FAO Schwartz standing guard in a corner. As far as I was concerned, no one actually owned toys like that. They only existed as kid bait, to be ogled through store windows.

Kate and Stewart bickered a ton—normal sibling stuff. She didn't want her stupid little brother in her face. But sometimes, on slow Sundays when no one better was around, she would take me by the hand and lead me away from Stewart's clutter of superheroes and smelly Nikes into the land of all things pink. We would bake muffins in her Easy-Bake Oven or have a tea party with her American Girl dolls. After the playdate ended, when I returned to my own ordinary bedroom, the expressions on the faces of my stuffed animals, piled high on the twin bed, looked sadder than before. The art supply bins looked more used. Later, as teens, Kate gave me and Stewart our first pot, put us on VIP lists for parties, talked trash with me about mean boys.

It had been more than a decade since we'd seen each other. Maybe the last time had been at Stewart's twenty-first birthday party? He was still a struggling actor then. He allowed his mother to throw him this tasteful dinner party at La Bernardin—all wrong. Afterward, he and I had snuck off to a nearby Bennigan's and gotten wasted and sick on whisky shots and chili fries.

Stewart. Gone.

I stared at Kate's message:

Wren, of course by now you've heard about Stewart. I'm afraid we lost him on Monday night. We're still trying to wrap our minds around all of this. I wanted to make sure to give you the funeral details (that feels so surreal to type—I wish I could delete it):

Riverside Memorial Chapel
180 West 76th Street
Thursday; 10:00 a.m.

At my mother's request, we've kept the list intimate, but if you know of anyone significant who we might have missed, please pass on the details.

I look forward to seeing you. I wish it was under better circumstances.

Best,
Kate

Riverside Memorial Chapel. *Of course.* For the Upper West Side Jewish set, it's the place to go when you're dead. I'd attended funerals there for my own grandfather, an ex-boyfriend's great aunt, a close friend's mother. I tried to picture walking in there to say goodbye to Stewart. I shut my eyes against the image. Despite my flight instinct, I reminded myself that the communal ritual was a chance for catharsis created to help mourners take their first shaky steps forward.

I adjusted my position on the couch cushions for the eight-hundredth time, my iPhone in hand. Every possible response to Kate's email seemed wrong. How do you express sadness without appropriating the family's tragedy? I didn't want her to feel like she had to comfort *me*.

"I'm sorry for your loss" seemed too formal.

"How can he be gone?" seemed too personal.

"This must be a difficult time" seemed too trite.

"I called him an 'asshat' the last time we spoke" didn't seem quite right either.

I also couldn't think of anyone they might have forgotten who should be invited. Stewart kept in better touch with our high school friends than I did. He had more tolerance for their antics as time passed. I talked to him regularly, but only saw the rest of our classmates at reunions and chance run-ins on the subway (when I didn't have time to hide). I'd come to drinks with his various hangers-on throughout the years, too, but had no clue who had stayed in the fold. These groups seemed to swarm in and out of his life like seasonal insects: his college friends, his LA friends, his famous friends. The relationship Stewart and I had was independent of all that, separate from his TV career and my grant writing job, from his many girlfriends and my occasional boyfriends, from his poker buddies and my book club ladies. (Why did I sound like such a loser in the unraveling of this?)

Our friendship, once we chose it for ourselves, had been its own entity. We'd known each other since birth, of course. Our families had been next-door neighbors, on the same floor of the same prewar apartment building, and our mothers had been inseparable while pregnant, sucking on lemon wedges to quell morning sickness and bonding over itchy bellies. But once Stewart's family moved to Central Park West, just blocks but also, in Helen's case, a world away, our mothers lost touch. Stewart and I drifted apart, too, despite being at the same school. Maybe we even avoided each other out of embarrassment, knowing that—literally and metaphorically—somewhere there existed photos of us in the bath together as babies. We had nothing in common—whatever that means when you're six or seven years old—and we never hung out, until one day our third-grade teacher, Mrs. Thompson, asked me to help Stewart with grammar homework during a "choice" period.

Resigned, we sat beside each other at a round wooden table, stained with colored ink. We were studying the Middle Ages and someone had left a dog-eared copy of *The Once and Future King* behind.

"What part of speech is 'running'?" I prompted.

"It's the part where I go play basketball instead of sit here."

"It's a verb. Because it's about action: I run, I'm running, I ran."

"As in, I'm running away from here to play basketball. Because grammar sucks."

I tried not to laugh. Grammar was serious business. But Stewart was charming, even then.

Our roles stayed the same from then on: I was cast as the voice of reason. He was the fun one.

Now, I was going to his funeral.

So far, the day had been a blur. One minute I was shutting the gate to my brownstone building, the next I was a block from the funeral home on Seventy-Sixth and Broadway, waiting for Gretchen, whom I had pleaded with to escort me. It felt like one of those strange, jittery mornings before taking the SATs or leaving on an early flight, unease humming under the surface.

I was dreading seeing Helen Beasley, especially. Poor Helen. She and Stewart were particularly close. What could I possibly say to his grieving mother that wasn't all wrong? The truth is, she had never been a huge fan of mine. She always seemed disappointed that Stewart had chosen me as a close friend.

I searched for Gretchen among the throngs of athleisure-clad mothers pushing strollers past towering apartment buildings. Five years ago, my parents moved out of my childhood two-bedroom, just blocks away. So exiting the subway up here was an emotional test on a good day, the smell of Gray's Papaya hot dogs wafting from the corner of Seventy-Second Street to deliver a sense memory of freer days. Today, the nostalgia was unbearable.

Stewart was everywhere. In Needle Park, which hadn't seen a hypodermic needle since Mayor Bloomberg. In the revolving space that was once an HMV in the days of CDs. In the elegant Apple Bank building where we played "jewel heist" while our parents conferred with tellers. I could barely breathe.

A skinny man, wearing a crumpled brown suit and a frown, caught my eye as he headed in my direction. Even from a distance, I could see that his hair was styled in the modern-day equivalent of a comb-over (spiky with product to disguise thinning). A scruffy Brooklyn beard did nothing to compensate. It took a moment for me to place that scowl: Keith Farber! *Of course.* Stewart had been tight with him since eighth grade—God knows why. Keith was so competitive, he'd probably even find a way to hate on Stewart's death: *An aneurysm? What a cop-out!*

An aneurysm. I couldn't stop thinking about the abruptness; your brain combusting from within. *Time's up.*

Keith was drawing closer. Just before he might have spotted me, I dove into the entryway of a nearby Duane Reade, pretending to be absorbed in my phone. The stench of pee wafted from all corners. I gagged.

"Why do you look so sketchy?" A voice rang out from a foot away.

I jumped, like a gun had gone off, and spun around, ready for . . . what? A run-in with a harmless, if annoying, high school acquaintance? Keith wasn't *that* bad. Or at least he hadn't been when Stewart was around to kick me under the table in commiseration.

The voice belonged to Gretchen, thank goodness, immaculate before me in a draped black jumpsuit and ankle boots.

I looked down at my own dress: Rebecca Taylor from a million summers ago and, okay, gray not black. Sorting through my closet, I'd discovered a deficit in "death" clothes. In the reflection of the pharmacy window, I looked pale. I examined my honey-colored hair—a bit too long—and my yellow-green eyes that sometimes were my favorite feature and sometimes made my dark circles more pronounced. Eyeliner was already smudged below one corner. I did my best to wipe it clean with the side of my hand. *Don't touch your face.* My mother's voice inside my head.

"Are you okay?" Gretchen's furrowed brows said she thought no.

"I'm fine." I toyed with a tassel that hung from my bag's zipper. "I guess I'm just nervous to see people. And deal. With the sadness and whatnot."

"And whatnot." She pursed her lips. "Have you cried yet?"

"Why?"

"So, no?"

"Why does that matter?"

"It doesn't. I'm just waiting for the moment of recognition."

"Recognition?"

"Yes. I'm just waiting for you to realize on a cellular level that one of your closest people just died and it's okay to be sad. You know, instead of psychotically anxious."

"I'm plenty sad, thank you. Now please act like the security blanket you're here to be."

"Okay!" She held her palms up in surrender, then took my hand. "Done."

Next thing I knew, we were pulling the glass funeral parlor doors open and being suctioned inside by heat. Polished cherrywood, bronze fixtures, and carpeting abounded. The walls were decorated with bright, abstract prints, referencing Old Testament stories. The permeating hush, a particular brand of quiet, reminded me of arriving at synagogue for bat mitzvahs as a preteen. And, all at once, I felt like I should have been arriving with Stewart instead of for him, pretending not to notice the oddity of a thirteen-year-old him in a suit, smelling like cologne. This felt like a poorly scripted performance. The way I was walking, with unnatural posture.

Except this was real. This was *real. Stewart. Gone. Forever.*

A bearded man in a boxy Men's Warehouse blazer stood in front of an elevator, directing people. I opened my mouth to speak, but failed.

"We're here for a service," Gretchen told him.

He gave a somber nod. "For whom?"

"Stewart Beasley." His name came out like a croak, against my throat's will. Surely this man would correct me—wrong name, wrong place, a case of mistaken identity.

"Third floor." Another day, another service, for him.

Once off the elevator, Gretchen and I shuffled with a crowd toward the chapel like patrons at a Broadway show. I knew I needed to buck up, but my throat was closing against the smell of expensive perfume, breath mints, and something rancid—grief. There were no open windows in sight.

I stood on tiptoe to check the progress ahead. One by one, people walked through gargantuan wooden doors and disappeared. I recognized a girl with brown curls and rosy doll cheeks as Stewart's younger cousin—Taryn, maybe? The last time I'd hung out with her, Stewart and I were teenagers and she was maybe eight. Now, so many years later, she appeared to me like a bizarro-land version of herself, face distorted and long.

She was looking down at the carpet. Everyone was looking down at the carpet. And it was so quiet, I had this impulse to shout. Stewart would have felt the same. Momentarily disoriented, I look for him in the crowd. *Stewart.*

Suddenly, my stomach churned like I was about to throw up. The back of my neck flashed hot beneath my hair; I stopped midstep. Gretchen squeezed my hand, sensing my panic. I tried to focus on the physicality of the moment—her fingers, still cold from outside. All around me, people sniffled; why couldn't I cry?

And everyone looked familiar. Did I actually recognize Stewart's relatives or did all families look alike? The great aunts in their oversized necklaces and "funky" colorful glasses; the preteen girls with their barrettes and jersey dresses; the nerdy young male cousins with their side parts and oversized puppy feet.

Ow! I jammed my thigh into the corner of a table, which I then realized held the sign in book. Rubbing my leg and cursing silently, I bent over to add my name. Holding that pen in my hand, I had a perverse urge to sign it like a middle school yearbook: *Have a great summer! Wish we'd hung out more! Too late now! Stay cool!*

Senior year of high school, fatigued from signing so many yearbooks, Stewart had scrawled something lame and perfunctory in mine and I'd complained, so he wrote a separate note and stuffed it between the pages just before I left to walk home that day: "I am amazed every day that someone as _____ as you, finds me as _____ as you do." I always remember that line because I knew what he meant. 'Cause I felt the same.

When I stood back up, my gaze rested on a face I did know well: James

Hernandez. As children, Jimmy was the third member of our tight trio. Now, he and I locked eyes. A look of recognition crossed his features—those far-set dark eyes and strong brows. We might have been the only two people in the room for our connection in that moment. He nodded, his lips curving into a tiny sad smile, almost like a frown. I nodded back, pressing my lips together. Tears began to flood his eyes. He looked away, then someone taller walked in front of him, obfuscating my view. I wanted to shove that person aside so I could see him again.

Fuck. This was real. My chest tightened.

"There's Jimmy," I murmured, though I could no longer see him.

"Where?" snapped Gretchen.

Right. I forgot. They had history, Gretchen and Jimmy. They hated each other, except when they were drunk and making out. I pretended as if I hadn't heard the question. I didn't feel like thinking about Jimmy that way right now. I wanted to think about the Jimmy I knew as a child, the one with whom I'd sat on brownstone steps and teased Stewart about some flashy new T-shirt; the one who teamed up with Stewart to mock my love of Joni Mitchell. The one who came to me for girl advice.

Gretchen and I neared the door to the chapel. When we finally entered, I was staring at a ripped seam at the back of some man's sports jacket. I figured he didn't know about the tear. People murmured as they slid into pews. The man in front of me moved off to the left down an aisle and, suddenly, before I was prepared, I was standing almost face to face with Helen Beasley.

She had formed a receiving line in a gap between the back and front sections. Of course, even in her most shattering moment, the woman would do things properly. I scanned the room for Stewart's father, Ted. He was standing at the far end of the space with other men in suits—probably business associates. He was always standing at the edges of rooms with business associates. His expression was impassive. His hair looked especially gray.

"My dad. Everyone's favorite Care Bear." I remembered Stewart delivering the line like he'd practiced it, pushing his glasses up the bridge of his nose, a habit that persisted long after the frames were replaced by contacts. We must have been twelve years old or so at that BBQ at their

Cape Cod house. We had snuck pineapple juice and spiced rum cocktails. My face was pulsing with warmth from the liquor and fear of being caught, as I reclined in a patio chair with my knees up, scratching a trio of mosquito bites. We watched his father from a distance across the green lawn. We were always watching him from a distance, it seemed to me, to the point where I could barely picture him close up.

Ted Beasley wasn't an unkind man. But when he bothered to notice, he looked at us kids with confusion, as if he couldn't figure out where we'd come from or what we wanted. Once, during dinner at their apartment, he'd set out these strange guava disks that he'd brought back from a business trip to China. I was the only one who liked them and told him so—perhaps with more enthusiasm than they merited. He was making an effort, and no one in his family seemed to care. After that, he brought some back for me from every trip to Asia. That was pretty much the extent of our relationship. I couldn't begin to imagine his experience of Stewart's death.

Helen was dressed in elegant black, her white bob coiffed. She was always small, but now, instead of delicate, she looked frail. She was talking to a plump, middle-aged woman, one of the great aunts, judging by her eggplant-colored caftan and enormous earrings. The woman was whispering right into her stoic face, barely giving her space to breathe. How horrible to have to be polite on a day like this. For a moment, Helen appeared to buckle, and I almost reached out, but the woman held her up while she righted herself. Then, reluctantly, the woman moved on.

Only a couple people were in front of me now. My heart thumped. I rehearsed possible things to say: "He was the best. I already miss him. How are you holding up? So this is what devastation feels like." None of it was right. Helen and I didn't commiserate; we'd never had that rapport. It felt almost condescending to express sympathy to someone who seemed so powerful. I bit my lip, tasting my sticky rose gloss. The two people in front of me delivered some quick words to Helen and moved on as a unit, exposing me.

It was my turn to step forward. Gretchen stepped back, giving us space. Helen wiped her cheeks with the side of her hand and then looked up and met my gaze. Tired blue eyes. Probing blue eyes. For a moment I felt like she couldn't compute, but then they focused as recognition set in.

"Wren." She said my name without inflection. Like a fact. Her chin wobbled. Was this bastion of strength about to cry at the sight of me?

"Helen. Mrs. Beasley. I'm—"

A monotone voice rang out, "Please find your seats."

I turned to see an older gentleman in a yarmulke standing at the podium across the room, speaking into a microphone. "We are a large group in a small space, so please move down if you have an empty seat next to you and allow others to sit."

I turned back to Helen, who, in that brief pause, had sharpened back into her old self.

"Helen," I began again.

"Good of you to come, Wren." She pursed her lips. "Stewart would have wanted you to be here." Then, before I could reply, she turned and walked in the direction of her seat.

I tracked her with my eyes as she made her way down the aisle, people's hands grazing her shoulders and arms, offering support, like she was a Torah paraded around at high holidays. She continued all the way to the front, past the pews, and laid her hand on what I realized—with alarm that rang through my entire body—was a shiny casket. *Stewart.*

I teetered on my heels. Gretchen caught me. And together we went to find a seat.

CHAPTER 5

Stewart,

The day you died, I became a funeral planner.

I don't mean that literally. I'm not planning any Indigo Girls–themed events for you—don't worry. I did get an email from Auburn Prep's alumni rep asking me to unearth old photos for a commemorative write-up in the newsletter and on their Facebook page. I know the school was always asking you for favors: tickets to your latest play for the fundraising raffle or an appearance at "career day." You avoided them like they might enlist you in jury duty or serve you a summons, so the postmortem behavior is consistent in a way you would have appreciated. I couldn't resist: I sent them that photo of you with the corn dog at Coney Island, which will no doubt get lots of "likes" online. It would get even more if people knew that you ate two more corn dogs and cotton candy after that, then puked in line for the Cyclone. #truth

No, what I mean by "funeral planning" is that I've been playing this involuntary game in my head since you've been gone: Whenever anyone talks to me—especially about how I'm feeling or more often about how they're feeling—instead of listening, I find myself choosing lunch spreads and songs for their funerals. What comes to mind is not the event I would want for them so much as what I feel in my bones it should actually be. On the music front, Leonard

Cohen's "Hallelujah" and Adele's "Hello" are often top contenders, although I know you would have chosen something more obscure by a band with "The" in the name.

This make-believe event planning has become constant. For receptions, I envision platters of smoked meats, lox, crudités, and cookies or entire old-school Italian spreads with meatballs and chicken Parmesan (unwieldy for a party, I know, but so delicious!). Did you know that Southerners traditionally bring deviled eggs and Jell-O molds when someone dies? My grandfather's Mexican nurse dropped off empanadas after Papa passed away. At your funeral reception, I wonder what the catering will be? Something refined, no doubt, courtesy of your mom. Caviar and blinis?

Sometimes, my plans don't stop at the food. As I lie in bed at night, one knee poking out from beneath my too-warm comforter, I plan touching but funny eulogies for everyone from Gretchen to my dad to our old history teacher, Mr. Harvey. Remember him? The guy with the giant 1970s glasses? I think he would have liked fondue and Jackson Browne's "Late for the Sky."

I plan how I'd find out that each person died too: a call, a text, a wildly inappropriate Snapchat, a premature social media post; from a mutual friend, from a family member, from an apologetic police officer showing up at my door.

I plan my reactions. My shock. My dismay. My aftermath. I plan. I plan. I plan for things one cannot plan. Like losing you.

CHAPTER 6

The service was cookie-cutter and so removed from anything to do with Stewart that I kept having to remind myself why I was there, awash in shaky exhalations and platitudes. Plenty of people were weeping, though, so maybe I was missing something. It wouldn't be the first time.

An older rabbi—his face lined with broken capillaries—stood at the bimah, punctuating boilerplate statements about losing loved ones too soon with Hebrew we all pretended to follow in the prayer books. Stewart would have been bored out of his mind, knees furiously bouncing. Up front, Helen sat with ramrod posture beside two small children, who I assumed were Stewart's niece and nephew. I couldn't tell how any of them were handling things from the back.

Toward the middle of the service, I zoned out and planned the rabbi's funeral:

CAUSE OF DEATH: Heart attack. Too much schmaltz.

AFTER-DEATH RITUAL: Burial.

SERVICE: A small private affair. Large memorial for his congregants a month later at the synagogue—so well-attended that the staff has to take down the temporary ballroom dividers. Presided over by his cantor and a chum from rabbinical school. (The two buddies almost got kicked out after that prank with the yarmulkes in the sukkah hut.)

PROCESSIONAL MUSIC: Chopin at the family event. At the memorial, the kids from the synagogue singing "Papa Can You Hear Me?" from *Yentl*.

MEMORIAL BUFFET: Brisket, kugel, three bean salad—the whole megillah. The kind of spread that demands you find a chair and sit down to eat. The kind of meal his grandmother used to make in the shtetl and his wife whipped up when important synagogue donors came to dinner. Maybe rainbow cookies at the end, the kosher ones covered in chocolate with raspberry jam and marzipan in the layers. I pictured him as one of those weird people who actually like those. (That's not a judgment: I'm one of those weird people too.)

I was jolted out of my reverie as the cantor took center stage. His voice was deep and powerful and commanded attention. Around his neck, he wore a garish tallit, too colorful for the occasion. I pictured him snapping at his wife in a panic that morning, "What do you mean my cream tallit is at the dry cleaner?!"

CAUSE OF DEATH: Tragic cancer.

AFTER-DEATH RITUAL: Burial. Obviously.

SERVICE: Medium-sized. Some congregants, some friends and family, definitely the guys from the interfaith softball league.

PROCESSIONAL MUSIC: "I Dreamed a Dream" from *Les Mis*. (I have a theory that most cantors are frustrated musical theater and opera singers.)

MEMORIAL BUFFET: Traditional. Bagel and lox spread. Not from a
high-end appetizing place like Russ & Daughters; just
from the bagel place he liked around the corner. Despite ribbing from his coworkers, the guy loved a blue-
berry bagel. Good ol' whoever-he-was.

The cantor's death made me sad to think about. He looked about
forty-five years old. I'm sure he had small children. I pictured their confused
faces and felt depressed. Then I remembered that he wasn't actually dead.
Stewart. Stewart was dead.

I tried to focus back on the actual service. The cantor was beginning
to sing a song I recognized, lodged in the back of my mind from countless family services as a kid. I don't know why, but as an adult any time I
hear the Hebrew songs from my childhood, I get emotional. Maybe it's
because they take me back to such a specific time and place in my personal
history: sitting in uncomfortable mauve-upholstered chairs, counting the
stars of David on the stained glass, waiting for songs to liven things up.
I was young; my parents were young. So, there's nothing like a rousing
rendition of "Bim Bom" to bring tears to my eyes.

As the cantor's voice gathered steam, filling the room and our chests,
my eyes welled. But I wasn't on the verge of crying for Stewart. Not really.
I was triggered by the passage of time—how brutal that reality can be.

It went on like that. I must have planned funerals for every mourner
within a five-chair radius. I kept waiting for a eulogy, during which we
all got to laugh and cry over stories that were "just so Stewart," but none
came. I guess Helen hadn't wanted that. If she had, I might have been
one of the people invited to speak. And it occurred to me that the Jewish
tradition of burying people within three days of their deaths doesn't leave
a lot of prep time. I guess it's designed to help people move on as quickly
as possible.

As I watched Keith emote from a couple of rows away, I decided that,
on second thought, speeches from friends would have been a terrible idea.
His expression was just a hair too pained. Maybe that wasn't fair. Maybe
he really was devastated. The dark circles under his eyes were certainly

cavernous. His neck looked extra bloated. But his repose—head cocked to one side, eyes squinting—was hard to buy.

I let my gaze sweep over the crowd. Stewart and his gaggle of followers. A little too much makeup. A little too much attention paid to hairstyles and blowouts. A little too much money spent on simple black dresses from Net-a-Porter—the Savile Row suits, the stacked rings. Some punctuated sobs for effect; a tissue requested at an unnatural volume. This was a funeral, yes, but it was also a social event. Even Gretchen had called me the night before for an outfit conferral.

"How formal do you think it will be?"

"It's a funeral, G. The dead don't care."

"Yes, but how formal a funeral? I'm-headed-back-to-work formal? I've-taken-the-day-off-for-this formal? I'll-wear-heels-all-day-in-solidarity-with-your-pain formal?"

"I-don't-care-what-you-wear formal."

"But—"

"Gretchen."

"Okay, fine. In honor of Stu and his propensity for overpriced clothing that looked sloppy as hell, I'll keep it subtle." She couldn't resist the dig.

I zoned out for the rest of the service, fixing my eyes on a stained glass window above the stage that depicted some kind of boat journey. I felt strange and numb and all I could think about was whether Stewart's uncle would want sushi or a Greek buffet at his funeral. Did they even allow spanakopita or raw fish at Jewish receptions, assuming it wasn't shellfish? Was yellowtail sashimi with jalapeños and ponzu sauce too awkward to share? That, and I kept saving up all the details I wanted to share with Stewart: the overdetermined outfits; the drama school friends who sat too close to his well-known agent; one random girl who I didn't recognize, doing such a dramatic performance of grief, that she drew curious glances even from the immediate family.

Eventually, it was over and people began to file out. And I thought, *Really? That's it? That's the celebration of Stewart's life?* Since Stewart's death, a few morning talk and E! news shows had done segments on him, though I hadn't watched. I wasn't ready. But those seemed to be over too. Now what? Just life without my friend? A telethon about aneurysm prevention?

How *did* you prevent aneurysms anyway? How did I know that I didn't have one now, just waiting to implode? My dull headache grew more intense. I needed to get out. I mumbled something to Gretchen about heading outside, which she may or may not have heard, and then pushed my way through the crowd to the door, eyes downcast to avoid meeting someone I knew. I had almost made it out the main doors and onto the street when I felt a hand settle on my upper arm.

"Wren."

Caught. I turned out around and found myself face to face with a woman I didn't recognize. She was middle-aged and frumpy in an ill-fitting black sweater and calf-length cigarette skirt, sapped of any sexiness by clunky boots. She was clutching a wool coat. Her blue eyes reminded me of someone—who was it?

Stewart.

And then I noticed her wavy red hair, chopped into a bob. "Kate."

It had been so long, I would never have recognized her. In my head, she was still the older, cooler twenty-something sister. The last time I saw her, she was leaving Stewart's birthday for some bar with an impenetrable list. She had been young; she had been electric; she had been wearing a miniskirt. This woman was—a woman. With children. And unchecked hips. Maybe a minivan. Of course, I knew that. She had moved out of the city with her wife Meryl years ago, when she was pregnant with their first.

"I'm not sure what upsets my mother more," Stewart had said, "that my sister is a lesbian or a suburbanite. Actually, I do know: definitely the suburban thing. And that's taking into account the phase when she stopped shaving her armpits."

Kate shot me a smile, at once warm and sad, and I felt guilty. Why was I judging her outfit or how much she had aged, which we all do? Her brother had just died. Her brother. *Stewart. Gone.* "I'm so sorry, Kate. I'm really so sorry. I can't express how—"

She rubbed my shoulder and nodded, eyes red-rimmed and flooding. "It's so nice to see you though, Wren. Have you been well?"

"I've been fine. Not great today." I felt like I should say more but could think of nothing to add. I had no kids, no life partner, no recent exciting work news, no items on the checklist to present as pleasantries. Everything in my life was status quo, fine. I could hear Stewart saying, "Low bar."

"How is Meryl?" I asked. "How are the kids?" Had she kept her American Girl dolls and rose tea set for her son and daughter?

"Oh," Kate glanced around as if the children might appear behind her at any moment to yank on that pencil skirt. "Did you see them inside? Meryl took them out halfway through. They were starting to lose it. It's all a bit intense."

"I'm sure. My God." I hadn't even noticed Meryl slipping out. I guess parents get good at that kind of thing, nipping agitation in the bud before it becomes a ruckus.

"They're handling it, I think," Kate was saying. "Telling them was horrible. Sabrina, you know, she's older, so she gets it more and is just very sad. She asked me yesterday if I was going to die too. But Matthew keeps assuring me that Stewart will wake up. He says, 'Don't be sad, Mommy. Uncle Stu probably just took Benadryl. Remember how that makes me sleepy?' Or he'll say, 'Mommy, maybe Uncle Stu is just *acting* dead.'"

"That's awful. I'm so sorry you all have to go through this."

"Yeah, me too."

There was a heavy silence that I felt compelled to fill. "But, otherwise? Life in Westchester . . . ?"

"Oh, yeah. It turns out that I love it! Who knew I'd be happy as a soccer mom?" she shrugged. Who indeed. "But you get it, Wren! The ease is seductive. Stewart always said that you were so practical! You'd probably love Westchester too!"

Stewart would have laughed for days if he heard his sister say that to me. It was like a gut punch from the grave.

"More like *complained* that I was *too* practical," I managed.

"That sounds right." She nodded absently; a light above us flickered. "Had you talked to Stewart lately? Were you guys . . . like still in regular touch?"

The question surprised me. She didn't know? Had some distance had developed between the siblings? Had Stewart chosen his fame and superficial friends over his own sister? "Yeah, totally," I recovered. "I mean, you know Stewart. He would disappear periodically, get busy with the show or whatever Hollywood scene and drop out for a while. But we stayed in touch, for sure. We just spoke a couple of days ago." *Fought.* We just *fought* a couple days ago. No—*argued.*

Don't get me wrong: I wasn't feeling tortured about the phone call. I mean, I wouldn't have chosen for our last interaction to be contentious, but it had been the sort of out-of-love debate that characterized our relationship forever. Stewart always pissed me off when he lectured me about settling; I always made him mad when I criticized his *Us Weekly* lifestyle. ("*Vanity Fair* lifestyle," he would correct. "At least give me that!")

"Right, right." Kate narrowed her eyes. "Did he say anything? When you talked to him?"

"Say anything? Like about . . . ?"

"Just anything of note, I guess. I don't know. Like anything that foreshadowed . . . all of this," she gestured around us. Most attendees were still on the third floor chatting, but a few outliers were starting to make their way down the carpeted stairs.

"Like that he had a headache or wasn't feeling well?" I strained, trying to remember the details of our conversation and failing. I had been too busy feeling defensive to listen.

Kate furrowed her brow, looking disoriented, but then recovered herself. "I guess that's a dumb question."

"No, no, it's not dumb at all! I totally get it. How could you not want to know whatever you could about the last days of his life?" That sounded so blasé. It dawned on me again: I'm talking about Stewart. *Stewart is dead.* "Sorry. That sounds trite. I'm having trouble making this feel real."

"No, it doesn't. There's no wrong here." Kate began sorting through her purse, a Proenza Schouler satchel that belied her trust fund and urban upbringing, no matter to what suburb she had absconded. "Hey, you don't have a cigarette, do you? God, I could really go for a smoke."

I wished I had one in that moment, a Parliament maybe. I felt like she'd given me a glimpse of that cool older girl I'd once known and still wanted to please. "I'm sorry. I don't smoke."

"No, no. Of course not. Nor should I. Nor *do* I. Normally. Stewart would not have approved." She rolled her eyes, returning her bag to her shoulder. "You know, he became so staunch after he quit. He could go from offender to preacher in a matter of seconds without an ounce of self-awareness."

I smiled. "Like no one else." It was nice to hear something true about Stewart, unromanticized.

"Are you coming to the reception now?" Kate asked.

My heart sank. "Oh. I didn't know about it." I'd figured there would be some sort of gathering, but I'd still harbored delusions of escaping home to the comfort of Chris Harrison's haughty mews.

"Yeah, it's my mother's nod to sitting shiva, but just one day and no actual religion. You know us: we barely pass as Jews. Ted could care less about his background and my mother's WASP roots run deep, no matter how many Passover seders she's hosted. Meryl knows more about Judaism than any of us and she's Irish Catholic. She studied religion at Wellesley." Kate brushed an imaginary strand of hair from her forehead, her mind elsewhere.

I noticed that she called her father by his first name. I tried to picture calling my own dad "Graham" and barely stifled a laugh imagining the look he'd give me. I really needed to pull myself together.

"Anyway, it's at my mother's place . . . well, our old place, you know. I should get going. I need to stop by and make sure the caterer has every-thing under control before I get back to Westchester."

"You're heading back? So soon?"

"Unfortunately. Duty calls. Meryl and the kids are waiting in the car. Book club tonight; I can't get out of it. I would normally cancel, but . . . it's a long story. Then, this week the kids have science fair and I'm head-ing up a school safety and gun control march. I don't want to disrupt their lives more than I have to, you know? Plans wait for no man—or woman!"

It was hard to imagine how a boozy book club could trump the reception for your only brother's funeral, but then suddenly more details flooded back about that last time I'd seen Kate: She *had* left Stewart's birthday party to meet friends at some sceney bar, as I initially recalled—but before the cake even arrived. I could remember Stewart's expression as she left: the frown before he saw me watching and rearranged his face into a grin. His big sister, always fleeing, especially from his mother.

"You know Kate," he'd said later. "First person in the lifeboat." He pretended not to care, but . . . Of course, he had his own lifeboats.

"Okay, I'm off." Kate slipped her arms through the sleeves of her coat. "Wren, thank you for coming. Seeing you, it's like a flashback to happier times with Stewart. That means a lot."

"You too, Kate. Truly."

"So you'll come to the reception? Make sure my mom seems okay and everything?"

"Your mom?"

"I know Stewart always felt he could depend on you entirely. It's so nice to know that I can too."

A wave of guilt crashed over me. I'd let Stewart fade away in the last few months. He'd disappeared into his Hollywood world and I didn't chase as hard as usual. Fatigue, I guess. I exhaled. I knew I wasn't the right person to look out for Helen Beasley. The woman barely tolerated me. But I couldn't say no. I nodded.

Kate looked at me and sighed. Then, before I realized what she was doing, she was wrapping her arms around me for what I realized was a much-needed hug. With my face buried in her red curls, something swelled in my chest—a connection that I'd been lacking since I'd found first out—to Stewart and our past. I really was fond of Kate, whatever her faults. Of course I would attend the reception for her. She was the big sister I always wanted.

Kate released me, and, with a wave, started out the glass doors. Cold air gusted through the crack. She turned back to face me. "Hey, Wren?"

"Yeah?"

"Don't tell my mom I asked you for a cigarette, okay?"

I smiled at her, assuming she was kidding. She was a mother herself, after all. She returned my gaze stone-faced. I cleared my throat. "Of course. No problem. You can count on me." I sounded like a girl scout.

"Thanks, Wren. You're a lifesaver." She pushed her way through the doors, leaving trails of her adolescent self behind.

CHAPTER 7

Stewart, how would you have pictured your funeral? Not like this, I bet. It was sterile—that's the only word for it. Lots of "What a waste" and "He'll be missed." No truisms about your pretentious movie taste or how much you hated beets or that weird habit you had of brushing your teeth with hot water. (I still say that can't be good for the enamel.)

I think I felt the worst for your drama school friends, cheated out of the chance to sing "Send in the Clowns" or songs from Hamilton *and* Dear Evan Hansen *to make us feel all the feelings in the heavy silence after the last cord.*

I'm joking-not-joking. I'm sure they would have done a beautiful job. But it doesn't matter because your mother didn't plan any of that. She hardly even invited any of your flashy Hollywood friends (no complaints from me, but still). The event was the opposite of you: It lacked charisma and spark. It wasn't alive like you once were. I couldn't feel you there, no matter how hard I tried.

You wouldn't have wanted me to plan your funeral either. You would have imagined a cat café with a Liz Phair playlist—which actually would be pretty cathartic between the cursing and the cuddling. Even that would have been more of a reflection of you. It's like your mother wanted to celebrate your facade. Did she want to protect you? Herself? The Helen Beasley I know (and don't exactly love) would never have drawn attention away from her brilliant son. That woman would have worn a T-shirt with a picture of your face on it, if Chanel made one.

I guess she planned what she could handle, something that skidded across your surface. The reception, on the other hand . . . that was filled to the brim with your leftovers.

CHAPTER 8

"Fourth floor," I said to the doorman, Gretchen towering at my side.

He had clearly been prepped about the nature of the event because he gave us an extra somber nod and gestured toward the elevators like a Buckingham Palace guard. I had pictured being greeted by a doorman I knew because I visited Stewart here so much growing up, but those friendly, goateed guys—Joey, Oswaldo, Victor—were either long gone or off today. This new guy returned to his post, never bending a limb.

I glanced around the lobby. It had been refurbished but looked essentially the same: same massive urn of hydrangea; same gilded mirrors and glossy console tables.

"Nice digs," Gretchen remarked.

It was an understatement. We were awash in a sea of white marble and open space, deco chandeliers tinkling above. It was the kind of fancy that made you correct your posture to demonstrate that you belong.

The old-fashioned elevator—now automatic but preserved in its wrought iron glory—arrived on the ground floor. We boarded and pressed the button, my stomach leading the way up on the slow ascent. It had been years since I'd ridden this thing, but I still felt like I was trapped inside an ornate music box. The smell was the same too. Silver polish? Floor wax? The musty apartments of fading beauties who welcomed few visitors? I glanced over at Gretchen, half expecting to find Stewart beside me instead.

She had discovered me shivering on the sidewalk outside Riverside

Chapel shortly after Kate left, my summer dress and wrap too flimsy to protect me against the elements. But I would have frozen to death rather than confront what milled about inside. I was standing off to one side, watching passing strangers go about their normal days, en route to shop for facial cleansers or meet friends for Cobb salads.

"There you are!" Gretchen threw her hands up—always with the drama. "I looked everywhere. I almost resorted to asking Jimmy if he'd seen you!"

I relayed the details of my exchange with Kate.

"Seriously? His sister asked you to stand in for her at her own brother's shiva? What is *wrong* with that girl?"

"Woman."

"Women don't bail on their brother's funerals."

"I guess people grieve in their own ways." I shrugged.

"Sure. But by outsourcing it?" She shook her head. "Rich people, man. I would be such a good one."

I needed to make an appearance at the reception regardless. But first, liquid courage: we stopped at a nearby bar on Amsterdam, where Stewart and I used to flash fake IDs as teenagers—me in a tattoo choker and halter top; him in a white T-shirt and Von Dutch trucker hat. *Oh, the sartorial shame.*

Inside, the light was dim and the paneled walls were hung with vintage beer ads. We had our choice of stools. Rag in hand, the bartender took our orders, his kind eyes like twin crescent moons dipping toward mountainous cheeks. Minutes later, as he slid me my Hot Toddy, he smiled: "One of those days." I wasn't sure if it was a question or a statement.

The drink was a bad call—too sweet. So Gretchen drank the rest plus her martini, which suited her fine. In the meantime, we sat, our elbows resting on the bar's ridge, and talked about everything but Stewart: how impossible it is to keep up with all the good TV, our friend Denise from college who overshares her gynecological mishaps on Instagram, how dressed up a person needs to get for remote meetings, the spoiled interns at Gretchen's office who think they're the next Mark Zuckerberg, but can't work a copier. Then, with a regretful glance back at the bar's warm recesses, we headed out.

And so here we were, riding up in the elevator I'd ridden a hundred times before beside ladies in pearls and my dead friend. I thought about where I would have been today if Stewart were still alive: at my corner coffee shop, eating avocado toast with pickled onions and red pepper flakes, researching new grants to apply for on behalf of my employer. It sounded safe and easy. *Like Westchester.*

I knew at the reception I'd have to approach Stewart's mother again—and make it through a full sentence this time. I needed a distraction from my surging anxiety: I examined Gretchen. I couldn't help myself.

CAUSE OF DEATH: Old age when she's 103.

AFTER-DEATH RITUAL: Cremation. (She hates clutter.) Ashes arranged in a Parisian ashtray.

SERVICE: Vodka martinis at a classic hotel bar, maybe the Carlyle or the Pierre. Attended by whomever she hasn't outlived. Especially her young lovers. With dancing afterward.

PROCESSIONAL MUSIC: "Only the Good Die Young" by Billy Joel.

MEMORIAL BUFFET: Who needs food when there's alcohol? Martinis! Champagne! And, okay, oysters. With super spicy horseradish—she loves spicy food. And truffle brie. And a perfect, crusty baguette.

"Why are you staring at me?" Gretchen narrowed her eyes in suspicion. "You're creeping me out."

I readjusted my focus on the bronze gates, remembering myself. "I wasn't. Nothing. *God.*"

I braced myself. The elevator would deliver us directly into the Beasleys' apartment, which monopolized the whole floor. No hallway for emotional prep here. I could picture Stewart waiting there on the other side, like so many times before, in a ratty T-shirt, jeans and socked feet—head cocked to one side like I was a delightful surprise.

Instead, the doors slid open to reveal a crowd gathered under mile-high ceilings. A single white orchid glared down at us from a lacquered, ebony table at center. Behind it hung an all-white painting I knew to be a Robert Ryman that the Beasleys had owned since the early '90s. I'd stood stoned in front of the artwork more than once as a teenager, captivated by its layers.

Guests had begun to tumble from the enormous, open plan living room into the foyer. As we got our bearings, a server stepped forward to take our coats; I handed my wrap over with regret. Surrendering your outerwear is like making a commitment.

Gretchen exhaled. "Okay. Drink?"

"Yes, please."

I led her toward the bar without having to search out its location—far left across from the piano. When we were teenagers, Stewart's parents had an annual New Year's Day party. Helen found New Year's Eve depressing, so a gathering the following afternoon was her compensation. That event was festive and tinsel-filled: hungover people, casually well-dressed in cowl-necked cashmere and winter white, enjoying hair of the dog.

There was no tinsel today, of course. Still, this felt jarringly reminiscent of those parties—the hardwood floors just as waxed, the light fixture still like a flapper's fringe, the Hockney painting just as bright. The unforgiving light of overcast skies fell through windows lined with draped silver treatments. Friends and family mingled amidst modernist pieces—chairs, tables, vases, clocks—that looked like characters. The women of the older set wore dark suits and dresses with mandarin collars and broaches; the men wore bespoke jackets with exposed stitching. They seemed more comfortable in this setting and their funeral attire than their younger counterparts, who shifted in conservative black.

People chatted quietly in clusters, sipping white wine, eating crudités off cocktail plates. Uniformed waiters passed hors d'oeuvres. Very civilized. Too civilized. I spotted a tray of blinis with caviar and made a mental note to tell Stewart that I'd predicted the catering menu. I knew he was gone, but I guess I still felt I was carrying him with me.

Gretchen followed my line of vision to a tray of what looked like pâté canapés. "In Germany, at funerals, they serve this sugary cake called a *zuckerkuchen*," she said. "Everyone stuffed their faces with it when we traveled back after my great uncle died." Gretchen has a German mother and a Jamaican father, which accounts for her stunning height and hair—and the fact that she's impossible to miss.

"Was it good? The cake?"

"It did the job as far as emotional eating goes." She crinkled her nose, accepting a mini cheese puff from a passing waiter. "Something just feels wrong about all these teeny tiny bites."

There was so much I didn't know about death and the diverse rituals meant to help people heal. "What was it like otherwise? A German funeral?"

"Like a regular old American Christian one," she shrugged. "But with more bratwurst. And German speakers."

"Right. I guess that makes sense. Have ever you been to a Jamaican funeral?"

"Yup."

"What's that like? The same?"

"No way," she smiled. "That's a party!"

Snippets of conversations trailed us as we edged past guests. "You know Linda," said a tiny woman with dyed-burgundy helmet hair and enough diamonds to topple someone less formidable. "She didn't develop chronic illness until late in life, but it was the role she was born to play." An older man with bushy eyebrows and a bowtie was holding court with what I assumed were tolerant younger relatives. "You know, I had malaria four times!" he bragged. "And the last time, I actually *died*." No one mentioned Stewart. The dead elephant in the room.

At the drink station, Gretchen and I were waiting for the bartender's attention, when a woman beside me nudged my arm, smiling kindly, "Excuse me, sweetie? Would you mind passing a napkin?" I complied, smiling back, until I looked down and noticed the mismatch between her reconstructed forty-five-year-old face and her eighty-year-old hands. I covered my surprise with a cough and hoped she thought I was choking back tears. I felt like I was in *Invasion of the Body Snatchers*.

I was just recovering from that exchange when I was startled by a tap on my shoulder. Jesus, I was jumpy. I turned to find Blair, Stewart's publicist, standing behind me. *Lord help me.*

Gretchen gestured that she'd grab our drinks, while Blair dragged me to the side.

"Wren," she said, frowning, eyes moist.

"Blair."

CAUSE OF DEATH: Stroke. At Dry Bar. Ninety-two years old. After reading a client's bad press.

AFTER-DEATH RITUAL: Burial. In only the most exclusive cemetery. Monogrammed coffin. Does Louis Vuitton make caskets?

SERVICE: Traditional. Dramatic. To provoke deep, unironic sadness.

PROCESSIONAL MUSIC: Celine Dion. "My Heart Will Go On."

MEMORIAL BUFFET: Canapés not unlike the ones here. And hostess napkins. Lots of hostess napkins.

Despite my disdain for Blair, the sadness in her face moved me. Both our eyes welled, but hers overflowed. And, just like that, mine dried up.

She hugged me, long and hard. I started to feel like she would never let go—and, after a while, I really wanted out. The lace of her white eyelet blouse was scratching my cheek; her sweet perfume was making me carsick.

Finally, she released me and we took each other in. I've never thought Blair was nice to look at; there's something unforgiving about her face—her wide, angular jaw, her close-set, hawkish eyes, her thin lips. Even her smile expressed more hunger than happiness. This harsh light wasn't doing her any favors: She wore too much foundation. Her highlighted hair, which lay in uniform waves well past her shoulders, was too yellow. She looked drawn and tired—and the way she was leaning toward me made me want to take a step back.

Because Stewart died, I reminded myself. *She looks drawn because Stewart died.*

I tried to think of something kind about her. I focused on the delicate gold *xo* studs in her ears. They were sort of pretty.

In my defense, I would have shown more generosity of spirit if I thought she was a good person, but her appearance was like an expression of her inner ugliness. Blair was Stewart's college theater friend. Once a wannabe actress (who realized she couldn't stomach the rejection), she had transitioned into publicity with Stewart as her first client. He had been fond of her, applauding her "loyalty" to him, but even he had to admit that she was challenging. Hanging out with her was like being trapped in a middle school girl's bathroom—with the *second* most popular girl in the grade. No matter how friendly she acted, she couldn't help eyeing you like prey. When she smiled, it was hard to tell if she was amused or reveling in the ways you were unwittingly humiliating yourself.

Blair had always been civil to me, recognizing, with that razor-sharp focus, that I was a permanent fixture. Stewart valued me, so she pretended that she did too. That was a punishment in its own way: she always behaved as if we were more intimately acquainted than we were, in together on some terribly girly secret.

"You know Stewart," she would smirk, as if to say, "No one knows him like we do." I often felt tempted to remind her that I'd known him for two decades longer. But I'm not petty like that. Out loud.

Now, tears hung on her eyelash extensions like raindrops on barren branches. "I just can't believe he's gone."

"I know." What was there to say? "Poor Stewart."

"Poor all of us! He was just the kindest, most wonderful person."

I nodded. Because that's what you do at funerals. Even if you don't agree.

I thought Stewart was wonderful, for sure. He was brilliant and amazing, and I already felt so alone in this crowd without him. But kind? That seemed like a reach. I could think of a snarky thing he'd said about every person I recognized in this room, especially Blair. I didn't value him for his sweetness, so much as his intelligence, humor, and kindred spirit. I swallowed hard, absorbing a wave of disbelief. I wished he was standing next to me, elbowing me in the side.

My temples throbbed. How long did your head hurt before an aneurysm gave way and your brain went to pieces? An hour? A day?

"How are we going to live without him!" Blair wailed. I snapped back to attention as she broke down sobbing, her face dropping into her well-manicured hands. Perfect neutral nails. Some stackable diamond rings she'd bought for herself (like me, she was single).

I patted her shoulder. Because that's what you do at funerals too. And, no matter what I thought of her, she was hurting. "I know. I really do, Blair." She loved Stewart, and he would have wanted me to play nice. "I already miss him so much."

"Me too." She looked up at me, brushing her smooth hair away from her face. Tears dripped down past her pronounced chin. I handed her a napkin from the bar. This was turning into a regular thing for me. Napkin girl. "I mean, I knew you'd understand," she continued. "All these people think they knew him, but not like us—"

She gestured to everyone else in the room. I felt confident that many of them knew him as well. His mother, for instance, who I spotted at a distance in conversation with some guy I didn't recognize—brown scruffy hair, crinkly eyes, five o'clock shadow, cute, about my age. I looked away, desperate to continue any conversation if it saved me from talking to Helen. Blair snorted loudly. Like Miss Piggy.

"Life is going to feel different now, for sure," I said.

"It is! Because, Wren, you know Stu! He and I talked *every day*, basically. I knew every single detail of his life. He and I were so close! So. Close."

"Right. Totally. So. Close."

"I know you guys didn't talk as much as we did, but you were so close too." *Ah.* There she was, the woman I knew. Let the pissing contest begin! "But I'm telling you, he didn't do one thing without running it by me. Like, every time I get a text now, I think it's him, asking for advice like normal. I'm just so brokenhearted. I mean, I've spent my whole adulthood with him, you know? We just connected—emotionally, ambitiously, intellectually."

Intellectually? I dropped my hand. I had a flashback to Stewart pushing his imaginary glasses up the bridge of his nose: "Blair thinks *Fifty Shades of Grey* is great literature."

She took a step toward me now, so we were only inches apart. You could just feel her ready to pounce. "Had you talked to him lately? I know you guys sometimes lost touch for periods." *Dig.*

"I talked to him two days ago." I wasn't about to share the details of our last conversation. Those were mine. No one else was going to own them. And I needed to change the subject to anything else, since I was starting to feel like kicking Blair's competitive ass. That seemed inappropriate in this setting; the living room rug was very white. "He didn't mention anything about feeling sick," I said quickly, moving on. "I wonder if he had any idea that something was up?"

I'd been thinking a lot about that: Is there a build up to an aneurysm? Like, do you feel tired for the days leading up to *dying*? Or do you just get a headache and *boom*! I guess, like Kate, I wanted to understand Stewart's last moments.

"Definitely not!" Blair snapped, drawing me out of my head again. "He would have told me if he felt bad! He would have asked me to bring him a cayenne wellness shot from Earthbar or somewhere."

"Right."

"The show was on hiatus. I'm pretty sure he was like sleeping a lot and taking it easy."

"You're *pretty* sure?"

"Oh, well, I mean, I hadn't talked to him in a couple weeks," she mumbled. "I was out of town with another client. Stu wasn't responding to texts, so I knew that meant he was either really busy or resting up. 'Cause he always answered my texts."

"Unless he was really busy. Or resting up."

"Yes."

The truth comes out. She hadn't talked to him in ages. She didn't know any more than I did. Now talking to her seemed like an even bigger waste of time.

"Oh, God!" she groaned again loudly, catching me off guard and drawing stares from nearby mourners. I offered an apologetic smile-frown to those whose gazes lingered and took a giant step back. Blair didn't seem to notice. "I can't believe I'll never get a text from him again! I just can't stop crying. I—"

"Hi, ladies," interrupted a voice from above. We both looked up. Keith was standing over us, doing a performance of compassion. His oblong head was tilted to the side, chapped lips squashed together, beard quivering. God, he was a terrible actor. He couldn't even do a decent impression of grieving his oldest friend. I mean, don't get me wrong, I'm sure he felt some legitimate sadness. But he delivered his condolences entirely to Blair because—Hollywood publicist.

CAUSE OF DEATH: Liver disease.

AFTER-DEATH RITUAL: Cremation. Because, drunk at a Korea Town karaoke bar on one of Stewart's birthdays, he told me he wanted to be scattered from the top of one of the world's tallest buildings, so he could be "caught by the wind." I suggested he be scattered from the world's *shortest* building instead, so he could be conveniently "caught by a garbage bin." He did not find that amusing.

SERVICE: He'd want a big, well-attended, theatrical affair. A small one at a dingy chapel would be more fitting. Maybe attended by some of the young acting students he'd coerced into fucking him. He was so #MeToo.

PROCESSIONAL MUSIC: "Born To Be Wild" by Steppenwolf. 'Cause poser.

MEMORIAL BUFFET: Cold coffee and Danish.

Fucker.
Maybe I was being harsh.
He leaned down and brushed his crusty lips against my cheek, leaving the stench of stale cigarettes and Drakkar Noir (or some other cheap cologne for thirteen-year-olds) in his wake. It took everything in my power not to pull out hand sanitizer and spray my face.

"Hi, Wren."

"Hi, Keith."

"It's been forever." Like I'd been deprived.

"It has." I gritted my teeth. "How have you been?"

He sighed—long and loud. "I've been better. My Snackables commercial is about to start airing nationally, but it's hard to feel happy about that today. Now I'll never get to share that with Stu. I know he would have been ecstatic."

I doubted that.

Keith laid a hand on Blair's shoulder. "Hi, Blair."

"Um, hi . . . sorry, remind me of your name?"

"It's Keith," he whined. "We hung out with Stu at the Chateau a couple of years ago when I was in town for pilot season? And, like, a few times before that. Don't worry. I know it's hard to keep anything straight today."

Blair looked from his face to his hand on her arm and crinkled her nose. For a blissful moment, I thought she might swat him off, affronted by his insubordination. But then he said the magic words: "I know how close you and Stu were. This must be *particularly* hard for you."

Suddenly, she was nodding. "We were so close," she groaned. "I mean, *so close*. I just can't believe it. How am I going to live without him?" With a wheeze, she started weeping again. Keith pulled her in close, a hand on the back of her head. You wouldn't catch my nose that close to his armpit.

He glanced at me over her head, forehead lined like ruled paper. "Tough day. Tough, tough day. We all have to band together and support each other now."

I dry-heaved.

He seemed to be peering over my shoulder, so I twisted to follow his gaze and realized I was standing in front of a framed portrait of Stewart and Kate. Stewart was probably ten years old. Gawky. Adorable. Wide smile. Crisp, white button down. Glasses. Glint in his eye. Kate was an early incarnation of that teenager I remembered. She looked pissed, stuffed into a navy blue velvet dress with a rope belt. Probably Ralph Lauren or something of that ilk. Something beautiful that a kid would hate.

Keith pointed to the photograph, his hand forming a gun. "Oh. Stu, old pal. You always used to say, 'Keith. Dude. You inspire me.' But the truth is we still had so much left to learn from each other."

Blair croaked out another moan and sobbed harder into Keith's shoulder. You had to be impressed by his commitment to performing the scene while Blair blew her nose on his sleeve. That suit was going to need a serious dry cleaning. Or a spit shine, knowing cheap-ass Keith.

I thought, *Stewart would have died to see this.* Unfortunately, he already had.

Actually, an aneurysm didn't sound like a bad alternative to witnessing this display. Thank the lord, Gretchen sensed my peril—or maybe, I imagined, Stewart used his heavenly influence to intervene. Either way, at that moment, my living, breathing best friend appeared at my side with a fifth of Scotch. Neat. How I like it. How Stewart liked it too. "I thought you might need this," she mumbled, looking from Keith to Blair and back to me with eyes wide.

Keith reached out a hand. "Keith. Farber. Old friend to Stu. And colleague. In the film biz."

Gretchen bit her lip to suppress a smile, then took his hand and shook it firmly, "Gretchen. Wren's college friend. We've met before."

"Apologies. It's a difficult day. I'm . . . not myself."

"How unfortunate for us all."

"Yeah, true. I'm amazed that I'm holding it together."

She stared at him. "Unbelievable."

"The turnout? I know, right? I'm surprised too. I didn't think this many people actually *liked* Stu." Keith caught himself mid smirk and ironed out his face. "I mean, I know how beloved he was, of course. But it was short notice. Typical Stu."

"Yes, sudden death is so inconvenient that way. No save-the-date!" Gretchen grabbed my hand and squeezed. Hard. "Hey Wren, can I steal you for a sec?"

"Yes. Yes, you can." *Please God.*

She pulled me toward the center of the room, hiding us behind a trio of older men in heated debate about superyachts. "Well, he's worse than

I remembered!" Gretchen raised both eyebrows in mock horror. "Who knew that was possible? Stewart really knew how to pick 'em."

"He sure did," came a voice from behind us—dry as hell. We turned to find Jimmy wearing a crooked, sad smile. He was like a giant teddy bear, meaty in his older age, eyes clear and brown. I exhaled. I was so happy to see him.

CAUSE OF DEATH: Lights out while playing poker at his Florida old-age home.

AFTER-DEATH RITUAL: Who gives a fuck? (That's what he would say—not me.)

SERVICE: BIG. Attended by the generations of Jimmys I have always believed would exist, plus his lifelong buddies. He's the kind of guy people keep around.

PROCESSIONAL MUSIC: Slick Rick's "Children's Story," or Frank Sinatra's "My Way."

MEMORIAL BUFFET: Three Words: Six. Foot. Hero.

He kissed me on the cheek, then let his eyes rest on Gretchen. "So. *You're* here." He frowned.

"Hello, James." No one calls Jimmy "James." She was trying to annoy him and probably succeeding. I couldn't even remember why there was so much tension between these two. They just loved to hate each other, I guess. I wasn't in the mood for their shtick.

He nodded his chin at her curtly. "Always a pleasure."

"Is it really though?"

"I was being polite."

"Oh! Is that a new trick? To go with that trim new haircut?" I had noticed too: Jimmy was shaving his head these days, surely because he'd gotten balder.

"Yeah. It's a trick called behaving like an adult. I would teach you about it, but you know what they say about *old dogs*."

Gretchen's mouth dropped open, then snapped shut. "Whatever. I'm going to top off my drink. And by that I mean escape before I catch something nasty from questionable company. See you in a minute, Wren."

Jimmy grunted, although I swear I saw him checking out her ass as she stalked away. When he turned back to face me, his expression softened. "Thank God you're here."

"Back at you. It's *so* good to see you. Seriously. All these people . . ." I ran a hand through my hair and down my cheek.

"I know. It's horrible. The situation is horrible. They're all horrible. Everything is pretty much horrible."

"I mean, it's been a long time since I saw all of these people in one place. Is it possible that they got worse?" Were Keith and Blair always this bad? Or were their most deplorable qualities on parade under the circumstances?

The circumstances. *Stewart. Gone.*

Jimmy nodded. "Looking around this room, I'm astounded by what bad taste Stu had in friends—*other* friends. Obviously."

"*Obviously.*" I was relieved not to be alone in my judgments. From a distance, I watched Keith rubbing Blair's back. Large, mushy, concentric circles. Better her than me. I pulled my attention back to Jimmy. "How are you doing, with all this?"

"I hadn't talked to Stu in a while." Tamping down emotion, Jimmy pulled his mouth to the right making a highway pileup of his lips. "I wish I had made more of an effort, but that seems to be going around. I was just talking to his grad school friends. None of them had spoken to him in ages either."

"I guess he was busy," I said. Not because I believed it.

"Busy star-fucking maybe."

I let out a single sharp laugh in surprise, then covered my mouth.

"Oh, c'mon, Wren. I wouldn't say it to anybody but you, but Stu wasn't exactly above being distracted by the fame."

"You don't have to tell me. He once blew me off for an Olsen twin."

Jimmy sighed, letting it all sink in. "Which twin though? 'Cause I feel like that's okay if it was Mary Kate. But Ashley? That's not cool."

"Which is the one who showers?"

Jimmy and I had migrated to a far wall between two windows. I glanced outside: cabs zoomed by between Central Park West's broken white lines.

"I can't believe it." Jimmy remarked, under his breath.

"I know." Not for the first time, an image popped into my head of a cartoon brain exploding into a mushroom cloud of particles, then disappearing into the ethos. *Mind blown.*

"It's like a part of our childhood just disappeared, you know? I keep picturing Stewart as a kid, like when we became tight, maybe in fourth grade. Who could have predicted this? He has—*had*—so much presence. I would have thought he'd outlive us all. He was always so . . . big."

That was funny coming from Jimmy, who was physically hulking by comparison, but I knew what he meant.

"When did you last talk to him?" he asked.

"A couple of days before . . ."

"That's good. If he was keeping in touch with you, he still knew some of what was important." I had this impulse to grab Jimmy's enormous arm and wrap it around my shoulders.

Instead, I asked, "Did you talk to his mom yet?"

"Yeah." He looked at his shiny shoes, avoiding eye contact as his grew teary. "She was really sweet. She said I was 'family.' It almost killed me. You?"

"I've been avoiding it." I shook my head. "She scares me. Especially today."

"You always said that. I never got it. She's a pussycat."

"With really sharp claws."

We got quiet again. It was comforting just to stand next to Jimmy, like this was the closest I would ever get to Stewart again. The old Stewart. The one I wanted to remember most. I never wanted to leave his side.

"We let too much time pass without seeing each other," Jimmy said finally.

"You and Stewart?"

"Me and you." He was staring hard at the ice clinking around in his almost empty glass. "Let's not do that again."

I nodded.

"Anyway," he coughed, changing course. "What's up with you? Boyfriend?"

"Not since Doug. Two years ago."

"That's the vegan do-gooder guy, right? What happened with him again?"

"He hooked up with a D-list celebrity chef on a media trip to build a well in Kenya."

Jimmy almost did a spit-take before choking out a loud laugh. "Wow. I don't where to begin."

"Yeah. It was pretty awesome. He asked me to contribute to his Kickstarter campaign later that same week."

"No. He didn't."

"He did. Although maybe it was GoFundMe?"

"Did you tell him to go fuck himself?"

"Nope. I sent him fifty dollars. I didn't want to punish the thirsty people. Plus, I wanted to be the bigger person."

"The bigger person or the bigger sucker?"

"Touché." I smoothed the front of my dress. "I was supposed to get a reusable water bottle for my donation, but it never came. That guy could never deliver, if you know what I mean."

Jimmy chuckled. "He sounds like a real gem."

"Yeah, it didn't feel like a *huge* loss. The relationship, I mean, not the water bottle. *That* I really wanted." I lifted my glass now, toasting no one. "I know how to pick 'em too! Stewart and I had that in common."

"Speaking of getting rid of trash, what about work? You still researching sewage?"

I shot Jimmy a dirty look. "Well, when you say it like that, it sounds so glamorous."

As a stockbroker, Jimmy could never wrap his mind around my job, writing grant proposals for a nonprofit that builds infrastructure in developing nations. Sometimes I suspected that my work sounded so boring that people in general just zoned out when it came up. It could be rewarding in practice, though, I told myself. At least, I think I believed that at some point. And it got more interesting once you rose through the ranks and began wooing big donors and traveling to the sites where the grant money was implemented. Or so I'd heard.

In truth, it had taken me awhile to find grant writing—and I wasn't sure where to go from here. At first, I tested the waters in marketing (too frat boy), PR (too Blair), and journalism (long story). But once I found the grant path, it seemed as inevitable as inheriting my mother's high cheekbones and my father's pointy chin. When you're the child of a poet and short-fiction writer respectively, you learn more about dangling participles than about economics—and maybe you're not so prepared for a nine-to-five office job. Maybe you find something that involves writing and allows you to work remotely and make the world a slightly better place. Maybe you find something safe, and, *okay*, tame, but reliable. Because you've seen what the unstable alternative looks like.

Jimmy must have been thinking the same thing. "Hey, do you remember that time you and Stu got into that huge argument 'cause he couldn't understand why you didn't want to be something flashy when you grew up?"

Did I? That would be a major *yes*. I had played that scene over in my head a thousand times throughout the years—and at least ten after my argument with Stewart the other night.

We were probably thirteen years old. Jimmy and I were sitting on the tall stone wall that divides Riverside Park from the sidewalk, mindless of the ten-foot drop behind us. We were only a block from Auburn Prep, but students came here to hang out and smoke, and the school pretended not to notice. The ground was littered with cigarette butts and the sprouts of plants so strong they'd pushed their way through the concrete. Stewart—in one of his perfect beat-up flannels—was pacing in front of us, ranting about how no one would ever be as talented as Kurt Cobain, and how he was an asshole for killing himself because he'd robbed the world of his gift. "I mean, what a dick? Am I right?"

We'd heard this one before. Jimmy nodded absently. It was hard to tear your eyes from Stewart when he was like this, despite the broken record.

He was magnetic, I guess a natural performer. Even a passing homeless man paused to listen.

"Maybe he was in a lot of pain, Stewart," I said, "and didn't want to be alive anymore."

Jimmy looked at me sideways like I was bonkers to engage. I knew it was pointless, but I was irritated. Enough with Stewart's sweeping statements! I wasn't in the mood to be agreeable.

"Fuck that. We're all in pain."

"We are?" Jimmy. He was never one for mining the emotional depths.

"Why should he have to live in service to other people if he's unhappy?" I argued.

"Because! The greater good! The world relies on artists and truth-tellers to elevate it! That's why we have to follow our dreams. Not just for ourselves! For everyone! We're all responsible for making the world more colorful, so other people can bear it. Right, Jimmy? Tell her!"

"The only thing I'm responsible for is myself and making a lot of money," Jimmy winked at me. "I'm gonna be crazy rich."

Stewart ignored that. "I'm gonna be someone important and make the world more interesting! I'm going to be an actor or an artist . . . or a musician!"

"You're tone-deaf."

To underline my jab, I puckered my lips, stained hot pink with perfumed lipstick.

"Who cares? I'm still gonna make the world more vibrant! What about you, Wren? You're not gonna do that as an investigative reporter? When you travel the world, uncovering political corruption and heart-wrenching instances of human kindness?"

I shrugged. "I don't know if I'm gonna be a reporter anymore."

"Wait, what? Why? That's what you've always wanted to do! You were born to write. Look at your parents!"

"Yeah, but it's hard and not very practical." I flipped my hair. I loved to flip my hair back then. Attitude for days. I didn't even believe what I was saying; I had every intention of traveling the globe as a journalist. I was just sick of listening to Stewart pontificate. Other people swooned for his "passionate side," but I knew the real him and liked to remind him of that. Take him down a notch.

"Seriously?" Stewart's face fell. He looked like an elementary school kid forgotten at pickup. "But what else would you do?"

"I don't know. Be a teacher?"

"A teacher?" He was incredulous, his face contorted in disbelief. "A *fucking teacher*? That's the *dream*?"

"Stewart. Leave me alone. Not everyone has to see the world like you do."

He stepped in front of me and rested his hands on my knees, looking up at my face through light lashes. "Wren. You're an amazing person. You have to have bigger dreams than that. For the good of mankind!"

"*Woman*kind. And no. I don't. I don't want to be like my parents, never knowing where rent is coming from. Always hustling to have 'experiences.' I want to be stable. That's the dream." My parents had been up until 2:30 a.m. the night before, applying for some artists' residency in Quebec City. Meanwhile, I wanted to go on the eighth-grade overnight trip to Washington, DC, and they couldn't afford to send me.

"But Wren, that's insane!"

That was it! A shot of red-hot rage coursed through me. I knocked his hands off my knees and jumped down to face him, ignoring the sting as I scraped my thigh in the process. "No, Stewart! It's not insane. Not everyone looks at the world through your penthouse windows!"

"Don't talk to me like I'm some clueless rich kid. Wren, you know that I—!"

"Hey, hey, hey folks, simmer down," said Jimmy, giant hands upraised as if to stop traffic. "I don't even understand what you're fighting about and I don't think you do either. Stewart, leave Wren alone. Wren, it's your own fault for trying to talk to him when he's like this."

"But—!" Stewart started again.

"No." Jimmy held up his hand and jumped down off the wall, brushing pebbles from his palms. "Lunch is over. We gotta get back. I have a pre-calc test and I haven't studied. It's gonna be a blood bath."

Stewart and I glowered at each other on the walk back to school and up the cement steps to our classrooms, his hands buried deep in his faded jean pockets. We made up a couple of days later, but it always remained a sore spot between us—my lack of big dreams and his lack of perspective.

I would give anything to be fighting with him about that now instead of standing here praying that I'd never forget his face. "Yeah," I said to Jimmy. "I remember."

"You guys could really piss each other off."

I put a finger to my lips. It had been a longtime since I wore lipstick that bright. "I keep hearing people call him 'kind.' Do you think he was kind?"

Jimmy considered that. "When he wanted to be." He swilled the last of his drink. "I should go find—"

"There you are!" A blond, hair pink at the tips, bopped in front of us like a pogo stick—very pretty, very bouncy, very young. Was she talking to me? She took a step forward, threw her arms around Jimmy's shoulders, giggled, and licked his ear. She was *not* talking to me. A tattoo on the inside of her arm read: *It is what it is.*

So true.

Flipping around to face the room, she pulled out her phone and positioned it in front of them for a selfie. "Jim! Look at the camera! But maybe look kind of, like, sad 'cause my post is gonna be about tragedy. Like hashtag YOLO. Or maybe about how lit this apartment is. 'Cause it's *so lit* I-M-H-O. One of those two topics."

Jimmy recoiled, then stared at the floor like he wanted to disappear beneath it. Without making eye contact with me, he said, "This is Britnee. We, uh, came together."

I'm sure my eyes were like saucers: "You brought a . . . date? To a funeral?"

"Oh, we're just hanging out!" Britnee assured me. "I don't do labels. I'm nonbinary. Except I'm definitely a cis girl 'cause, well, that's a long story about my journey, but, like, in other ways. Like I'm not a vegan or carnivore—that depends on my mood and if I have my period and need a burger. And, like, I like Kanye *and* Taylor Swift. And sometimes even Blake Shelton. Everyone gives country music a bad rap in NYC, but I'm, like, open—to all possibilities. You have to make space for and invite in whatever brings inner bliss, you know? That's how you find your truth." Britnee powered down, considering that for a minute, then she seemed to wake up again, like someone swiped up on her back. "Anyway, hi! Who are you?"

"Um, I'm Wren." I shot Jimmy an amused look. "Nice to meet you. How do you guys know each other again?" *Been hanging out at the playground, Jim?*

"We met at a Yankee game. My dormmate's dad gave us tickets and we were in the box next to Jimmy's company! Her father is like super important in tech or something. Isn't that cool? That's another example of how I'm open, 'cause I would watch any sports team, as long as I'm in a box."

"Right."

Suddenly, Britnee assumed what presumably was meant to be a serious expression—her eyes wide, mouth puckered—and leaned toward me. It just made her look goofier. "Do you know Stanley?"

I was genuinely confused by everything about her. "Stanley? No, I don't know Stanley. At least I don't think I know Stanley." I looked at Jimmy. "Who is Stanley?"

He shrugged. *Got me.*

"The guy who *died*!" Britnee stage-whispered. "You know—*Stanley*!"

At that choice moment, Gretchen returned. Bad timing for Jimmy. She took one look at Britnee, then at Jimmy and grinned big.

"Oh!" I said. "You mean, Stewart. Yes. I did. He was my friend from childhood, like Jimmy."

"Right, *Stewart*. I always confuse him with that Stanley guy from *CSI*." Britnee pushed her bottom lip out into a pout. "But, anyway, it's so sad. Isn't it so sad? Like *so* sad?"

"It is so sad," Gretchen nodded. "About Stanley."

"But I mean like, sooooo sad, right?"

"Yes. Very, very sad."

"I didn't even get to meet him, but I like, cried when I heard. 'Cause also he was famous and super cute. Poor Jimmy. It's just so so so . . . I don't know . . ."

"Sad?" Gretchen offered.

"Yes! It's so sad!" Britnee got distracted by a passing tray of tuna tartare cones. "Ooh! Is that raw? I'm only eating raw food this month, while I intermittent fast. It really helps with digestion and longevity. Is that the word? For living for a long time? I always get it confused with 'gingivitis.' Oh, shoot. Is that weird to say here?"

"Gingivitis?" I was trying to keep up.

"Was he into raw food?"

"Who?"

"Stanley."

I turned to Jimmy. *You take this one.* "No," he shook his head. "He ate real food."

"Oh. Maybe that's why he died. It's so sad." She stepped toward the server. "Excuse me. Is that raw?"

The waiter looked down at the tray. "It's ceviche."

"Oh. Rad. Is that raw?"

"Well, kind of. I mean, I guess ceviche is technically 'cooked' with lime juice."

"Wait, so it's cooked or it's not cooked? Because the thing about raw food is . . ." Britnee began lecturing the confused cocktail server, a captive audience. She followed him as he inched away toward other attendees.

CAUSE OF DEATH: Spontaneous combustion.

AFTER-DEATH RITUAL: Evaporation. They'll have that by the time she dies.

SERVICE: A carnival with a ball pit and Instagram photo booth.

PROCESSIONAL MUSIC: "Wolves" by Selena Gomez.

MEMORIAL BUFFET: Raw food, obviously. Unless she has her period when she dies.

"Who's the brain trust?" Gretchen smiled at Jimmy. "Your fiancée?" She had won the battle for superiority by default.

"Whatever," he scowled. "She's hot."

"Sure. If you like preschoolers. Which you probably do."

Abruptly, the classical playlist stopped—only then did I realize it had been ambient the whole time. I scanned the room. In the corner, by a Jeff Koons balloon animal, four of Stewart's theater school friends were huddled around the baby grand. The opening cords for "Someone Like You" by Adele rang out. I hoped these were the more talented members of his class. Otherwise this would be brutal.

"HI, GUYS!" a voice boomed behind me.

I whipped around to discover Stewart's friends Mallory and Brian holding hands beside us. *Of course. How could I have forgotten?* It always amazed me how identical this couple looked—and how much like Muppets—with matching grins and features that looked molded from clay. As usual, they appeared more costumed than dressed, like subjects from some Japanese fashion photo book. Brian was monochromatic in a black newsboy cap, a button-down and tie, and suspenders above pants cuffed as high waters. Even his wallet chain was matte black. Mallory was draped in dark layers with snake-inspired bracelets climbing up her tattooed arm like she was about to perform Medusa. Ten different studs dotted her ears.

The duo, now married, had been attached at the hip since I first met them when Stewart was in college. They had both been studying stage management then. I wasn't sure what either of them did now, but they were always together and in perpetual good humor. Today seemed like no exception. "THIS IS SO TERRIBLE!" Mallory grinned. She had trouble modulating her voice and tended to draw glares in public. I imagined a lot of shushing backstage when she worked on plays. She embraced me in a warm hug. "WREN, IT'S SO GOOD TO SEE YOU! IT'S BEEN TOO LONG!"

The Adele cover singers shot us dirty looks. We were disrupting their show. Meanwhile, had anyone asked the dead guy's mother if it was okay to perform? I scanned the room and spotted Helen, now sitting on the far corner of a severe couch—all angles, no give. It was draped with a camel hair throw blanket, the cashmere kind that had never been thrown. A

circle of people surrounded her; a balding middle-aged man knelt closest. He was speaking about something with apparent passion, and she
was nodding, but, even from here, I could see that her eyes looked miles
away—somewhere in the past with her son.

"WREN, YOU MUST BE SO SAD!" Mallory boomed. I snapped back to
attention.

"We're all sad," whispered Brian. It was almost inaudible. He was very,
very quiet, even on a good day.

"IT'S TRUE! YOU'D HAVE TO BE A FUCKING ROBOT NOT TO BE SAD!"
bellowed Mallory.

"Shhhhhhh." Jimmy rolled his eyes. "This is a goddamn shiva. Have
some respect!"

"OOPS! Sorry, Jimmy." Mallory shrugged. We all listened to the singing
for a minute. It was pretty. Then Mallory picked up where she'd left off.
"DID YOU GUYS KNOW THAT IN SOUTH KOREA, PEOPLE HAVE MOCK FUNER-
ALS SO THEY CAN, LIKE, EXPERIENCE THEIR OWN FUNERALS? MY MOM TOLD
ME. SHE JUST DID SOME ANCESTRY.COM THINGY, AND IT TURNS OUT WE'RE
ONE-EIGHTEENTH KOREAN!"

No one responded. All I could think was that, if Stewart were here
right now, he would have suggested ditching his own funeral reception
and heading to a dive bar.

"YOU GUYS, THIS IS SO *TERRIBLE*!" Mallory boomed. I'm sure she
thought she was whispering. Tears streamed down her face even as she
smiled. I figured she was incapable of frowning.

"It's the worst," whispered Brian, rubbing her back. At least I think
that's what he said. It might have been, "Where's your purse?" They both
looked really stoned.

CAUSE OF DEATH: Suicide pact.

AFTER-DEATH RITUAL: Cremation together into a single urn, then
            sprinkled over the set of *Game of Thrones* in Iceland.

SERVICE: A screening of *The Big Lebowski*.

PROCESSIONAL MUSIC: "Broken" by lovelytheband.

MEMORIAL BUFFET: THC-laced edibles.

"It really has been so long," I said because I had to eventually say something. "How are you guys?"

"WE'RE OKAY," laughed Mallory, "EXCEPT FOR THIS. IT'S JUST . . . THERE ARE SO MANY THINGS I NEVER GOT TO SAY!"

Not to be ungenerous, but I wondered what those things might be: "Cool T-shirt, Stu"? "Are you bingeing that new Marvel show on Netflix?"

"IT'S JUST SO CRAZY! REMEMBER STU HAD THAT LINE IN THE SCI-FI THRILLER ABOUT AMAZON ECHOS TAKING OVER ON MARS? 'ONE DAY, EVERY-ONE'S TIME COMES! NOTHING TO DO ABOUT IT!'" Mallory actually lowered her voice. "It's like he knew."

"I can't believe you memorized that line." Jimmy shook his head, and not in admiration.

"OF COURSE I DID! BRIAN AND I SAW EVERY MOVIE AND TV SHOW THAT STU WAS EVER IN! WE WERE HIS BIGGEST FANS! BRIAN WOULDN'T SHUT UP LAST NIGHT, QUOTING EVERY SINGLE EPISODE OF *MANIC MONDAYS*! I WAS LIKE, ENOUGH ALREADY, HONEY! I NEED SOME QUIET! STOP TALKING MY EAR OFF, YOU CHATTERBOX!"

Brian shot us a crooked grin and looked at his shoes.

"WHEN DID YOU GUYS LAST SEE STU? WE TRIED TO VISIT HIM ON SET LAST TIME WE WERE IN LA, BUT HE WAS SO BUSY, WE NEVER EVEN GOT TO SEE HIM. BUT I GUESS THAT'S THE DEAL WHEN YOU'RE A MOVIE STAR. HE SAID HE WOULD HAVE PREFERRED TO HANG WITH US THAN GO TO THE WORK THING HE HAD AT THE IVY WITH SOME STUDIO PEOPLE. I DON'T BLAME HIM! WHO WOULDN'T RATHER CHILL AND GET STONED WITH OLD FRIENDS THAN GO TO SOME OBLIGATORY DINNER WITH HOLLYWOOD HONCHOS?" I scanned the nearby crowd for now affronted studio execs. Mallory sighed, loudly. "IF ONLY WE HAD SEEN HIM, MAYBE . . ."

"Maybe it would have staved off his aneurysm?" commented Gretchen. She couldn't help herself.

It was just like Stewart to prioritize cooler plans with cooler people.

And it was just like Mallory not to realize she'd been dissed. Still, I was surprised that he hadn't made any time at all for Mallory and Brian when they were in LA. They were weirdos, but they were lovable, and he'd been friends with them for a million years. They would have traversed the Earth—and Echo-controlled Mars—just to meet him at his apartment. He wouldn't have needed to leave home.

"I saw him just after New Year's," Jimmy frowned. "But I hadn't talked or texted with him in a month or so." He shook his head, focusing hard on his feet, eyes welling. "Seems like Wren spoke to him last."

Mallory and Brian turned their coordinated gaze on me. "WHEN WAS THAT?"

Why did it feel like an accusation? I felt hunger in their eyes like I might be withholding. I swallowed. "Like, two days before—"

"WHAT DID YOU TALK ABOUT? DID HE TELL YOU IF THEY WERE PLANNING ANOTHER SEASON OF THE SHOW? I READ SOMETHING THAT SAID THEY WEREN'T SURE—UNREST AMONG THE CAST OR WHATEVER. I BET THAT TRISH MCKEN-ZIE IS A HUGE PAIN IN THE ASS! MAYBE SHE WAS THE PROBLEM. WHO ACTUALLY SAW HIM LAST? WREN, WHEN DID YOU LAST SEE HIM, LIKE, IN PERSON?" I felt like I was being interrogated. By someone who didn't need a bullhorn.

I thought back. I had been so preoccupied with keeping my last phone conversation with Stewart private that I'd forgotten to think about the last time I'd laid eyes on him. That lovable face. The truth is, he was away so much, we could often go a couple of months without grabbing dinner or hanging out. "I guess when he was in New York last. When was that? A month or two ago?"

Brian and Mallory looked at each other and shook their heads. "NO WAY! IT WAS SPRING, BEFORE PILOT SEASON. MAY, MAYBE EVEN APRIL."

"Really?" I counted back: Had it been five months since I'd seen him? "Jesus. Time goes so fast."

No one was listening.

"I WONDER IF THEY'LL CANCEL *MANIC MONDAYS* NOW WITHOUT HIM. THEY KINDA HAVE TO, I GUESS. REMEMBER WHEN HE FIRST GOT THE SHOW, BRI? REMEMBER THAT? HIS MOM GOT THAT FIRST PAGE OF THE FIRST SCRIPT FRAMED FOR HIM? THAT WAS SO SWEET. HUH. I WONDER WHAT THEY'LL DO WITH THAT MEMORABILIA NOW? I WONDER WHAT THEY'LL DO WITH ALL HIS STUFF?"

"I heard he didn't have a will." And, on that lovely note, Keith inserted himself into the conversation. As if from nowhere, he and Blair appeared beside us, shoulder to shoulder, like they'd been best friends forever. "Typical Stewart to be unprepared." Keith rolled his eyes. I wanted to punch him in his dumb face.

"He probably didn't think he was about to die," Jimmy snapped. "He was thirty-six, not eighty. He went to the gym all the time, drank those nasty green juices."

"HOW DO YOU KNOW THERE'S NO WILL?" Mallory. That hungry look in her eyes again.

"It's true." Blair. Like she was the last word. "I would have organized it for him. I would have known about it."

"WHAT WILL HAPPEN TO ALL HIS STUFF THEN?"

"Probably his mom will go through it. Or someone will."

"BUT WHAT IF WHOEVER GOES THROUGH IT DOESN'T REALIZE AND THROWS AWAY PRECIOUS STUFF? LIKE, THEY MIGHT NOT KNOW WHAT'S VALUABLE—TO US!"

I was starting to feel uncomfortable. Mallory's voice was cutting through the throng; people were looking at us.

"I'll handle it, I'm sure." Blair. Flipping her hair over her shoulder like she was a shoo-in for Harvest Princess. "Don't worry, Mal. I got you. We were so close. I know everything that was important to Stewart."

Brian rubbed Mallory's back again, as she nodded, unsure. "DO YOU THINK THEY'LL KEEP HIS COSTUMES?"

"This is literally the dumbest conversation of all time." Jimmy grumbled.

"For once, we agree." Gretchen.

"Why is it dumb?" Keith threw his chin up, Blair's new bodyguard. I noticed an ingrown hair coming to a white head beneath his beard. No way he ever washed his face.

"Because Stewart just died. He's gone! And you're talking about his stupid TV show costumes!"

The group began to bicker. Grossed out and not wanting to be associated with any of them, I took the opportunity to slip away. I needed to talk to Helen anyway. The longer I put it off, the worse it would loom.

CHAPTER 9

Stewart. Here goes nothing.

CHAPTER 10

I took a swig of my whisky and marched toward Stewart's mother and her surrounding semicircle. It wasn't until I'd almost arrived that I realized I'd have to interrupt and deliver my inadequate sentiments in front of all those onlookers. On second thought, I was about to duck away, when Helen noticed me approaching. "Ah, Wren. Hello, dear."

Caught. I righted my course and wound up squeezing awkwardly between the coffee table—a real Noguchi, of course—and a chair, still feet from where she perched, so I had to yelp to be heard. The tribe of supporters around her gazed up at me like she was their captain and I was a planetary interloper. "Hi, Helen . . . Mrs. Beasley. Um. I just wanted to come over—" I swear the whole group leaned forward.

"Yes, dear? Speak up! It's difficult to hear above the noise."

"I just wanted to say . . . that I'm sorry!"

She nodded, her chin wrinkling. "Well, it wasn't your fault. It's no one's fault." Why did it feel like she meant the opposite?

I wanted to ask if Stewart had been under the weather beforehand: Was there any warning? How did she get the news? I kept having these terrible flashes of what it must have been like for Helen to find out. Who told her? Who discovered him and when? Where was he in the apartment? Was he alone? Did aneurysms run in their family? Were they genetic? Why did this happen to her son, of all people? Was it because of the lead paint they may have used at that temporary LA apartment complex? Because of the ecstasy we did together in high school? The coke he experimented with in college? Because he fell off the jungle gym when we were eight? He had needed six stitches across his eyebrow.

The questions choked me so I couldn't get a single word out. After a beat of deafening silence, Helen addressed the group, "This is Wren, a very old friend of Stewart's. Stewart had so many longtime friends. He was very loyal."

They all turned and looked at me expectantly.

"It's true! As evidenced by all the people here." I swept my arm outward to indicate the room like a spokesmodel for funerals. I sounded dumber than a bag of hair.

"Wren and Stewart were just platonic," Helen explained to the group. My mouth dropped open. I hadn't expected her to share that tidbit. Then she turned back to me, her hair just brushing her shoulders like an upscale car wash. "But you had one of those arrangements, didn't you? If you didn't find anyone else by the time you were forty and so forth?"

I was taken aback, first that she knew and second that she was bringing it up. In front of all these people. Before I could respond, she continued, "It's so nice to have friends you can rely on that way. Of course, Stewart could have found a million women to end up with—and several men—if he chose." She laughed ruefully.

The implication about my comparative prospects might as well have been erected in neon lights. Apparently, Helen shared her son's belief that I was destined for life as a cat lady.

"What is that called?" she went on. "That kind of agreement? You were his . . ." she snapped her fingers, "'last resort!' That's it, right? That's what it's called? Wren was Stewart's last resort."

That was definitely not what it was called—at least not in polite circles. I would have even taken "backup plan" or "consolation prize" over that.

The members of the semicircle nodded in unison. No one corrected her or even reacted.

Well, almost no one: The crinkly-eyed guy I'd seen her talking to earlier, who now leaned against the couch's left arm, choked back a laugh. Either that or he was coughing, but the delight in his eyes suggested otherwise. I exhaled and tried to stand up taller. 'Cause things are less humiliating with good posture.

"But anyway, they've always been very close. Right, Wren? Even up until recently."

"Yes." I looked down. "We were." The past tense seemed to echo throughout the room, bouncing off walls and leaving noxious gas in its wake. I needed to say something else—to erase the act of referring to Stewart as no longer—and clear the air. "We just texted a couple days ago."

Helen leveled her gaze at me, the corners of her lips curling inward like shriveling petals. "Yes. They gave me his phone. I saw your conversation."

I stopped breathing. In that moment, two words reverberated through my head: *Ass. Hat.* I just had to use that expression in my last text to him! *Christ.* I wanted to curl up in a ball and roll away like a pill bug. Why did I always end up acting like a moron in front of this woman?

The tribe's eyes were still on me and I needed to escape. "Um, I know Kate had to go back to Westchester. I just wanted to offer myself up for any help you might need. I have your number in an old email, so I'll be in touch."

Helen's expression softened. "Thank you, sweetie. That's very nice. I'm taken care of."

"Okay, well, I'll email you my information anyway, just in case. I have some old pictures you might like to see—of me and Stewart as kids mostly."

As terrified as I was, I shuffled around the coffee table, brushing against people's legs as they flushed them sideways. Finally, I leaned down, across the older bald man and all, and kissed Helen's cheek. I thought, *She smells like Saks Fifth Avenue.* My stylish great-aunt and my mother used to take me there as a child to trail them while they shopped. I thought it was the fanciest place in the world, with its shiny marble floors and mirrors reflecting shards of light. If glamour has a smell, I'm pretty sure that's it.

When I straightened back up, I could see Helen's eyes were flooded. I had no idea if I had made things worse or better, but at least I had said something.

She smiled weakly—as if by some miracle she had appreciated it—and then grimaced, perhaps realizing anew that Stewart was gone. I was poor compensation. "Thank you, Wren. Maybe you'll be my last resort too."

Ouch. I backed away, injuring several people's shins in the process, then turned my back to them, shutting my eyes against the humiliation. *Ass hat.* It was time to leave.

But my security blanket was nowhere to be found.

Frantically, I scanned the crowd for Gretchen. All around me, people were growing progressively animated and unmodulated; eye makeup was getting smeared. Blazers were coming off to reveal damp armpit stains and loose cuffs. Things were getting good and ugly, the way I suppose they do in the aftermath of a tragedy. Everybody wants to celebrate the life they still have, maybe? That's the nicest spin on it. More likely they want to drown their existential fear like a mouse in a bucket.

Either way, the group was getting toasty. If Helen Beasley didn't kick this crowd out soon, she'd have a proper Irish—well, semi-Jewish—wake on her hands. I watched two dark-haired women at the entrance to the living room propping each other up. Hands flew to heads, as mourners tried to stop their own aneurysms from materializing. Everyone was on the verge of telling their versions of the truth, and that seemed dangerous in a setting like this one. At the piano, Stewart's theater friends had moved onto "Memory" from *Cats.* Things were going downhill quickly.

I noticed that Keith and Blair looked good and drunk now, huddled in the corner of a backless love seat against a windowed wall. I had half a mind to stop Blair from making a regrettable decision with that human embodiment of bad breath, but I figured she was a grown-up.

"We were just *so* close," I could hear her repeating now for the hundredth time as I snuck past.

I suppose I could have joined the throng, but the louder the voices got, the less interested I became. So many versions of Stewart filtered through so many lenses. It was overwhelming.

All I could imagine was that tomorrow I'd wake up with a horrible hangover and Stewart would still be dead. That sounded even lonelier than this. I just wanted to hang out and make fun of everything with him. And cry about losing someone I loved with him. And talk about how weird this situation was with him. It reminded me of a bad breakup, when you wake up devastated the next morning and realize that the only person who could possibly offer you comfort is the one person you just agreed never to speak to again.

"Miniature chocolate cream pie?" I was startled by a server who stood in stark contrast to the debauched mourners in a pressed white button down and tight bun. She looked at me hopefully—or so I felt. I always feel bad about rejecting passed hors d'oeuvres like it's a personal affront to the waiter (which has resulted in me eating some very questionable dim sum), but I shook my head. Stewart hated chocolate. I would skip in solidarity.

I turned in a circle, starting to wonder if I'd ever find my friend. Instead, my eyes settled on a girl—or, woman, maybe?—with a mess of light brown hair. She stood in a corner facing the wall like she'd been punished, wracked with sobs. Right. I had noticed her at the funeral service too, where she was equally hysterical. I wondered if she was someone Stewart dated for fifteen minutes. I sighed. Everyone seemed more in tune with their sadness than I did, even the sycophants.

I was so busy berating myself as I turned toward the foyer that I completely missed the approach of Willow, Stewart's kooky ex-girlfriend from LA, until she was fully invading my personal space.

"Uh huh!" she said.

"Whoa!" I took a startled step back.

"Wren! Sorry. I was just noticing you from across the room looking so pale. I felt worried and wanted to get a closer look. Have you tried turmeric? You can drink it in warm almond milk—the good kind you make from scratch at home without preservatives and additives—and it neutralizes free radicals and takes down inflammation. It has an unusual taste, but it's pleasant after a while. Kind of like a pumpkin latte!"

I doubted that.

Willow was probably Stewart's most serious girlfriend throughout the years. I've always found her amusing and harmless. Even now, her eyes were all earnest concern. An ex-model (with what had to be a made-up name), she had a successful line of healing essential oil blends and was always offering up natural cures to ailments I didn't know I had. As usual, she looked amazing in a batik Ulla Johnson dress and perfectly distressed Isabel Marant ankle boots, both of which I had been coveting. Her long, unbrushed hair should have looked ratty, but instead read as free-spirited. Basically, she was Bohemian Barbie.

CAUSE OF DEATH: A disease that allows her to fade away slowly, finding acceptance and peace with the hereafter. The physical body is only a vessel for the spirit, after all.

AFTER-DEATH RITUAL: Floated out on the Ganges River, surrounded by marigolds. (I saw a ceremony like this on a trip to India with my parents once. Very romantic.)

SERVICE: Medicine ceremony with drumming, sound baths, breathwork, and a meditation circle.

PROCESSIONAL MUSIC: John Tesh. (Or, okay, "Funeral" by Phoebe Bridgers. Stewart notwithstanding, she mostly hung with hipster musicians.)

MEMORIAL BUFFET: Ayahuasca. And, for when the hallucinations wear off, turmeric lattes. *Ohm Shanti.*

I realized she was waiting for me to speak. "Oh! Thanks, Willow. I'll be sure to try the turmeric." I would not try the turmeric. "How are you?"

She bobbled her head from side to side, considering the question. This is what I've always liked about Willow: she doesn't do small talk. She takes every conversation seriously. "I'm holding up, I suppose. This is a hard day for us all. I can't even begin to imagine what Helen must be feeling. That connection between mother and child—it's the most sacred bond that exists!"

"I know. It's kind of all I can think about." I toyed with the waist of my dress, running my fingertip against a raw edge, and felt a pang of guilt about avoiding my own mother's calls over the last few days.

"I wonder if Helen kept his placenta?" Willow continued. "She could have it made into a tincture to drink in hot lemon water and create a sense of deep spiritual connection."

I tried not to gag. This is what I've always disliked about Willow: the same part. She is so earnest. She thinks we'd all find enlightenment if we just switched to nontoxic cleaning products.

Regardless, I could not picture Helen drinking Stewart-flavored tea, no matter how much she missed him. "I'm not sure that they saved those . . . parts back in the day, when we were born?"

"Ah, maybe not." Willow shook her head. I'm not sure if she was lamenting Stewart's passing or the loss of his placenta thirty-six years before. "This is a super tough one. Of course, we all wish we'd made more of an effort to see him recently. It seems like he was too trapped on the hamster wheel for everyone at the end. You know, I tried to get him into kundalini, but he refused. I felt it could have been uplifting! It's difficult for any of us to sit still and just be, but it's that ability to stay present in what is uncomfortable that keeps us alert to our authentic selves."

The idea of Stewart keeping a regular kundalini practice was laughable— cross-legged in a white turban for hours on end. He could barely sit through a slice at Ray's Pizza. I said, "I imagine he would have had a hard time with that."

Willow wasn't really listening though; she was gnawing on a nail. Even her pillaged nail beds somehow looked cool. She stopped and gazed upward for a moment, as if a vision had just appeared to her out of the ether. "Do you think he was happy? At the end? Was there bliss in his life?"

The question surprised me. I thought about that for a second. I wondered if there was bliss in my life. The word "no" popped into my head and refused to budge. I didn't want to be a downer though, so I said, "He claimed he was. It's hard to know what was really going on."

"We are all unknowable in our completeness. Maybe he was distancing himself from people who cared because he could sense his impending exit."

Maybe. Or maybe he was hanging out with famous people in VIP rooms and dissing his old friends.

Willow somehow ran her fingers effortlessly through her tangled hair. "It's such a loss—for everyone left on this astral plane."

"Yeah." I sighed. "I guess it's always harder to be left than to leave."

"Well, yes. Although, Wren," she lowered her voice, "I'm a bit concerned about his crossing."

"Sorry? Crossing to . . . ?" I realized I still had a headache and it was making me nauseous. Was I creeping closer to my own aneurysm?

"His crossing into the next realm!" Willow leaned forward, her hair falling into her face, making her look unhinged. She smelled like some essential oil blend that reminded me of earth and black-lit college dorm rooms. "My intuitive says that he's confused and stuck. He doesn't know how to transcend. We all need to help him do that."

I felt deflated. In a moment of delusion, I had imagined that Willow and I might be able to commiserate in a real way about loving Stewart, but no. This was *Willow*. In the end, Stewart had broken it off because—as much as he appreciated her positive attitude toward life—he couldn't take her seriously. Why did he surround himself with people he didn't respect? Did it make him feel better about himself?

"It's fun to float along with Willow for a while, but then the irony-free zone gets old," Stewart told me once. "If she ever comes down from the mountaintop, I'd love to share a bourbon with her."

My flight instinct was kicking in again. I scanned the room for any excuse to walk away. Stalling, I said, "How can we help him . . . cross over?"

"Pray as much as possible to the great Source to help guide him on his prescribed path. I've just been saying, 'Go on your journey, Stu! It's okay to leave!'" She threw her arms in the air, chin tipped up toward the ceiling. "Go into the light . . ."

I looked at Willow as she swayed and then at the others in the room behind her—Keith, Blair, Mallory, and Brian (who I now realized were wearing matching pins bearing Stewart's face). There was Helen on the couch, a photo of the absent Kate, the theater friends belting at the piano, their voices worse for the drunken wear. I felt anger pulsing to the surface. I couldn't believe Stewart had left me alone with these fuckers. No wonder his head had exploded.

I couldn't take another minute. "Willow, I really have to pee," I interrupted, leaving her mouth stranded open in midsentence. "But I'll find you later. Great to see you!" I hurried away to hide.

"If you want, later I can check your tongue to see how your liver is fairing!" she shouted after me. "Grief can be very hard on the organs! And persistent urination can be a symptom of an unbalanced vaginal pH!"

The huddle of superyacht owners looked at me with alarm.

Humiliation complete, I decided I really would head to the bathroom—I did have to pee. Then I'd find Gretchen and get the hell out of dodge. The door was locked. *Damn.* Standing there out in the open, I was a sitting duck for anyone who felt like approaching to project their bullshit all over me (not to mention my dead friend).

That's when I remembered another, more discreet bathroom in the former maid's quarters. *Yes!* I slipped down the hall and made my way through what was now a converted laundry room. At the far end, I saw that the bathroom door was a few inches ajar, thank *goodness*. I grabbed the deco doorknob and threw the door wide. Then, just as abruptly, I stopped short, my mouth dropping open: Gretchen had Jimmy pinned up against the subway tiled wall and they were making out with a voracity that I never needed to see. *So. Much. Tongue.*

"Christ!" I yelped. *Right. Jimmy.* The only other guest who would have known the layout of this house as well as I did.

They broke apart, looking at me and then at each other.

"Seriously, you guys? I thought you hated each other!"

"We do," Gretchen shrugged. "We're just embracing life while we have it."

I cocked my head to the side. *Give me a break.* "And your raw foodist friend, Jimmy? What about her?"

"Ah. The dingbat." Gretchen brought the heel of her hand to her forehead. "We plum forgot."

They were wasted.

"Oh, right." Jimmy scratched his head, having forgotten about Britnee's existence until now. "Would you tell her I'm not feeling well and that she should go?"

Gretchen nodded in support. "It will make a dramatic ending to her Insta-story."

I stared at Jimmy, with his shirt askew, and then at Gretchen, who seemed not to give two shits, and I closed the door and left. I'd pee later. I needed to get the fuck out.

I flagged down the server with the bun and begged her to retrieve my wrap as quickly as possible. Then, to kill time, I crossed to the dessert table, picked up a linzer tart and took a rage bite. Raspberry. It was fucking delicious. I took another cookie, then thought, *screw it*, and took five. I shoved them into a napkin and inside my purse. It was the first thing that make me feel better all day.

"Your scarf, miss?" I jumped like I'd been stealing silver.

The server held my wrap aloft, her eyes darting for just a split second to my napkin full of cookies.

"I'm eating my feelings," I announced with as much grace as I could muster.

"There's powdered sugar on your nose."

I swiped at my face, balling the wrap up in my arms, and made a beeline for the elevator, cursing the fact that I was still inside the apartment. Was it not possible to leave this godforsaken place? To make matters worse, the more time that passed, the more I had to pee. I crossed my legs and listened for the creak of the slow-motion lift. Miracle of miracles, it finally arrived with a chipper *bing!*, welcoming me into its recesses. Freedom!

But before the door could close, a hand popped into the gap, alerting the sensor to snap back open. *For the love of God!* If one exists, please let me leave this hellish place! And please let this be someone I don't know!

In walked the guy I'd seen talking to Helen earlier: Mr. Crinkly Smile. He flashed me a subdued grin, then moved to the spot beside me, playing that universal game of elevator Tetris, and stood facing the doors. Out of the corner of my eye, I saw him glance at me, then I cursed the heavens as he parted his lips to speak. I was in no mood.

"So," the guy said. "You're the 'last resort'?"

That I wasn't expecting.

I whipped around to face him. "I'm sorry?"

"I heard Helen call you Stu's 'last resort.' Catchy nickname, by the way."

I rolled my eyes. "I'm hoping it doesn't stick."

"Joke."

"Funny." There was an awkward silence. Before I realized it, I heard myself add, "That's not how it was—with me and Stewart."

He nodded. "Oh, I know."

I knew I shouldn't take the bait, but I couldn't help myself. I looked his way. Up close, his eyes were twinkling for sure—with even more mischief than I'd realized before—and they were brown and flecked with yellow. *Trouble*. That was my first thought. I said, "Oh, yeah? What do you know?"

"Stu thought you were the greatest person alive," he shrugged. "He used to bore the pants off me telling stories about you guys as kids and even as adults. He said you were brilliant and beautiful and sharp and had so much integrity, blah, blah, blah."

I felt my breath catch. His words were the first thing since Stewart died to almost break me, despite the delivery. *Stewart. Gone.* The only person in the world who thought I was that amazing. Maybe the only person who really, truly knew me and loved me anyway, flaws and all. Pressure rose in my chest. With all my emotional might, I shoved it down. No breakdowns in elevators with strangers, thank you very much. "I appreciate you saying that."

"No problem. It's the truth. About what he said. No idea if it's actually true."

I smiled.

The stranger smiled back and then faced forward again. After a moment of silence, he cleared his throat. "He also said you were kind of a loser though."

The elevator jolted and then settled into its destination; the metallic doors swept open to reveal the lobby. He motioned for me to step out first, but I was frozen with my mouth hanging open, so he shrugged and exited. Shaking my head clear, I scrambled after him as he pulled on his coat. "Are you for real? Who talks to people that way? At a funeral?" I demanded. "Who *are* you?"

"Have a good day," he nodded to the doorman as the uniformed man opened the glass doors to the street. The insanely rude stranger sauntered through, taking his time, then turned back to face me. "I'm George." He held out his hand. I looked at it without moving. He grinned and put it back in his pocket.

"I've never heard of you," I mumbled, trying to think back. I tended to zone out when Stewart talked about his random buddies, since they came and went and mostly sucked. There was something vaguely familiar about the name—had Stewart mentioned a George? Had I been listening? Like ever *really* listening? "You're what? Like an aspiring actor?"

"I am not."

"A working actor?"

"No."

"A restaurant investor?"

"Nope."

"A club promoter?"

"Nope. Jeez. Why don't you just cut to the chase and ask if I'm a douchebag. That's basically what you're suggesting."

"Okay," I agreed. "Are you a douchebag? 'Cause you seem like one."

George considered the question. "Maybe a little. But in more of an Adam Levine, well-intentioned kind of way. Seriously, I'm a friend from LA."

"Clearly," I snorted, gesturing toward his hair—perfectly mussed with product.

"What does *that* mean?"

Outside, the wind had picked up and small droplets of rain had begun falling from the sky, forming pointillist patterns on the concrete. We were protected under the navy blue and gold-trimmed awning, but the air felt damp when the wind blew—sharp gusts that cut through layers. I shivered.

"You might want to put on your scarf thing."

I'd been cuddling my wrap like a teddy bear, and, if I hadn't been so cold, I would have refused to put it on out of spite. Resigned, I attempted to pull it across my shoulders, getting repeatedly tangled in my purse strap. Finally, George held out his hands, and, despite misgivings, I shoved my bag in his direction while I slipped the wrap on. Then I yanked my purse back without a thank you.

"You seem kind of pissed," he said. "Maybe we got off on the wrong foot."

I glared at him, dumbfounded. "Be honest: you're actually some deranged fan, aren't you?"

He ran a hand through his Bradley Cooper hair. "Look, I'm sorry," he groaned. "Stu always said you had a killer sense of humor; I thought you'd take a joke. But you're right—it's a funeral. I tend to make inappropriate jokes when I'm uncomfortable. Very low emotional IQ."

"You think?"

"But, to be fair, he did describe you as a kind of loser. I didn't want to be untruthful."

I looked to the heavens. "Oh my God!"

"What?" George glanced over his shoulder like he'd like to run in the other direction. "Sorry. I have this bad habit of speaking when I should shut up—no filter. Anyway, nice meeting you and I should—"

"Um, no! You can't just drop that bomb and walk away. Now you have to tell me: What did he say? If he really said anything."

"Are you sure?" George exhaled, trapped. "Look, he just mentioned that you don't go out much and are risk averse. And that you're like the living embodiment of wasted potential. And that you haven't had a boyfriend in forever—except some guy who dumped you and asked for money on Indiegogo for libraries in Africa. And then there was a whole thing about *The Bachelor* and cats, I think? But that part I didn't really follow 'cause he said there were two Chris Harrisons or something? And we'd had a lot of beer by then." He scratched his head, confused.

I've never felt so exposed. And the worst part was that this George person was telling the truth: He and Stewart were close friends. And Stewart had said all that stuff about me. I knew it. Otherwise this dude wouldn't have known the details. How come I didn't know about *him*? I mean, I know I wasn't as much in Stewart's everyday life lately—especially in his LA world—but wouldn't he at least have mentioned this guy?

Most of all, I was pissed that I couldn't defend myself to Stewart—he was dead. Now, because I didn't know what else to say, I grunted, "It was Kickstarter and wells, not libraries. And there's nothing wrong with cats."

"Sure. Okay. I like cats," George said like he was placating a deranged lunatic. "I grew up with one named Melba. Like the toast."

As George eyed me nervously, I shoved my hands in my dress pockets. My fingers were starting to sting from the cold. Across the street, I watched a female jogger lope by, apparently concerned enough about her BMI to run in a storm.

"Hey," George tried. "If it's any consolation, I don't think you seem *that* bad—as last resorts go."

All the rage I'd been projecting on the linzer tarts came bubbling up in that moment. All the injustice of having to endure Stewart's terrible friends. Why had Kate bailed? Why had Gretchen and Jimmy left me stranded for a cheap hookup?

"Who asked you?" I spat at George. I didn't need this, today of all days. Like the situation wasn't horrible enough? Done, I turned and stormed down the sidewalk, so I was being pelted by raindrops.

"Wait! Um, Last Resort!"

I whirled around. "What?" I could have kicked myself for responding.

"Sorry. I forgot your name?"

"Wren!"

"Right. Wren. One last thing!"

"What? What more could you possibly have to say to me?"

"Your cookies are falling out of your purse."

I looked down. Indeed, the napkin stuffed with tarts was hanging out the side pocket of my bag. I pulled my wrap up over my head like a babushka. "My cookies are just fine, thank you."

With that, I turned to leave. The momentum sent the napkin and cookies falling to the pavement. There they sat, broken into infinitesimal pieces, turning to soggy pulp in the downpour. And all I could think was, is this what the inside of Stewart's brain looked like after the aneurysm? All his beautiful thoughts reduced to a pile of mush? The idea was so dark that I almost laughed.

George moved toward me, but I shot him a glare that stopped him in his tracks. He put his hands up in self-defense.

"I just wanted to help."

"You *can* help. By going away. Forever."

I took a shuttered breath, bending to gather the napkin to throw in the trash. When I stood up, George was gone. And I still had to pee.

CHAPTER 11

Dear Stewart,

Thanks for dying.

It's just like you to bail without notice and leave me alone with all these assholes.

Love,
Wren

CHAPTER 12

I woke up the next morning with the dim light of dawn. That's unlike me. I'm a late riser, but I couldn't get back to sleep.

I was uncomfortable. My tank top was bunched up, my head was sore from an all-night ponytail, the radiator was expressing relentless heat into my bedroom. That's what happens in old New York City apartments; they suck you dry. I tried to will myself to stand up and fold a pile of clothes that had been slumped on the one nice chair I owned—an Eames reproduction—for days. I didn't move.

Instead, unable to stop myself, I played a fictional reenactment of Helen Beasley finding out that her son was dead on repeat in my head: As she was scrutinizing a prize orchid, her phone rang and she reached for it, perhaps assuming the call was from a telemarketer, her Pilates instructor, or maybe even Stewart. That's when the person spoke—but *who*? I kept getting stuck there. Who found Stewart's body? I both needed to know the details and was terrified to find out. I sure as hell wasn't going to ask Blair. She could only be smug if she knew and useless if she didn't.

I kept picturing Stewart in those last moments too—before and after the life left his body: Was he sitting on the bed or on the couch? Had he felt sick enough to lie down or had he fallen to the floor? Was he looking up at a popcorn stucco ceiling or out the window at the tip of a palm tree frond and a section of blue sky? Was he wearing a T-shirt? Jeans? What color is brain fluid? Did it leak out his ears? Is that a thing? That's a thing, right?

I closed my eyes against that image—too gruesome. But, with them shut, I saw Helen's face projected against my hooded lids. The shock in her blue eyes. Sharp features folding into a wobble. A veined hand to her chest.

When they spoke the words, "Your son is dead," did she collapse? Or is that something people only do in Hallmark movies? Did she shake her head in disbelief? Did she throw up? No, women like Helen don't throw up— they *vomit*. Did she cry? Did she think, "My life is over. That's it. I'm just done"? Did she sense the news in advance, intuiting a shift in the cosmos?

"It's too horrible," I sighed to no one at all. "Stewart. Gone. Forever." I said the refrain out loud this time, testing its resonance. My mind was still rejecting the information like a vending machine with a beat-up dollar bill.

I couldn't even distract myself with funeral planning, as I was stuck on a song for that guy George's service. Maybe something lame by Counting Crows. Who *was* that dude anyway?

I picked up my phone: 6:43 a.m. I ignored some *New York Times* alert as I typed in my password. Somewhere, across the world, a bunch of other people had died. Bengalese refugees. Helpless citizens in Syria. Children in Darfur. The world is a dangerous place. But not to *my* people, right? Not here, right now, in my safe Brooklyn bubble?

Suddenly, I felt scared. I didn't even know of what: loss, death—my own, someone else's, the people I love. I moved to dial, then realized I couldn't call the one person I needed: *Stewart*. What a dumbass I was. What a disorienting realization, like looking for your glasses when they're on your face.

I held down my iPhone's home button just to hear Siri's voice: "What can I help you with? Go ahead. I'm listening."

I exhaled. Then, I gave in, navigating to Facebook and typing in Stewart's name. I'd been resisting social media for days, but I was out of ideas for ways to feel close to him. I knew what I risked finding: tributes from strangers, page-long rants about how much he'd meant to people I'd never met. I was worried it would make me feel like I didn't know Stewart at all. I guess in some ways I never did know the person who chose that public life.

I remembered too clearly the ownership people on my feeds had taken over the deaths of other celebrities throughout the years—long, overwrought tribute posts about childhood memories of movies or songs. There was so little restraint or sense that, perhaps, the losses didn't belong to the whole wide world. The emoting felt like a competition to prove who felt the most hurt or had a right to the most sadness—about the absence of someone who most people had never met, whose identity was merely a projection. Stewart wasn't an icon; just a TV actor with a budding "serious" film career. Still, I feared the unchecked outpouring.

My prediction was sort of accurate. On his private personal page, there were no messages from crazy fans, but there were several posts that began with descriptions of the authors' tears. Why do people—especially ones named "Ginger"—think they deserve applause for crying? I don't trust people named after spices.

I guess I was being cynical. Maybe I was jealous because my post would have had to say, "I haven't cried since I heard! I'm a fraud!" But then I thought about Helen and decided I was okay. She'd shown more stoicism than most of his so-called friends.

There were pictures posted, too, of course: Stewart on set with craft service people. Stewart at a gastropub with his arm around some "bro" in aviators. Stewart by a pool in Palm Springs, holding a cigar and an alcoholic slushy. Stewart laughing at a bowling alley. Stewart on a mountaintop looking deep. He hated the fucking mountains. He thought hiking was a waste of time because it "got you nowhere." When the photo was taken, he was likely calculating how many minutes he'd waste walking down.

He looked handsome though. The afternoon sun caught his angles nicely. And he had had nice angles, if imperfect ones. He wasn't some standard Hollywood hunk. A nose just big enough to be considered prominent, eyes that narrowed like crescents, a lithe build, a scar over his eyebrow from the jungle gym fall. Did these people know that? Where his scar was from?

I scrolled through a few more posts. One girl had posted a blood oath: "stu, only u and i understand the depths of what life can be like. u were my partner, i can't live without you."

Jesus. Who was this person? I hoped she had a therapist. I clicked on her profile picture and realized she was the same sobbing girl from the semishiva.

The comments on the posts were just as cringe-worthy:

"OMG. Stu is dead? I just saw him at a Sundance gifting suite like seven months ago!"

I stared at my ceiling; a crack radiated from one corner. Was their Stewart real or was mine? Would the real Stewart please stand up?

I had several private messages waiting in my Facebook inbox, I realized, including one from Morgan Tobler, the high school acquaintance I was afraid might spoil my *Bachelor* screening the other night. I couldn't face them right now. I didn't have answers anyway.

My phone *bonged*; a text from a number I didn't recognize, to me and another unknown number:

> Hello. I'd like to talk to you both. Please be at the apartment at 2 today for tea. Let me know if that's a problem. Otherwise, I'll expect to see you then.

I stared at the message. *The* apartment? What apartment?
The other, more astute, recipient responded quickly.

> Of course. I'll be there. May I bring anything?

Who were these people? I wracked my brain. My boss? No. He was scouting project sites in Panama.

> Just yourself. Thank you.

I sighed and looked toward the heavens. *Are you there* Stewart? *It's me, Wren!*

What choice did I have? I typed, "Who dis?" Then I reconsidered, erased it and wrote,

> I'm so sorry, but who is this? I don't seem to have your number in my phone.

A blinking ellipses appeared, then:

> Wren, it's Helen Beasley. Remember yesterday when you said to contact you if I needed anything? I'd like your help.

Ah. *That* apartment. *Damn.* What was wrong with me? Who else would text me this week, at 7:00 a.m., in that formal tone?

> Yes. Of course. I'll be there. You can count on me.

> So you've said, despite neglecting to log my information in your phone.

I sighed, unbunching my tank top for the five-hundredth time. I could only fail with this woman.

The dots appeared again as if she was thinking of typing more, but nothing came. I wondered what she wanted. Maybe my old photos? I'd gather them together.

On the upside, maybe I could glean some details about what happened to Stewart, fill in the gaps. I saved Helen's information in my phone, then peeled back my comforter and forced myself up to shower. It was the least I could do.

CHAPTER 13

Stewart,

The strange thing about your loss is that I'm praying to feel its sting.

This dull ache—the constant unease, nausea, and jumpiness at the sound of honking trucks or backfiring busses—it's like being teased. To always be on the brink of severe pain, but not to know when it might arrive. To peer over your shoulder for fear that a sharp blade of sadness is about to penetrate. It's like being seasick and waiting to puke.

I am praying to puke, Stewart. Like we both did into buckets on that overnight whale-watching trip in ninth grade.

Well, maybe not quite like that.

The worst part—aside from missing you—is my inability to wrap my mind around what happened, to make it real, so that I can begin to understand what this new normal might look like. I wake up every day, surprised again by the reality of your absence. Is it true? Are you really gone? Forever?

But I need you, Stewart. What about that? What about me?

xo - W.

CHAPTER 14

I was back in Helen Beasley's lobby, that shimmering crystal palace, and I was dressed in my most polished jeans. I looked in the mirror, my image disjointed by a seam. It was the best I could do.

What did one wear to tea with their dead friend's very proper mother anyway? The floor of my apartment—littered with dismissed outfits—was a monument to my cluelessness. I tucked my chin inside the cowl neck of my chunky gray cashmere sweater, turtle-style, and wished I could hide.

I thought with regret back to my morning. I should have spent those hours being productive, packing my laptop and power cord into my leather backpack and trudging the three blocks to my regular coffee shop. I should have put my stuff down on a wooden table by an outlet, then crossed to the white slatted counter. I should have smiled and said, "Hi!" to the girl in the maroon baseball cap who takes my order daily—plus or minus a poached egg on top—and said, "That's right!" when she remembered it should be dairy-free. I should have taken my order number and utensils to my table and sat down to check my email, responding first to the proposed date and location for my next book club meeting. (I had left the thread hanging as the last person to confirm, except for Betsey, who never shows up anyway). I should have rescheduled my dermatologist appointment and my dinner with Gretchen and our other college friends. I should have read the day's *New York Times* morning briefing. Then, I should have started working because ever since Stewart died, I'd been useless.

But I was unfocused and not hungry and nervous about meeting with Helen. After trying on eighty-five outfits, I had pored over old yearbooks, staring into the eyes of Stewart's photographs for a hint of premonition.

As I waited for the elevator now, tapping my foot against the marble floor with a pleasing clacking sound, I realized I felt like I was going in for a job interview instead of tea.

What had Helen's tone been when the doorman called to say I'd arrived? I could have sworn his nod was reluctant, like he was allowing me up against his better judgment. Maybe he thought I was "the help." Maybe I was.

Why was I so anxious? What was the horrible thing I thought might transpire? After all, the worst had already happened. Was I afraid of making things harder for Helen? Of disappointing her? Of proving her right?

In my peripheral vision, I caught the doorman scowling at my tapping foot. I stood up as straight as I could, sucked in my cheeks and gave him my best haughty once-over; he looked away. Stewart would have enjoyed that. "You do a strangely accurate Queen Elizabeth impression," he once said, when I was giving him the silent treatment. Of course, that made me laugh and I instantly forgave him.

As the elevator rose, so did my stress level. By the time the doors were about to open, I was doing full-on breathing exercises. *One, two, three. Exhale.* I had the irrational thought that, if only Stewart were waiting on the other side, I would be okay.

Stewart. Gone. Forever.

I'd heard people say that grief comes in waves. If that was true, I could feel a fourteen-footer crashing over me now. No tears came—nothing as easily explained as that. No, this was devastation that stole my breath. I braced myself with a palm against the cool bronze of the elevator wall. Then, the doors opened with a flood of light from the apartment's mile-high windows.

Given no other choice, I stepped inside, looking back over my shoulder to watch the door slide closed behind me.

"Hello!" In place of Stewart, a plump young woman in a button down and pleated skirt stood waiting for me. Her expression was aggressively cheerful, even by nonmourning standards.

"Hi," I wheezed.

"You must be Wren!" She yanked the jacket off my shoulders. "I'm Madison, Helen's assistant. It's so nice to meet you! Stewart always spoke *so* highly of you!"

"Oh, thank you. Nice to meet you too."

"You'll be having tea in Helen's office! You do like tea, don't you? We have honey, lemon, sugar, milk, and even almond milk because, well, I know you're"—she dropped her voice to a whisper—"lactose intolerant." (She said it like she was saying "Jewish" in Nazi Germany.)

I was impressed that she knew that detail about me and sensed that she wasn't one to miss a step. She continued moving as she spoke, "I can eat cheese, but maybe it would be better if I couldn't. I eat it by the barrels! That's probably why I'm not a size four, but the heart wants what it wants! And mine wants triple-cream brie!"

CAUSE OF DEATH: By falling cartoon anvil. Or maybe an overdose on cheese?

AFTER-DEATH RITUAL: Cremation, so someone can make one of those creepy diamonds from her ashes.

SERVICE: Landmark Forum meeting.

PROCESSIONAL MUSIC: "Happy" by Pharrell Williams.

MEMORIAL BUFFET: Marzipan fruits and petit fours. Sickly sweet.

Madison gestured for me to follow and, when I hesitated, she prodded me forward with a series of taps on the back of my shoulder. *Come, come.* "So you're a writer, right? What kind again? I love magazines."

"Just a grant writer."

I could read her disappointment even from the back of her head, the way it settled into her neck. Maybe I was projecting.

"Oh. Grant writing. What does that mean exactly?"

I scurried to keep up with her as she zoomed down the hallway. The one thing I'll say for the whirlwind that was Madison is that I didn't have time for panic; I was winded from exertion instead. "I write applications, so that people or organizations—one organization in particular right now—is awarded money for research and program initiatives. That kind of thing."

"Uh, huh. Totally." She wasn't listening. "Did you used to write for magazines? I thought I remembered that? Stewart was in a lot of the good ones. I loved looking for him in them while getting my weekly pedicure. It's so sad!" She said it like, "It's so awesome!" I wasn't sure if she meant Stewart's death or the fact that she couldn't find him in magazines anymore.

"I wrote for a few. Magazines. In the beginning. But editorial is very unreliable, I—"

"Uh-huh. Totally." Madison didn't turn around as she said, "I don't know how you do it! I do not enjoy writing. No, sir! As soon as I was done with that last college term paper, I thought, 'Thank God! I'm never doing that again!' No offense. I'm sure it's great for you!"

Was it great for me? It was more like part of me. Writing was the language of my household. I grew up in a cluttered but well-loved rent-controlled apartment—the kind with piles of first edition books and not enough storage. The bookshelves we did have were finds from flea markets and antique shops, although my parents are discerning, so many were of Danish modern and other design movements. My mother and father left each other—and eventually me—Post-it notes on surfaces all over the house: *Don't forget fennel for tonight's dinner party. Take out the garbage. Remind me to tell you about this Hannah Arendt passage I rediscovered.* It's how we communicated. Sometimes, especially in comparison to Stewart's home—or *homes*—I found our lifestyle embarrassing and avoided having friends over.

"Your parents are the real deal," Stewart used to assure me. "They just don't have real furniture."

He loved them. How could he not? My parents were the diametric opposite of his. Back in the day, he never missed a Passover at our house.

CAUSE OF DEATH: Simultaneous.

AFTER-DEATH RITUAL: Cremation. There is no God. Lifelong

atheists. Also: "I tell you the past is a bucket of ashes, so live not in your yesterdays, not just for tomorrow, but in the here and now." (Carl Sandburg)

SERVICE: All their weird literary friends—and me, of course. Maybe at the local library.

PROCESSIONAL MUSIC: Neil Young and Talking Heads. For days.

MEMORIAL BUFFET: Italian subs, for sure. With dill pickle–flavored chips. My dad wouldn't have it any other way.

My parents—who were both adjunct professors—took their time in the mornings, listened to NPR, scheduled time for "thinking." The only things that inspired urgency in them were the residency and fellowship applications they were always filling out, so that one or both of them (and often me, too, unless my grandparents watched me) could go work on their craft somewhere remote for a period of time. Generally, that meant a monastic setting in the middle of nowhere with lots of trees, no TV, no internet, and scratchy sheets on uncomfortable Victorian cots. There, they spent their time reading theory and fiction, writing and attending readings—which is how they spent time in their everyday lives anyway. If you think about it, it's no surprise that my one skill turned out to be writing grant proposals.

My mother was thrilled that I chose a more stable career than they had; my father less so. He thought, in less intense terms than Stewart, that I might be wasting my "talents." For some reason, he dreamed of me writing screenplays, maybe because I wrote one semidecent one in college. For the millionth time in the last few days—okay, maybe much longer than that, if I was honest—I had a sinking feeling like somehow I'd failed. Like maybe my career wasn't what it should be, and everyone knew it but me. Did Stewart's criticisms bug me because I sensed the kernel of truth in them?

Madison stopped before a closed door, her hand on the knob. "Oh, shoot! I just realized that I got popovers to go with the tea, but you won't be able to eat them. Eggs!"

"Oh, no. I can have eggs. I just—"

"Anyway! Can't keep them waiting!"

"Wait, *them*? I meant to ask, who is the other—?"

She flung the door open to reveal Helen, sitting on a mauve love seat next to George, the jerk from the day before. Of course. Because—my luck. He was holding her hand. Her head was bowed. Maybe she was crying.

The pop of the door opening had startled them both, though, and Helen looked up. Spotting me, she pursed her lips and dropped George's hand, erasing any signs of vulnerability. She raised her palm in a flourish to gesture me in. "Wren. You've arrived."

My Queen Elizabeth had nothing on hers.

"Sorry if I'm late. The train . . ." Why had I even said that? I knew I wasn't late. It was like I wanted to give her reason to hate me.

"Let me know if you need anything!" Madison chirped. She shut the door behind me. For all her annoyingness, I wished her back. This place felt like a trap.

Still, I had to admit, it was a beautiful dungeon. The walls were vaguely pink and the furniture was all by recognizable modernist designers—angular and embodied. But there was also a warmth here. The neutral rugs and textiles were woven into muted patterns, creating a yogic effect, as if we'd been transported to an Asian-inspired wellness retreat. Of course, there was a signature orchid on Helen's desk.

Once, when I was a kid, I knocked one of her flowers over while Stewart and I were playing some make-believe dragon game. I was terrified, but Stewart took the blame. It was the only time I ever heard her raise her voice at him. "You know my mother," he would say sardonically years later. "She's a delicate flower herself."

My sweater was starting to feel like its own little prison. Like I was being cultivated in a greenhouse like her orchids.

"Have a seat." Helen's voice quivered. At least I thought it did. "Do you know George?"

I nodded, sitting down in a chair to their left and allowing my eyes to stray to his face. What was he doing here? He nodded back without smiling, no indication that he remembered yesterday's exchange. Maybe it had never happened. Maybe none of this was happening.

"I'm sorry to be abrupt," Helen continued, "but I have an appointment with my estate lawyer shortly, so I'm afraid I need to dispense with pleasantries." I'm not sure if she meant the word *pleasantries* ironically, but it sure felt off in this context.

"Whatever you need."

"So, as you know, Stewart's passing was very sudden." George and I nodded solemnly. "As a result, we're left with some messes to clean up. He wasn't . . . prepared. Well, none of us were. And, as you also know, he wouldn't have been one to worry much about the fallout from such things. He would have figured when you're gone, you're gone." I thought I saw the faintest trace of a smile cross her lips, as she recalled how maddening her son could be.

"I asked you both here because I'd like you to take on the most literal mess: his apartment."

This was not what I'd expected. I figured whatever Helen asked would be deeply peripheral like informing his old classmates or helping to cancel his subscriptions to *Variety* and Blue Apron. But *this*? This seemed like a major undertaking, from both an emotional and practical standpoint. I was at once horrified and honored to be entrusted with the task.

"You want us to . . . sorry, do what in his apartment?" asked George. Turns out I wasn't the only one caught off guard.

"Go through his stuff," Helen said, massaging her temple. Maybe she had a headache too. "Decide what should be kept, donated, or discarded. Decide who should get what, after I've reserved whatever Kate and Ted and I might like to keep."

George and I looked at each other, then back at Helen.

"But how will we know?" I heard myself say. "What has value? To you?"

"Wren, you were his best friend for three decades. If you don't know, then who would?"

To my horror, I felt flattered. "What about Kate? She doesn't want to see what's there?"

"She's too busy. Or upset. I don't know."

"But—"

"You'll have George here to help you figure out how best to disseminate things—what, if anything, has monetary value or should go to a specific person based on Stewart's very vague will. Some of Stewart's other friends have reached out about retrieving mementos. I'll let them know that you'll be handling things."

"He had a will?" I blurted out, instantly regretting it. "I didn't realize." Every revelation was like a knife to the gut. I guess it just made it all more real. I furrowed my brow in confusion. "But why would"—I gestured at George without looking his way—"*he* know what Stewart cared about?"

Helen stared at me like I was the world's biggest moron. "Because George was Stewart's lawyer. He drew up the will."

I'm sure my eyes opened wide at that. I looked at George, as he avoided my gaze. "His lawyer? Oh. I *see*."

As my mind reeled, processing that information, Helen continued, "The Institute of Television Arts has expressed interest in hosting a memorial in Stewart's honor—some speakers and the like to highlight his work. Very short notice; they like to do these things quickly. There will be a curated display of certain objects, some photographs, et cetera, in a small gallery by the auditorium there, for attendees to peruse, so you should also be on the lookout for anything to include."

"Anything?"

"Photographs, costumes, objects, his Emmy. Anything that reflects his career trajectory, his inspirations. Anything that screams, 'Stewart.' You understand." She looked away quickly.

We do? An image came to mind of Stewart as Friar Tuck in our fifth-grade production of *Robin Hood*. And a postcard he kept propped on his adolescent desk of Robert De Niro in *Raging Bull*. So there would be something beyond the boilerplate funeral. Thank God.

Helen rose and walked to her desk. She opened a drawer and pulled out a set of keys on a brown leather Balenciaga keychain. She crossed back to us and held them out. "Here." George and I stared at the dangling cluster without moving. "Take these, so you can let yourselves into the apartment and start sorting everything tomorrow. Who wants them?"

I said, "I can—"

"George. You take them. There's only one set."

She'll only lose them.

"Of course." He stood and accepted the keys, which had started to feel totemic to me. So I stood too.

"One last thing: Wren, the Institute likes to partner with a charity for these events to donate proceeds from ticket sales. In this case, an aneurysm organization seems to make the most sense. I can't recall—are you writing for magazines or working in the nonprofit sector these days?"

"No, I stopped the journalism stuff a while ago. The industry is dying, I—"

"Good. Then you'll be in charge of figuring out which aneurysm nonprofit is the best fit. Be in touch if you have any questions." The idea of delving into the details of the affliction was both terrifying and enticing.

This was our cue to leave. George opened the door and I hurried through, almost slamming into Madison, who waited on the other side with a gigantic smile frozen on her face. I stifled a shriek. I bet she slept with her eyes open.

"Can I show you out?"

Minutes later, George and I were back in our coats and riding down in the elevator together.

I couldn't restrain myself for long: "His lawyer, huh? You said 'douche bag friend.'"

"First of all, I never actually called myself a 'douchebag friend.'" George looked sheepish, stuffing his hands in his pockets. "And I was both. Friend and attorney."

"Sure."

"I didn't mention the lawyer thing because I didn't want you to react like you are now, thinking I was some bottom feeder. Stu and I were close."

"Right, right. *Close.* You're an entertainment lawyer, I imagine, then?"

"Yeah. I just drew up a boilerplate will because he said the studio insisted he have something basic. That's partially why it's not as detailed as it should be."

"Uh-huh." I sighed. "I can't fucking believe this."

"That you have to go through his apartment? Or that you have to do it with me?"

"Both."

The truth is I was shocked that Helen had chosen me and acknowledged me as Stewart's "best friend." Had I been wrong? Did she see my value in Stewart's life, after all?

"I'm not thrilled either," George frowned. "I have a job. This is going to be really time-consuming and the partners at the firm aren't going to be happy about me working remotely for even longer. Plus I loved Stewart, but I really don't need to go through his underwear drawer."

"You know, I have a job too."

"No, but I have a *real* job."

I stared at him. "You're the worst, you know that?"

"Oh, and you're a ray of sunshine?"

I clenched my hands into fists. The doors swept open. Sensing my rage, George backed out of the way as I stomped from the elevator like I might run him over. If only I'd had a car.

Behind me, I heard a groan, then he jogged to catch up. "Wait! Wren, wait." He stopped me in the middle of the lobby, resting a gentle hand on my shoulder. I almost shrugged it off, but the contact felt oddly calming. "Look," his voice softened, "I know we haven't exactly hit it off so far, but this . . . it's going to be tough. On many levels. Let's try to make the best of it and help each other, okay?"

I exhaled. That sounded reasonable. It was maybe the first thing out of his mouth that did. "Fine."

He pulled his phone from his back pocket. "What's your number? I'll call you now, so we have each other's info." I recited it; my phone rang.

"You would use that old-fashioned phone ringtone." I opened my mouth to protest, but George held up a hand. "I mean, because it's so quaint, not because it's played out. And grandma." He shot me a fake smile. "Okay. Let's leave it at that before I make things worse. Tomorrow at ten a.m.?"

I rolled my eyes but nodded begrudgingly. The doorman opened the lobby doors wide in obvious deference to George, but, as I walked past, he scrutinized me. I looked down at my jeans and then at George's navy peacoat and pressed button-down. I guess he was dressed as if he merited respect. Was that the difference?

"See ya, Bill!" George waved to the doorman, who waved back. *Oh.* Or maybe George had made a buddy.

I crossed my arms. "Why is that guy such a dick to me?"

"Who? Bill? What did he do?"

"He just glares at me."

"I think he's just being cautious."

"Cautious? Why? Do I look like I might mug a tenant?"

George shook his head. He gestured across the street, to the park side of Central Park West, where a cluster of men lingered with cameras. *Paparazzi.* I started. I don't know why I was surprised. Sometimes I was so busy thinking about where Stewart started that I forgot who he had become. "Oh! Oh, I see."

"They've been loitering out there waiting for photos. One doorman caught them paying off a garbage man, so they could rifle through the Beasleys' trash. Slow gossip week, I guess."

"But that's disgusting!"

"Sure is."

It was like there was my universe and then this foreign Hollywood one, and I didn't even speak that language. But then I had never been able to understand Stewart's world of fame or his attraction to it. Even back when he started making theater friends in high school and dedicating so much time to acting, I couldn't comprehend the appeal.

"Okay. I'll see you tomorrow," George said. For him, apparently the tabloid scavengers were no big thing. "Should I bring coffee? How do you take it?"

"I think Stewart was gifted one of those fancy Nespresso things with the pods after doing a commercial," I said, tearing my eyes away from the photographers. "He probably never used it. I'm sure there's plenty."

"Okay. We can play it by ear then. Oh, and I'll call the police detective who's lead on the case and make sure we're clear to get through the crime scene tape."

I swear my heart stopped. Just for a moment. Maybe I died and came back to life like that older guy with the bow tie from the shiva. I couldn't speak—and I wanted to so badly. I looked from the blue sky to the sidewalk, where the first fallen leaves were collecting beneath the curb's lip, and tried to find my breath. "Wait, what?" I finally managed. "Why police?"

"There're always police when someone dies suddenly like this. Apparently, it's standard."

"But why would you need to call?"

"Well, it's possible that they haven't closed the case file."

I shut my eyes. "Stop. What are you talking about? I don't understand. Why would there be police tape at his New York apartment?"

"Because that's where he died." George's eyes opened wide in surprise. "Did you not know that?"

CHAPTER 15

You were here? Stewart. You were here. And you didn't call me.
   How come?

CHAPTER 16

Before I was able to answer George, my phone *bing*'d. I looked at the screen without seeing. *Stewart was in town when he died? I was going to have to sort through the crime scene?*

I snapped back to reality. The text was from yet another number I didn't recognize.

> Wren. It's Blair. We need to talk. Keith and I heard that you're—

Another *bing*. Another text.

> It's Keith. It's so generous of you to go through Stewart's crap. I'm sure there's endless piles of it. He was such a slob. I don't even want the job, but I think we can both agree that there are certain things that only I, as a fellow—

Bing.

> WREN, HI HI! IT'S MALLORY! SO, HELEN MENTIONED THAT YOU'LL BE THE ONE GOING THROUGH—

Bing.

> Cheers, Wren! It's Willow. Hope you're having a
> beautiful and peaceful day. I was just wondering
> if you'd like me to bring sage for a clearing
> ceremony for—

The texts kept coming. I was tempted to throw my phone into oncoming traffic. And then maybe follow it.

"What's with your phone?" George cocked his head. "Is it having a psychotic break?"

I looked up at him, suddenly too exhausted to speak.

"Are *you* having a psychotic break?"

I exhaled. "I'm guessing that Helen sent an email to the vultures about cleaning out the apartment."

"The vultures?"

"Stewart's 'friends.'" I formed air quotes with my free hand.

"Aren't they your friends too?"

I shrugged. *Not really.*

"What are they saying?"

"That they want to help."

He shrugged his broad shoulders. "So?"

"So that's bullshit. It's code for wanting to prove that they knew him best. That they have sobbing rights. They want to carve out a piece for themselves, soak up what's left of his celebrity. Maybe they want *stuff.* I don't know."

George narrowed his eyes, channeling Atticus Finch. "Like what kind of stuff?"

"Who knows? His watches, his photos, his old socks. A piece of Stewart."

"Ah," George exhaled. "I thought you meant money or things of substantial monetary value."

"Who knows?" I shrugged. "That's your department."

"Well, let's just assume the best for now, okay?" George let his shoulders drop, slipping his hands inside his coat pockets. "You're probably overreacting. Maybe they all just want to be in his place and absorb the fact that he's gone. Maybe they each want a memento in order to feel close to him."

Oh, George. He was so innocent—and condescending. My mouth said, "Maybe." My tone said, "Maybe not." I ran a hand through my hair, which I'd taken the time to curl into a wave earlier. "Look, you didn't hear that crew talking at the funeral."

"No. I didn't."

"Well, it was gross. And—"

"Look, no offense, but—"

"Oh, this should be good," I crossed my arms over my chest. "Sentences that start with 'no offense' are generally not at all offensive."

"Can I give you some advice?"

"Seriously? No."

"Case and point: You're a little negative. You're always assuming the worst."

"Always?" I threw my hands in the air. "We're on an 'always' basis now?"

"Always. In the two times that I've met you."

"Not much of a straw poll."

"I think Nate Silver would still agree with me."

I took a deep breath of cool air and tried to contain my seething anger. "Look, I know these people."

"Okay, fine. That's true. But, for the record, I've worked with Blair before on Stu's behalf and she's been just fine."

"By Hollywood standards?"

"But forget that. Just imagine for a moment that maybe these people loved Stewart too and aren't going to make this all about themselves. Think about how much better you'd feel in this moment if you trusted that they were offering you earnest support in this difficult task." I felt like I was trapped in the world's worst self-help seminar.

"Fine. Maybe they're not self-serving. Maybe they're not trying to milk this thing for all it's worth—from a status, career, and monetary standpoint. Maybe they're not trying to demonstrate that their grief is the most valid. Maybe they're not all about getting attention and feeling important—and sucking the blood out of my dead friend's memory."

"*Our* dead friend's memory."

"*My* dead friend. *Your* dead client."

George groaned and slapped a hand to his forehead in frustration. "Whatever. The point is, maybe! Maybe they do have decent intentions!"

I looked blankly back at him.

"See?" he grinned. "Don't you feel better now?"

"Yes. I always feel better after a man who knows less than I do explains why I'm wrong."

"This isn't a gender thing," George sighed. "I'm just trying to stay positive."

"Why don't you leave that to your STD tests?"

"I give up."

"Awesome."

"I'll see you at ten a.m. If you want, I'll email the group and ask them to join us at noon, after we've had a couple of hours to sort through things. That way you don't have to deal with them when we first arrive, and we'll have some control over the situation."

I forced a fake smile. "Works for me. Can't wait!"

Without a goodbye between us, George and I turned and walked in opposite directions. I wasn't even heading toward the right train stop. I just wanted to escape. I could feel our energy dividing, as I walked on, as if pressure was releasing.

On the subway ride home, as the car jostled and tossed me around, I read Helen's email, which she had sent to Blair, Keith, Mallory, Brian, George, Willow, Jimmy, and me. I guess we represented Stewart's inner circle in her mind. Inner circle of hell, if you asked me. But no one did.

Dear All,

Thank you again for being at the funeral and reception. It meant a lot to see you there. Your friendship is a credit to Stewart's memory and reminded me of simpler times.

Several of you have reached out to ask what might happen to Stewart's memorabilia, photos, and other possessions. I have asked George and Wren—Stewart's attorney and friend, in case you haven't met—to take a cursory look and organize the possessions at Stewart's New York apartment. After that, we can decide how to disseminate things. Let me know if there are specific items by which you'd like to remember my son and I will keep that in mind.

Best,
Helen

I sighed. So this was my new reality. How did I wind up without Stewart, but with all of these nightmarish people? When he was alive, they had seemed like the comic relief I put up with in order to spend time with him. He would shoot me a knowing look across a restaurant banquette or bar, and then resume whatever silly conversation with a sip of his vodka. Later, we would joke about the absurdity of it all. Now there was only absurdity and no touchstone.

In retrospect, it was hard not to question Stewart's values for having chosen these friends. But none of that even mattered. Because he had been here. In New York City. And not only hadn't he mentioned it, he had pretended to be in LA. I tried to think back: Had he actually said he was in California when we talked on the phone or had I just assumed? Was I the only one who didn't know or were we all in the dark?

You're probably shooting today. Wasn't that what I had texted him? Was he already dead by then? Did he forget to tell me he was in town because his brain wasn't working at full capacity as it readied to explode? Had he decided he didn't want to see me after our argument? Had he been more fed up than I'd realized? Or had I not been high status enough to merit his time? To me, the conversation had been vintage us. Maybe it was a bit more charged than usual; he had less sense of humor about my "limitations." But I figured he was just in one of his moods.

The worst part was that I had no reliable narrator. My own memory was the only record, and it was proving hard to trust.

The subway screeched to a halt. Across the train, a bearded man in a skullcap—homeless or hipster?—groaned in his sleep, head falling onto the shoulder of the revolted woman next to him.

We are being held momentarily by the train's dispatcher.

The lights blinked off and on again. A split second of darkness, then a blast of fluorescents. A minute passed and then another. Was I about to get stuck on this train for the long haul? Passengers started to shift in their seats. A man nearby began talking to himself—or was he on his phone's earbuds? Were we trapped with someone unstable or was he completely normal?

We are delayed because of train traffic ahead of us.

I felt paranoid. I looked at the people around me—and I didn't trust them. My eyes strained against the light. The air smelled like something rotten; I hoped it wasn't emanating from nearby. Being trapped on the subway is a nightmare. *Please no*, I thought. But then something else occurred to me: *You are lucky to be stuck on this subway.*

You could be Stewart. You could be dead. You could never be stuck on a subway again—or even ride one. You could have vanished off the face of the Earth. You could be gone.

CHAPTER 17

Dear Stewart,

I wonder where you are, if anywhere. When it comes to the afterlife, I've always believed whatever was most comfortable at a given time: reincarnation and karma (to explain away an asshole who somehow comes out a winner), another stage of existence, a heaven that is whatever your unconscious mind decides. Maybe just being dead and gone is the most realistic outcome, but I guess that makes me uncomfortable.

Whenever we talked about this stuff, you claimed to be an atheist. Remember when I came home from Florida after my grandfather died? I pestered you until you admitted what you believed about the afterlife: "When you're dead, you're dead. That's it. No encore." Even then, I'm not sure I believed you. Sure, that fit your cooler-than-thou misanthropic image. But how could someone who lived life with such intensity believe that everything just goes black? What then was the point of expending all that energy?

So where are you, Stewart? Are you just gone? Or will your soul be hovering over your apartment tomorrow, your essence permeating the negative space as we invade your privacy, leafing through your Arthur Miller collection and emptying the half-finished pressed juices—the ones you drank out of obligation—from your fridge? Will you be watching over us? Do you even care? Or are you too enlightened now to have time for petty grievances?

Sometimes you even acted that way while alive—above it all.

"Wren," you would groan, impatient with my intolerance, even as you felt intolerant of me. But most of the time, you were right there with me, Stewart. Snarky as hell. I miss that.

So I'm wondering, when you die, do you lose your sense of humor? If not, I bet you think my life is pretty hilarious right now.

xo - W.

CHAPTER 18

That evening, George sent an email, as promised, inviting Stewart's nearest and dearest monsters to join us at noon the next day for a cathartic last visit to his apartment. Their responses flooded my inbox within minutes:

7:51 p.m.

Thanks for handling this, George. Stu would have really appreciated it. And I'm sure he left a big mess, if I know him. We'll be able to offer some unique insight into what has value, no doubt. I still can't believe the loss we've suffered. Cheers, Keith

---

7:52 p.m.

George, it means the world that you're able to support Helen in this difficult time. I know because I talked to her twice today and she told me. She keeps reaching out to me, which is very difficult, but I would never say no. Of course we'll meet you at the apartment and say a real goodbye to our best friend. I know Stu would have wanted it. I am practically OCD when it comes to organizing, so I can help in any way.

Have you gotten bins from IKEA? A label maker? It will be very trying for us all, but I'm so important. xx - Blair

7:53 p.m.

Sorry. I meant "it's" so important. Obviously. xx - B.

7:55 p.m.

GEORGE, you're our HERO for taking on this HORRIBLE task. OF COURSE WE WILL HELP YOU. I'm actually GREAT at this kind of thing and know everything about the *Manic Mondays* stuff especially. I know Wren could never have handled this alone; I'm so glad she doesn't have to now. I CANNOT stop CRYING onto this keyboard; I'm going to damage my COMPUTER. Brian and I will both be there. We wouldn't miss it for the world! Brian will not stop talking about it! You know how he is. Should I bring beer? It seems like we could use some liquid courage. Maybe some snacks too? I could pick up truffle popcorn? Chips and salsa? Also, will we be taking items home with us? Should we bring empty totes? Can't wait to see you all! - MAL & BRIAN

7:57 p.m.

Mal, that is so sweet, but I don't think beer is really appropriate as it will be early afternoon. It's not a party, right? Love you, honey. xx - Blair

---

7:59 p.m.

Okay. You're so right, B. My bad. - MAL & BRIAN

9:14 p.m.

George, thank you for the honor of joining you at our beloved Stu's physical space one last time. I know we will all feel his presence there though his soul is en route elsewhere. I'll bring some sage to clear out his spirit and encourage the crossover. Mal, I have some Kava-infused supplements, if you'd like to take something for anxiety in lieu of alcohol. I'll bring them too. Have a blessed day. Love & Light. - Willow

---

9:15 p.m.

Willow, if you're bringing sage to burn, please remember to bring matches in case Stu doesn't have any. That said, I'm not sure if burning herbs is a co-op code violation, so perhaps consider a sage mist spray or diffuser instead? You're so thoughtful! I'll let Helen know that we've got this under control. xx - Blair

---

11:03 p.m. [only to me]

No way I'm going to this fucking thing. Not on your life; not on Stewart's death. - Jimmy

To say that I was disappointed about Jimmy bailing was an understatement. I was desperate for solidarity, especially from someone who remembered the same Stewart as I did. I had fantasies of unearthing relics from our childhood together amidst Stewart's things and finding shared comfort in tears and laughter. But I knew better than to try to convince Jimmy to come. He was immovable when he made a decision. Stewart knew that better than anyone. I had seen him try to argue, cajole, flatter, threaten, and shame his gentle giant of a pal into everything from lip syncing to De La Soul at a seventh-grade talent show, to dressing up as Austin Powers and Mini-Me for Halloween, to attending Morgan's *Josie and the Pussycats*–themed birthday party, promising they would "make it fun." (Stewart never wanted to miss a celebration.) Jimmy always shot him down.

Instead of responding, I forwarded the thread to Gretchen without comment.

She answered right away:

FML. Well, actually FYL. These people should be euthanized.
Love ya! - G (Seriously, sending you love. How are you handling
everything? Have you cried yet? Who is George?)

Just another spoiled sycophant suckling at Stewart's
pseudofamous teat.

Well, that's vivid. But don't mince words. How do you *really* feel?

Needless to say, when I awoke the next morning, I was not looking forward to the day.

As I sat at my computer, checking my email, my mother tried me again. I ignored the call and instead texted that I'd try her later. I knew I was taking avoidance to the next level, but I just couldn't deal.

After staring at the log of her "missed" calls, I let my gaze fall on a framed photograph that I kept on my desk: It was of my parents and me—at maybe five years old—in a Nigerian village. This particular artist-in-residence position involved both my parents teaching reading to Nigerian children. I don't remember the trip that well, having been so young, but I have a couple distinct memories of sitting on a dusty porch with village kids, eating some version of jerky. I looked happy in the photograph. We all did. It had been so long since I'd been somewhere that different. It seemed like a thousand years ago.

I got dressed and left the house, stopping at my corner bodega for a bruised banana and coconut water. I hadn't done my usual grocery shopping that week for obvious reasons. And, anyway, I loved the couple who owned the store. Today, the wife was working alone. As she rung me up, she scrutinized my face. "You're tired?"

I nodded. "It's been a long week."

"Take care of yourself," she shook her head. "Cold weather is coming."

CAUSE OF DEATH: Rheumatism.

AFTER-DEATH RITUAL: Cremation with last rights by monks.

SERVICE: A celebration, attended by countless relatives.

PROCESSIONAL MUSIC: "Wind Beneath My Wings" by Bette
       Midler. Unexpected, I know, but she once told me that
       she loves *Beaches* when I mentioned that I was going
       home to watch a movie.

MEMORIAL BUFFET: Banchan to the max: kimchi, bibimbap, spicy
       tofu stew.

Waiting on the subway platform, I fished inside the plastic grocery bag
for my makeshift breakfast and found that she'd slipped me an Emergen-C
packet. See? *Kind.* I was so touched that I almost cried. *Almost.*

Thirty minutes later, I made my way from the train to Stewart's apartment, dodging Soho street traffic—homeless guys milling on corners with
empty cups, worker bees en route to design showrooms and meetings. As
I neared the building, I spotted George waiting for me outside, dressed in
a slate-gray hoodie, jeans, and high-tops. He looked freshly showered, but
he hadn't bothered to shave. Five o'clock shadow hid the faint cleft in his
chin. When had I noticed it?

He smiled at me. "Twinsies."

I guess he was referring to my hoodie and jeans too—more fitted,
but similarly neutral. I mustered a half smile instead of rolling my eyes,
though it took restraint.

I had promised myself I'd be more patient with George today. He was
right about one thing: this process was not going to be fun. Better not to add
extra tension. I needed to make him an ally against the vultures. Plus, I was so
nervous that I felt like I was about to throw up. I didn't have it in me to spar.

I stopped in front of him; he bent down and kissed me softly on the
cheek. It surprised me, partially because it was almost tender and partially

because it set off a fresh wave of butterflies. He was just being polite, but I recoiled in confusion. "Oh, sorry," he said. "I didn't mean . . . I was just saying hello. It seemed . . . whatever. 'Cause we're here and this is so, I don't know." He exhaled. *I can't win with this girl.* It was written all over his face.

"No, no," I said, wringing my hands. "It's totally fine. I'm just on edge."

"Me too." He peered up at the building's facade with a mixture of respect and fear, like he was checking out an intimidating woman. I had the sudden urge to have someone look that way at me.

Instead, I stared at the building too. It was new construction—minimal and industrial brick—with nods to its prewar neighbors in the form of deco-style edges.

We stood there in silence. Not the comfortable kind of quiet; the awkward kind. What was there to say?

"Sorry. I'm really out of it," I started. "I didn't sleep—"

"I hear you. I was up too. You should have called me. We could have watched *Gilmore Girls* reruns together on the phone."

"You watch *Gilmore Girls*?"

"Joke."

"Right."

"'Cause you know, we wouldn't call each other and watch anything. 'Cause we don't know each other very well. And also you don't like me."

"Yeah, I get it." I exhaled, not bothering to disagree. "Funny." I think things had been more comfortable when we were sniping at each other. At least that was honest.

"I assume you saw the email exchange with Stu's friends about coming here to take a last look at the apartment and help clear things out—or, what did you call them again? 'The vultures.'" He repeated the nickname in a mocking tone, with accompanying jazz hands, like I'd suggested that as a lame name for a band—like I was the crazy one.

"Of course. How could I miss all three-hundred-forty-five emails about how touched they were that you reached out, so they could put their stamp on everything? How devastated they are? How essential to the process? How appreciative? How moved?"

"You think they're not?"

"Who knows?" I shrugged. "Each email was an attempt to sound more grateful and despondent than the last person—and to speak for everyone else including Stewart. And also to act as if *you* wanted them there, as opposed to the other way around. They're each desperate for you to believe that Stewart was closest to them. I don't know why they care so much what you think." I knew I was scowling. Just thinking about the litany of messages made me mad.

"Really?" George furrowed his brow. "You thought their responses were annoying? I totally didn't take them that way. They were gracious."

"Are you serious?" Was this guy oblivious or just hell-bent on disagreeing with me? If he was anything like Stewart, it was the latter. But then I wasn't sure he *was* anything like Stewart. Why should he be, really? Why did I find myself comparing them? And why, I wondered for the hundredth time, hadn't Stewart told me more about him, if they were supposedly so tight? I shook that off, addressing the issue at hand. "I know Blair was okay when you worked with her, but that was a different context. You don't mind that she kept saying that she would 'report to Helen,' despite the fact that Helen put us in charge?"

"I don't really care to be in charge. Do you? I think you're seeing this in the worst possible light. They're just trying to help."

"Mallory practically suggested bringing a keg! At least before Queen Bee Blair shamed her out of it!"

"I mean, I wouldn't say no to some blurring of edges. I'm feeling pretty jittery right now." He glanced up at the building's facade again as if it might crumble down on top of him.

I kicked at a can on the sidewalk. "Look, maybe they do a good performance of normal. Trust me: they're not. With the exception of Jimmy, of course."

"What makes Jimmy so different?" George asked, his tone contentious.

"Because. Jimmy is the best. Have you met him?"

"Once with Stewart when he was in LA for work."

"Did you like him?"

"Sure." He shrugged. "He seemed cool."

"Jimmy is a real person, not like the others. He's everything. The rest of them are pond scum."

"Okay," George sighed. "We'll agree to disagree. I think you're under-estimating them. People come together during times like this. But, either way, I told them not to come until noon, so we'll have two hours—just us—to take it all in and set the groundwork for a smooth process."

Just us. That wasn't much of a consolation. I felt like he was final argument-ing me. "If you say so." The truth is, I was terrified of going into that apartment, being alone with its familiarity and emptiness, but I didn't want them there either, polluting what was left of my friend.

A large man walked by with a small dog on a leash, which got tangled for a moment on my leg. I shook myself loose.

"Sorry, sorry," he apologized. "You okay?"

"I'm fine, really." I felt dumb.

I watched the man and his puppy lope away; I wished I could join them. I turned to George instead. "Do they all know now that Stewart died here? And not in LA?"

"I emailed them each individually after I realized you didn't know. It seemed more appropriate than a mass email—and I asked for their discretion on future details."

"I'm confused. Why not tell the truth? To everyone?"

George rubbed the side of his neck, toggling his head. "It's not that we want to lie; it's just that we think the details should be private, despite Stu being a somewhat public figure."

"We?"

"Helen."

"Right." *We. Helen. Of course.* I felt the understanding steal my breath. I thought about the paparazzi photographers lurking across from her building. "I guess I get that."

"She just lost her son. So, whatever her reasons, it's our job to respect her wishes."

"Of course. Obviously." This guy was so damn preachy.

We stood there silently again, only this time I think we were both deep in thought. I'm not sure what George was thinking about; maybe getting as far away from me as possible. I was imagining Helen finding out for the eight-hundredth time. But now the scene was set in New York: she found out and ran right over. Or took a cab to the hospital. Did she know that Stewart was in town? Of course she did. If losing a friend felt this bad, what must it be like to wake up every day and remember your son is gone? I hoped I'd never find out. *Stewart. Gone.*

The pulsing shriek of a delivery truck backing up at the curb in front of us jolted me out of my reverie. I watched the wheels back over some garbage in the gutter: an empty Starbucks cup, a single glove grayed with dirt and rainwater, then baked in the sun.

I looked up. George was watching me. I thought I detected a glint of sympathy in his expression. As if he was afraid I might bite, he touched my elbow ever so gently, like a whisper. "You ready?" He didn't move. Jerk that he was, I could tell he would have waited all day if I needed. He confused me.

I exhaled and nodded. We headed inside. The lobby was much more spare than at Helen's uptown digs. It smelled like coffee—the kind in a disposable blue cup—and breakfast sausage. George approached the doorman, who appeared to be watching a YouTube video of a shark attack on his phone. The guy didn't notice us.

Finally, George cleared his throat. "Hey, we're going to 2B. Stewart Beasley's loft?"

The doorman shot to standing, tucking away his screen, and winced. "Of course! I'm so sorry, man." I wasn't sure if he was apologizing for Stewart's death or for ignoring us. "Mrs. Beasley mentioned that you'd be coming. Go right up."

We headed toward the elevator. George pressed the button. It lit up, bright and cheery like a tiny moon.

I don't know why, but it reminded me of a school trip Stewart and I took to the planetarium at the Museum of Natural History when we were maybe ten years old. I loved it there, probably because my father treated me to astronaut ice cream whenever we visited together. It was like eating a brick of Neapolitan Lucky Charms marshmallows.

About halfway through the show on this occasion, I realized I had to pee. Regretfully, I tore myself away from the projected constellations on the ceiling, craning my neck to see them until I had backed all the way out the door. It was always jarring to emerge back into the light and leave that booming voice behind—like the voice of God. Or Spock. Spock-God.

I was rushing back from the restroom, so I wouldn't miss too much, when I heard someone call, "Hey! Wren!"

I flipped around and there was Stewart, sitting against the wall outside the theater doors, leafing through some pamphlet about current exhibitions, sub-Saharan sand vipers and all that.

"What are you doing out here?" I asked.

"I had to get out. It's too much."

"What is?"

"Infinite space. I can't wrap my mind around it. It's too massive. It freaks me out."

"Seriously?"

He nodded. "You know what I mean?" He seemed anxious for commiseration.

"Yeah, I guess so," I lied. "I never thought about space that way. But don't you also think it's cool?"

"Sure! In a, we're-all-going-to-get-swallowed-up-by-a-black-hole-someday, kind of way."

I wanted to go back in—bad. My hand was resting on the theater's door handle, but Stewart looked pretty bummed. I dropped the knob and crossed to him instead, leaning my shoulder against the wall beside him. "Are you okay?"

"Yeah, totally. I'm fine." He crinkled his nose. "I just really don't like the planetarium."

I slid my back down the wall until I was seated next to him, my legs bent in front of me. Crumbs dotted the carpet. I wondered if they were the remnants of astronaut ice cream.

"So what now?"

My mind was so deep in the past that I was barely cognizant as George and I boarded the elevator. The door was about to close when the doorman pressed the button to reopen it. It snapped back like a Hungry Hungry Hippo. "Hey, please let me know if you need anything—supplies or like a dolly or anything to help move things. I told the lady who went up there before you, but I wanted to make sure to tell you too: I'm here if you need a hand."

Neither George nor I managed to speak before the doors closed with an accordion sigh.

We stared at each other. "Who is he talking about?"

George frowned. "I guess Helen came by this morning."

"I thought the whole point was that she didn't want to have to deal with this?"

"I know. But she must have changed her mind."

"Or maybe it's Kate?" I hoped that might be the case, both because I felt more comfortable with Stewart's sister and because I felt weird about the fact that she wasn't participating. Wasn't this the family's purview? I planned on emailing her for approval on any items we chose for the tribute.

Indeed, the police tape on the door had already been cut. *Police tape. On Stewart's door.*

Stewart. Gone.

I felt sick to my stomach. I readied myself for an onslaught of emotion and for the remnants of anything gruesome. If there was one thing I did understand about death, having watched my grandfather leave this planet, it's that it's not pretty.

I had a plan: I would walk in. I would stand in the middle of Stewart's space, preserved from the night he died. I would breathe in reality; breathe out grief. I would absorb what had happened as fact. I would stop feeling shocked. I would finally believe that he was gone. I would feel him in the silence of the place. I realized I was afraid of the smell.

George turned the key in the lock and swung the door open. But inside, instead of quiet, there was a bustle of activity. Music was playing—something by Lady Gaga. The air smelled like mochaccino and Method cucumber spray cleaner. A stocky housekeeper was stuffing an old comforter into a garbage bag. Piles of items, from clothing to books to artworks, were leaning against walls, categorized. I looked at George; he looked back at me and shrugged.

There was a rustle from a nearby closet and out popped Blair, her artificial waves pulled into an immaculate ponytail. Even her T-shirt was perfectly worn but also pressed, as if chosen out of a J. Crew catalogue for the occasion: *The Dead Friend Tee, cotton, $68.*

A rush of heat flooded my face. Rage. I thought, *What the fuck is she doing here?* But I knew. Of course I knew. She wasn't going to take no for an answer. She would run this show, regardless of Helen's wishes.

"Oh!" she said. "You're finally here." Like we were late. She grinned at us. She actually grinned. And put her hands on her hips like she was supposed to be there. Like it was painting day on some fixer-upper TV show about starter homes. Like she was about to start talking about backsplashes.

I said, "We thought you were Kate."

She said, "Who's Kate?"

"Stewart's sister."

"Oh, right! He never mentioned her. Were they even close? They must not have been."

"Well, they were . . . siblings."

"Well, he barely ever mentioned her to me."

George's mouth gaped open like the hood of his sweatshirt. I swear I heard him swallow, hard. The sound of eating crow. I sucked in my cheeks. Let them go with a pop. I was half-horrified, half-vindicated.

"The vultures," I whispered.

He didn't respond.

CHAPTER 19

How on Earth did you tolerate these people, Stewart? They are horrible, horrible humans. Okay, maybe not "Russian collusion, take healthcare from babies, ignore global warming, rape teenagers, #MeToo, slave to the NRA even when kids die" terrible, but despicable nonetheless.

And, yes, Stewart, I am "on one of my high horses," as you liked to say. Because I deserve to be. Because—monsters! Why did you choose these people as friends? What did they offer you? Their loyalty? Their social status at some point? A sense of superiority? How did you not punch Blair in the overly injected face?

You once said, "Sometimes it's nice to be the coolest person in the room." You could have been the coolest without these animals, Stewart. At least when you weren't saying stupid shit like that.

Didn't you realize that?

They bust in and emote all over everything—their need viscous and sticky. They demand attention; they demand recognition. They use up all the oxygen in the room and then demand more.

Is that why you died, Stewart? Was there no more oxygen left for you to breathe? But more importantly: How am I supposed to grieve with all this noise?

CHAPTER 20

George recovered from the shock of seeing Blair and, to his credit, played it off like he was fine with her presence. Better not to show that you're rattled. That's when animals attack.

"I thought you could go through all that," she said, gesturing toward Stewart's paperwork, already sorted (and no doubt read) on the window-sill. "That's your thing! Right, George? All those papers?" She banished him to a far corner of the living room. He went to work, looking confused about how he'd landed there.

I wanted to ask Blair if there was anything interesting in the stacks, just to watch her lie about not having snooped, but it wasn't worth enduring some sanctimonious response about it being none of her business. As if she had respect for boundaries.

"You guys, I am so sad! I can barely breathe," Blair groaned. "This is so hard! I just want to like collapse!"

Then go home. Please.

George grunted.

I wanted to say that no one asked her to be here, but I figured that wouldn't improve the situation. So I didn't respond; I just hovered in the entryway, close to the exit. I wasn't ready to give up that option. Apparently overcome, she sprinted over, embraced me, and started rubbing my back. I endured it with my arms hanging. I really wanted to knee her in the groin.

"Are you okay?" she asked, probably because my body was rigid.

"I'm fine. This is just a lot." *You are a lot.*

Blair let me go, nodding with saccharine sympathy.

Released, I looked around, too distracted by the pop soundtrack to meaningfully digest that I was standing inside Stewart's apartment, the place where he *died*. I walked myself over to his bookshelf, running my hands over his collection of plays—thin colorful bindings, sharp staples glinting. I could feel Blair's eyes on me.

"Totally," she said. "Go through his plays. That's what I was going to tell you to do."

To spite her, without a word, I continued past them, running my hand along his other books. A bright red tome called, *Unearthing the Answer: Manifesting Your Authentic Self*, popped out at me. Would Stewart have really read something cultish like that? Once upon a time, it would have been fodder for our shared jokes. Then again, "The Answer" had been a Hollywood self-help trend a few years back and didn't that explain it? I wondered if he'd really bought into that bullshit or if he'd just played along in exchange for inclusion.

Some more familiar objects dotted the shelves: a conch shell, a Batman figurine, an old-school Transformer, a Monchichi doll I once gave him when we were kids during a playdate—just because he liked it. I could remember his face, all surprise at the gesture.

There was a series of framed pictures too: One of him and Kate as teenagers with snowboards and oversized teeth on top of some mountain. One of them sunburned as twentysomethings at a luau in Hawaii. There was a photo of Stewart at the beach, sun shimmering along the plains of his face. His features had gotten more chiseled as he got older. He was always a thin kid, but these angles were the stuff of men. There was a still from some set—maybe the first season of *Manic Mondays*. That's when I spotted that picture I'd been thinking of: him and me, arm in arm, after our elementary school production of *Robin Hood*. Seeing it stole my breath for a second. I picked it up to examine it more closely.

"That's cute," said Blair from over my shoulder. Why was she following me around? *Stalker.* "Halloween, I assume?"

"No, it's from a class play we did when we were in fourth grade." The theater teacher cast me as Robin Hood for some reason; Stewart was Friar Tuck. He was so mad about the part at first, but, of course, he stole the show. Probably that was when he first got bitten by the acting bug. He realized how much positive attention he could get. I stared at a young Stewart—giant shit-eating grin, glasses. He was a wiry boy who made himself strong, but he was already adorable then. Charisma emanated from every pore. He wore a burlap costume, slung like a sandwich board over his chest. He had his arm around my shoulders, pulling me sideways like we might topple over. I was wearing a dumb green hat and carrying a sad cardboard sword, and I looked like I knew it. But Stewart wasn't embarrassed at all.

How had that boy arrived here as an adult? I had this irrational urge to find and warn the kid in the photo. *There's something wrong with your brain!* I thought, *What a tragedy.*

I must have said it out loud because Blair said, "I know. I can't even, Wren. I'm just so upset." Her voice was like a commercial interruption at the climax of a movie—wholly unwelcome. She started to well up again. I clenched my fists and placed the picture back down on the shelf.

Stewart's apartment. No Stewart. *Stewart. Gone.* I tried to force myself to believe it. I felt like something was missing. I felt lonely, like someone had burrowed a hole in my chest that was growing more gaping by the day. *A black hole.* But I still couldn't make the fact that I'd never see him again real.

"Well, *that* picture has to go in the tribute exhibition, obviously, since it was his first acting gig," Blair was saying, picking it up off the shelf and moving it to a stack on the dining room table. "Then you can take it home, unless Helen wants it."

Why did she think she was in a position to dole out Stewart's possessions?

I sighed. Maybe I needed to shock myself into recognition. I hated to even engage her, but what choice did I have? I exhaled a rattled breath. "So where is the scene?"

"The scene?"

"Where Stewart . . . where it happened. Where they found him?"

"Oh! I see. In the den. We already cleaned that up."

"You already—?"

"Yeah, Bianca, the housekeeper, and I. We just got rid of everything and cleaned and whatever." I wanted to smack her for being so blasé, for assuming she had the right, but she was already back inside one of his closets. "He had so many pairs of snow boots! Like how much skiing can one guy do? Especially a guy who hates being cold?"

I stood there, stunned. So much for having a moment to say goodbye. So much for making it real.

I had the urge to throw Blair out of the way and take the closet for my own—to hide inside and escape from her piercing existence. Then, suddenly, I was struck so strongly by a memory that I reached out for a chair back to brace myself.

The game was "Seven Minutes in Heaven." We were sitting in a craggy circle on the floor of Dev Singh's den—all black lacquer and gold fixtures—drinking Alizé and watching duo after duo disappear into the dark depths of the hall linen closet. His parents were out at some event or maybe even away at their Hamptons house.

Matthew Simonsson sat beside me, his right hand—twice as big as mine and most often seen palming a basketball—resting just centimeters from my own. I'd spent the night pretending not to feel him next to me like a vibration, his backward baseball cap tipped carelessly on his head, his T-shirt riding up above low-slung jeans as he slouched over his bent knees, revealing a band of boxers and smooth skin.

I wasn't paying much attention as Amanda Cassin and Ryan Cunningham emerged. I didn't much care what they'd done. Jimmy was DJing the music across the room. My friend Cynthia was sitting on my other side, complaining about how we were too old for this dumb game, clicking open and closed the silver clips holding back her pixie cut, messing with her bicycle chain necklace. I was only pretending to listen because Matthew had started tapping his fingers against my whiteout-painted nails, then pulling his hand back and looking the other way when I glanced down. He was pursing his lips, trying not to laugh. He'd been paying me attention like this all night; I could feel our future coming like a thunderstorm in summer.

The third time, I caught him turning away. "I saw that, you know," I said, rolling my eyes like I thought what he was doing was stupid instead of the best thing that happened to me that month. "I'm not actually an idiot."

He shrugged. "No clue what you're talking about."

"Oh, yeah? That's how you want to play it?"

He grinned at me—that giant beautiful grin that had monopolized my daydreams during weeks of boring algebra classes. That smile was the reason I didn't understand fractions. "Yup. That's exactly how I want to play it . . . homie."

"Dude," Cynthia said. I turned back to face her. "Can we leave soon? This is wack. So seventh grade."

"Okay, soon," I lied.

Tap. Tap. Tap. I whipped around, catching Matthew's hand in my own before he could move it away. "Got you."

He raised his eyebrows; shot me a killer smile. "Yup. You got me."

We were staring at each other. I didn't even hear Kim Yu say my name. Suddenly, Stewart was standing over me, sighing. He looked gangly and childish next to Matthew. "You coming?"

"Coming?"

"Wren! Hurry up! My turn to pick and I picked you and Stu for heeee-aaaven. You know it's about time, you guys!" *Fucking Kim.* Of course. She liked Matthew too. It was obvious. She'd been at all his games lately. And we'd never been big fans of each other's. This was her way of getting rid of me. No doubt I'd come out to find she'd taken my seat. Still. *No choice.*

"Okay. Heaven it is." I shrugged at Matthew, as if dropping his hand wasn't like unplugging from my lone power source. I stood up, pulling down my cropped baby tee, and nodded at Stewart. "Let's do this."

He looked as resigned as I felt. Thank God Kim had chosen him and not someone with actual expectations, who I'd have to reject. We walked to the closet; he opened the door. "After you, my lady."

Once inside, we settled onto the floor of the narrow walk-in, surrounded on either side by neatly folded cloth napkins, sheets, towels, and duvets. I leaned my back against the door and stretched my legs out in front of me; Stewart did the same opposite me. In the dark, I could just make out a tub of silver polish and a digital alarm clock perched on a shelf above his head. The only light fell in from the hallway through cracks between the door and its frame. He was in silhouette.

"So, this is where the magic happens, huh? If these walls could talk . . . they'd talk about some really repulsive Frenching."

I laughed. "I know! Did you see Jamal's face when he walked out of here? I think Jenny tried to puree him with her braces!"

"Pretty nasty." Stewart sighed, running a hand through his hair. It was long for him, hanging in his face. "So, we have about six minutes and forty-five seconds left to sit in the dark. What should we do?"

"I have no idea."

"Well, there's not enough light for shadow puppetry. We could tie a bunch of dish towels together and lower ourselves down to Eighty-Third Street and Riverside, then make a run for it?"

"That sounds exciting, but maybe too ambitious in my platforms." I was wearing a precious pair of brand-new John Fluevog sandals with super clunky wooden heels. *Shit kickers.*

"That does sound like a problem. And I assume we're not making out since you've basically been sitting in Matthew's lap all night?"

I sat upright. "Shhhhhh! Don't say that!" I hissed, afraid that someone might hear.

"So we *are* making out?"

"Stewart!"

"You sound like my mom when I put my shoes on the sofa: *Stewart!*" His parody of Helen's voice was perfect. He was always a good mimic.

I felt anxious. Was I being that obvious about liking Matthew? Were my feelings as one-sided as Stewart was making them sound?

He and I didn't really talk about who we liked. Actually, that wasn't totally true. We talked about *his* crushes, just not the other way around. In middle school, I'd had the more dramatic romantic life, but now, in early high school, Stewart's stock was shooting up along with his height. We'd had plenty of advice sessions about his prospects lately.

"What percentage of people who come in here actually hook up, you think? Fifty percent? Seventy-five percent?" He grimaced, squinting at the ground. "Do you think we're sitting in fluids?"

My nerves won out over pride. "Does it really seem like I'm all over Matthew?"

He shrugged. "Probably only to me."

"Why?"

"Because I know every tiny thing about you."

"But I'm not like embarrassing myself?"

"No. I mean, unless you think it's embarrassing to like a tool like Matthew Simonsson."

"Stewart!"

"I'm kidding. I get it. Everyone likes him."

"That's not why I like him," I said, tipping my head to the side. "You have to know that!"

"I do?"

"Yeah. I don't care about what everyone else thinks. I mean, he's cute. But did you know that he volunteers downtown at a Boy's Club for under-privileged kids?"

Stewart threw his head back and slapped a hand over his eyes. "Of course. *Now* it makes sense! You heard that, so now you think he's a 'good person.'"

"Yes. I do."

"Only you, man. Wren, he has to do community service because he got busted shoplifting."

"I don't believe that," I frowned. "That's just a rumor. Why are you trying to change my mind about him?"

"I'm not," Stewart shook his head. "Matthew is fine. He's great. I just hate the way he wears that hat. Why can't he just put it all the way on?"

"I'm not even sure he likes me anyway."

Stewart groaned. "Oh, please. Of course he likes you."

"Why?"

"Because. You're *you*."

Most of the time, I knew I was pretty. I felt good about my newly plat-inum hair, like Courtney Love but girlie. Boys liked me; I was cool and comfortable around them. But I was fourteen. I barely knew what any of it meant, and I was smart enough to see I was out of my depth with Matthew. Was Stewart right? Was Matthew not a good person?

"Thanks, Stewart."

"You're welcome. So, *now* are we making out?"

I laughed, bent my knee and knocked his Jordan-clad foot with my giant sandal. "Stewart!"

"Just double checking. I'm a teenage boy. We have to exploit all possible options." We were silent for a beat. I could hear the other kids' excited voices from the other room. A Tribe Called Quest blasted from Dev's dad's stereo. *Check the rhyme . . .*

"You know what, Wren?"

"What, Stewart?"

"I think sitting in the dark with you right now for seven minutes might actually be heaven. It's kind of nice and peaceful in here."

I leaned my head back against the door. "I couldn't agree more."

"At least we don't have to listen to Kim squeal. She's like a velociraptor on crack. What is wrong with that girl?"

Stewart would go on to date that drug-addled dinosaur in twelfth grade. He said she was "misunderstood."

Now, I watched Blair step in and out of the closet with armfuls of Stewart's belongings. What was she if not another Kim?

Resigned, I walked over to the plays and began pulling them down, one by one. What else could I do?

Too soon, the rest of the crew began to arrive.

I was sitting cross-legged on the floor, absorbed in sorting: Tennessee Williams, Arthur Miller, August Wilson, Lillian Hellman, Sam Shepard, Neil Labute, Annie Baker, Shakespeare, Chekov, Brecht, Mamet. Stewart's collection seemed endless.

Keith appeared first in some shitty corduroy jacket that reeked of mothballs even from across the room, and when he entered, he crossed straight to Blair. I could feel him like a bitter wind, changing the chemical makeup of the room. He kissed her cheek and held her gaze with meaning. "How are you holding up, honey?"

"Okay, I guess." She looked down. "It's been hard."

He nodded, rubbing her shoulder. "I brought you a matcha latte with almond milk. I figured you might need it. Coming here was very brave of you."

He handed her one hot drink and took a sip from the other, dispelling any illusion George and I might have had about him considering our needs too.

Blair started to cry, sort of. At least she ran a finger under each eye in a performance of squelching tears. Keith completed a final revolution of his hand on her back and began circling the living room. I got the sense that he hadn't been here before, which was interesting. Had Stewart never invited Keith over? When, exactly, was the last time they'd hung out? When was the last time he'd mentioned Keith's name? I was starting to think that Stewart might have exorcised this guy from his life. Maybe my dead friend had some standards, after all.

George looked up, his face impassive. "Hey, Keith."

"Hey." Keith was too busy scrutinizing the space to look his way. "I guess they hired an interior designer to do this place up 'cause no way Stu had taste this good. Although, I would have added more pops of color."

"Oh yeah, Keith?" I couldn't help myself. "Is that what you would have done?"

He looked down, as if just noticing me. "What are you doing?"

"Sorting through Stewart's plays to see if any are significant for the family to keep or for the tribute gallery. We'll donate the rest."

"Huh."

"What's 'huh'?"

"Just that it might have made more sense for a real actor to do that."

"Define 'real.'"

"HI, GUYS!" Mallory and Brian swung the door open with a slam, interrupting us just as I was about to go all uncensored.

"OMG. THIS IS SO FUCKING CRAZY!" Mallory crossed to Blair and kissed her on the cheek, then she made her way to me, kneeling down to give me a big hug. At least she was sweet. Brian waved.

She peeled off her coat—a faux fur, I assumed—and threw it over the kitchen island. She scanned the apartment. "THIS IS SO SAD!" she grinned. Just as suddenly, her face collapsed like smushed Play-Doh and she started sloppy sobbing. I moved to get up and make my way to her; she seemed genuinely broken. But Brian got there first, rightly, and she buried her head in his shoulder. He half-frowned in a way that reminded me of a cartoon.

That's when Willow arrived, wafting through the door like an essence. She paused to absorb her surroundings. "Hey, guys," she whispered. She walked over to where Mallory and Brian were locked in an embrace and placed a hand on each of their heads. Then she rested her own forehead against both of theirs. "It's going to be all right," she hushed. Both of their eyes popped open, surprised, but she didn't seem to notice. She released them and crossed the room in slo-mo, taking deep breaths as she floated. When she got to me, she placed a hand on my head too. I hoped none of us had lice 'cause she would definitely have been spreading it. Actually, it kind of felt good. I had another headache and the pressure of her palm offered some relief. "Hi, Wren," she whispered, kneeling beside me.

"Hi, Willow."

"How are you?" I could barely hear her, her voice was so quiet.

"I'm okay. You?"

"I am meeting myself where I am today, Wren. Where. I. Am. That's all any of us can do."

"So true."

Her hand was still resting on my head, and I could smell her perfume—some essential oil blend of maybe neroli and rose. This one was nicer than the one from the funeral.

"Hey, Willow?" I said.

"Yes," she whispered.

"He's already dead. You can't wake him up. You don't have to whisper."

"Oh." She took her hand off my head. "I was just trying to be respectful. In many ways, this is a sacred space."

"Okay. You do you." I felt a little bad for poking fun, especially since she wasn't known for her sense of humor. "Sorry."

"No worries. Jokes are a common way to cope with confronting the great beyond. We've all come face-to-face with our perfect mortality. We need to make space for our fear and sadness." She closed her eyes and took a deep breath. "Okay." She shot to standing. "Where was Stewart's final resting place? I need to be in that space."

Blair popped up for that—always first with the information. "The den. I'll show you." They disappeared into the recesses of the apartment, and I went back to sorting plays.

There were a few from high school: *Cat on a Hot Tin Roof* with notes for a term paper in the margins; *Major Barbara,* which I remembered reading in senior English during a section on Shaw; *Our Town,* which I think we first read in ninth grade. I once saw Stewart play the Stage Manager in a graduate school production of it. He was great.

That play has always been one of my favorites, no matter how many times it gets performed. I opened it to skim. He had highlighted some of the major passages like when Emily returns to say goodbye to the world after she's died, only to discover how blindly human beings live.

Maybe someone should read from the play during the tribute—or would that be too on the nose? Stewart might have scoffed, even though he loved it. I flipped to the next page and noticed a piece of paper stuffed in the crease like a bookmark. I plucked it out and studied it: It was a prescription for 200 mg of Zoloft. That in itself wasn't strange. I mean, everyone is on medication these days and Stewart definitely had his highs and lows. I had my own anxiety-fueled dalliances with Zoloft and Clonopin. But the dosage was high. And there was a second prescription, too, for Cymbalta. Why would you need two?

I had this gut sense in that moment that I didn't know Stewart—at least not everything about him—and it made me feel even sadder and more empty. I stuffed the paper in my pocket. I told myself I didn't want someone else to find it because it was private, but, if I was honest, I also didn't want someone else to find it and know something I hadn't about him.

Feet away, I could hear Blair talking to Keith about Stewart's art collection. "Well, he really liked contemporary portraiture. I know that because I advised him on what to buy. We always went to the LA Art Fair together. Stu loved art, you know."

"Well, he's lucky he had you to advise him. He wouldn't have had any instincts on his own." Fucking Keith.

"I was the one to recommend that he buy Elizabeth Peyton early on," Blair continued. "Now her paintings are worth a ton. This wasn't the one I recommended, but he wanted it for some reason."

They were all so sure they knew him—the real Stewart. How come I was the only one doubting my relationship with him? He liked "portraiture"? Really? He was a deeply untalented artist and disinterested viewer. The last time I dragged him to the Whitney Biennial, he whined his way through the galleries and made me leave before I was finished.

I watched the vultures for a moment, absorbing their aggression from a distance like radiation. It was like I could see the thought bubbles above their heads:

I am sadder than you.

I loved him more than you.

I knew him better than you.

My tailbone was sore from sitting on the wood floor for so long. It was hot in the apartment—the heat blasting like it was winter when it was only fall—and my jeans were stuck to the backs of my knees. I stretched my legs out and my arms above my head, looking up just in time to see Mallory emerge from Stewart's bedroom wearing his favorite Pixies T-shirt. I was so stunned that it took me a moment to realize she was also wearing his gray skullcap. I recognized it because I had teased him for wearing it in warm weather and so far back on his head—such a LA actor move and very Matthew Simonsson. Mallory made her way over to a shelf to my right and started examining Stewart's knickknacks like she was shopping at a thrift store. "THIS IS COOL!" She picked up the Transformer. "OOH, LOOK BRI! HE HAS THE ORIGINAL MEGATRON! YOU DON'T HAVE THIS ONE IN YOUR COLLECTION!" She began sorting through Stewart's records, flipping from vinyl to vinyl. My mouth hung open like I was catching flies.

Suddenly, I felt a rough tug on my arm. Startled, I look up to find George standing over me. "Can I talk to you?" he said, through gritted teeth.

"Oh. Um, sure."

Once I was standing, he practically yanked me across the room. Blair and Keith were still surveying the art collection like a couple shopping for their new McMansion. I craned my neck to see the portrait they'd been discussing: It was of Kurt Cobain. That's why Stewart had wanted it. Not because he loved portraiture—because he worshipped Nirvana. That made me feel a little better. Or at least a little smug.

George dragged me past the entrance to the den, where Willow was performing a ceremony with a metal bowl. The air had an unpleasant familiar smell. I sniffed and did a double take. Was she taking the hair from Stewart's brush and burning it?

Watching her reminded me of when my grandfather was in a nursing home with dementia. One day, I went to visit him and caught his born-again nurse, Dolores, wheeling his chair out of a Christian church service. We're Jewish and my grandfather was an atheist, but I guess Dolores wanted to save his soul. Her heart was in the right place, but he wouldn't have knowingly signed up for that. Just as Stewart would not have sanctioned New Age chanting in the wake of his death. This was why he had broken up with Willow in the first place. Her orthodoxy didn't sit right with him. Now, these people were turning his home into their personal playground. They had subsumed his energy. There wasn't a trace of him left here anymore—only his former stuff dusted in their bullshit and fingerprints.

Apparently, George and I were headed to the bathroom. Once inside, he dropped my arm, slammed the door like a monster was chasing us and leaned his back against it. "Wren."

I glanced over my shoulder, crinkling my nose. "Was she actually burning Stewart's hair or did I imagine that?"

"Wren. Look at me!"

I turned to face him. "Yes? What's up? What's wrong?"

George's eyes were wild and his face was flushed. He brought his hands to his head and dug his fingers into his hair. "These people are *the worst*."

I felt my shoulders relax. So I wasn't crazy. I parted my lips to agree, but, to my surprise, a sharp laugh shot from my mouth instead. I started cracking up, softly at first and then hard. The first tears I had shed since Stewart's death fell from my eyes, but they were tears of laughter.

George looked at me like I had lost my mind, but then his lips curved into a half smile. I couldn't help but think it: he was kind of cute.

"Okay, okay. I get it. You were right. Blair is a demon," he was saying, as I caught my breath. "But, Wren, in my defense, I could never have imagined that people could be this bad! I mean, I think vultures as a species should be offended by the comparison!"

I nodded, wiping my eyes. "They're horrible."

"First of all, they're all so obsessed with Stewart's death, showing up at a moment's notice so they don't miss anything. Don't they have jobs? Or families? Or lives?"

"I mean, Blair must have other clients."

"Blair! She's like a super villain!" He leaned in. "And did I imagine it or was that girl Mallory wearing Stu's clothing just now? Like she just walked into his room, opened a drawer or, worse, dug in his dirty laundry and started putting on his T-shirts?"

That sent me on another laughing jag. George sighed and sat down on the closed toilet. "How did Stewart tolerate these people?"

"I don't know. I never understood it. I guess he was a sucker for people who worshipped him." I leaned against the sink, picking up the basil-scented Meyer's hand wash and sniffing it. It's my favorite.

"And *yes*! Willow was burning his hair! And that guy, Keith? What a dick!"

"I guess Stewart was also a sucker for people who were jealous of him."

George shook his head. "They're horrendous. Helen has no idea! How're we going to get through this process with these animals?"

"Alcohol?"

George ran a hand through his hair. Today, it looked softer, with less product. I had the weirdest impulse to touch it. "Losing Stewart is already so depressing, but this? It's so gross."

"Hiding by the toilet is gross or the whole situation?"

He didn't laugh. We stayed quiet for a minute, processing the day. Finally, George sighed. "What time is it? I'm starving."

"Me too."

"Let's get out of here."

"The bathroom? Or—?"

"The bathroom, the apartment, the building, the whole horrible atmosphere—their whole galaxy!"

"Done."

Standing, he turned the silver knob and the door opened with a satisfying pop. That's the thing about new apartments: everything works as it should. Stewart's life in a nutshell. Unlike my brownstone apartment where, at least once a week, I panicked that I was locked in my bathroom.

Back in the living room, George grabbed both our jackets as I picked up my bag. "We're going out!"

"OOOH, GOOD IDEA!" boomed Mallory. "ARE YOU GETTING FOOD? I'M SO HUNGRY! I'LL COME!"

"Nope," George lied. "Bins. Just bins. For sorting . . . stuff."

"AH, THAT'S COOL. I'LL JUST CHECK STU'S FRIDGE! I'M SURE HE HAD SOMETHING YUMMY! DIDN'T HE HAVE ONE OF THOSE AWESOME FROZEN MEAL PLANS? ARE THEY STILL BEING DELIVERED? WE SHOULD HAVE THEM REDIRECTED TO ONE OF OUR HOUSES! NO SENSE IN THEM GOING TO WASTE." Mallory charged toward the kitchen. No crevice of this house would be left unpillaged. "OH, GEORGE? WILL YOU GET EXTRA GARBAGE BAGS?"

"Sure."

We ran out the door before anything or anyone else could stop us, the musk of Willow's ceremony in our wake.

CHAPTER 21

You owe me big time, Stewart. I'm not sure how I'll collect, but—for this bullshit and so much more—you owe me.

CHAPTER 22

Outside, George and I gasped for fresh air like we'd survived drowning. The warm breeze had crisp edges; the sky was blue. It was one of those beautiful New York fall days—perfect for going through your dead friend's bathroom cabinets!

We paused to bask in our escape, then started walking. "Wow," I managed. "And I thought the funeral was bad."

"You did?"

"Just kind of cold. And depressing. Like a bunch of people just staring at this giant coffin."

"Like a funeral, you mean?"

I shrugged.

"Well, I consider us fortunate. It was nothing compared to an open casket wake."

Against my will, an image popped into my mind of Stewart's dead body embalmed and stuffed in his favorite Band of Outsiders suit. "That sounds terrifying! I've never been to one of those. Jewish funerals aren't like that."

The truth is, I was sort of obsessed with the idea of open caskets. I had been reading up on different funeral traditions, so I could more accurately plan rituals for people. I'd just learned about this "extreme embalming" trend in Puerto Rico, where, for visitations, they'd set dead people up as if they were playing poker or reading magazines or smoking cigarettes or whatever they spent their time doing—as if they were still alive. The families said it made them feel less sad. I thought it sounded like visiting a dead relative at Madame Tussauds. Like people might take selfies.

"Oh, yeah," George was saying. "I'm a nice Catholic boy, half Irish, a quarter Italian and a quarter Chilean. I've got open caskets on all sides."

I stopped and turned to face George. "You're part Chilean?"

"Yeah, I know. I don't really look it."

"Do you speak Spanish?"

"*Un poquito*. But barely."

"Have you been to Chile?"

"Yes."

"Are you from Chile?"

He looked at me like I was an alien. "I'm from Pittsburgh."

"And your parents? They're still . . . in Pittsburgh?"

"Yup."

"What do they do there?"

"My mom is a law professor. My father is an engineer."

"Huh."

"What is 'huh'?"

"I just thought—"

"You just thought what?"

It was too late to turn back. "I just assumed you were, you know, like an LA version of Stewart." I wanted to evaporate into thin air.

"Ah." George cocked his head to the side to display his angles. "Good looking and talented?"

I flushed, embarrassed to my core, and shook my head. "No. One percent and white. With all kinds of legacy."

"Oh, I see. No. More like middle class—and tan. With legacy in academia."

I felt like the world's biggest idiot. I don't know why I'd assumed that George was Stewart's twin, moving through the world with unlimited resources, privilege, charm. I'd filed him away without knowing a thing about him.

He was grinning at me like he knew I felt stupid and was enjoying it. Pittsburgh or no, he was still smug. "Can we go eat now? All this talk about dead bodies is making me ravenous."

The closest restaurant was a corner bagel shop. We made our way toward it as I stared down at the gum-spotted sidewalk, struggling to recover from my humiliation.

George opened the glass door for me. "Are you sure it wasn't the 'good-looking' thing that made you think I was like Stewart?"

I groaned.

Inside, the decor was stark and minimal, more upscale than your average deli. The air smelled of toasted onions and slightly rancid fruit, thanks, I assumed, to their pressed juice bar. While we waited in line to order, I gazed at a display of artisanal donuts in flavors like matcha, pistachio, and hibiscus that no doubt looked prettier than they tasted. We placed our orders: salt bagel with turkey for me; sesame with lox spread for him. I grabbed a Dr. Brown's Black Cherry soda as he chose some carrot-and-ginger pressed juice, then we sat down to wait. Someone had knocked over the pepper shaker and black granules were scattered on the table.

"Salt bagel, huh? You shouldn't eat that much salt."

"No?"

"Nope. It's not healthy."

"As opposed to lox spread, which is very low in sodium?"

He smiled. "Yes. Much healthier. Protein in salmon. Omega-3s."

"Right. What's going to happen to me without Omega-3s again?"

"You might . . . be Omega deficient."

"That sounds like a serious disorder."

"It is. It causes snap judgments, rosy cheeks, and bad taste in bagels." My hands flew to my face. Was I still blushing? "It comes full circle."

"It does."

"Well, as long as I don't drop dead from too few Omegas."

That shut us both up. I cursed myself for making things awkward.

The truth is that it was hard for me to think about anything but death—and my still-pounding head, which, rationally, I knew was from the overzealous heat in Stewart's apartment. Stewart always liked things warm, but I had never noticed it being this sweltering the countless times I sat on his couch in the den—the den where he *died*—and watched TV. I wondered again if I had an aneurysm that was about to burst too. Would

I collapse and die on the speckled floor of this bagel place? What is it they say you smell when you're about to have a stroke? Burnt toast? Does burnt everything bagel count?

"How do you know if you're having an aneurysm?" I asked out loud, unable to let the topic lie.

George looked confused. "I don't know. Why?"

"Why? Because our friend's brain just exploded, and I want to make sure I see it coming if the same thing is about to happen to me."

"Ah. I think the odds are not good that it would happen to both of you in the same week."

The guy behind the bagel counter—with a face so shiny and round that it looked like its own tiny sun—called George's name and he went up to retrieve our sandwiches. As he handed the bagels over, the counter man winked at me. I don't know what he was suggesting. Maybe he thought we were on a date? I winked back at him.

CAUSE OF DEATH: Complications from bagel-induced diabetes.

AFTER-DEATH RITUAL: Burial.

SERVICE: Traditional, Catholic, many relatives.

PROCESSIONAL MUSIC: "Fernando Pando" by the Virgins.

MEMORIAL BUFFET: His grandmother's tamales.

I unzipped my bag, searching my wallet, overstuffed with receipts, for cash. I don't know why I bothered; I never have any. I stuck my hands in my pockets to plum their depths, which was even less likely to be fruitful, and came out with that prescription. *Oh, right.* I panicked and shoved it into the front pocket of my purse as George returned, bagels in hand.

"I'm so sorry. I don't have any cash. Can I Venmo you?"

"I got it." He waved my imaginary money away. "Don't worry."

"Are you sure?"

"Yes. I am positive that I don't mind paying for your extremely inexpensive bagel."

"I just don't want you to feel obligated to pay for me."

"I don't. I *want* to pay for your lunch."

"You do? Why?"

He rolled his eyes. "Are you serious? It's not 1952. I don't expect you to put out because I bought you a bagel or something!"

I don't know why the joke made me nervous. "Right. Totally. Fine."

"Anyway, it's the least I can do for doubting your vultures intel."

"That's true."

He raised his eyebrows. "Okay? So, can we eat now and stop talking about your four dollar bagel?"

"And soda."

"And soda. Which is also not healthy, by the way."

"Yes. Fine. Eat. If it means you'll stop lecturing me." All preachy, George sounded like . . . Stewart. I realized it with a jolt.

Unaware, George took a bite of his sandwich, shaking his head at me. "I've never met someone so on the defensive! For all the talking Stu did about you, he never mentioned that you were this much of a pain in the ass."

"Yeah, well, for all the talking Stewart *never* did about you . . ." I smiled, despite myself. "Anyway, maybe he didn't think I was a pain in the ass."

"No. I feel confident that he did."

I did too. I sighed. It occurred to me that I should have been sitting here having a bagel with Stewart and talking about his friend George, not the other way around. I glanced back toward the door, as if I might spot my lifelong friend lingering at the beverage display in the corner, picking out a Snapple Half & Half. He loved an Arnold Palmer.

"Why only have iced tea or lemonade, when you could have *both*? Two experiences in one!" he once enthused. Stewart had been in one of his top-of-the-world moods. I think he had just gotten cast as "Convenience Store Witness #2" in a *Law & Order* episode—one of his first TV appearances. "Sometimes the universe just gets it right."

I'd ordered a water. He was disappointed in my choice. As usual.

I still remember his line from that episode: "I was picking out chips and, the next thing I knew, that dude was busting through here!"

Mariska Hargitay was no doubt impressed.

I looked at George now, wondering what his relationship with Stewart had been like. When I really compared, they didn't seem similar exactly, but I could see where they overlapped. At least they both found me infuriating. "Why *do* you think Stewart didn't tell me about you?"

George considered the question for a moment, resting a cheek on his propped-up fist. "I've been asking myself the same thing, honestly. We certainly spent enough time together. But I guess Stu wasn't really one to overlap friend groups too much. Maybe because it allowed him to be different versions of himself with different people? He kept things . . . compartmentalized. Don't you think?"

I did think that was true. I'd witnessed it firsthand. "But then why did he talk to you about me?"

"Well, that's easy. Because he got homesick sometimes and, for him, you were home."

I let that sink in. Is that part of why I was so thrown? Was Stewart home for me too? Finally, I asked, "How long ago did you guys meet?"

"About three years ago. He was already a client at our firm. Someone passed him off to me, I guess because we were around the same age and seemed like a match. Whoever thought of it was right. We hit it off from day one. I was like his straight man."

"I know all about that role."

"You know Stu. First time we met, he insisted that we shoot hoops at some gym. He told me I needed to get more exercise, giving me some lecture about too many hours sitting at desks—not that he knew a single thing about me. Then he took me to some taco stand and insisted I taste this cactus burrito that he said was the best in LA, like he was the expert. On Monday, a standing desk was delivered to my office. I kid you not."

"That sounds on brand." I took a bite of my sandwich and realized I was hungry for the first time in days. "Did you go to college in LA?"

"No. Virginia. But I had been in California a lot longer than he had! He was always trying to get me to expand my horizons, loosen up. I kept trying to explain that I wasn't closed off; I just have a job. At an office. With windows and desks and computers. And bosses. And I have to be there sometimes. And take meetings. Or I won't have a job anymore."

"That sounds like vintage Stewart," I laughed. "He never understood why everyone couldn't live like him—wasn't as charming and charmed."

"Even you?"

"Especially me."

George considered that for a moment. Behind him, a mounted TV was playing some terrible talk show. "I notice you always use his full name. You never call him 'Stu' like everyone else."

"Yeah, I know." I don't know why, but that made me feel self-conscious, like the weird, uptight friend. I started pushing the black pepper particles into a pile with a napkin, just for somewhere else to focus. I guess it was PTSD from feeling that way with Stewart himself. But George was the uptight friend too, I reminded myself. We were kindred in our lameness. "Stewart and I met when we were so little. Helen hated the nickname, so we always called him by his full name. Once he got older and adopted the shorter version against her will, it was too late for me to adapt."

"So you met in elementary school?"

"Technically in utero. Our mothers were next door neighbors when they were pregnant."

"You grew up in that swanky building?"

"Ha. No. I wish. This was ages ago on Eighty-Sixth Street between West End and Riverside. Before Ted made his real money and they moved to the park. Their next-door neighbor is probably Bruce Willis or someone now."

"They don't have a next-door neighbor; they have the whole floor."

"Ha! True." I liked talking about my history with Stewart. There was something nice about remembering how long we had known each other; about how complicated and uncomplicated our entanglement had been. "Anyway, our mothers realized they were due around the same time, so they became friends—went to prenatal classes together or whatever people did in those days. Lamaze? And so Stewart and I knew each other from birth. I guess as toddlers we spent every second together. I have these great photos of us at the playground, popsicles dripping all over our faces. But then we didn't see as much of each other for a while."

"Because?"

"Because my mother and Helen had nothing in common besides having kids the same age. I think my mother felt that Helen was competitive and thought she was better than us—and she demonstrated that via me and Stewart."

George raised an eyebrow. "Meaning?"

I didn't know if he was actually interested or being polite, but I hadn't gotten to talk about my past with Stewart since he died. Gretchen already knew the details. The vultures weren't interested since it didn't involve them. This felt good. Like an opportunity to expel some of the sadness swirling inside of me. So I continued. "According to my mother, Helen was always disparaging of me. I guess Stewart walked first. And she tells a story about me reaching for a toy on a shelf and Helen saying, 'I'll help her. I forgot that she's limited.' At one point, when we joined the same playgroup, she suggested that maybe I wasn't mature enough for it, though Stewart is only two weeks older than me. He would punch me, I'd cry and Helen would call me, 'sensitive.' It went on like that."

"Did she ever get over it?"

"Helen? I mean, I don't think so. She doesn't like me, if you haven't noticed. The last time my mother ran into her at Zabar's, Helen asked, 'How is Wren?' My mother said, 'Working hard.' And Helen said, 'Yes. She always was aggressive.'"

George did a spit-take, almost spewing the juice he had just sipped. He managed to get it down, then choked, "Sorry. Wow. That's amazing. She really doesn't like you."

"Couldn't you tell from our meeting?"

"I guess she seemed tense, but her son just died," he shrugged. "I'm not sure how she's managing to get out of bed and put on clothes, let alone dealing with all she's handling. I would be curled up on the floor in fetal position."

I considered that. "I think handling things makes her feel better, which is why it's weird that she outsourced the sorting of Stewart's apartment."

George toggled his head, side-to-side, and I caught a whiff of something. "What is that?"

"What is what?"

I pointed. "That noncommittal thing you just did with your head."

George looked up, all innocence. "No clue."

"Wow. You're a terrible liar for a lawyer. You should work on that. Especially if you're going to survive in Hollywood." I squinted my eyes at him. "What do you know?"

He stared hard at his lap. "Nothing."

"George, why did Helen assign us the job of going through the apartment?"

"I don't know!"

"George! Why us and not his sister, Kate?"

George threw his hands up—palms facing the ceiling—in a kind of comical performance of ignorance.

I planted both of my own hands on the table. "*George!* I'm not going back there unless you tell me!"

"You would leave me alone with those assholes?"

"I would. Try me."

"Jeez. Harsh." He picked up a napkin and wiped imaginary cream cheese residue from his face, stalling. Finally, he met my eyes. "Look, in all seriousness, I can't tell you everything. Attorney-client privilege."

"Seriously? Your client is dead."

"It's still a gray area, but also I'm helping Helen and she's very much alive."

"Fine." I stared at him. "Tell me what you can." Adrenaline pumped through my body. Any new information was precious, but also frightening.

George hesitated. "The will. One of the stipulations was that you take part in whatever planning and sorting needed to be done."

I wasn't expecting that at all. I was stunned. "Wait. Are you serious?"

"As a heart attack." He coughed. "Sorry. Poor choice of words."

"Why would Stewart do that?"

George shot me a sad smile. "It seems he had faith in you knowing him best."

"But what if we'd grown apart by the time he died?"

"I guess he didn't consider that a possibility. Frankly, neither would I."

I tried to absorb that. I was tempted to tell George about the prescription, proof that there were some things you didn't know about a person, no matter how close you were. Stewart didn't even tell me he was in New York! But then he didn't know this trip would be significant. How often had he come and not called me? "So Helen didn't choose me. Stewart did. That makes a lot more sense. She would honor his request, no matter what." I felt a bit of disappointment rise in me; she still didn't like me. Why did I care? "And he stipulated that you had to help too?"

"Not to my knowledge. That's on Helen. I guess because I'm his lawyer . . . and friend."

"Right. 'Friend.' So you keep claiming. What else did the will say?"

George shook his head. "Sorry. I can't tell you. Seriously, Wren. Don't make me. I shouldn't have even told you that much. I don't know everything anyway. Any additional paperwork was for the family's eyes only."

I stared at my lap, contemplating this new piece of information. George confused me. He embodied such a strange combination of qualities. He did work that seemed vapid, but he approached it with all this integrity. "Did the will say that Kate shouldn't be involved?"

"No. Not at all! I get the sense that that's between Kate and her mom." He cleared his garbage and stood to throw it out, pointing a finger at me. "That's it! Don't ask me another thing. Dammit. I'm usually a steel trap for secrets. What is it about you?"

"I'm relentless and annoying?"

"Right. That. Look, don't tell anyone. Please." His brow was furrowed in earnest guilt and concern.

"I won't. You can trust me."

"Yeah." He stared at me for a beat. "I know."

George crossed to the trash, then returned and sat back down. The wrought iron metal chair looked small beneath him. I noticed a blond at a nearby table eyeing him from behind her wavy locks. I avoided guys like George like the plague—their sports cars and button downs and table service at cheesy clubs. Still, he was good-looking. I couldn't blame the girl. But I could plan her funeral.

CAUSE OF DEATH: Choking on bagel.

AFTER-DEATH RITUAL: Cryogenic freezing.

SERVICE: A wake. Full makeup. All her sisters from Delta Delta Delta.

PROCESSIONAL MUSIC: Taylor Swift. "I Don't Wanna Live Forever."

MEMORIAL BUFFET: Jello shots. Anything solid would be a trigger about the bagel mishap—and her past bulimia.

I eyed George. Why couldn't I decide on his funeral details? Cause of Death: Hmm. Taxi accident? Crash while driving through Malibu on PCH? Helicopter accident on set? No. That was all wrong. Bagels with lox spread? I was at a loss. It usually came to me so organically.

That girl was still trying to catch his eye. She sat up straighter and arched her back. At first, he seemed oblivious, but then I saw him glance quickly her way and ignore her smile. *Interesting.* I narrowed my eyes at him, trying to figure him out.

"What? Why are you looking at me like that?"

"You have a girlfriend? Waiting at home in LA?"

"Me? No. Not at present."

"A boyfriend? I don't want to presume."

"Thanks. No. Not a boyfriend either. Or a polyamorous union. Thank you for not presuming though." He rolled his eyes. "You?"

"Stewart told you about my water charity ex."

"I figured by now maybe you'd found someone who builds libraries for Bolivian children or houses for Haitian refugees? Or talks about one day maybe doing those things while hoarding vegan hors d'oeuvres and sustainable gift bags at launch parties?"

I wished George was more off base about my past, but he had the history of my love life pegged. So many do-gooders who had not done me any good. "Not recently. Nothing serious."

I took a bite of my sandwich, which I'd been neglecting. George eyed me like he could osmose my truth. He had this unnerving way of scrutinizing a person's face, as if he were reading it. I felt my heart begin to beat faster. I smoothed my hair. "To be honest, when Helen seemed uptight in front of you, I assumed it was because you and Stewart had dated. Maybe you broke his heart. But you didn't? Never anything romantic between you guys?"

I flashed to that night—the one I always used to want to forget. Did I still want to forget it now? Us. On his bed. Not this apartment; the one before. Stewart without a shirt; me wrapped in a sheet. Alcohol pungent and sour in the air. The way he looked at me. Naked. His face.

I shook my head. "Nope. Nothing romantic."

"Huh. Surprising."

"Why?"

"All those years. So much closeness. And you're not, you know, super unappealing."

"Wow. Thanks. That's so generous. Anyway, it wasn't just the two of us. We were also always with Jimmy."

"Right. Jimmy. Who is the best." George screwed the top back on his drink. "Okay! Ready to get back in there?"

I groaned. "Do we have to?"

"I'm afraid so. Otherwise, we risk Blair growing even more sanctimonious. And no one wants that."

I pictured her blowing up like the Stay Puft Marshmallow Man from *Ghost Busters* in giant Repetto ballet flats and flooding the city with crocodile tears.

I stood, grabbing my garbage, shredded lettuce and mustard remnants clinging to the tinfoil and paper, and tossed it in the bin. I turned back to face George, who was now standing directly next to me. I could smell his shampoo—athletic, soapy, uncomplicated. It reminded me of something I couldn't quite define—a flashback to a safer time. For a second, I was tempted to bury my face in his neck and breathe it in. Since that was out of the question, I said, "You know, Stewart is dead."

"I am aware of that, yeah."

"He'll never know if we don't handle this."

"Yeah, that's true," George nodded. "But *we'll* know." *And we are the suckers who always do the right thing.*

He was right, of course. We couldn't let the vultures pick Stewart's memory apart, piece by piece. We had a responsibility, if not to our dead friend or his mother, then to ourselves.

As I'd frozen, lost in thought again, George placed a hand on my back, sending a strange charge shooting through me, and steered me out the door. At his touch, I was reminded of high school drama class trust exercises. I felt something I hadn't in a long time: a desire to lean back and let someone else hold me up.

CHAPTER 23

Is it true, Stewart? Did you really choose me to handle the fallout from your death? I'm honored but also confused. You hated everything I liked. It was one of your favorite things about us. Didn't you worry that I'd choose everything wrong?

You always had more faith in me than I had in myself. What will I do without you to pronounce—with undisguised irritation—that I can do anything I want? Be anything I want? Go anywhere I want? Who will I disagree with about my potential?

You were my confidence—my entitlement—my self-aggrandizement. You were my healthy delusion. My Jerry Maguire speech. My hot air balloon.

That said, I know you thought I lived a tame life, but I'm almost offended. How could you be so confident that you would die first? That I would outlive you?

CHAPTER 24

Is that a joke?

I left Gretchen hanging over text while I watched where I was walking. Once I hit Third Street, the landscape on my walk from the R train on Union to my apartment was industrial at best, decrepit at worst. Giant trashed buildings and warehouses lined the street, suspicious rubble entrails tumbling onto the sidewalk from their neglected innards. Brooklyn's flagship Whole Foods rose above it all like an overpriced refuge, its own mini sanctuary city. Its very existence gave residents confidence that, even in the apocalypse, they'd still have access to their organic, non-GMO, fair trade truffle goat cheese.

I was just past the greener-than-thou supermarket and was about to cross the Gowanus Canal—it's proximity ironic, maybe even ominous. I always pay attention when crossing the short bridge over that murky cauldron of toxic waste out of fear of tripping and falling in, though it made a decent origin story for a radioactive superhero. The air reeked of sulfur and dead bodies; I held my breath. It always confounds me that some people choose to kayak here.

I started toward the chic prefab-style row houses that had popped up off Bond Street. Back on safe ground, I returned my attention to my phone and typed:

I wish I were kidding.

But Wren. How much were they really taking? Like a couple of T-shirts? 'Cause that's weird, but I guess it's not the end of the world.

No! I kid you not, G. They had three garbage bags worth of stuff—memorabilia from the show, everything. They'd asked us to pick up more trash bags and, when we got back from the bagel place, we realized why! We thought they were for cleaning things out, but Mallory was on her way to ask the doorman for A LUGGAGE RACK!!!!! 🙀

I am literally covering my eyes to shield myself from what you're telling me.

I KNOW. No words. Luckily, we got back from lunch just in time. George stopped them in the hallway and pulled out the charm. He was super diplomatic, which is good because I would have lost my mind. He explained that, even if Blair put this stuff in the donation pile, that fact wasn't confirmed until the family made sure they didn't want to keep it for themselves or for the tribute. That she and Brian and Keith couldn't just leave with Stewart's stuff! I think they still snuck a bag or two. Mallory was a bit TOO willing to take out the trash at the end.

I mean. I can't even. That that even needed to be said! I'm appalled.

Oh, I know. Trust me. Me too. It's worse than I even imagined.

Grotesque. And so so dark.

I could picture Gretchen at her desk, clear but for her laptop, Tata Harper hand cream, and the dregs of her afternoon coffee.

And, of course, Blair and Keith claimed they didn't realize what was happening because they were in the other room sorting Stewart's art collection. They're circling those paintings like prey. And Blair said—even though she supposedly didn't sanction them taking Stewart's stuff—that she was confident that SHE knew Stewart and his family well enough to decide what was valuable and what was disposable.

It must be so nice to know everything about everything.

Must be. Meanwhile, Mal kept talking about how it was all going to be donated anyway. Did it ever occur to her that there are people who need that stuff more than she does? It's called, 'a good cause!' CHARITY!

She thinks her hoarding IS a good cause.

OMG—I can't believe I forgot to mention the best part: When George and I walked into the den to assess what damage they'd done, we found Keith alone HOLDING STEWART'S EMMY!! He was gazing at it like some girl he'd roofied.

Stop.

I wish I could.

I did stop at the curb, as I waited for the light. I swear it blinked a thousand times before changing. I was impatient to get home and was almost to my block, a tiny street tucked between Hoyt and Smith.

These people are next level. Where was Willow?

By then, she had left to go to her holistic healing workshop, but not before making the whole apartment smell of fried hair. G, I'm not even sure what else she burned of Stewart's. She kept taking stuff and lighting it on fire in this portable kiln thing! Now, she wants us all to get together for a goodbye ceremony in his honor.

That sounds like a lot of quinoa and Moon Juice powders. You're obviously not going to that.

I think I'll probably have to.

Why?

I could sense the irritation in Gretchen's tone, even without hearing her voice. She could never understand why I didn't say "Screw it!" more often and refuse to care.

I don't know. Willow means well, I think, even if she's forcing her beliefs down everyone else's throats. She's the least of the problem. Anyway, if I didn't go, they'd all probably never speak to me again.

And that would be bad because—?

Fair question.

Just opt out of all of it.

I thought about Stewart's will, his request that I be part of determining his epilogue. I couldn't tell Gretchen because I had promised George I'd keep the secret.

I can't without abdicating all control over how Stewart is remembered. George and I decided we would just get in and out. But I don't care what Willow says. I'm not doing ayahuasca. I'm out of my head enough without Peruvian acid.

Interesting.

Not really. I've never been big on hallucinogenics. Remember that time I did mushrooms and spent the entire night rocking on Gabriel's bathroom floor, insisting that I'd seen a shark in the toilet?

Not the drugs! You and Geeeeeeorge.

Gretchen stretched out his name like she was about to launch into a rousing rendition of "Sitting in a Tree, K-I-S-S-I-N-G."

I stopped short, almost slamming into a woman pushing a stroller. I mumbled an apology; she barely noticed.

What about me and George?

You're going to lunch together, stopping the Mallory heist together, suffering through weird New Age ceremonies together? Suddenly, he has CHARM. I thought we hated him.

Well, we don't love him, but he's our . . . my . . . best option at the moment. At least he's not trying to steal Stewart's belongings, while pretending to preserve his memory. Plus, I have no choice but to meet with him and Helen again, and I'd rather not have everyone in the room hate me.

If you say so.

I could feel Gretchen's sly smile and I wanted to give her a gentle shove.

> Believe it or not, I don't see my friend's death
> as an opportunity for a fling with some cheesy
> LA lawyer.

There was a pause while Gretchen typed and then, I assume, erased something and started over. My brownstone was in sight, the soft yellow filter of magic hour lighting it up like a treasure chest. I wanted to break into a run. The temperature was dropping by degrees. Why I couldn't get myself to dress appropriately?

Finally, she wrote,

> Totally.

That took a long time.

Maybe Gretchen was annoyed. Could I blame her? I was conscious that Stewart's death was becoming an obsession for me. Was that normal or was it getting out of hand? Either way, I needed to at least pretend I cared about what was happening with the other people in my life too.

I typed,

> So, what's up with you?

> Nada. Just the usual. Work.

> Do you want to grab a drink tomorrow
> night?

> Ah. I can't tomorrow, sadly.

> You've been so busy this last week!

I know, I know. Work is just insane. Next weekend though?

I climbed the steps to my building's front door and opened my purse to rummage for keys. Stewart's prescription was stuffed in there; I'd forgotten. I paused. I wanted to tell Gretchen, but that seemed like an invasion of Stewart's privacy. Also, I didn't know if pocketing it had been a questionable move. I typed,

I'll let you go work. But, hey, Gretch, what do you know about Cymbalta?

Cymbalta can help.

Very funny. I've seen the commercials. But, I mean, do you know why someone would take it?

Gretchen's parents were psychiatrists, so she'd osmosed this kind of information.

You'd take it if you were depressed and SSRIs weren't doing enough. Why? Are you taking Cymbalta?

No. Just curious. Although maybe after dealing with these horrible people, I'll need to look into it.

Well, for what it's worth, I don't recommend it. One of the supposed side effects is something called "brain zaps."

Ack! What's that? That's a real thing?

I don't know, lady. But it doesn't sound good.

Once upstairs in my apartment, I sent Jimmy a text about what he'd missed that day: The bags of figurines, records, and clothes with which Mallory and Brian had tried to abscond. I figured he'd appreciate it, but he didn't answer. For someone who said we should be better about prioritizing time together, he wasn't being very attentive—and this was only week one. I felt a pang of disappointment, but told myself not to feel hurt. This part of Jimmy—the self-absorbed side—was what Stewart had struggled with most. It was probably the reason they'd drifted a bit in recent years.

I opened my fridge and contemplated dinner. A pruned green pepper stared back at me. I gave up and closed it. In my cabinet sat a loan bag of rice cakes. Maybe I wasn't hungry after all. Chris Harrison gave me an impatient head butt. *Just because* you're *not eating* . . .

Leaning against my kitchen counter after feeding him, I thought about calling my mother. I knew she was desperate to be in touch. I wasn't sure why I was avoiding her anymore. I don't know if I thought that hearing her voice would demolish my defenses or if I was worried she'd be blasé about what happened—too quick to try to move past the issue.

The truth is, Helen had her negative feelings about me, but my mother had her opinions about Stewart too. I was worried she'd try to tell me that there were silver linings to his death when it came to my openness and making new friends. I didn't want to hear that right now. She always felt I allowed Stewart to live for me, while I played the background. *The straight man.*

Sated, Chris Harrison flopped to the ground in front of me and bared his white fluffy stomach (although I knew he'd be affronted if I rubbed it). I bent down and nuzzled his nose with my own. Sometimes I felt jealous of his simple life—less so when I smelled his food.

I scrolled through my phone to check my email. Sometime in the midst of sorting Stewart's Philip Roth novels and packing up his Heath Ceramics dishware, I had glimpsed a message in my inbox from my boss, Anton.

He rarely checked in. He had this philosophy about giving his employees autonomy, which I appreciated. I scrolled through and found the note:

> Hi Wren,
> Greetings from sunny Panama!
>
> As we discussed, I'm here in a remote southern area scouting out possible project sites. There are no indoor toilets, but there's plenty of sun—just how I like it! Looks likely that this will be our next Operation Sewage destination. The infrastructure here is crap—ha! Just a bit of plumbing and drainage humor.
>
> Checking in to make sure you don't need anything from me for the Collins Foundation grant this go around. I know you're old hat at this, but Wi-Fi is spotty here and I want to make sure I can make myself available in a timely fashion, if needed.
>
> Thanks,
> Anton

CAUSE OF DEATH: A rare flesh-eating disease—or a rock climbing accident. Maybe both.

AFTER-DEATH RITUAL: Tribal burning.

SERVICE: At IHOP. He is a citizen of the world and happens to love their chocolate chip pancakes. Win-win.

PROCESSIONAL MUSIC: Seneca Indians' funeral chant.

MEMORIAL BUFFET: Gorp. Or those pancakes.

To say I had been neglecting my job was an understatement. The deadline for one of our most substantial biannual grants was coming up and—although we were awarded it every year and the application was a formality—there was a bunch of paperwork involved. It was paperwork I had done a thousand times before. I was bored just thinking about it; it seemed so insignificant in the wake of Stewart's death. I'm sure the thousands of people who now had indoor plumbing because of Anton's work would disagree. But a person, besides my boss, could only get so stimulated at the thought of sewer systems. I tried to force myself to start on it. I even sat down on my couch, pulled my soft gray blanket over my lap, and opened my computer. But then I remembered that I needed to find a charity partner for Stewart's tribute—the perfect procrastination!

Unfortunately, one google of "aneurysm research" yielded me the results I needed: the Brain Aneurysm Foundation. Clearly the perfect organization with which to partner. I copied and pasted the link and emailed it to Helen with a quick note. Then I stared at the site's homepage. Here, in front of me, was everything I needed to know about what happened to Stewart. Was I ready for answers? I took a deep breath and clicked on "Risk Factors." That seemed like a manageable place to start. *Smoking, cocaine use, traumatic head injury.* I flashed back again to Stewart falling off the monkey bars at recess. I was being crazy, right?

I closed the browser tab. This was not healthy. I considered working after all, but the siren call of Facebook won out. *As long as I was making poor decisions.* I navigated to Stewart's page like it was beyond my control, my trackpad like an Ouija board. My stomach fluttered with anticipation as it loaded, but I only needed to catch a glimpse of a post that began, "Oh, dearest Stu!" to want to flee the outpouring of noxious grief. I don't know what I'd hoped to find. I stared at Stewart's profile picture, sitting on the sidewalk against a graffitied building somewhere in either Brooklyn, Manhattan, or Downtown LA. Hard to tell. Some urban scape. He had Ray-Bans on, his sandy hair disheveled to perfection like windblown grass. He was wearing earbuds, throwback Nikes, and that Pixies T-shirt that he loved. I wanted to reach inside the photograph and tap him so he turned toward me. I wanted to crawl inside the image and curl up in his lap—something I hadn't done in years, probably since that one night— and drop my head onto his shoulder. God, I missed him. And it had been less than a week. Suddenly, my body felt like it weighed five hundred pounds. I could barely lift my arm. I almost shut my eyes and tried drift-ing off, but I don't do naps. If by some miracle I fell asleep, I knew I'd wake up groggy and feeling worse than before.

Desperate for escape, I navigated to my Facebook messages, realizing that I hadn't checked them since the night Gretchen had broken the news to me. I hadn't even opened Instagram. There were five or six notes from old middle and high school friends with whom we hadn't kept in regular touch:

I can't believe it.

It seems impossible.

He was so alive.

A piece of our childhood, our shared history.

Do you know the details?

Did he suffer?

I could hear Stewart's voice now, so *knowledgeable* after this course he took a few years ago at UCLA's Mindful Awareness Research Center. (Sarah Paulson, Michelle Williams, and Busy Philipps all recommended it.) He didn't take to the meditation for long, which is why I'd scoffed at Willow's reference to kundalini, but the underlying concepts made sense to him as guidelines for life. I was complaining about my stomach hurt-ing. I went through a period when it always did, before I knew about the lactose intolerance and stopped eating so much cheddar cheese.

"Pain is a part of life," he preached. "But suffering is a choice."

"Except for your lectures. Those I have no choice but to suffer through."

He was undeterred. "I'm just saying, you don't have to let the pain upset you. You can sit with it and find peace in the stillness; find equanimity in accepting how you feel in this moment, even if it's not entirely comfortable."

"I'm less upset about the pain and more upset that I have to give up coffee because it's too acidic. What does the Dalai Lama say about caffeine?"

He rolled his eyes. "I'm serious."

"I know."

"Life is hard. But you don't have to let that fact ruin everything."

It was a typical Stewart rhapsody. When he got into something, he invested fully and became obsessed with bringing everyone he loved along for the ride. I felt a pang of regret. Maybe I should have taken him more seriously? Maybe I should take a mindfulness course as a tribute to him? I felt plenty uncomfortable right now. Could I sit with it? Did I want to?

I shifted my computer on my lap. My joints felt achy. I seemed to have inherited Stewart's hypochondria in the wake of his death. Did he pass it onto me as he breezed, like a whisper, past my shoulder on his way to the next realm?

I answered the messages from top to bottom—most recent to oldest—winding up back at Morgan Tobler's note from the day Stewart died. Navigating to her message, it occurred to me that Morgan knew before I did—and that felt bad. Everyone knew before me. Social media has changed the nature of death, of breaking even the most personal news.

Oh, Morgan. She was a nice girl, however bland and accident prone. You know those people who trip over air?

CAUSE OF DEATH: Freak accident. There are too many possibilities to consider.

AFTER-DEATH RITUAL: Burial. Jewish cemetery.

SERVICE: Suburban synagogue. Family, congregation, school fund-raising committee members, book (don't you mean Trader Joe's *wine*?) club friends.

PROCESSIONAL MUSIC: Whitney Houston. "The Greatest Love of All." (Spoiler alert: It's inside of you.)

MEMORIAL BUFFET: Potluck. Multiple couscous salads due to a miscommunication between the organizers. All of them under-salted.

I opened her Facebook message, prepared to cut and paste the same basic explanation. After all, I didn't know much myself. There wasn't much *to* know—except that sometimes life can really "*f* you in the *a*," as they say. Bad things happen.

I read her note:

Wren,

I'm so sorry to bother you at what has to be an awful time. I know how close you and Stu were. Oy. What horrible news! I can't remember the last time I saw him; it must have been our ten-year reunion? He gave that funny speech in tribute to Mr. Bender. They always had a funny shtick. Anyway, this is kind of strange: I know it's none of my business really, but they didn't include the cause of death in the article. Was it an accident? What happened? I figured you might know, as you guys were so tight back in the day.

Sending hugs,

Morgan

In some ways, Morgan's email was much like the others: *horrible news, sorry to bug, what happened?* Clearly, she had written it before news broke about Stewart's aneurysm. But something about that question, "Was it an accident?" threw me off. As opposed to what? Murder? Why did that make me angry, considering I had thought the same thing at first?

I wrote her back:

Hi Morgan,

Good to hear from you.

I debated for an absurd amount of time about whether to add an exclamation point and decided to be more subdued. Because—death and all.

I'm so sorry that it took me a moment to get back to you. I've been a bit overwhelmed with the logistics of

> cleaning out Stewart's apartment and
> helping plan a tribute for him.

Why did I feel the need to mention all my death-related responsibilities? Sure, it was a good excuse for having ignored her message, but, if I was honest, I also wanted her to know that Stewart and I had still been close. Our friendship wasn't past tense.

> By now, I'm sure you've read about the
> aneurysm. I don't have a lot of additional
> details, but, essentially, he got a terrible
> headache—and that was it. It's so hard to
> fathom, isn't it? That one second you could
> be complaining about your sinuses and the
> next just be erased? Life without Stewart
> seems pretty unimaginable.

> A black hole.

I stopped typing. Why was I now confiding in Morgan? The pendulum was swinging pretty wide and fast on this one. I guess I felt resentful of her intrusion, but also grateful that she could confirm memories of me and Stewart in our early days—like she could help make my time with Stewart real.

> Anyway, you should definitely come to the
> tribute next week. In the meantime, I hope
> you're doing well. It looks like you're happy,
> judging by Instagram at least. Your trip to
> the Jersey Shore this past summer looked
> delightful.

> xo - Wren.

I was about to close my computer, but then three dots—that flickering ellipses—appeared. Apparently, Morgan was online and already responding.

> Thanks, Wren. So good to hear from you too!

(She went for the exclamation point.)

> Yes, I heard about the aneurysm and, as sad as that is, I was relieved to hear that he didn't suffer and that he'd been happy and thriving until the end.

> We should try to get a group of high school people together soon and have a toast in his honor! And, yes, thank you. The Jersey Shore was awesome. Turns out NJ isn't all garbage like they told us growing up. My kids loved it! I miss summer already!

> Best,

> Morgan

She was relieved that he was happy and thriving? He was a famous actor with a ton of successes—a rising star.

> Morgan, is there some reason why you thought Stewart wouldn't be thriving?

Maybe she had read about turmoil between the *Manic Mondays* cast in *Us Weekly* and took that seriously. Maybe she was perusing tabloids at weekly pedicures like Madison. I saw the dots appear, then disappear, then appear again. There was a lag, a pause, and then her response posted:

Well, I don't know if this is okay for me to talk about. I guess he's gone, so it doesn't hurt anyone. But between you and me, I just always wondered how he was doing because of that month he missed in ninth grade—you know what I mean.

I did not know what she meant. At all. I mean, I remembered the month he was sick; he'd had a terrible bout of mono. Was she worried that his body was frail after that? Surely not.

You mean when he had mono?

Yes. "Mono."

What did "mono" mean? Why the air quotes?

Hey Morgan, I'm sorry. I feel like an idiot, but I'm not sure what you're saying.

Oh, no, *I'm* sorry. I was being too vague. I mean because of what really kept him out of school.

???

Wait, Wren. I'm so confused. Did you not know? I just assumed you knew 'cause you guys were inseparable and your mothers were friends. You know he was absent because of the breakdown, right?

The breakdown? My heart started pounding—or maybe it already had been and I was only alert to it now. How much was there about Stewart's life that I didn't know? How close were we really?

I was torn: I didn't want to seem clueless about Stewart, but I needed to know more. Maybe Morgan was confused. Maybe she'd come unhinged in the years since I last saw her, all evidence to the contrary? I rubbed my eyes, as a tug-of-war played out in my mind. What was I afraid would happen if I admitted that I didn't have all the answers about Stewart's life? I gave in.

> Honestly, Morgan, I don't know about that. What makes you think he had a breakdown?

> Okay. Did Stu ever mention that he and I saw therapists in adjoining offices? And that we used to talk?

My world was being rocked. Stewart had a secret friendship with *Morgan Tobler*? He used to call her "Fluffy" behind her back because of her wild hair. No wonder she'd wanted more information. They'd been legit friends. I thought about how ardently Stewart had argued with Jimmy about going to one of Morgan's birthday parties so many years ago.

> I knew he went to a therapist, but that's it. Morgan, is there any way that I could call you?

> Of course! I'm just getting the kids down and then I have a planning committee meeting at their school, but I'm headed into the city tomorrow for a dentist appointment and then I'm free. Do you want to meet for coffee, by any chance? Maybe at like three at Cafe Lalo?

I could swing it if I ran from there to Helen Beasley's apartment to meet George at 5:00 p.m. to discuss the tribute planning. I had to see her.

Yes. I'll be there. Can't wait to catch up!

I closed my computer. What the hell was going on? Who was the real Stewart Beasley?

CHAPTER 25

Stewart. Are you for real? How much did you keep from me? And, more importantly, why? I wouldn't have judged you. I would have been there. You know that! I loved you!

I can't believe that I'm going for lattes tomorrow with fucking Morgan "Fluffy" Tobler to learn more about the real you. Am I making up how close we were? Was I imagining our connection all this time? Am I just one of many people who overestimated their closeness with you?

The worst part is that you're not even here to verify what I thought were the facts. Who really knew you, Stewart? Because I'm starting to worry that it wasn't me.

CHAPTER 26

The minute I saw Morgan's moon face, I felt like a horrible person for projecting my anger onto her. I made a mental note to replan her funeral with an upgrade. *Premium package.*

She stood on the sidewalk right off Amsterdam Avenue, the lights from the café twinkling behind her even in the light of day. A lot had changed on the Upper West Side since we were kids. Mom-and-pop businesses, from knish and halva shops to shoemakers, had been replaced by basic chain stores. Amsterdam, once a dangerous stretch, was now home to sports bars and neighborhood eateries serving artisan fried pickles and Asian-inspired tacos. It was late afternoon and clusters of middle and high school kids romped by, postdismissal. Squealing and laughing with shoelaces untied, they chased each other in circles, free from the confines of grown-up rules. As I approached Morgan, one boy shoved another in jest, sending him flying in my direction. I jumped out of the way before he crashed into me.

"Sorry, ma'am!" He cavorted away, backpack hanging off one shoulder.

I looked at Morgan. "Ma'am? Did he just call me 'ma'am'? Jesus. Like I wasn't having a bad enough week."

She giggled, cupping her hand over her mouth, the mannerism reminiscent of her girlhood self. She wore a Patagonia fleece, straight-leg jeans, and sporty sneakers, the colorful kind you wear to the gym, not out. Apparently, she had ceased to care. In some ways, I envied her that. Her puffy hair was tamed into a bun and maybe even keratin flattened, revealing her ruddy face.

We exchanged a quick kiss on the cheek and mounted the steps to the door. Inside, the restaurant was buzzing, more so than I expected. When we were kids, this had been a neighborhood spot, known for its extravagant pastries and desserts. But then Nora Ephron featured it in *You've Got Mail* and it became not only a tourist destination, but also a symbol of the old guard Upper West Side, standing staunchly on the right side of history.

We were led to a small round table. I ordered peppermint tea with almond milk and honey; Morgan ordered a cappuccino and tiramisu. I would have loved to inhale every sweet in the place, but my lactose intolerance means I'm out of luck at heavenly spots like this. I inhaled, though, and let the smell of chocolate and cream envelop me. Stewart lived for the key lime cheesecake here.

Lived for . . . Stewart. Gone.

Morgan and I exchanged pleasantries as we waited for our drinks. She asked after my parents. I asked after her husband and kids. Then, once she'd mixed a packet of stevia into her coffee, I decided it was time to dive in.

"So, Morgan, I was so surprised by what you said—about Stewart and his break from school. The thing is, I assume I know everything about him, but it's starting to feel like maybe that isn't the case. Like, at all." I heard my voice shake and willed to it stabilize.

Her face folded like a consternated bulldog's—a cute one. "Oh, Wren. I'm so sorry. The last thing I want to do is mess with your memories of him!"

"No, no. Not at all. Truly!" I stirred the honey into my tea for longer than necessary, then pushed on. "I mean, I want to know. Now that he's gone, I'm finding I have this impulse to investigate him. To understand every single detail about his life because in some ways I feel like maybe I didn't. We were still close at the end, but I feel like I let too much time pass between really checking in. I took for granted that we were in each other's lives. That we always would be."

"And why wouldn't you have? You should have had much more time. It's such a horrible, shocking thing, death. Especially when it's sudden and arbitrary like this." She looked down at her coffee cup, wiping a bit of foam off the lip and licking it from her finger. Only then did I remember that she'd lost her father to cancer about five years before. My stomach dropped. I was so self-involved.

Poor Morgan. Was she still shocked daily by her father's absence? How long did that feeling linger? A few weeks? Forever? "You're right. It is . . . shocking . . . again and again. Speaking of which, how is your mother holding up?"

"She's good. Thanks for asking. But the thing is, it doesn't go away, the sadness. It just moves toward the back of the closet, if that makes sense. You still keep it with you always, but, eventually, it's not the only thing you think about—not every day, all day. You're no longer angry and confused about how the world can continue to spin and people can go on with their days, even though you're shattered. So that's a long way of saying, my mom is still sad sometimes and she misses my dad every day, but she's okay. She has this hiking club she loves. That's very helpful—like a sisterhood."

"That makes sense. I'm glad she found that."

Morgan sighed. Then she seemed to remember herself. She took a big forkful of her tiramisu and groaned, "Oh my God. It's so good."

Life is funny. There is pleasure; there is pain. Sometimes they're back-to-back. Sometimes they are one and the same.

"Are you sure you don't want any?"

I shook my head. "Lactard." I wanted to punch myself in the face. I vowed that I'd never use that expression again. I felt like Morgan was one-thousand times the person I was—or at least I'd been acting like lately.

"Ah. Too bad. I didn't know. That must have started after high school?" Morgan took another bite and closed her eyes to luxuriate in the dessert. Suddenly, her eyes popped open. "You know, I've been so focused on Stewart, I forgot to even ask you what you're doing with yourself! You wanted to be a journalist, right?"

"Good memory. Yeah. An international correspondent, as a kid. I wanted to travel the world."

"That's right! I think the last time I saw you—at the five-year reunion—maybe you were writing for magazines? *Cosmo* and *ELLE* maybe? And talking about applying to Columbia's School of Journalism to move into more 'serious' stuff? Did you end up going? I remember that your dad taught there."

I had a pat answer that I normally recited to this question—which people from my past asked from time to time—all about how I worked as a fashion and beauty writer for a while before realizing how frivolous and difficult editorial could be. *Magazines are dying blah, blah, blah.* Today, though, I looked Morgan in the eyes and worked up the courage to speak the truth aloud for maybe the first time ever. "I applied, but I didn't get in. They rejected me."

I waited for the world to shrivel up and drop off its axis—or at least a look of shock to register on Morgan's face. Instead, she took a sip of her cappuccino, leaving a trail of foam on her upper lip. "Oh! Their loss! So, did you study somewhere else? Or continue working your way up in magazines?"

"No," I shook my head. "I kind of took it as a sign—and did something else."

"Oh. That's too bad. I remember you being a really good writer!" Morgan peered at me through glassy eyes. I felt like she could see too much.

I shifted in my seat. "Anyway, so Stewart? And his break . . . down?"

"Oh, right! Sorry, I got off track. So, when my dad got sick the first time, during our ninth-grade year, my parents sent me to a therapist. I guess they wanted me to have professional help processing what was happening."

"That was probably a good idea, right?"

"Sure. My parents love a therapist. Anyway, I arrived for my first appointment and the waiting room had one of those boards where you press the button and it lights up to let your therapist know that you've arrived. But I didn't understand the system. I was standing frozen in this empty waiting room surrounded by framed floral prints and ancient magazines strewn on side tables and, suddenly, I hear this familiar voice from behind me say, 'Just push the button, Fluffy.'"

"Stewart." Morgan knew about the nickname, and she didn't mind. I realized now that it was probably a term of endearment. *Stupid, Wren.*

"Yeah, I was, of course, very surprised. It was awkward. I mean, we were thirteen or whatever, and Stewart was one of the cool kids at school. I was—well, never quite that."

I started to disagree, but she swatted at the air like it didn't matter and continued. "Anyway, that's the funny thing about therapists' offices, right? You're waiting to talk to a professional yourself, but you still assume that everyone else there must be crazy. Stewart and I were uncomfortable at first, but then it became clear that we had the same appointment time and that our therapists shared an office. We couldn't avoid each other. So we started talking while we waited each week. First, it was just about school—teachers we liked or hated, impossible homework, some funny prank at assembly that morning. But then, we started to open up about why we were both there. I think it felt good to talk to another kid, who understood the nature of our lives, but who wasn't in our immediate social circle. I remember, he mentioned his father being somewhat absent?" She looked to me for confirmation.

I nodded. "Yes. That remained true."

"The other stuff was normal adolescent angst: his parents put pressure on him, his sister and mother fought, he was sick of playing peacemaker. But then he started to talk about how hard he found it to get out of bed some days. At first, I agreed. I thought I knew what he was talking about. What teenager doesn't want to stay in bed? But, then it became clear to me that he was experiencing something more intense than I understood. Now, as an adult, I would be better equipped to wrap my mind around the idea, but we were only kids. So I just listened. I told him you'd never know it from watching at him at school. Everyone loved him. He always seemed so energetic and upbeat."

"Yeah," I agreed. "He often was. And what did he say?"

She smoothed her bun. "He said he felt like it was weak to give into the sadness and lethargy, but that sometimes he felt exhausted by everything. I remember he said he wanted to curl up in bed and stay there for a month. He laughed afterward, but I didn't feel like he was kidding."

I pictured Stewart in his king-size bed, which seemed giant to me then, too big for a child to fill—navy sheets and gray duvet splayed around him, shades drawn. Morrissey playing in the dark. I had laid beside him in this state many times. I knew the Stewart who moped and festered. But it just seemed part of the performance of his being, and also part of growing up for us all. I could remember the feeling now, as a physical sensation, of lying next to him, his body warm beside mine as we stared at the ceiling in silence.

I knew that boy well. He wasn't a stranger. I felt the tension in my shoulders release at that recognition. "What happened then?"

"Then he stopped showing up for a couple weeks straight, and he didn't come to school either. I thought it was mono like everyone else, but then, one day, I went to use the bathroom before my therapy session and saw Helen Beasley and Stewart's therapist in the hallway talking. They were clearly at the end of a meeting. Helen was wearing this amazing mink coat—you know that one she had? She looked like a 1940s movie star. Anyway, I heard her say, 'How long do these sort of episodes usually last?' The therapist said, 'It depends. I'll be honest: Stewart has been battling this for a while. After a breakdown, a person may take time to repair himself and get back to normal. Some people are never quite the same.' Then they noticed me and I ducked past them into the restroom. Of course, I pretended I hadn't heard a thing. But I never forgot those words because they scared me: never quite the same."

Sheesh. A *breakdown*? I tried to wrap my mind around it. Poor Stewart. I remember trying to get in to see him during that time, but I was told he was too sick and contagious. That seemed absurd to me. It was the "kissing disease," right? I wasn't going to stick my tongue down his throat; neither was Jimmy. But the Beasleys had said no, and that was around the time that Matthew Simonsson became my boyfriend. I was deeply focused on flirting with him by Riverside Park, taking off his baseball cap and threatening to throw it over the stone wall, then letting him kiss me against it instead.

"Anyway, then Stu came back to school," Morgan went on. "And he *was* the same, so I figured all's well. He didn't come back to that therapist though. At least not at our regular time. So when I heard this terrible news, I wanted to make sure he'd been happy. I hated to think of him being miserable this whole time. I wanted to know that he'd spent his life before the aneurysm feeling like he could get out of bed."

"Well, he definitely made it out of bed—for every B-list celebrity with an Instagram account." The joke didn't have a shelf life. It turned rancid out there in the silence. Morgan smiled out of generosity, but I could tell that more hid behind her expression. Stewart had been kind to her. I was being unkind to him now.

Had I underestimated him? Was Stewart kind, after all?

I watched as a couple of teenage girls tumbled inside the café now, giggling together at the counter as they debated the selection of sweets and counted their pooled money. It was hard to believe we had ever been that young. "Thank you, Morgan. I really appreciate you telling me all this— about Stewart, I mean."

"Of course, Wren! You really didn't know?"

I shook my head and shrugged. "I don't know why he didn't tell me."

"We were kids."

That was true. And there is a lot that we hide from each other as teenagers—it's a matter of survival. We know each other as our parents and siblings never could, but there are limits on the other side. In some ways, we all lead secret home lives—parents sleeping in separate bedrooms, sex toys stumbled upon in bedside tables, the infidelities, the rehab stints, the tumbles off wagons, the abuses and criticisms, the disagreements, the unusual foods with strange smells, the illnesses, the nerdy game nights—even the proliferation of Post-it notes and thrift store furniture. We protect ourselves.

At some point, though, don't we let our guards down and reveal the truth to our closest people? Once we grow up and realize how screwed up everyone else is too?

"No, but later," I insisted. "When we were adults, confessing every horrible thought and impulse to each other. At four a.m., drunk and miserable in the best way in our twenties. I don't know why he never told me then."

Morgan sighed, her lips forming a sad smile. "Old habits die hard, Wren."

"What do you mean?"

"Meaning maybe he didn't want you, of all people, to see him that way. No matter how much time had passed. Maybe he wanted to preserve your image of him. Maybe those weren't your roles in the dynamic. I mean, you know how he felt about you." She laughed suddenly. "Or maybe I've seen too many therapists!"

I thought about the deep shame I felt when I was rejected from Columbia, how I still hid that fact from others though I was the only one who cared. How that shame had shaped my life, the dreams I hadn't pursued. I thought about the people we want others to see us as versus the people we really are.

I thought about Stewart, about how he was my bright spot, my cheerleader. I thought about how cheerleaders can't do their jobs when they're too sad to move. I thought about lying in bed next to him in the dark, how I thought we were just wallowing in teen angst. I thought we were bummed because our parents were annoying and our friends could be dumb and there was too much American History reading and we didn't understand precalculus. I didn't understand if he was in real pain.

I had sensed him near me then—his fingers inches from my own. I wished I could take his hand now. Our arms flush against each other, emanating warmth. Why didn't I just grab his hand and weave my fingers through? Why didn't I press my palm against his and let him know he wasn't alone?

CHAPTER 27

Stewart. Grab my hand.

CHAPTER 28

I could have walked to the Beasleys' apartment from Cafe Lalo, I was that close. I *should* have walked. But I felt like I needed to be propelled by some other form of motion, while I sat and thought—about Stewart, about friendship, about Morgan, who was a more quality person than anyone I'd interacted with in a while. Including myself. So I hailed a cab.

I tried Gretchen. Voicemail. Again. She was so hard to reach lately. That job was working her to the bone. I made a mental note to force her to see a shitty movie with me soon. Something with Seth Rogen and anyone else. She needed downtime to space out and, frankly, so did I.

That left one last person to call: I took a steadying breath, dialed and the phone rang. I got voicemail.

"You've reached Margaret Pinkus. I can't come to the phone right now, but leave your name and number and, if I'm not off-the-grid, I'll call you back. Remember: 'The medium is the message.' Thanks!"

Just hearing my mother's voice on her outgoing message stole my breath. I knew this was going to happen. I squeezed my eyes shut. It was more than I could take.

"Hey, Mom, it's me," I managed. "Hope you guys are good. I got your messages. I'm so sorry we haven't connected in the last week since . . . It's been crazy, as you would imagine. Everyone is behaving . . . badly. That's the nicest way to put it. Anyway, I have a random question for you about Stewart: Do you remember when he was out of school for a month when we were like thirteen or fourteen? They said it was mono. Is it possible that it was something else? Did Helen hint at anything? It's not important, but it just came up with Morgan Tobler—yup, I saw Morgan; she's good—and, well, anyway, I thought you might remember, having been an adult and all. Actually, come to think of it, maybe you were on that retreat in the Berkshires that month? I can't remember. Anyway. Love you. Miss you. I promise I'll make it up there soon to see you guys. Tell Dad I said, what-up! Talk to you later."

I pressed end and stared at my phone, hard. Having finally tried and failed to reach my mother, I felt as alone as ever in my life.

I gazed out at the streets, blurred as we passed. It didn't matter. I knew them by heart. The route to the Beasleys' house. Each corner and stoop, with its particular slopes and divots, was as much a part of me as the cells in my body.

The taxi driver kept accelerating then stopping short at each red light, as if that might somehow get us to our destination faster. It was making my stomach drop like a roller coaster that I wanted off. I kept a hand to my chest, holding my heart inside. I tried to see the driver's face, but I couldn't make him out through the thick glass littered with stickers. He was in silhouette against the windshield. At a stop, he pushed his glasses up on his face and for one brief, heart-stopping, irrational instant, I thought he was Stewart.

CAUSE OF DEATH: Car crash (duh.) Hopefully not in the next ten minutes.

AFTER-DEATH RITUAL: Burial. With a procession of taxicabs.

SERVICE: Something casual, but big enough to include all of driver friends. All dressed up and wearing aftershave.

PROCESSIONAL MUSIC: A rousing rendition of the Beatles' "Drive My Car."

MEMORIAL BUFFET: Road trip snacks. Beef jerky. Doritos. Gatorade.

We stopped short again, the breaks squealing. I grabbed the door handle and held on tight. Maybe a cab had been a bad idea. The leather seat felt stiff beneath me. The air smelled heavy with aftershave and mildew. I cracked the window, inviting in a blast of cool atmosphere. We zoomed up tree-lined streets past brownstones in various states of grandness or disrepair—mostly well-kept these days—then past Columbus and up to Central Park West. Lush trees came into view. I noticed the leaves were starting to change. Sometimes they fall off before they turn vibrant reds, purples, and yellows, but it looked like this would be a beautiful year. A year full of political upheaval and insane headlines and natural disasters and sickness and health and small miracles and resistance and beautiful fall foliage. A year Stewart would never see.

"Near corner, please."

My mysterious driver did not respond. I spotted George waiting for me outside, shaded underneath the awning, staring down at his phone. Despite what I knew awaited upstairs, I felt myself smile, a different kind of butterflies fluttering in my stomach, and it surprised me. With George, at least I didn't have to pretend.

The driver pushed the plexiglass aside and turned to face me, offering me my receipt. He was an older guy with wire rim glasses, pockmarked skin, and a goatee. Definitely not Stewart. I said goodbye and closed the cab door.

George still hadn't realized he was being observed. He rubbed the back of his neck, shifting on his feet. I came to a stop in front of him. "Hey. Know a good lawyer?" You would have thought I'd screamed, "Fire!" from the way he jumped.

He put a hand to his head. "Jesus. I didn't see you there."

"Stressed much?" I nodded toward his phone.

"Yeah. Just work stuff."

"Real job and all."

"Right."

"So just work stress? Nothing to do with meeting with our dead friend's mother upstairs?"

He frowned. "You love to call him 'our dead friend.'"

"Sorry. 'Your dead client's mom'? Is that better?"

"Not really."

Is this thing on? I pulled my jacket tighter around me to protect against the cold. "George. I'm joking. Don't tell me I actually offended you?"

"No." He exhaled, shook his head. "Look, I'm sorry. I do find meeting with Helen anxiety-provoking, especially with you."

"With me? How come?"

"Oh. I didn't even mean—"

"It's okay. You can say it: because she doesn't like me."

George looked flummoxed, but then recovered. "Yeah, I guess that's why. I don't know."

"It's okay," I said, resting my palm on his upper arm. "It's not your problem. Don't feel like you have to try to fix things." I knew I should move my hand, but his muscle flexed underneath and I liked how it felt. He was wearing a navy blue sweater; it was a good color on him.

He looked me in the eyes, then looked down at my hand on his arm, then looked back up at me again and smiled. I dropped it.

"Let's start over." He leaned down and kissed my cheek, sending a shiver down my body.

It's chilly out, I told myself. *That's all.* "Hello. Nice to see you. How's your day going?"

"Weird. But what isn't these days?"

"Well, I'd love to hear more about the weirdness later because we haven't had enough of that lately, but we should head upstairs."

He gestured toward the doors. "After you."

"Gentlemanly."

"That or it's a #MeToo move," he said. "You don't know. I could be trying to catch a glimpse of your butt."

I rolled my eyes. He grinned and gestured toward the door. "Let's go."

"Nope. You first."

On our way up in the elevator, he debriefed me: "So I talked to Blair. She's back at Stewart's place again today, finishing up going through everything."

"Wait, what? I thought we were done!"

"So did I, but apparently she felt that it wasn't quite organized enough, so she's doing a last appraisal with her label maker."

"You mean correcting our choices, recategorizing, and putting her stamp on absolutely everything?"

"Right."

I threw my hands up. "George! You're such a sucker!"

"I know, I know. Though I prefer 'nice guy.' I told her that Mallory and the other vultures were not permitted inside under any circumstances."

"I assume you didn't call them 'vultures.'"

"You mean, did I reveal your affectionate nickname? Maybe I did; maybe I didn't. You'll never know. Unless you ask them next time you see them. Like, 'Did George tell you that I call you 'the vultures?' That's a good idea."

The elevator *pinged* its arrival and the doors opened. Why did the entrance to this apartment always remind me of stepping onto a massive ship in Star Wars, the doors sliding open to reveal so much blinding white? I half expected an army of storm troopers to march up with Bellinis and cocktail napkins.

As if on cue, Madison appeared. "Hi, guys! Fantastic to see you both. Can I take your coats? Let me take them. It's warm in here and cold out there! Come, come, come."

I hustled out of my jacket, handing it to a housekeeper, who appeared as if from nowhere. I noticed that George took his time. I guess he wasn't as rattled by Madison's frenetic energy.

"Hi," he smiled. "Always a pleasure."

"Nice to see you too." She blushed. "Both of you, of course." *Not convincing.* Madison cleared her throat. "Anyway, come this way. Helen is in her office. It's so chilly today, isn't it? Fall is here!"

George was able to match her stride without much effort, being taller than I. He leaned in toward her conspiratorially, as I shuffled behind them. "How's she doing today?"

"It's a hard one!" Madison beamed. "She's been locked in her study all day, dealing with estate issues—Stu's trust fund, what have you. We found an old album from a family trip to the Amalfi Coast when the kids were small. She's been poring over that. I tried to open a window for fresh air, but she wasn't having it. Too cold, apparently!"

Madison knocked on the door of Helen's office, lightly enough that I guessed she'd been reprimanded for being too loud in the past.

"Come in."

Helen was seated behind her desk, wearing a white sweater and riding pants—not for riding. She looked "dressed" by anyone else's standards, but it was as casual as I'd seen her in years. My first thought was, *she looks tired. Like something has gone out of her face. Like she's lost something.*

Of course she had.

"Good of you both to stop by." She pulled off her tortoiseshell reading glasses. "Have a seat."

George crossed and gave her a kiss on the cheek, so I did the same. It was more of an air kiss in her vicinity really; her cheek smelled of expensive face cream.

"So everything got sorted?" Helen asked.

"It should be," George said, settling on the love seat beside me. "We separated out what we thought you, Ted, and Kate might like to keep and then everything that seemed appropriate to display at the tribute."

"Yes. Blair mentioned that she was finishing up today. What a lovely girl she is. She's been so helpful. How lucky that she could make the time."

I restrained myself from gagging but couldn't help stealing a glance at George. He was avoiding my eyes as he nodded. "Yes. She was . . . there."

"She and Stewart spent so much time together. I wonder why they never dated. Do *you* know?"

I figured Helen was asking George, but when I looked up, she was eying me expectantly. "Me?" I put a hand to my chest. "Oh. I think Blair probably wasn't his type. Kind of . . ." I struggled for a nice way to say it: controlling, insecure, aggressive, vapid, high-strung, materialistic, full-of-shit, star fucker. "Tightly wound."

Helen squinted at me. "Huh. Really? She just seems effective to me. Like an adult."

I was at a loss. Stewart didn't date adults. Not in that way. But I wasn't going to argue with his mother.

George swooped in to save me. "Eh. She was probably just too tall."

Helen turned her gaze on him and smiled with genuine affection, even warmth. I was catching a glimpse of the "pussycat" Jimmy knew. "Probably. Anyway, I'll be able to stop by tomorrow morning to look through what you found, then we can send what's necessary to the TV Institute. After that, you can have Stewart's friends back over in the evening to pick out the memorabilia they'd like."

The idea of watching the vultures pick over Stewart's belongings like raw flesh made my head hurt. Again.

"And Kate will be able to get there before that too?" I asked. "I put some items aside that I thought she'd particularly want—old photos of them together and stuff like that."

Helen avoided my eyes, shuffling papers on her desk. "I'll make sure anything Kate might want is brought here."

So Kate wasn't going to see Stewart's apartment one last time? Or go through her brother's belongings herself? What was wrong with this family? Were they trying to outsource their pain like Gretchen suggested? Or did Kate just not care? Was that possible? I knew how close they'd been as kids, having survived a kind of boot camp with their parents.

I was upset. My face felt hot. I'm sure it was flushed. I unbuttoned my chunky cardigan sweater. Why did this family keep their homes so hot?

"I can liaise with Madison about having everything messengered, if that's helpful," George was saying. *Liaise. Lawyer mode.*

"Thank you, George. You're a lifesaver. Oh, that reminds me. I wanted to give you this." Helen bent down and began rifling through her Goyard tote.

I shifted in my seat. I was desperate to get out of there. Nothing felt further from Stewart than sitting in this stifling office with this ice queen. The family never appreciated the real him. They never understood him! He always felt that way.

George stole a glance at me and mouthed, "Are you okay?" I shook my head. He stood.

"Helen, I'm so sorry to rush us, but we should go. I have a client call that I couldn't reschedule. Apologies."

She looked up. "Not at all. I know you have an important job. Wren can stay and get the rest of the information from me."

I looked up at him in panic.

"No, no. I promised her a ride downtown. I can wait until we have everything we need from you. My client will just have to understand."

"Okay. Thank you."

With a small shrug, he sat back down. Without looking at me, he placed his hand on top of my own and squeezed once, then moved it away. I wanted it back.

"Ah, here it is. I wanted to give you two a program from another recent TV Institute tribute, so you know how they usually go. Most of it will be organized by the staff there—they're pros at this. They'll reach out to invite his professional contacts, etcetera. But, in order to introduce a personal element, they'd like us to choose someone to speak—about Stewart as a person. Wren, I'll let you choose whom, if you think you're up to it. You did a good job finding the aneurysm organization. As I understand it, the partnership is good to go."

I cursed Stewart for choosing me to help with his aftermath. I knew Helen Beasley would never have asked me otherwise. "Sure," I managed. "I can find someone. Unless . . . were you hoping to speak?"

"Me? Oh, God no." She looked down at her desk and seemed to say to herself, "I wish I could, but I couldn't."

"And Ted?"

It was a silly question. I wasn't even sure that Stewart's father would know how to describe his son. She shook her head. "Maybe Blair or . . . I don't know, Keith. He knew Stewart for a long time."

I flinched. Over my dead body. Not over Stewart's. "Okay. Thank you, Helen. I'll give it some thought. Maybe Jimmy." I pictured Jimmy demurring, if I could even get him to respond. Public speaking was not his jam.

"Yes!" her face brightened at the thought. "Maybe Jimmy. Okay. That should be it. George, have a good meeting. If you don't mind calling me later to discuss some minor life insurance issues, I won't bore Wren with that now."

He nodded. "Of course."

Once dismissed, we blew past Madison. George gathered our coats and, in no time, we were outside in the fresh air. I wanted to bow to the trees in gratitude for their oxygen.

He pulled on his jacket. "Does it seem to you like we've spent the days since Stewart's death constantly trying to escape?"

"It does. Thanks for rushing us out of there."

"Feeling any better?"

"Yes. Thank you."

"No problem. I thought you were about to turn into a tomato."

"Gee. Thanks a lot."

"A cute tomato. One with a face."

"Oh, that's much better." The word "cute" hung in the air between us like a balloon; I blew it off. He probably called Madison "cute" too. "It's just strange to be in Stewart's childhood home. Without him, it feels like everything he wasn't—cold, stiff. It's odd. It makes me feel even lonelier. Like he was the life of that place and without him—"

"Yeah, I get it. He was the family's heart."

"Yes! And they're so odd. I know they're mourning and I shouldn't judge and all families are insane, but why don't they want to help more? I expect his father to be too busy, as usual, but why won't Kate get over whatever is happening and come visit Stewart's apartment one last time? Pick up the photographs of them as kids?"

"I don't know. Families are nuts. Especially at times like these."

Nearby, a teenage girl was checking her phone while walking a giant dog in a sweater across the street. A squirrel darted in front of them, catching the girl unaware. She yelped as the dog dragged her after him. It would have been funny, under other circumstances. I used to have a sense of humor.

I blurted out, "I can't stop thinking about how she found out." It felt like an admission.

"She?"

"Helen."

"Right."

"Do you know . . . the details?"

George studied me, maybe wondering how much to share, his jaw flexing and releasing. I was making him nervous. "Well, I know that his downstairs neighbor found him," he said gently. "They had some sort of arrangement where he allowed her to use his cable when he was away. She didn't realize that he was home. After she found him, she called the door-man to come up. I think maybe it was that guy watching the game on his phone when we arrived the other day. And then he called the police. I imagine they called Helen."

I thought about that for a moment. It was as I pictured, only now I had a whole new scenario to consider: the neighbor walking in. Horri-fying. *Stewart. Lifeless. Blue. What happens when your brain explodes?* I almost asked George. Thus far, I had been wise enough not to look it up online. I was afraid of the images that might appear.

Behind George, the sky was turning a soft pink, warming and dark-ening as evening set in. I looked up at his face, half in shadows. "How did *you* find out?"

He cleared his throat, eyes downcast. "She called me. Right afterward."

"Where were you?"

"At my office. LA time. It was earlier there, of course. I was drinking my morning coffee, which was, of course, some special Ethiopian blend that Stewart had insisted I try. My day had just started." The day had begun like normal, then everything flipped upside down.

"I wonder how she knew—to call you."

"She knew I was his lawyer," he shrugged, "even if I wasn't the right kind."

I bit my lip. "When I found out, I was eating vegan taco salad and watching *The Bachelor*."

George's eyes widened. I saw him try not to laugh. "That's . . . I feel like I should say something somber, but I can't think of what."

"I was super excited for my relaxing evening! It was the finale!"

"I can't believe you watch that show."

"Why does everyone say that? It's quality TV!"

"You are a complicated woman."

"That probably wasn't meant as a compliment but thank you."

He looked at me, hard. "Of course it was a compliment."

Something about the way he was examining my face—refusing to look away—made me feel exposed. A flutter of nerves reverberated through me. "Hey, are you hungry? I'm hungry!"

"As far as I can tell, you're always hungry."

I rolled my eyes. "I know you're used to LA models on intermittent juice fasts, but, yes. I'm a human being. I need food to live. Preferably fried food."

"Fair enough. Let's walk downtown. We'll find something around Columbus Circle."

We started to walk, the magic hour settling over us like an enchanted spell. The behemoth prewar buildings were like mystical mansions of a bygone era. I half expected the glitterati to emerge from them in stoles and shimmering diamonds on their way to the Harvard Club or the Algonquin or some such playground where the likes of Dorothy Parker quipped. George was walking beside me like some handsome costar. I wondered why he'd chosen a job behind the camera instead of in front of it. But I knew. Because—responsible. And he didn't need the spotlight. I took a deep breath. "I have to tell you something." I heard myself say it before I understood that I would confide in him. "It's a confession. It might be silly."

He raised his eyebrows, "You have my full attention."

I exhaled. "I've been doing some digging and I think that Stewart may have struggled with depression and anxiety. And he never told me."

George stopped walking and cocked his head. "That's your confession? I was hoping for something tawdry."

"Well, you'll have to settle for maudlin."

"Seriously, though, what makes you think that?"

"I talked to a high school friend who remembers a bout he had with it. And I found a prescription for meds tucked inside one of his plays."

George toggled his head. "High school was a long time ago. And a prescription for antidepressants doesn't seem unusual. Plus, if you found it, it means he might not even have filled it. These days, doctors, especially in LA, dole that stuff out like candy!"

"Why do I feel like I'm about to get a lecture on the opioid epidemic?"

"It's a serious problem."

"Sometimes you *do* remind me of Stewart." *Preachy.* I shoved my hands in my pockets. "Anyway, I know it doesn't even matter. He's gone. It's just upsetting me that I somehow didn't know—like he had this whole world I was oblivious to."

George brought his hand to my shoulder, stopping me. "Wren, you knew him. As well as anyone. He adored you. You can't possibly know every single facet of any human being. That doesn't mean that your relationship wasn't legitimate."

Across the street, a trio of children shrieked with excitement. Their father stood watching them climb up onto a green park bench and then jump down off of it. I thought about sitting on benches like that with Stewart. Never again.

Stewart. Gone.

George was right. I was overreacting. I gazed up toward the swanky hotels on Central Park South, across Columbus Circle toward Time Warner Center. Trump Tower slumped—a gold and gaudy blight—at its edge. That's when I spotted it! The antidote for all my woes: Nathan's!

"Oooh." I made a beeline for the shiny green cart.

"Where are we going?"

"Hot dogs."

"Hot dogs?"

"Yes."

"I thought you were vegan."

"Really? Why?"

"You said when you found out about Stewart—"

"Oh!" I laughed. "No, I'm not vegan. I ate a turkey sandwich at the bagel place with you, dummy. I'm just—" I stopped myself from saying *lactard*, thank God. George wouldn't have let me hear the end of it. "I can't eat dairy. But I *love* hot dogs."

"I should have known. For all of Stewart's health nuttiness, the man loved a Dodger Dog. During baseball season, we went to all the games together. You should have seen the shit he gave me for wearing my lucky Pirates hat in the box."

"Um. Lucky Pirates hat?"

"I told you. I'm from Pittsburgh. The hat's maybe a little old. And decrepit."

I stepped up to the ordering window. "Stewart and I were regulars at Gray's Papaya as kids. He actually hated healthy food, as you saw. He just had to look good for TV. Luckily, I don't have that problem."

Minutes later, we were leaning against the stone park wall, halfway through our hot dogs on doughy buns with mustard and sauerkraut. George ordered relish on his too, even though I scrunched up my nose in disapproval. Gilding the lily.

It was almost fully dark out now—time to head home. I was spending a lot of time below ground lately, as the subway shuttled me, on a daily basis, up and away from my everyday life and into my past. Or was it my uncertain future? Obviously, the loss of Stewart was terrible, but what about the interruption to my life? Was that so bad? I realized that there wasn't anything, except for my grouchy cat, that I was missing about my routine.

"This must be weird," George said, startling me out of my reverie. "For you."

"What? Eating hot dogs?"

"Um, no. I get the feeling that you do that a lot." He smirked. "I meant hanging out with me. I'm another remnant of Stewart's life with which you have to contend. A reminder of his absence." He tossed his white cardboard tray in the garbage. *Swish.*

I thought about that. "You know, for some reason, you feel separate. Maybe it's because I never knew you guys together. Like I can talk about him and you can remind me that he was real, which I appreciate. You're more like a super inept therapist who appeared in his wake."

"Gee, thanks."

"I'm sure he would have thought it was weird, though—us hanging out."

George's dimple appeared beneath his stubble, an open-ended parenthesis. I wanted to trace it with my finger. "Oh, he would have been horribly jealous."

"You think?"

"Sure! He didn't share well. He and I went to out to beers with a friend of his from set once—the first AD on the show, Gary something. The guy and I connected about old noir movies; turns out we both love them. Gary mentioned a Raymond Chandler screening at this old movie theater in Hollywood. Stewart basically freaked out thinking we might hang out without him. He made me promise we would call him if we ever went."

I giggled. "Yeah, he liked to be the main event."

I pulled out a pack of cherry Lifesavers from my purse. I have thing for old-school candy; I popped one in my mouth. I offered one to George.

"Wow. These take me back."

"They're so good, right? It's easy to forget how good they can be. Life's simple pleasures." I thought about Morgan and her tiramisu.

We were quiet for a beat again, watching people rush by on their way home to children or out to drinks, only now it wasn't awkward. I snuck a glimpse at George and saw that he was watching me. He scratched his head, like he was figuring out how to approach something. I wondered if he did that in court. "The other thing is, with Stewart . . . and you, I mean, he would have been jealous because you were special to him."

"He relied on me to keep him grounded, I guess."

"Yeah, there's that." George narrowed his eyes—even then they seemed to twinkle. "But he also loved you a little—don't you think?"

I inhaled.

George had rendered me speechless. In the silence, I searched his face. He looked like he was trying hard not to look like anything. I wasn't sure what he wanted me to say.

I thought about the question—looked at it hard without a filter, tried to find the truth I understood at my core. Did Stewart love me a little? Could I have loved him if I tried?

"No. I don't think so," I said finally. "Not the way you mean."

I felt a tightness in my chest, but George looked relieved. It made him even more handsome. Those amused eyes brightened. The semicircle crease by his mouth grew more pronounced. I resisted the urge to bury my face in that navy blue sweater peeking out from beneath his jacket.

When I started down into the subway, a few minutes later, I glanced back over my shoulder and saw him watching me descend.

On the train back downtown, the car was crowded. I stood, leaning over other passengers—a teenage girl with a pimple on her cheek (her funeral: hiking accident, "I'll Be Missing You" by P. Diddy, gummy candy) and an older man with paint on his pants (his funeral: diabetes, "Precious Lord, Take My Hand" by Aretha Franklin, chocolate cake). I felt sick to my stomach. I'd done all I could to avoid thinking about that night, but now it was consuming me.

He loved you a little, don't you think?

There were several times throughout the years when I decided I liked Stewart as more than a friend. Or maybe you could argue that I always wondered what that might be like. It remained there, humming under the surface as we went about our lives: When he got a haircut in seventh grade and looked like Zac Efron. In high school, when he comforted me through my breakup with Matthew Simonsson (apparently I didn't handle rejection well). In early college, when he got cast in *Streetcar* and was brilliant. That time, I think he must have known. I came close to telling him at drinks afterward. I even launched into a whole prepared speech about how long we'd been friends, how I'd never want to "mess that up" and how "change is confusing." But, before I got to the part about how lately I'd been "feeling different" about us, he made it clear he had feelings for his costar, Carolina White. Maybe he was trying to stop me from confessing.

I imagine he felt conflicted and wondered about me sometimes too. When Stewart was on a winning streak, I always had the sense that he was flying somewhere above me. It was during his losing streaks that he searched me out, or so I felt.

This particular night was different—and the same. We were maybe twenty-five. He was in one of his moods, which I wrote off as self-pity. Auditioning wasn't going well. He wasn't yet in grad school. I was on an upswing—or so it seemed to the untrained eye. In fact, the reality that my magazine writing career might not prove sustainable had begun seeping into my consciousness. I'd soon realize that I'd have to write a hundred features about plumping lip gloss a month at fifty dollars a pop in order to survive. And I was running out of synonyms for "glowing." I was starting to feel like I wanted something more, starting to think about journalism school.

We got dressed up, went out to a fancy dinner at a preposterous restaurant (that was often Stewart's move to cheer us up) and got sloppy drunk. The place wasn't cool or trendy, only expensive and stodgy—a special occasion restaurant for the wealthier bridge-and-tunnel set. We stuffed our faces with steak, creamed spinach, and corn bread.

Around the middle of our second bottle of absurd Burgundy, we were laughing—hard—about something dumb and Stewart leaned in: "What if we live our whole lives and never find anyone else who we can go out to a terrible restaurant with and have the best night ever? What if we end up alone? Or, *worse*, bored?"

"Oh, I fully expect to be bored."

"No!" he slammed his hand down way too loud. The Republican delegate types at the next table over shot us a dirty look. "Don't just lie down and accept that!"

"I'm not lying down. I am fully upright. I am an upright citizen." I guess I was buzzed too.

"Look." He took my hand. "I, Stewart Theodore Beasley, do solemnly swear that, if we haven't found anyone else—"

"Anyone *better*!"

"By age forty, we should marry each other."

"Hmm."

"What? I'm not enough of a do-gooder to deserve you? I solemnly swear to do good deeds—"

"I'm not sure why you're solemnly swearing. That's more of an oath than a proposal."

"Fine! Do you want me to get down on one knee? 'Cause I'll do it!" He started to lift out of his Louis VII chair.

I held up my hands. "No! Please don't! Yes. Okay. Fine. When we're super ancient. Like forty." It seemed like we would never be that old.

Later, we took a cab back to his house—like a million other nights—and got drunker on Scotch. Spent, we lay in bed beside each other.

In the dark, I felt the world rushing by without me. I had the sense of being immobile. I could feel his arm against mine. Just Stewart, always there, like an extension of myself. It was hot in the room. Stewart liked things tropical, of course. I got tired. I rolled over on my side, facing away from him. A minute later, he spooned me, curving his body around mine.

That in itself was nothing out of the ordinary, until he rested a hand on my side and moved that hand down the length of my thigh—and then back up again. Then again. Maybe I'd been sleepy, but every nerve in my body woke up then. I was alert to the most minute twitches and sounds. I held my breath. This was a mistake, I knew, but in that moment I wasn't sure I cared. He slid his hand onto my stomach. Snuggled in closer. It felt good. I pushed my bottom up against him. I guess that was my way of saying *yes*. Because then his lips were on my neck, sending shivers down my body, and his hand was sliding up my dry-clean only top (as befit the fancy evening).

"What's happening?" I murmured.

"If we're going to get married—"

"*Maybe* get married."

"Then we should make sure this part works."

In a half-hearted attempt to stop us, I said, "Are things going to be weird?"

He nuzzled closer. "I hope so."

I decided to accept that, adopt his attitude. Stewart always said I ovethought things. With a kind of lazy amusement, I tracked his hand as it traveled back down to my belly and unsnapped my jeans, finding its way inside. Just like that, he pushed my underwear aside, closing the curtain on our friendship as we knew it.

We stopped short of having sex. I'm not sure how; we both just stopped. I think that probably made things more awkward in the end— at least in my head. Afterward, we lay in bed. He lit a cigarette. I always thought it was gross when he smoked in his room. The smell saturated everything, finding its way into crevices and staging a sit-in. I felt pissed at him suddenly. Probably I knew we had done something dumb and I wanted to place the blame on anyone but myself.

He said, "Wren, can I tell you something?"

I said, "Sure."

He said, "I think I love you."

And I said, "You don't."

He said, "I don't?"

I thought he was feeling bad for himself, reaching for me because he felt at bottom. Maybe he was. I thought I deserved more than that from him. Maybe I did.

It was uncomfortable for a while after that between us—first, because it wasn't clear if it would happen again, and then because it didn't. Maybe things were never quite as relaxed between us again. As I stood on the train now, staring down at some lady's dandruff-littered part, I tried to remember if we'd ever found ourselves alone in a dark room in bed together again, just as friends. Probably not. When it came to our seamless closeness, to sharing a brain, maybe that was the beginning of our end.

CHAPTER 29

Stewart. Last night I dreamed that you were gone, but I could see you. You were wearing one of your white T-shirts, that signature of your high school wardrobe. I got to hang out with you for hours upon hours in a random hotel room while I packed up my stuff to leave. You were funny, just like always, annoying, just like you. It was the best. I like to pretend that you gave me that dream—a gift of unconsciousness. If so, can we do that again tomorrow night?

Only this time, can we go somewhere nice, like the Caribbean or Capri?

CHAPTER 30

The next morning, I sat at the desk I never use and scrolled through the thousands of emails in my inbox, searching for the one from the Collins Foundation. I had woken up on a mission to get back to work, but realized that I didn't have this year's forms.

I gave up. If they had sent it, the email was missing. I sent a message to my contact—a sweet executive assistant named Angeline who had been there forever (heart attack from sedentary work, "Tears in Heaven" by Eric Clapton, finger sandwiches)—and asked for the updated materials. Then I scanned my other messages to see if anything important had come up. I also checked my grant deadline spreadsheet to confirm that I hadn't forgotten any upcoming applications. The Collins Foundation award was one of many on which we relied. While most of our funding was cobbled together from $25,000 to $50,000 grants, the Collins money was bigger: $175,000. I checked the list. I was good. I didn't have another application due for a few weeks.

I should have been trolling the Giving Report for new possible grants; my job was 50 percent grant applications and 50 percent research, a cultivation of relationships and stewardship, so we could win new donors. Anton had been talking about promoting me to a "foundation relations" title for over a year, which was even more about networking. It was the natural course of growth for someone like me. I probably should have made the move ages ago, but it involves a lot less writing, which was the part I liked best. I was ambivalent.

My computer chimed with an email from Angeline. I knew I should open it and get started on the paperwork, as planned, but all my morning energy—my get-up-and-go—had already gotten up and left. I had another week, so I promised myself I'd start tomorrow. Right now, I needed to sit and obsess about Stewart—again.

I had decided on who I thought was the best speaker for the tribute. I opened a new blank email and addressed it to Stewart's sister:

Kate,

I hope you're doing as well as possible. I'm sure your mother mentioned that George and I put aside some items from Stewart's apartment that we thought you might want. (Do you know George?) There were some sweet photos of you and Stewart as kids, etc. Let me know if for some reason you don't get them. I know Blair went through everything after the fact, so hopefully she didn't get confused.

For better or worse, your mother has assigned me the task of choosing a personal friend or family member to speak at the tribute. I thought Jimmy would be great, but he isn't comfortable doing it. Of course, I also thought of you. You and Stewart were so tight; I know how much he idolized you. You obviously have a unique perspective on him, having known him since birth and sharing DNA and all. Anyway, I wanted to reach out to you and see if you'd like to do it.

Love, Wren

The email sent with a loud swoosh. Next up: text Jimmy.

> Please tell me that you're coming to Stewart's tonight. You have to, actually, because otherwise you'll be letting those vultures pick over his shit before you get

> anything to remember him by. Also, you'll be leaving me alone, and you promised we'd spend more time together. Was that a successful guilt trip? I hope so.

I felt an irrational wave of my own guilt for saying I'd be alone when George would be there. I hated to lump him in with *them*.

For once, Jimmy answered right away:

> I'll be there. Wouldn't miss it. If there's anything left. After what you sent me about Mallory and Brian, I'm wondering what they pocketed. No way they emptied those garbage bags and left with nothing.

> Ugh. You're probably right. So gross!

> Gross is an understatement. It's deplorable. I probably don't want much, but there were a few pictures and, I know this sounds dumb, but I feel like his Little League trophy could be cool to have, since we did that together.

> Not dumb.

> Thanks. Anyway, 7:00 p.m.?

> 7:30 p.m. Maybe we can grab a drink afterward?

Maybe. I have somewhere I have to be, I think, but let's see how long it takes.

Big date with the raw-food Mensa?

I am never going to live her down.

You are never going to live her down.

I texted Gretchen next. I was calling for reinforcements:

Dude. Please tell me you're free tonight and I can drag you to this horrible thing at Stewart's. 🙄 Apparently, Willow is going ahead with that farewell ceremony before we choose items to remember Stewart by. The last thing I feel like doing is listening to these people share about Stewart. 🙄🙄🙄

Hi! I was going to text you. I figured you'd be dreading tonight. Wouldn't it be weird if I came though? An outsider and all?

Who cares? I need you at the ready to tell these people to fuck off.

Ha. Well, I would enjoy that. That is my great skill in life. I have a work thing later in the evening, but maybe I could make it happen. Who is going to be there?

> Usual suspects. Vultures, plus George and Jimmy.

Jimmy is definitely going?

> Well, if he doesn't bail. But don't feel weird! I know whatever happened at the funeral between you guys and you hate him, but I figure you guys make bad choices together every five years or so. It's a semiannual tradition.

She took a minute to respond, so I walked over to the mirror in my hall and started examining my face for imperfections. My skin looked dull. Change of seasons. During my freelance journalist stint, I had accidentally fallen into beauty writing and learned just enough to keep me paranoid about aging for a lifetime. I wondered if I could pull off red lipstick tonight. I was feeling the need for a powerful color. A "teenage Wren" color.

Gretchen finally responded:

I don't feel weird about Jimmy. Don't worry! But you'll have him at least? If I can't make it?

> Yeah. But he already said he can't stay long and you know he's going to flee the second he finds out that there's a shamanic ceremony. I intentionally left that detail out.

Wise plan. I'll do what I can. Let me call you in a few and we can talk about timing! -xo

I set my phone down, stood, and stretched. I had hours to kill before heading uptown to face the inevitable shit show of doling out Stewart's stuff. George had told everyone to arrive at 8:00 p.m., but I was no dummy: I would be early this time.

I contemplated watching some YouTube videos of Stewart's TV interviews over the years. He had done appearances on most of the big talk shows. I thought it might make me feel close to him, but I had so far only been able to bring myself to play one very old appearance on *Ellen*. I watched long enough to see him start to dance—very goofy—and then I gave up. It was too strange. He seemed like someone I knew and someone I didn't. It made my stomach flip. I hadn't been ready then. I probably still wasn't now.

I wandered over to the couch and plopped down next to Chris Harrison. He opened one eye to take stock of me, was apparently unimpressed and went back to sleep. I turned on the TV, scrolling through my list of recorded shows. I still hadn't watched *The Bachelor* finale. I never would. I deleted it. I had about three thousand episodes of *Veep* that I hadn't gotten around to yet. It sounded like it required too much brain power. I decided to turn on an old *Gilmore Girls* episode, which always made me feel safe in an unsafe world. George had pegged me right on that front. I felt sure that Stewart would not have approved. What did he know? I lay back on the couch.

Before I could begin, my phone rang, startling me. Probably Gretchen. I jumped up, scanning the various surfaces in my apartment. It's amazing how quickly I'm capable of losing things. Distracted much? I grabbed it off my desk.

It wasn't Gretchen.

George. My heart started to pound. What was my problem? I swatted at myself in the mirror and then pressed Accept. "Hello?"

"Hey." His voice sounded lower over the phone, gravelly.

"Hey."

"It's George."

"Yeah, I know. Hey."

"I would say 'hey' again, but I'm afraid we'll never move past that point."

"Okay. Let's try, how are you?" I walked over to my desk, picked up an organic peppermint ChapStick and began applying it in the mirror. I'm not sure why.

"I'm fine. How are you?"

"Fantastic! Trying to avoid thinking about tonight, but too distracted to be able to think about anything else."

He grunted. "Yeah. I'm trying to redline a contract for a client. I think I've read the first sentence eight times now without absorbing a word of it. I figured you might be in a similar fugue state."

"Ah. So no official news to report?"

"Nope. Just checking in."

Huh. I was rubbing my lips together hard, I guess, because they came apart with a loud pop.

"What was that?"

I bit my lip. "Um. Nothing. Just my cat."

"Your cat. Chris Harrison."

"Yes. Please do not ask me again why he's named that."

"I wouldn't dare."

"Can I ask *you* something instead?"

"Sure?" George's tone was dubious.

"Did Stewart really call me a loser?" I shut my eyes as the words flew from mouth, so I didn't have to look at my humiliated face. I'd been thinking about what George said a lot since the funeral and had promised myself that I wouldn't bring it up. I didn't want to come off as even more pathetic than Stewart made me sound, but my need to understand won out.

"You really want to talk about this again?"

I sighed and collapsed onto my couch. "I guess not."

"He didn't call you a loser," George said softly. "You know how he felt. He had grand visions for you. For all of us. But he didn't always live in reality."

"True story."

"I should probably go deal with this contract," he sighed wearily. "And by that I mean stare at the pages without making progress until it's 6:30 p.m. and I have to leave to meet you."

I desperately didn't want the conversation to end on that note. "Where are you working?" I blurted out because I couldn't think of anything else.

"Where? My hotel room."

"Is it a suite?"

"It is."

"So there's a desk?" Honestly, it was such a dumb question. I smacked a hand over my eyes.

"There is, but I'm working on the bed. In clothes. Not in a robe. I want to be clear about that."

"Is it nice?"

"The robe?"

I rolled my eyes, although he couldn't see. "Yes, the robe. No! The hotel room."

"Oh. Yes. I'm at the Crosby, right by Stewart's place. Why? Are you angling for an invite?"

I sat up straight. I know I flushed red, which was silly since I was alone. "No, Harvey Weinstein. I just love a hotel and was curious."

"Ouch!" George laughed. "Man. I think I would have preferred a Louis C.K. comparison at least. Actually, maybe not." He paused. "This conversation has gotten off track."

I smiled. "Conversations with you often do."

"Well, you distract me. It makes me say dumb shit."

I stood and walked to the mirror again, examining my reflection as I raised a doubtful eyebrow. Apparently he could sense it.

"Okay. Dumb*er* shit. Anyway, I'm gonna go before I make things worse. Do you want to meet outside tonight? I figure you're dreading dealing with Blair and her crew."

"That's so sweet. Truly. But I talked to Jimmy and he's coming, so I'll probably be fine. I'll meet him outside."

"Oh. I didn't realize you and Jimmy were close like that these days."

"We're trying to spend more time together."

"Oh." I could hear the surprise in his voice. "Okay. Got it."

"You could meet us outside too? I'm happy to wait for you!"

"No. That's okay. You meet Jimmy. I'll see you in there."

We hung up then. Glancing in the mirror one last time, I decided on red lipstick, for sure. It wasn't until a few minutes later, as I sat on the couch watching Logan and Rory banter on *Gilmore Girls*, that I wondered why I was planning my makeup to go pick over my dead friend's belongings.

CHAPTER 31

Stewart, what piece of you should I take?

The snow globe you bought at that gift shop during our seventh grade Boston trip (the one where you kissed Rachel Amari in that cheesy hotel's indoor pool)? The crooked aviators you wore around LA during the first season of Manic Mondays *like you were a superstitious athlete on a winning streak? Your framed black-and-white photo of Eugene O'Neill that frowned down from the wall of every apartment you ever inhabited?*

Or should I just grab your platinum and diamond cuff links and sell them on eBay? Who am I kidding? With this crew, those are long gone.

It's all so absurd.

Is an object really supposed to keep you close to me? Is that how to keep you real?

CHAPTER 32

I was waiting outside for Jimmy when he texted me to say he'd be late.

> Not sure how delayed. Go in without me.

So much for our united front. I wish I could say I was surprised. He certainly hadn't turned out to be the partner in crime I'd anticipated after the funeral.

I walked through the building's glass doors. That same doorman was on his phone again and barely looked up. Stewart wasn't receiving the same level of service as at his mother's uptown building. Down here, they were too cool to try that hard.

On the elevator ride up, I was texting Jimmy to *hurry*, when I got a text from Gretchen bailing too. She had too much work to finish but would check in on me later. None of this seemed auspicious.

So I stood on the threshold of Stewart's apartment alone, my arms crossed over my leather jacket in a kind of self-hug. Knocking didn't seem right. I tried the knob and it turned. Inside, I saw immediately that the "event" was in full swing. So much for an 8:00 p.m. start. So much for a somber gathering.

The vibe felt like some twisted art gallery opening: Mallory and Brian—each wearing an old trucker hat of Stewart's—were cozied up on our dead friend's couch with *Manic Mondays* mugs and a half-empty bottle of vodka on the coffee table in front of them. Modest Mouse was playing over the speakers—at least a Stewart-approved band. Blair and Willow were huddled by the floor-to-ceiling living room bookcases, which had been cleared out and were now stacked with categorized items that were up for grabs. Willow's hand on Blair's shoulder and Blair's head dipped in tears suggested that the yogi was playing therapist again. Keith was in a corner talking emphatically to Madison, his arms waving. I hadn't realized that Helen's assistant would be here. As intense as she was, I was happy to see her. Maybe she would bring order to this chaos. Maybe people would be on better behavior in front of her.

No one noticed me walk in. With relief, I spotted George standing by the marble kitchen island, drinking Lagavulin, Stewart's and my favorite Scotch. He looked lazily in my direction as if he'd known I'd been there all along and hadn't bothered to greet me. Taking a swig of his drink, he said, "You're dressed up."

"No, I'm not!" I heard myself snap. *Damn red lipstick.*

"Okay, then." He raised his eyebrows. "Where's Jimmy?"

"Late."

"Ah. Is that why you're grumpy?"

"What makes you think I'm grumpy?" I exhaled, pulling my jacket off and throwing it over the back of a chair. "Yeah, that's part of it. Among other things." I gestured to the surrounding scene.

He took another swill of his whisky, finishing the rest, and began pouring again.

"Save me some."

He grabbed one of several clean glasses from the counter—etched tumblers I'd always loved, no doubt one of Helen's selections—and doled out a hefty pour. I raised my glass, "To Stewart."

"He would have crapped his pants to see this."

We clinked glasses, then stopped to watch the others. I caught sight of myself in the entryway mirror—a circular art deco thing. I did look dressed up, more than I'd intended. I was wearing tight black jeans that riffed on motorcycle pants and a fitted black sweater. My hair was in shaggy waves. I'd spent real time on it, since I couldn't get it together to accomplish anything else. With the lipstick, it seemed somehow wrong.

I felt a rush of wind, or maybe just a bustling energy, as Madison hurried up to George and me. In her defense, she wasn't the first woman to sprint away from Keith. She was clearly uneasy, her eyes darting from object to object, around the room. "Hi, Wren. Welcome. I'm glad to see you." I felt like she really meant it.

"Hi, Madison. It's good to see you too." She stood in front of us, rocking back and forth on her feet—toe to heel, heel to toe. She was white-knuckling her phone. I lowered my voice and leaned in, tipping my chin, "Are you okay?"

"Oh, yeah. Yeah. I'm fine, I'm great. I mean, I didn't realize . . . I guess they . . . Keith, well, he didn't understand. But you know the family came and they had to take what they wanted."

George had been resting against the counter, but, at that, he stood straight up. "Madison, what are you saying? Was Keith demanding something that the family took?"

She waved it off, but her face told a different story. "He was just upset. I guess he didn't know that the family would claim all the art. He says he thought he might get a particular piece that reminded him of Stewart. He's sure Stewart would have wanted him to have it and that Blair said it was his and is now reneging. I told him he was free to email Helen, although I wish he wouldn't. She has enough on her plate without . . . well. She puts up a tough front, I know, but she's a grieving mother. She's barely left the house since . . . She's in pieces."

"That's unacceptable." George slammed down his drink with a clank. I almost told him to be careful; the glasses were so delicate. But he looked mad, and I didn't want to get in his way. "I'm going to talk to Keith."

"No, no, no!" Madison shook her head. "It's okay. I'm sure he didn't mean to snap. We're all on edge, these days."

"That's no excuse for getting aggressive with you." George was pissed, his jawed clenched. I liked this side of him. This was one way in which he and Stewart were different. Stewart's sense of justice wasn't that strong. He would have cheered Madison up, but he would not have defended her.

"Was it a valuable work?" I asked. "The one he wanted?"

"The most valuable of the bunch," she nodded. "Stewart's collection was mostly from emerging artists, but do you know the portrait artist, Elizabeth Peyton? This is a seminal work for her. It's a painting of Kurt Cobain."

"Of course it is." I felt sick to my stomach. "And did Keith say why it had so much sentimental value for him?" I shot a pointed look at George, and he growled.

Madison shook her head, lips tight. She looked deeply freaked out.

I flashed to the other day, when Blair was describing how much the value of the work had increased since Stewart bought it. Keith obviously went home and googled the approximate sale price. There was his sentimentality for you.

"I was just planning to make sure everything was set up, bring over some last items from Helen and then leave to go to a dinner with friends, but now I feel like maybe I should stay." Madison peered over her shoulder at the vultures, like one of them might attack her—or Stewart's memory.

Mallory was telling some story, loudly as usual. "I WAS LIKE, 'NO! NOT THE PURPLE ONE!'"

George shook his head, resting a hand on Madison's upper arm. "We've got this. Don't worry. You can go to your dinner."

She gazed up at him, adoringly. "Thank you, George. I don't know what I—what any of us—would do without you." She put her opposite hand over his, so that her claddagh ring was on full display. If she had a hulking Irish boyfriend somewhere, she wasn't thinking about him right now. She glanced at me. "You too, Wren."

"Thanks, Madison."

"Alexa, off, please!" commanded Willow from the middle of the living room. The music continued. "Alexa! Off!" Apparently, Willow's voice was not discernible beneath the din of Mallory's storytelling. The song played on. "ALEXA!" the yogi yelped. "I said, OFF!"

The music stopped and so did all the talking. Everyone glanced up to see what was happening. The bohemian goddess was standing at the center in a tie-dyed maxi dress with a giant, sweeping cardigan over it, one with an open weave like a hammock. "Hi, everyone! I think we can now get started with our peaceful parting ceremony! If you can all gather in a circle here, I've cleared a space."

George dropped his hand from Madison's shoulder. She watched it fall mournfully like a long-distance boyfriend boarding the plane home. I swear I heard her whisper, *Come back.*

"Here we go," George muttered, oblivious. He grabbed his glass, refilled it (though it was pretty full) and headed toward the middle of the room, where the group was beginning to convene.

"We're sitting on the floor?" Blair. Of course. In her cropped white jeans.

"Yes. To stay grounded," Willow explained. Blair nodded, but, when Willow looked away, she rolled her eyes conspiratorially at Keith. *Assholes.*

Peripherally, I saw Madison grab her wool trench and slip out. I wanted to yell, "Yes! Save yourself!" Instead, I chugged my drink like a shot, my chest burning. What a waste. That's not how you drink Scotch this good. But I hoped the inebriation would get me through this crap without punching someone—unless it *inspired* violence instead. I was fine either way.

"C'mon, guys! Just head over here and sit on the Oriental rug!"

I refilled my pretty glass, then walked over and settled in a space between George and Mallory. The rug was Turkish, in fact. I knew because I remember when Stewart picked it up. He was shooting a small part in some Chris Pine movie in Istanbul. He loved it there. When he came home, he went on and on about how he would take me back there with him someday, how I would love the food and the vibe. I had visited with my parents as a kid once, but I didn't remember it very well—just the haunting prayer bells that reverberated throughout the city each day.

I ran my hand along the rug's textured surface, woven in muted blues, greens, and creams with a shimmering golden thread that hinted at the magic carpet. Suddenly, I missed Stewart so much, I felt like the wind had been knocked out of my body, like when I once slipped on slick stone steps as a kid and landed on my back. But even then, Stewart had been there to pick me up and sit with me while my breath returned.

I wanted to tell someone. I turned to George, but he was staring intently at the floor. Why was he being so weird?

"Everyone take a deep inhalation," Willow was saying, "and then we'll begin."

"What about Jimmy?" George said.

"Jimmy?"

"Wren might want to wait for him." I don't know why, but it sounded like George was mocking me.

"It's okay," I said to the group. "I don't think this would be his speed."

"He's too cool to say goodbye to his oldest friend?" George challenged.

"I don't think it's about that. If he could have gotten away, he would have. He'll be here later." And not wanting to hurt Willow's feelings, I added, "He didn't know how late he'd be at work; he said not to wait. I think we're good." I shot George a dirty look.

Willow nodded. In front of her, she had laid out an embroidered prayer mat with several crystals and a few rocks bearing words like FREE-DOM, TRUTH, and BLISS in hexagonal formations. She pulled out a small blue glass bottle with a spritzer on top. "Is anyone allergic to lavender?"

No one was. Willow began walking around the circle, asking permission and then spraying the mist in a cloud above each person's head.

"As Blair so rightly pointed out, using an actual diffuser or incense in the apartment might create a mess like the other day, so I brought this little mister. It's just rose water with lavender essential oil—to create a sense of balance and calm." From the other side of Mallory, I heard Keith snort.

Willow arrived in front of me and I nodded that she was clear to spray. The mist settled over me in tiny prickles and, I have to admit, it smelled and felt good.

"THIS IS FUN!" Mallory boomed. "IS THIS A BUDDHIST CEREMONY? I'VE BEEN REALLY INTERESTED IN BUDDHISM SINCE I FOUND OUT ABOUT MY KOREAN HERITAGE!"

Blair suppressed a smile at Mallory's inappropriate exclamation, one side of her mouth tugging upward in a mirthless grin. She was such a bitch.

Willow finished her rounds. "Everyone good?"

"CAN I SEE THAT REALLY QUICK?" Mallory said. "I KIND OF WANT ONE TO USE ON THE TRAIN WHEN IT SMELLS NASTY! SO SMART, RIGHT?"

Ever ethereal, Willow glided over and handed the bottle to Mallory with a smile. "It's great because it comes with multiple tops—one for mist, a roller for applying to chakra points and then you can open it up fully to pour out and mix with coconut oil and apply directly to the feet. That's the most powerful entry point for aromatherapy."

Mallory held the bottle up in front of her. "I CAN'T GET IT TO SPRAY!"

"Oh, yeah. Careful. Sometimes it gets stuck and then—"

There was a loud spritz, and Keith let out a scream like he'd been attacked. "My eyes! You sprayed my fucking eyes! MALLORY! What the fuck!"

"OOPS."

"Oh, dear!" Willow ran for the kitchen. "Hold on, Keith! I'm coming!"

"Sorry," chirped Alexa from the Echo at full volume. "I'm having trouble understanding you right now! Here's a station that plays '70s folk music!"

"ALEXA! STOP! NO ONE IS TALKING TO YOU!" Willow shouted. She grabbed a bowl from a cabinet and filled it with water, then ripped a paper towel off the roll and rushed back over to Keith. He was folded over his lap with his hands covering his face. "Don't worry! It won't do any damage, but it burns like hell. That can't feel good."

"It's like great-smelling pepper spray!" I said a little too cheerfully. "Probably less calming in this application." I stole a glance at George and smiled. He raised his eyebrows, then looked away.

In my head, I sent a secret thank-you to Stewart, wherever he was, for bringing me that moment of levity. And for mildly injuring Keith, who was a piece of shit.

Willow set Keith up with a wet paper towel like a cold compress against his eyes and the bowl in front of him for more water, as needed. Pure comedy. She stood up. "Okay! Everyone good? Let's begin!"

"SORRY!" Mallory said. I assumed the sentiment was directed at Keith, but she was looking out at the circle, so it was unclear. She leaned over to me and said, in what I imagine she thought was a whisper, "THE THING GOT STUCK, YOU KNOW?"

I nodded, then pointed to Willow, who was beginning, and brought a finger to my lips.

"Okay. Nothing like a small trauma to bring us all together. Everyone grab hands!"

Keith snarled as Mallory reached for his hand, which was occupied, holding the damp compress to his face. I swear he almost smacked her.

"Oh, right! Not you, Keith. You're exempt!" our leader continued.

Mallory grabbed my hand instead. Hers was hot and sweaty. I wouldn't have expected anything else. I looked down and noticed an old lanyard bracelet of Stewart's hanging at her wrist. Some girl—maybe Rachel Amari, actually—had made it for him in middle school. Was there anything these people wouldn't take?

I turned to George, who offered his hand, palm up. I don't know why I was hesitant to take it. As soon as I did, and he closed his fingers around mine, I felt a warmth spread through me—one that made me want to let go and hold on forever at the same time. *Gotta love Lagavulin*, I told myself. George winked at me like he could read my thoughts. Then he lifted his glass with the other hand, took another sip and set it back down. "Shall we?" he said to Blair, taking her manicured fingers in his own. Blair looked at him over one raised shoulder and practically batted her eyelash extensions. What was it with the women here? Was everyone so hard up? Sure, George was cute and gainfully employed—and funny and smart and kind and single—but he wasn't perfect! Suddenly, I felt stressed out and I wasn't sure why. I cleared my throat, shifted on my butt, and waited for Willow to begin.

"Close your eyes, everyone, and take a moment to find quiet. Look deep within and find a center of calm there."

I looked deep within and found that I needed to pee. *Damn*. Oh well. Better hold it.

"Okay. This is going to be more brief than my usual moon circles because Blair pointed out that people might not want to commit quite that much time, so not to worry. Short and sweet."

It sounded like Blair had been a buzzkill as Willow tried to organize this thing. The ceremony wasn't my scene, but Willow was trying to put something nice together—and also find her own catharsis.

"We're going to begin by asking the Source to remove our egos from the room." That seemed like a gargantuan task for this Source guy.

"Now, we're going to chant *ohm* three times, together."

I have always liked chanting *ohm* at the beginning or end of a yoga class. It sounds so harmonious no matter who sings the sound. When I hear that, I get why people believe in something more than just happenstance and chaos.

Oooooooohm. Ooooooohm. Ooooohm. Even now, it brought a kind of calm to the space.

"Okay. Everyone open your eyes. Sorry. Not to discriminate. Everyone who *can*, open their eyes, open their eyes. Not you, Keith!" Willow smiled benevolently at all of us. She really was beautiful and well-intentioned. I could understand what Stewart saw in her. If you didn't mind a little sanctimony—which he shouldn't have because he had some of his own—she was a catch. "I want to thank you all for taking the time to be here to remember our friend. We live busy, complicated lives and it means so much that you've taken this moment to pay homage to this beautiful soul who we all loved."

Maybe this wouldn't be that bad?

"To begin, we're going to go around and each share our most significant memory of Stu, so we can support each other in our shared pain and meet each other where we are in our grief."

This was going to be horrible.

Now I had to listen to them all share their stupid memories? Hear about the Stewart they wanted to remember through the filter of their own self-important narcissism? Good times.

"Maybe share the memory of Stu that's coming up most often for you. That might be one way that he's sending you a message about what you meant to him. Whatever you share is fine. It's just about connecting with your authentic truth."

As if the universe could sense my worst-case scenario, Keith said, "I think it would be appropriate if I went first." His eyes were bloodshot from the lavender spray and his skin was blotchy, but apparently the pain had subsided.

Willow looked delighted—everyone was participating! "Keith, you have our collective ear."

"Well, um, I keep thinking about when we both auditioned for our high school production of *Grease.*"

I was so busy staring at Keith in wonder that it took me a minute to realize that George was clearing his throat repeatedly, trying to get my attention.

"What?"

He gestured with his chin down at our clasped hands, flexing his palm. "I think we can let go now."

I hadn't realized I'd still been holding on. Everyone, including Mallory, had indeed dropped hands. I released him, embarrassed. "Sorry."

"It's fine." But he wasn't looking at me. Why was he being so distant? I saw Blair notice and smile faintly. Of course.

"Are you guys listening? I don't feel respected!" Keith demanded. "Anyway, it was junior year and we both tried out for the part of Danny. The list went up and we went to check it together and he got the part, which was bullshit because my audition had definitely been better, and I had a better voice. Plus I look more like John Travolta." *Nope.* Keith cleared his throat and worked to relax his angry expression, his face coming vaguely unscrunched. "Anyway, it wasn't a big deal to me 'cause I didn't even really want the part, and it was just a stupid high school production. I was already auditioning for real plays and movies and getting lots of attention and buzz. But it did kind of piss me off, just because Stu never worked hard at anything and things just came easily to him, and the teacher hated me, and it wasn't fair!"

Did this guy hear himself? Willow was nodding, active listening. "Uh-huh. We are here with you, Keith."

Speak for yourself.

"So he turned to me and said, 'Keith. Dude. I'm sorry. It should have been you.' And I appreciated that because, you know, he was big enough to admit that my audition had been better and that I was better suited to the part. And that takes some balls, you know? Stu was good like that. That's it." Keith teared up, but I wasn't sure if it was from the burning sensation or the sadness or the fact that he'd wound up with the part of Nerd #5 in *Grease*. Oh, yeah. I remembered it well.

"Insightful share, Keith. Who would like to go next? Blair?"

She shifted, adjusting her floral top across her shoulders. "Oh, me? No, I think I need more time. My memories of Stu just kind of blend into this one feeling that we were just so important to each other—just like two sides of the same coin, you know? I can't think of a specific story, probably because we spent like every single day together. This is just really hard for me right now."

"Totally," Willow said, and leaned over to rub Blair's knee. "It's hard for us all."

"Right. But especially for me."

I could barely take another moment of this. No way was I sharing one of my important stories with this crowd. My memories were sacred to me. They were all I had left.

"I'LL GO NEXT!" said Mallory. "I REMEMBER WHEN WE WENT ON A TRIP TO LA DURING THE FIRST SEASON OF MANIC MONDAYS, AND STU INVITED US TO SET AND LET US EAT ALL THIS CRAFT SERVICE—LIKE CANDY AND STUFF—AND LIKE MEET THE OTHER CAST MEMBERS. AND HE EVEN GOT US BOTH T-SHIRTS WITH THE SHOW'S NAME ON IT. YOU KNOW THE ONES, BRI? THAT I CUT INTO TANK TOPS FOR US? WITH THE SUPER WIDE ARMHOLES?" Then she burst into tears. I was flabbergasted. Brian was nodding.

Willow gestured toward him. "Would you like to go next?"

He shook his head. I leaned in to hear him as he mumbled, "That was going to be my share too." He tugged his hat down on his head.

"Okay. George? Wren?"

I shook my head. "No, thank you. I'm just taking it all in for now."

Willow nodded and looked at George, who said, "Sure. Okay. I'll go." He rested a hand on each of his knees and exhaled. "I just keep thinking about the first time I met Stu. He was so magnetic. I thought I'd never known someone so alive—energetic and caring and warm and brilliant and intense and bouncing off the walls, drumming on the tables. You know how he was. He told me all about his background that day, where he came from. He was so open in certain ways. He told me about many of you all and how much he loved you. You guys meant so much to him. That keeps popping into my head."

Classy. And not about himself. Of course.

"That was beautiful, George," Willow purred. "Thank you."

"It really was," said Blair.

"SO SWEET!" sobbed Mallory.

Brian bobbed his head.

"I didn't know we were talking about stuff like that. Otherwise I would have said something like that too." Keith was such a charmer. "Anyway, this is dumb. When you're dead, you're dead."

Willow's cheeks flushed; she looked pissed. *Don't cross a true believer.* I saw George open his mouth to reprimand Keith, but Willow beat him to it. "Keith, we are all entitled to our belief systems. If it makes you more comfortable, you can think of this as an exercise for us as survivors. It's a way to help your friends. Help *others*. Look outside *yourself*." She exhaled, long and hard, and forced a smile at him through gritted teeth. "Now. Are your eyes feeling better?"

He scowled like a ferret.

She turned back to face the rest of us. "Okay. Thank you all so much for sharing such amazing, vibrant memories of Stu. If you don't mind, I'd like to share a memory too." She closed her eyes, took a deep breath, and began: "As you all know, Stewart and I had a romantic and sexual kind of soul connection."

Uh oh. Where was she going with this? Because if I was going to have to hear about their "tantric love making," I might have to leave.

She continued, "But we didn't always have the same interests." *Thank God.* "One Sunday morning, we woke up and he was in one of his down moods. It was a dark day."

My ears pricked up. One of his down moods. Like they were a regular thing. This wasn't in ninth grade; this was maybe five years ago.

"Usually, I kind of had to leave him alone and let him work those out. But I was feeling brave and so I asked him—begged him, if I'm honest—to please come on a walk with me. At the time, I was living in a guest house in Topanga Canyon. Do you know the area?"

"Of course," Blair snapped.

"Right, so it's very bucolic. Lots of gentleman farms and the smell of night jasmine and the ocean and old VW busses parked by the sides of the road."

"Isn't that where Charles Manson lived?" Keith.

Willow ignored him. "Anyway, I don't remember how I coerced Stu, but I did. Maybe he wasn't feeling that bad? Either way, we wound up in our coziest T-shirts, sweatpants, and hoodies, walking up the road. We walked and walked. He wasn't complaining and I wouldn't dare break the spell since he basically never wanted to go outdoors on days like that."

I felt a pang of sympathy for Willow in that moment. It wasn't easy to be with Stewart; that much was clear. I hadn't thought about it much from her perspective, but he could be a challenging person. He took up a lot of space. And she was only trying to bring positivity into his life.

"Finally, we reached a summit. The marine layer was lifting and the air was getting warmer. He closed his eyes against the sun," she closed her eyes in demonstration, tilting her chin toward the ceiling, "and took a deep breath. Then he looked out and said, 'The world can be a truly magnificent place.' We turned around and started back a few minutes after that, but I think that moment was transcendent for him. When we got back to my little bungalow, he was still feeling down. He got in bed and went back to sleep, while I stayed up and worked in my herb garden and on my tinctures. But he referenced that moment several times over the next months. I think it became a kind of reservoir for him—a place in his mind where he could return for a sense of peace, gratitude, and joy."

I could barely breathe. Everyone was nodding and thanking Willow for her story. I was frozen stiff. What had been happening with Stewart? Why didn't I know?

Willow had us all close our eyes again for a few minutes of silence, just thinking about Stewart and breathing in his "essence" in the space, then she rang some bell as a final note, but all I could think about were his "dark days" and this supposed transcendent experience.

I was rocked to my core. I swigged from my Scotch and didn't flinch. I realized I was sort of drunk and still really had to pee. I stood up.

"Oh, Wren. Are you going somewhere?" Willow peered up at me like a schoolmarm asking for a hall pass.

"Oh! Sorry, Willow. I thought we were done. Are we not?" I pointed toward the bathroom. "I have to go."

She held up a hand. "Actually, there's one last element to this ceremony. But it's quick, I promise. Don't bother sitting down. In fact, you can lead us."

I stood there, dumbly, as everyone else looked up at me from their seated positions on the rug. I felt like an unprepared preschool teacher. "Okay. What do I do?"

"Well, I believe, as Stewart is passing onto the next plane, his soul must leave his old body behind and transcend to the next level. We want to encourage this forward motion and his rebirth as a new incarnation of himself."

I shifted from one foot to the other. I *really* had to pee. "How do we do that?"

"Well, there are many ways: Buddhist chants, mantras, and such. But we're going to do something a bit more familiar to all of us—something I thought would be more playful. We're going to sing 'Happy Birthday' to him, as he is being reborn as his new self!"

For a millisecond, I waited for the punchline before I realized none would come.

Everyone averted their eyes. Some looked at the floor; others at the ceiling. I imagined they were doing anything they could to avoid looking at each other. I was about to start laughing uncontrollably; I could feel it rising in my chest.

"So, Wren, if you could start us off? You know how it goes!"

They all looked up at me with wide eyes. I brought a hand to my throat. I couldn't believe I was about to do this. *Please, hold it together.* "Um. Okay. So, I'll just start then. So, um: *H—Happy Birthday to you . . .*"

Slowly, everyone joined in. *Happy Birthday to you . . .* We sounded awful. Like dying goats. In our defense, it was hard to commit.

I could feel the hysteria bubbling up inside of me. I croaked, as a laugh threatened to escape from my throat and I fought to shove it down. I was desperate to stay somber. The last thing I wanted was to belittle Willow; and they were all still watching me.

Happy Birthday, dear . . . Stewart. We all stumbled over his name—choosing different incarnations—*Stu, Stewart, Stewy,* speeding past it or hesitating.

Happy Birthday to yo—u!

AND MANY MORE! We all looked at Mallory, who had belted the coda. She covered her mouth with her hand.

Willow gritted her teeth and forced an expression of serenity. "Thank you all for participating."

The others had begun to stand up, brushing imaginary carpet dust from their bottoms. I felt paralyzed. "So, guys," said Blair. "Now is your chance to peruse what's here and decide what you want as a memento. Take a look around and let me know if you need help because Helen has invited Stewart's extended family and other friends over tomorrow to choose what they would like. This is your chance."

Was she running a sample sale? What the fuck? I felt like she was about to ask me to check my bag. Were there colored dots delineating price ranges?

Mallory and Brian darted for the hanging rack. George rested a hand on my shoulder. Then, before I could speak, he seemed to remember that he didn't want to be near me and made a beeline over to Stewart's book and record collections.

At a loss, I went to pee.

CHAPTER 33

Stewart. Well, that was fun.

Would it have killed you to choose a couple of sane friends? Why did you keep these idiots around? Were you really the kind of person who would shrug, "She's always been nice to me," about someone who is clearly unkind to others? I used to think maybe you had become that, but now—I'm not sure what motivated you.

Remember that game you made up when we were kids? "Where would you go?" You dreamed up all these fantastical destinations. I remember you got so pissed that time I said I'd go to New Jersey because there was less sales tax. You told me I was banned from the game. God, I loved to make you mad.

Right now, I wish I could hop on your pretty Turkish rug and take a magic carpet ride anywhere else.

If you were alive, I would wait until everyone else left and then I'd make you lie down on the rug beside me. I would stare up at the crown moldings until my lids felt heavy, listening as you made up some elaborate story about the trips we'd take, flying in the dark past clusters of stars. We would open our mouths to catch the vapors of clouds.

CHAPTER 34

I left the bathroom and went in search of Willow. I couldn't just let her story lie. I needed to know more. I needed to understand what I hadn't understood about Stewart.

She was crouched on the floor by the enormous windows, packing her ceremonial items into a woven Columbian satchel. I crossed to her. "Hey, thank you for that, Willow. It was really nice."

She looked up at me and then stood, draping a giant streaked scarf around her neck. "Thanks, Wren. I wanted it to be cathartic. I hope it was for you, even though you chose not to share."

She was evidently displeased with my level of participation. "It *was* cathartic. Thank you." She nodded once and started to turn away. "Hey, can I ask you, that story about Stewart? When was that from? About five years ago, when you guys were dating?"

"Oh. No, no. It was during that brief stint when we got back together about eighteen months ago. It's so crazy. If only I'd known that he had such limited time left on this plane."

I tried to remember if I knew about that—their period of reconciliation. I didn't think Stewart had mentioned it. I shouldn't have been surprised by his omissions anymore.

"Wow, okay. That was recent," I recovered. "Those 'down days' you mentioned—they happened a lot? I'm asking because, well, to be honest, I barely knew about them."

Willow didn't look surprised. "Oh. Yeah, well, it wasn't the kind of thing he would have wanted to share. Especially not with someone like you." She tucked her hair behind her ear, pursing her lips.

"Someone like me?"

"Someone he wanted to see the best in him all the time. Someone from whom he wanted approval. Someone with impossibly high standards with whom he exchanged judgment."

I digested that, trying not to be offended. My head was swimming, from the characterization, from the alcohol. "You're saying he only wanted me to see a certain version of himself because he was afraid I would judge him?"

"Well, we all do that. Don't we? Tailor ourselves for our audience instead of behaving like our authentic selves and living our truth?"

"I thought we were being our authentic selves with each other."

She shrugged. "Well, maybe you were. But only portions of them."

I stared at the floor. "I just wish I would have known that he was sad."

"He only was sometimes! You know, Stu. He believed that being sad was giving in. And he never wanted *you* to think he gave in."

I nodded, only half sure I knew Stewart at all anymore. I looked beyond her, out the window, but it was dark outside and light indoors and I could only see my own reflection, distorted by the angle.

"Wren," Willow commanded. I trained my gaze back on her. "Everything happens for a reason."

"Does it?"

"Yes!" she insisted, her eyes blazing. She seemed to believe what she said without question. She was one fixed free spirit. We regarded each other. She stood tall, fists balled, like she was ready for a fight. I realized in that moment that her belief was the tissue paper that separated her from total meltdown. Exhaling, she kneeled back down to finish packing. "Plus, there was always going to be a power imbalance with you two."

"There was? Why?" I held my breath. Was this the insight for which I'd been waiting? The truth about me and Stewart?

"Aren't you a Sagittarius with Scorpio rising? He was an Aquarius with Cancer. He was too sensitive a soul for you. You would have had to align your chakras weekly to meet each other's needs. And even then . . ."

"Right." Disappointment rose and fell in me. I felt it physically, the hope draining from my body. How absurd I had been to expect real guidance from Willow. She meant well, but she saw the world in such narrow terms. I wished I could find answers that appeased me in the stars. "Thanks again, Willow." I wandered toward the center of the living room in a daze.

All I could think about was this terrible trip I had once taken to visit Stewart. We were in our late twenties, right after his show had hit and become huge. I was out in LA to see him because it had been a while and things were still a little strained between us. I wanted us to be *us* again. Also, I was still doing some editorial writing—I hadn't heard from Columbia yet—and was talking to a fashion website out there about possibly becoming their East Coast editor.

Stewart invited me to the set, where I was served Vitamin Water and craft service sushi by friendly interns with acne and eager smiles, but mostly I spent a long day watching him shoot the same scene again and again from an uncomfortable folding chair. Afterward, he invited me out for drinks with the cast; we drove in a packed car. When we walked onto the restaurant's back patio as a group, the atomic makeup of the air shifted. Everyone around us grew more animated—performing themselves, pretending not to care, hoping for a juicy story to attach to their star-sighting.

I felt conspicuous in that world, all those eyes on us and me nobody notable, but Stewart soaked it up. It made him a nuclear reactor. He didn't bother babysitting me; in fact, he barely spoke to me. Instead, he made the rounds, patting people's backs and spreading that snarky smile like herpes. I sat on the wooden bench at our upscale picnic table and drank cucumber sake mojitos with his female costars. They were friendly and inclusive, minus the birdlike one he had briefly dated; she must have been confused about the nature of our relationship. They regaled me with outrageous audition stories, funny now that they'd transcended, and asked me for beauty tips, because of my job, and to describe Stewart as a kid. I told them about his rare penny collection, a small act of revenge for his neglect. After a couple of hours, I approached Stewart and stood at his side like an idiot for several minutes until he finally took a break from his conversation with some young agent. Then I pecked him on the cheek and said good-bye. He didn't ask me how long I'd be in town. When I looked back from the doorway, he was standing below the fairy lights talking to an Olsen twin. I left, feeling that it would be a long time before I visited him again.

My hotel room had one wall of floor-to-ceiling windows. Later, I stood before them in a thin gray tank top and underwear, goosebumps raised on my skin, knowing I could be seen but no one was looking. I watched the city twinkle and sprawl, unconcerned about encroachment. My neighbor on the plane ride over—with a boyish face but receding hair-line—had a similar attitude, his elbows jutting further across the border of our shared armrest each time he attacked his laptop keyboard.

I had opted to book a room instead of staying at Stewart's, which, with hindsight, I saw as an act of self-preservation. Now hoping for sleep, I slipped in between the bed's crisp sheets, the oversized furniture cast-ing cartoon shadows across the floor. All around me, it seemed, the city vibrated, like bass from cruising cars on Sunset Boulevard, and reminded me that I had retreated, no real place to go. They say New York is a solitary place, but no place makes more aliens of people than Los Angeles.

I waited for a text from Stewart, thanking me for coming or pretend-ing we'd had a nice time. It never came.

I can't remember the next time we spoke after that. I'm sure he let me know he was coming to New York, and I went to meet him, never acknowledging my hurt feelings. I know we never talked about that visit. For me, that evening was the moment of our greatest divide, the time we strayed farthest from each other. There was the Stewart he wanted people to see, and there was my Stewart—the complicated person with the penny collection and some questionable past haircuts.

I was so sure about his motivation in those days: bad values and a need for attention, insecurity and a fragile ego. Now, I felt less sure. What had he been looking for in all those handshakes? What was it about me that he'd wanted to avoid? Was it really that I was too regular? Or was it some-thing more? I had been so sure that I understood the real Stewart, but had I been looking at him with open eyes?

Now, gazing at George across the room, I reminded myself that he came from that strange LA planet too. He understood its blunt rules. Something about its desert landscape attracted him. Yet he seemed like such a different breed. He and Stewart shared a kind of good-natured openness maybe, but George had standards and limits. Stewart collected these foul types; George seemed to look for the best in people, but when they demonstrated otherwise, he wasn't interested in keeping them around. In fact, considering the way he was acting toward me tonight, I wondered if he'd somehow deemed me unworthy of his time.

"So! What's it going to be?" I jumped at the sound of Blair's voice. She appeared in front of me as if from nowhere.

"Be?"

"What are you going to take? There are first edition books you might like. Some beautiful scarves. Some of his old notebooks. Not journals or anything private, but acting notes. A couple of cool skateboards. Maybe you remember him riding them? Some lovely Alessi vases."

I felt like she was offering me parting gifts on some horrible game show where we all competed to prove our closeness to Stewart: *Whose Grief Is This Anyway?* Like she was playing both Vanna and the winning contestant, somehow in a position to decide who deserved what and dole it out too. How had this happened? Stewart had asked for *my* help.

In that moment, I decided that I wanted nothing. Not now that Blair had touched it all. "I'm good," I said.

She furrowed her brow, as much as was possible with the Botox. "Good?"

"Yeah. I don't need anything."

"But you have to take something!" She leaned in, lowering her voice and pointing her thumb over her shoulder toward Mallory and Brian. "Otherwise these guys will take everything and start some creepy fan club, charging for tickets to see it—if they haven't already." She scrunched up her nose, as if she smelled something foul. "Can you believe them? Terrible. No sense of propriety."

I wanted to say, "Isn't Mallory one of your best friends?" Instead, I said, "That's okay." Suddenly, I felt like it really was. I didn't need the stuff; I didn't want to be part of divvying it up. I just wanted to walk away clean and remember Stewart how I could in my head. My Stewart. The boy I knew—or thought I knew—and loved. "I'll just take that picture of us from after *Robin Hood* once the tribute gallery display is over and they're done with it, and I'll be good."

"Wait, actually, there was one thing I really thought you should have!" What was with the hard sell? It's like I had sapped her of power and she wanted it back. Blair crossed to a shelf and began rearranging objects toward the back: a conch shell, a tofu man figurine, a picture of the *Manic Mondays* cast. "Ah, here!" She swiveled around and tried to shove a giant chunk of glass into my arms.

I just looked at it. "What is this?"

"It's Stu's People's Choice Award!" she said as if it was the most obvious thing in the world. "I'm sure Mallory and Brian would die for it, but I know he would have wanted you to keep it. Here! Take it!"

I looked down at the thing. I reached out to take it because I didn't know what else to do and I thought it might drop. That's when I saw it; just as she transferred that award into my hands. On her finger. A reflection of light that drew my eye—a sparkle. My mouth dropped open.

Stewart was not a jewelry guy. That wasn't his vibe. But he wore one item every single day: a diamond and platinum pinkie ring that had belonged to his grandfather. His mother's father had died young, but Stewart had enjoyed eight good years with him, during which he was more like an actual dad than Ted had ever been. Stewart wore it to remember his "G-pa."

Blair was wearing that ring. My stomach dropped, as rage boiled up inside me, my body recalibrating in every direction at once.

"What. Is. That?" But I knew. Of course I knew.

Blair smiled, feigning ambivalence. She could barely contain her glee. "Oh, this? This is just that ring that Stewart liked to wear."

"No, I know. But did Helen get it back from the coroner?" *How did you get it?* That's what I wanted to ask.

"Nope. I found it when I came back the other day to finish organizing. It was in the back of his bedside table drawer. Thank goodness I found it."

"That's weird." I never knew him to take that thing off. Not ever. He showered in it.

"Not really," she shrugged. "I think he kept it there when he slept. Anyway, I returned it to Helen's when I went there for lunch."

'Cause Blair and Helen have lunch all the time. *What a lovely girl.* I felt it like a punch to the gut.

"And she said I should just keep it! As a thank-you for all the work I've put into packing up Stu's apartment. Isn't that so sweet? So I've just been wearing it. I think it's pretty cool actually." She splayed her hand in front of her and eyed it like a new engagement ring—one that was notably missing from her life. She had no idea what it meant to Stewart. I doubted if she even knew its origin. She just knew it was the winning item in the Stewart's stuff contest—and a cool accessory to boot.

I looked at that ring—the closest thing to a Stewart talisman that might exist—on her veiny hands. I looked down at the People's Choice Award cradled in my own arms: What she had decided that I deserved. And it took everything in my power not to pick it up and bring it down over her head.

The force of my anger scared me, so I backed away from her, murmuring something about going to the bathroom, again. She turned on her heal and went off to ruin someone else's day. The room was spinning. It felt like a head rush from a first cigarette: Was this from the alcohol or the world tipping off its axis?

I felt, for the first time, like I might cry for real. Not from sadness, but from frustration and rage. I needed a moment of quiet. I rushed down the narrow hall toward Stewart's bedroom, almost slamming into George as he left the bathroom.

"Whoa. No running in the halls, kids."

"Excuse me," I mumbled, moving to pass him.

His brow furrowed. "What's wrong?"

"Can I just get past?"

He tilted his head and took a more intent look at my face. A line etched its way across his forehead when he was worried; one day, it would leave a crease and make him look wise. *Must be nice.* "Wren, are you okay?"

I couldn't speak. I looked at the floor, then, when I had gathered enough courage, up into his handsome face. I shook my head.

He took me by the hand and walked me into the bedroom, closing the door behind us. Despite my current state, I felt a stir of something besides anger and sadness.

We sat down next to each other at the foot of the Design Within Reach platform bed with its pricey Hästens mattress. These were the items Stewart had carried from place to place. I hadn't spent as much time in here as I had in Stewart's previous bedrooms—or even apartments. Neither had he. He moved in after a couple seasons of the show and was in LA a lot. The Egyptian-cotton sheets and duvet and the space itself—with its high ceilings, large windows, and dark Venetian blinds—didn't elicit a visceral reaction from me. They weren't familiar. But it still smelled like Stewart's aftershave or hair product, something artisanal that I always loved with fig and basil notes. Or was that George's? The two scents had intermingled and fused in a complicated way in my mind. I couldn't tell one from the other anymore, but I craved them both.

I looked around the room. The art had been taken off the walls and most of the objects had been removed so that Stewart's friends and loved ones could pick through them. Only a faded globe still sat on his wide windowsill.

"I love Earth; way more manageable than outer space," he told me the day he bought it. We were browsing at the Smithsonian gift shop on a high school trip to Washington, DC. Stewart was in one of his grandiose moods. "All over this giant world, people are experiencing moments of tragedy, brutality, triumph, joy, and boredom," he raved, rotating the globe with his thumb.

I pulled myself away from the quartz jewelry display I'd been examining with my mother's birthday in mind and crossed to him. "That seems more manageable to you? It seems more overwhelming to me."

"It's a reminder that my problems aren't that big." He shrugged, tipping the brim of his Yankees cap up with his pointer finger. "Also, globes are fun to spin. I'm getting it!"

"What is that?" George said now, referencing the award in my hands—not the globe. It took me a moment to realize what he meant.

"This? My consolation prize."

"You don't even get the Emmy?"

"Apparently not."

"Lame." George sighed. "So tell me why you're upset? Because Jimmy isn't here?" He rubbed his cheek. I'd never noticed how defined his jaw was before.

"Jimmy? No. I mean, maybe it would have been helpful to have him here to deflect."

"But you're not upset that he didn't show up for you?"

I shook my head. "I mean, I've sort of given up. I don't really expect that from him. I love him, but Jimmy does what's good for Jimmy."

George cringed. "And you don't mind dating someone like that? 'Cause, based on what you said about your other ex-boyfriend, maybe that's a pattern for you. Just because a guy says the right thing, doesn't mean he's a good person."

"Wait, what?" My brain was not operating at full capacity. "Are you saying you think Jimmy is my boyfriend?"

"Well, I don't know about boyfriend," he shrugged, "but whatever the kids are calling it these days."

"I think the kids would call us 'friends.' Jimmy spent Stewart's funeral reception locked in a bathroom with Gretchen."

"Wait, seriously?" George opened his eyes wide, and I could see the constellation of specks in them—speaking of outer space. *A galaxy far, far away.*

I tried to focus back on the conversation. "Yup. Not their classiest moment."

"Huh." George scratched his head, absorbed that information. "Wow. I really misjudged this whole situation. But then why are you so upset? If it's not about Jimmy, what is it about? Is it being in Stewart's apartment?"

I held up the People's Choice Award, then resettled it on my lap. I was starting to get attached to it like a really sharp, heavy security blanket.

"Ah. Yeah, that's not the memento I would have expected you to pick."

"Oh no? You didn't think I'd want to spend every day for the rest of my life staring at proof that random strangers thought famous Stewart seemed dreamy?"

"So, how did you—?"

"Queen Vulture bestowed it upon me." I regarded it sadly.

"That woman is a nightmare." George tipped his head to the ceiling for commiseration—maybe from God? Maybe from the universe? Maybe from Stewart's ghost? He leveled his gaze back at me. "You don't have to accept this. You have a right to whatever you want."

I shook my head. "It's not that." I was drunk, I was delirious, I was tired, George's toned and tanned forearms were distracting me. I missed my best friend. "This is just a symbol, you know? A really, really ugly one."

"Okay. So what is it a symbol of?"

It was hard to explain. I couldn't totally connect to the feeling. What was it? Sadness? Anger? Envy, even? I thought about Stewart's ring. If I closed my eyes against this reality, I could see him wearing it, his hands wildly gesticulating while he told some hilarious story. How could I put my feelings into words? "I feel like . . . they're stealing him from me."

George's face fell. He closed his eyes for an almost imperceptible moment, then took my hand. When he looked at me, his eyes were watery. "Not them, Wren. They didn't steal him. It was his own body. His own brain."

The truth hit me like a ton of bricks, heavy and real. Death. *Stewart. Gone. Forever.*

Just gone? Forever? Abandoned? Forever?

"I'm so sorry, Wren. I hate that you're in so much pain. I wish I could—" George exhaled. "Look, they can't take what you had with Stewart away. They can't erase your memories and replace them with their own. They can't disappear him. It was his own body that did that. Just dumb, tragic, unfortunate bad luck. A glitch in his code. A mechanical malfunction."

A glitch in his code. The wrong sequence of zeros and ones. I dropped my face into my hands. Was I malfunctioning too? Life seemed so tenuous. What separates one of us from the other? Why was I alive and Stewart dead? Why one person and not another? George slipped his arm around my shoulders and rocked me. I wanted to crawl onto his lap and stay there forever; bury my face in his neck and smell that delightful cologne.

But then, abruptly, I remembered his behavior all evening—his dry welcome, his flat affect, the way he'd been avoiding my eyes when we were supposed to be partners in opposition to the vultures. The way he'd dropped my hand during Willow's circle.

I pulled away, far enough to look up into his face which was only inches from my own. I smelled honey on his breath. "Why have you been so weird all night?"

"Weird?"

"Unfriendly."

"Oh, that." He looked hangdog, as he bit his lip. "I kinda thought you were dating Jimmy."

"Yeah. So?"

"So I was disappointed and confused. I guess I was sort of pissed. I realize that's not the most evolved reaction."

I was starting to get the picture, one in whose outcome I'd been too invested to look closely. I'd been too afraid of a letdown, too conflicted about having a crush in the midst of all this loss. "Because?"

He cocked his head. "Wren. Because I like you. Despite your terrible attitude and bad taste in bagels. I like you a lot. I thought that was clear."

I allowed myself the smallest smile; he scowled at me playfully. I felt a rush of nerves. I wasn't used to taking leaps like this. I wasn't used to men like George. "Can I ask you a question?"

"Open book. Sort of. Unless it's privileged information."

"Why did you become an entertainment lawyer? You don't find that world gross?"

"Oh! Because I love movies. My dad is a total film nerd. I spent my whole childhood obsessed. Why?"

How had I not allowed for a simple explanation like that? Why did I assume that George had some pernicious motivation, all evidence to the contrary? Why did I always imagine the worst?

I raised a hand to his chest, toying with a shirt button. I could feel his body rise and fall with each breath, warm beneath the thin fabric. Finally, I said, "I have another question."

"Of course you do."

"Tell me the truth: When we were talking on the phone earlier, you *were* wearing the hotel robe, weren't you?"

George laughed—like hiccups. I realized I loved his stupid laugh.

I sensed his kiss coming long before he took the award off my lap and moved it to the floor, making my legs feels so light that they might float up in the air: *light as a feather, stiff as a board.* I felt it before he leaned in, his lips finding mine, his scruffy facial hair scratching my face. And when he kissed me, I still wasn't prepared for the shiver that ran down the length of my body, inspiring something that felt like necessity. I experienced him like a forgone conclusion long before he ran his hand from my cheek, down my neck, across the plane of my collarbones and down the length of my side. I wanted him to hurry, even as he arrived. His body felt strong, warm, as it closed around me. I nuzzled my way into his neck, the way I'd wanted to since we met.

My mind was sending thousands of messages to nerves around my body to get woke, jump into action. They set off explosions in my brain, demolishing old neural pathways as new ones etched their way into prominence—a path of destruction to make way for this new sensation: *George.*

So this is what it feels like when your brain explodes, I thought, as his hand traveled up my thigh. *This is oblivion.*

CHAPTER 35

Stewart. I finally listened to you: I made a decision without debating the pros and cons. I just went for it. And all it took was your permanent absence!

That's what Mr. Nowak—of AP English fame—would have called "legitimate irony." (I think he's dead too, BTW.)

I like the idea that maybe you're watching over me, beaming with pride. Maybe Mr. Nowak is there with you too.

That said, I really hope death doesn't give you access to round-the-clock visuals.

CHAPTER 36

Things would have gotten out of hand if George and I hadn't heard Mallory approaching from the hallway: "BRI! DID YOU SEE I GOT ALL THE SCRIPTS FROM *MANIC MONDAYS* SEASON I? NO ONE ELSE WANTED THEM! CAN YOU BELIEVE IT? MAKE SURE YOU TRY ON THAT SUEDE JACKET BEFORE WE LEAVE. IT'S SAINT LAURENT AND WE COULD GET IT TAILORED TO FIT YOU! I'M RUNNING TO THE BATHROOM. BLAIR! IS THERE ANYTHING LEFT IN THE BEDROOM?"

George and I froze. We were intertwined on the bed in stages of near, but not total, undress. We looked at the door and then at each other, then both started to laugh, hard. Once again, I was shedding the wrong kind of tears.

"HEY! IS ANYONE IN THERE?"

I took my hand off George's chest and covered my mouth, trying to erase all humor from my voice. "Um. It's me, Mal! Just taking a moment to reflect."

George made a face at me, like, *really*?

I choked back another laugh, but it sounded enough like a sob to stop her.

"OH! ARE YOU OKAY?"

"Yeah! I just need a second."

"OKAY, HONEY. LET ME KNOW IF YOU WANT COMPANY!" We heard her footsteps fading away and then, "YOU GUYS! DON'T TELL HER I TOLD YOU, BUT I THINK WREN IS REALLY UPSET!"

George collapsed on top of me and groaned. I kissed his neck. Why did he smell so good? Like vanilla and beach and hot cocoa?

"All right," he said, sitting up. "I guess we better get back out there." He looked down at his lap. "Well, in a minute."

I sat up too. "I think we're lucky we got interrupted."

"Yeah." George looked around the room, smoothing down his ruffled hair. "This feels pretty macabre. And yet . . ." He kissed me again.

I left the bedroom first. When I reappeared, I half expected Mallory and Willow to try to comfort me, believing that I'd been alone and upset. They didn't look up. Mal was fitting the suede jacket on Brian and had a mountain of other clothing next to her too. Willow was sitting on the floor by the bookshelf with her eyes closed, holding a pair of brown leather gloves to her lips. I didn't have the heart to tell her that I recognized them as a gift from Ted that Stewart made a point never to wear.

It was Keith who approached as I started to search for my leather jacket. He slouched in front of me, all greasy with his patchy beard and blackhead-spotted nose. "What's that?"

I looked behind me. "What's what?"

"In your hands." He gestured with his chin.

"Oh, this? It's Stewart's People's Choice Award."

Keith stared at me. "You just took it without asking anyone?" *Was he for real?*

"No, Keith. Blair suggested that I take it."

"Well, it was supposed to be mine."

I looked down at the award. "You wanted this?" I had a vision of him in a stained Hanes T-shirt and loose boxers in front of his mirror at home, accepting it and thanking his imaginary fans over and over again.

He shrugged. "I don't care. I'm just saying, Blair gave that to me when I first got here tonight. She keeps taking shit back. She also gave me a DVD of season one of *Manic Mondays*, but Mallory took that, so now what the fuck am I supposed to take?"

"I'm pretty sure you can watch *Manic Mondays* on Hulu. Or order the DVD box set on Amazon. And there are a million other things here."

"That's not the point."

"What *is* the point, Keith?" Normally, I would have handed the statue over. I never wanted it anyway, and he seemed to feel ownership. It was entirely possible that Blair had promised it to him. But I was over his nasty behavior and his stupid face; I was done being nice. There was no way in hell anyone was leaving with that hideous hunk of glass but me.

"It was supposed to be mine," Keith repeated.

"I'm surprised you even want it. I would have thought you felt Stewart didn't deserve the recognition."

"Whether he did or didn't isn't the point. He would have wanted me to have it."

"He would have laughed in your face."

We both knew it was true. Stewart would never have abided this behavior.

Keith glared at me. "You've always acted like you think you're better than me."

"Almost anyone is better than you."

"You're being a selfish—"

"A selfish *what*, Keith? Choose your words carefully. 'Cause I'm not one of your underage 'acting students.'"

Keith took a step toward me.

"Okay, okay," said George, appearing beside me with arms outstretched like a referee. "Keith. Get a grip, dude. What the hell? It's a People's Choice Award. Back the hell up!"

I'm not sure if Keith checked himself and realized he was being a douche, or if he didn't want a successful Hollywood lawyer to think ill of him. "Whatever," he snarled. "It's no big deal." Then he slunk back into some dark corner.

George flashed me a forced a smile. "Okay, then. On that note. Ready?"

I felt happier than I should. I wanted to lean over and kiss him, but it seemed wrong to flaunt. "Just need my jacket."

I was slipping it on, when Blair approached. "Are you leaving already?"

"Yeah, I'm tired."

She rolled her eyes. "You're no fun. Right, George?"

"Wren? She's a barrel of laughs." He was pulling on his beat-up Pirates cap, which made me smile.

Blair was not deterred. She took a step toward him and tugged at the arm of his coat. Apparently, holding his hand during Willow's ceremony had given her the impression that he might be interested in more than just planning tributes with her. "Don't tell me you're leaving too?"

"Yeah, I'm following Wren's example. I've got work to do."

"Wren should learn to live a little. Why don't you follow my example instead?"

Unbelievable. "Um. I'm standing right here," I said. "Can anyone see me?"

Blair allowed her gaze to travel to me. She looked me up and down and did not seem pleased. "We see you, Wren. Don't worry. Everyone sees you."

I wanted to punch her. I figured she could take me after those countless hours of Taryn Toomey and Tracy Anderson classes, but I was willing to chance it.

Before I could move, George said, "We're gonna go." He stepped toward the door, yanking his jacket from Blair's clutches harder than he intended. That was better than any punch I could have thrown. Her mouth dropped open and her cheeks flushed. She shook her head as if to erase the moment. Her hand remained suspended in air, as if she didn't know where to put it.

I was about to follow George through the open door when something red and glossy caught my attention, and I felt an inexplicable pull. "One sec," I told him, as I crossed the room and grabbed a book off the shelf. I felt everyone's eyes on me, but I didn't care. Probably they were wondering if I was taking something valuable. I wasn't. It was just that self-help guide, *Unearthing the Answer*. I don't know why it called to me. Maybe because it seemed to represent everything that I didn't understand about Stewart. Maybe because *The Answer* sounded like a neat solution. I tucked it into my Operation Sewage tote alongside my emergency umbrella, then returned to George's side.

He rested a hand on my back, "Ready?"

"Ready. Bye, guys." I said. No one responded.

George and I made it to the other side of Stewart's door before we looked at each other and lost it, laughing uncontrollably.

"I don't even know what's funny!" I gasped.

"It's funny because it's horrible!"

As we walked out the front doors of the building, wiping tears of laughter from our eyes, I finally got a text from Jimmy:

> Sorry! Got caught up. Be there in 5.

"Ah. Of course."

"What is it?"

I showed George.

"Are we going back in there? Because I don't know if I can handle that."

I appreciated the "we." "I definitely don't want to."

"Did you see Willow collecting lint from his bed? Did you see the rolling suitcases that Mallory and Brian brought?"

"And they're the nicest of the bunch."

"What is wrong with these scavengers? Were they raised in a barn?"

"Not in a barn. In extreme privilege, I think." Was that true? I had only a vague sense.

"Well, apparently that's worse."

I wiped a final tear from my cheek. "You know what? Let's go. Jimmy is a big boy. He can handle himself."

"Thank God." George took my hand and we started to walk. When we arrived in front of the Crosby only a minute later, he stopped and turned to face me. "We didn't discuss where we're going. Am I putting you in a cab? Or do you want to come up? No pressure, of course, but I do have a desk. And I know you like that in a hotel room."

We were blocking street traffic on the sidewalk. Pedestrians wove around us, rushing toward their destinations: hipster bars, farm-to-table eateries, HIIT classes, media events, coffee and pressed-juice shops. A group of three tall, thin, women in leather pants and mile-high boots dragged on cigarettes as they walked past (lung cancer, "In Memory" by Ed Sheeran, lemon cayenne water).

It was dark, but the city was light. It sparkled and pulsed, enlivened by the crisp fall air smelling of exhaust, beer, perfume, and Halal carts. *The world rushes by fast.* That's what Stewart would have said. *Recognize your moments when they arrive and seize them—without looking back.* I had never been good at that. I decided to take his advice in absentia.

"Maybe I'll come in for a minute." I took George's hand; we went inside.

Upstairs, in the pristine suite, I wandered around, absorbing the decor—sleek, but plush. "Wow. So pretty."

"It's not much, but it's home," George joked. "No, seriously, the firm is generous in the hotel department. I always stay here. I love it."

He shrugged off his jacket, throwing it over the side of the quilted couch. Then he leaned against the far wall, hands in his pockets, and watched me as I ran my fingers along the various surfaces. The windows were truly floor-to-ceiling and, for a brief instant, I was reminded of a fancy hotel room that Stewart and I shared during a trip to Paris when we were twenty, the year we all went abroad. That had similar windows with sheer white curtains that blew inward with the breeze.

Stewart and I had met up after separate travels with our respective friends. I'd been looking forward to it for weeks, but the trip turned out to be stiff and odd, uncharacteristic for us. He kept ordering more alcohol to the room like he was assuaging nerves. I wanted to get outside and wander the city. We couldn't find our groove.

I pushed the memories from my mind. I needed an escape from the vultures, from the sadness and confusion. I would leave Stewart outside these walls.

I wandered past a fireplace mantle and arrived in front of the desk. I looked over my shoulder across the room at George and smiled. He looked down and laughed. *Adorable.*

"Good desk?"

"Great desk." I thought, *I bet George would have wanted to explore Paris.*

I turned and leaned my bottom up against the table, eyeing him. I was nervous in a way I couldn't remember feeling for eons. After what felt like forever, George crossed to me, moving closer until we were only inches apart, but still not touching. I tilted my face up toward his. His arms hung at his sides. I gripped the desk.

"I'm glad you came up," he said.

"Me too."

"I like your red lipstick."

"Oh, thanks. I was worried that it was too much."

He shook his head, shot me a half smile. "Not for you."

I reached up, then, and traced that little semicircle by his mouth with my fingertip—a crescent moon.

He rested a hand on either side of my waist. Then, he leaned down and kissed me—gently at first, then harder as I kissed him back. He lifted me up onto the desk, his hands finding my bare lower back. I pulled him toward me, wrapping my legs around him and tugging at his button-down shirt, a rush of anticipation coursing through my body.

Great desk.

CHAPTER 37

Stewart! Last night, I was lying in George's plush white hotel bed after he fell asleep (more on that later!) and I finally had the guts to google, "What happens in your brain when you have an aneurysm?" It wasn't as scary as I imagined. No images came up at all.

It turns that an aneurysm is just a weak section in a blood vessel wall. Many people live with them for their whole lives without knowing it—just doing the laundry, crying at cheesy commercials, complaining about their bosses. They don't realize it could all go south at any moment! If one ruptures, however, blood leaks out and begins to flood the brain, causing a headache—and you know the rest. That's called a "subarachnoid hemorrhage." Like George said, it's a structural defect, a mechanical malfunction.

Here's the crazy thing: I don't know why, but I also looked up, "What happens in your brain when you fall in love?" The answer is that the pleasure center—which is also the part associated with Obsessive Compulsive Disorder! What?—floods with all these chemicals like dopamine, adrenaline, and norepinephrine. And there's also this rush of extra blood flow.

It made me think two things: First, it wasn't my fault that I liked Matthew Simonsson so much that I kind of stalked him, going out of my way to walk past his apartment building every day after school for a month after he dumped me. Second, maybe you just had too much love to give and it busted down your walls.

CHAPTER 38

I woke up beneath a cloud of comforter and bliss. Sun streamed in through the wide hotel windows, illuminating the room—immaculate save our clothes on the floor and a single fork that must have fallen from the room service tray when we decided we needed molten chocolate cake and French fries at 1:00 a.m. I rolled onto my side, facing George, who was sitting propped up against several pillows, glaring at his iPhone.

I propped myself up on my elbow, watching him. "What did that phone ever do to you?"

He started. "You're up! I thought you were still asleep. Why are you always sneaking up on me?"

"Um. I'm not." I cocked my head to the side. "Aw. This is so cute. Are you already composing your next text to me even though I haven't left yet? I think *The Rules* stipulates that you should wait three days so as not to appear overeager."

"Yeah, but they didn't know you," he smirked. "Three days is way too long. By then, you might have fled the country."

"True story."

He set his phone down on the comforter beside him and turned to face me, leaning over to kiss my head, then my cheek, then my neck.

"No, but seriously. What was with the phone?"

"Nothing."

"That was an angry kind of nothing."

He groaned and fell back against his pillows. "Are you sure you want to know? 'Cause it's been kind of a perfect night and I don't see any reason to bring all this awful crap up, when instead we could just—"

"George." I gathered the comforter up around my chest and sat up. "What's happening?"

"Ugh. Keith gave an interview."

My stomach dropped. "What does *that* mean? To who?"

"*Star*. Who else? I'm sure *People* and *Us Weekly* wouldn't have him. It just posted online."

I'm sure I got crazy eyes then—I felt insane. "That self-serving maggot! Just when I think these people can't get worse, they prove me wrong! What did he say?"

George picked up his phone and scrolled to the top of the post. "The article—if you can call it that—is titled, 'Five Things I'll Miss Most About My Best Buddy, Stewart Beasley.' The intro describes Keith as his 'grieving best friend, whose life will never be the same.' Then Keith talks about Stu's final hours, which he completely invented, by the way. So much for discretion and privacy. I hope Helen doesn't find out."

"I kind of hope she does." My heart was pounding with rage. "So basically, he couldn't get the artwork to turn around and sell, so he sold whatever story he could make up and bought himself some publicity too? As if anyone would care who he was."

"Basically."

"Ugh! I'm not even sure that he and Stewart were still in touch." I peered over George's shoulder to see the article for myself. All I could make out was the hot pink header; my contacts were foggy from sleeping in them. "Keep reading, please!"

"I'm trying, but it's hard not to throw up. The rest is just bullshit about how Stu's 'friends' are commemorating him."

"How? By stealing his shit? Did he mention Willow burning Stewart's hair? I hope he didn't leave that gem out."

"He skipped that, though he did drop Willow's name since, you know, she's known in her way."

"Of course he did."

"Then he answers the final question about Stu's legacy by claiming that he and Stu were collaborating on a project together—a thirty-minute comedy—that he's now shopping to 'several interested networks.'"

I picked up a pillow lodged between me and the headboard and threw it across the room, only I didn't have a lot of leverage and it landed at the foot of the bed. George raised an eyebrow. "So maybe not the Yankees' next pitcher."

"As far as I know, they don't throw pillows," I grumbled.

"Anyway," Stewart bit his lip. "Um, I feel like I'm going to regret telling you this, but—that's not the worst of it."

With force, I flipped over onto my stomach and buried my face in the remaining pillow, which smelled like orange-blossom linen spray. I knew because there was a bottle of it sitting on the bathroom sink; it was lovely. I wished I could spray it in Keith's eyes. "Go ahead," I mumbled into the cotton and down.

"Okay, here goes: Madison emailed me about Keith's story. So to find it, I googled Stu's name . . . and something else came up." He bit his lip. I was starting to recognize that as a tell. "Are you ready for this?"

I turned onto one cheek, so I could be bolstered by the sight of George's strong upper arms and angular face. Even his ears were nice. "Why not?"

He passed me his phone. It took me a second to understand what I was seeing: an eBay listing for a *Manic Mondays* hoodie described as "a crew gift worn by the official Stewart Beasley." The seller was MalGal1984. I stared at it without reacting for a minute. Then I stuffed my face back into the pillow and screamed.

George eventually coaxed me out of my catatonic state with a combination of kisses down my back and coffee. Also, I didn't want to overstay my welcome, no matter how traumatized I felt. I knew he had work to do. I did too—if I could get myself to focus. Plus, he was headed back to LA in a few days. I was trying to remind myself not to get too attached.

Not long after, I packed up my things and readied to head toward the elevators. George opened the suite's door for me and leaned against the door frame, ushering in some intoxicating gardenia-like signature fragrance the hotel pumped through the vents. I turned to face him, "But *why* are they so horrible?"

"The vultures?" He shook his head. "I think maybe they just want to feel acknowledged."

"By selling Stewart's stuff?"

"By feeling like the arbiters of his story. By trying to make the death amount to something material. So it has some silver lining. They're not happy people."

"That's generous." I raised an eyebrow. "Too generous." George wanted to see the best in everyone.

I tried to channel Stewart's reaction, if I'd asked him the same question under the same circumstances, but about strangers: "Because they're atrocious people without an ounce of class." That seemed more on target to me.

As I moved to leave, George pulled me back and kissed me. "About last night—"

But I was already retreating down the hall. "Oh, yeah. You owe me a bagel. A salt one. I never put out without being compensated with bread."

"I already bought you one."

"Yeah, but that doesn't really count because it was before you had intent."

"So you think." He smiled. "But seriously—"

"It's okay," I called. "Let's talk later. Tonight, at the preview for the tribute."

"Right. Fuck," he covered his eyes with his palm. "That sounds awful."

"I won't take that personally." I stuck my tongue out, then walked around the corner to the elevator vestibule.

On the train ride home, I couldn't stop searching through Mallory's listings of Stewart's stuff. There were at least ten items posted within the last twenty-four hours: some additional *Manic Mondays* paraphernalia; some high-end items of clothing listed without Stewart's name attached. The brands—Alexander Wang, Derek Lam, Martin Margiela—were enough to sell them on their own.

I was revolted—physically nauseous—and angry enough to flatten a city block in my monster fantasies. But there wasn't anything we could do; the stuff now belonged to them. They weren't embarrassed enough to even disguise their names. How do you explain to people that they've done something wrong when they don't know enough to feel mortified in the first place? How do you shame someone who feels no shame?

I would have to see the vultures again tonight. We were all meeting at the Institute of Television Arts to preview the tribute gallery before it opened to the public, to make sure everything looked as it should and nothing was misattributed. The curators also wanted to give us a chance to see it without the hubbub of a crowd.

The following evening would be the event itself, and then I would be free of these terrible humans forever. I tried not to think about what that meant in terms of George. He would be going back to California, of course. But I was the new Wren, who didn't think about consequences like that. I pushed the thought from my mind, shooting Kate a quick follow-up email instead:

Hi Kate,

Just want to make sure you got my message about speaking at Stewart's tribute tomorrow. I'm sure you did. I just want to confirm that you feel comfortable. I know it might be very difficult. Looking forward to seeing you there, regardless.

Best,
Wren

Chris Harrison, for one, was not pleased about my recent inattention or my absence the night before. When I opened my apartment door, instead of jumping up and sauntering over, he stayed curled up on the couch, wearing a look of scorn on his fluffy face. He was an easy mark, though. He came running as soon as I opened a can of chicken in gravy. I gave him a pet and wished him "bon appétit!" as he dug into the brown muck. Relationship successfully repaired, I dug through my tote and pulled out Stewart's People's Choice Award, placing it on top of my white IKEA bookshelf next to a glass dove from my mom. It no longer felt like a slap in the face from Blair—or Helen, by proxy. It had morphed into an inside joke between me and George. George. *George. George. George.*

Could I possibly think about anything else? I grabbed my computer and plopped down on the couch.

Kate had answered right away.

> Wren, sweetie, I'm so sorry that I wasn't quicker to respond.
> Meryl has been working insane hours these last few weeks—I'm
> so proud of her activism, but it is time-consuming—and I am, as
> you can imagine, deeply distracted.
>
> I don't think I would feel comfortable speaking at the tribute,
> although I am hoping to be there. It would be hard for me to
> know what to say and I think anything I did choose would upset
> my mother.
>
> She and I are not on fantastic terms, to be blunt, so I haven't yet
> seen what you put aside for me, but whatever it is, I'm sure it's
> perfect. Stewart was so lucky to have you and, now, so are we.
>
> I'm sure it seems odd that I haven't done more to help with
> disseminating Stewart's worldly possessions and planning
> his memorial. Hopefully you won't judge me too harshly.
> Someday, when we have more time, I'll explain. You deserve to
> understand—you've done so much in my stead. In some ways,
> you were the sister he never really had.
>
> Love, Kate

As I stared at the screen in wonder, it seemed to blink back at me. She was "hoping" to be there? I *was* judging her; I couldn't help it. I understood what a nightmare Helen could be and I knew that they never saw eye to eye, but to completely bail on your only brother's aftermath? What could I possibly understand that would change any of this? It was bizarre. And selfish.

I sighed. I needed to figure out who else could speak by this evening. No way was I asking any one of those vultures. Maybe Blair hadn't auctioned off Stewart's stuff or burned his lint or sold his story for a millisecond of attention, but—through her competitive energy—she had rendered the whole experience toxic, taken the focus off Stewart and onto herself. They were all awful.

I thought about Stewart—no wonder he was sad sometimes. He was surrounded by assholes. I navigated to his Facebook page, now my go-to procrastination destination. George was going to post the details of the event tomorrow for anyone who wanted to attend and I wanted to share the information with some people too.

Before I could get to that, I noticed another post from the bereft girl from the funeral. Her name appeared to be "Belle Rose." That sounded made up. Her previous posts—written almost daily like tiny cries for help and invoking her and Stewart's "twin souls"—had garnered sympathetic comments from friends and even strangers. But it seemed like people had now tired of consoling her. The most recent gem had only won her a few frown emojis. In everyone's defense, the messages were almost incomprehensible with as many typos as complete words. *Who is this girl?*

This one started out much like the rest:

Stu, don't know how to continue w/pot u. i look in the miror
+ don't even no muself I still can't believe your gone 4ever.
Listening to this on repete + thinking of u.

Below, she had printed all the lyrics to "Might as Well Be Gone" by the Pixies.

It may not be attractive to admit, but I had been enjoying the inanity of her posts in a schadenfreude kind of way—like reading a seventh grader's diary. But then I read those lyrics. My stomach dropped and I sat bolt upright. I said, "What the fuck?!" aloud to nobody. Chris Harrison glared at me like I'd offended his delicate sensibilities.

That was Stewart's favorite song. Everyone knew he loved the Pixies, but that song—it was his private anthem. This girl wasn't some nutball fan. She knew him. She *really* knew him.

Before I understood what I was doing, I was typing a private message to her:

Belle,

We don't know each other. I was—

I stopped myself and edited that.

—am a very old friend of Stewart's. It seems like you guys had a deep connection too. Is there any way we could meet and talk? I'm trying to know the parts of his life that I somehow missed.

Thanks,

Wren

Instantly, she started typing a message back:

Yeah. I think Stu maybe talked about you once.

I thought, *gee, thanks.* I wrote:

Yeah. We knew each other for a long time. Would you be down to talk? It seems like you're struggling.

Sure. I can talk. Not always the best at getting out of bed rt now. But I prolly should anywya.

Great! I mean, not the part about you being in bed. That's no good, but I really get it. This is so tough. Where are you based?

Staying with my parents on the UWS right now.

Okay, perfect. Do you want to maybe meet at like 3:30 p.m. today?

Sure. City Diner on 90th?

That works for me. See you then.

I wouldn't have called Belle enthusiastic, but she was willing. I would stop by the tribute gallery in midtown to make an appearance and then run to meet her uptown. Maybe she was only some girl Stewart dated for a second, who got obsessed. But, even if that was the case, at least I would learn *something*. Who was this person who was so sure that she and Stewart were soulmates, when even I was beginning to doubt the depth of our relationship? Was she delusional? Or was I?

Hours later, on the train to the Institute of Television Arts, my phone *binged*. George.

Wren. I'm so sorry, but I have to skip the gallery walkthrough. A big client is having an emergency. Studio says she's in breach of contract and they're threatening legal action. I need to comb through the contract, talk to their counsel and figure out a resolution. I know this is worst-case scenario, leaving you alone with the vultures, especially after what we discovered this morning.

It was definitely the worst-case scenario, since seeing George had been the only silver lining about attending this thing—and it felt like a bad omen. But what could I do? He had a work emergency.

Wait. He really did have a work emergency, right? He wasn't making up an excuse to avoid me? After very little consideration, I decided to at least pretend not to be psycho. *It's cool. I'm cool.*

> Ugh. That sucks. For both of us. Maybe more for me. But I get it. No worries.

See? *No worries.* So chill.

> Okay. Thanks for being cool about this.

> What's the alternative?

> I don't know. Freaking out at me and calling me an asshole for deserting you in your hour of need, especially after last night?

> You're an asshole. For deserting me. In my hour of need. Especially after last night.

> Right. Like that.

> Wait, what happened last night again?

I smiled, despite myself. Then I made the mistake of looking up. A large, bald man in Carhartt overalls across the car seemed to think I was smiling at him. He grinned back—in all his gold toothed glory—and raised an eyebrow, licking his lips (accidental decapitation during construction work, "Jump Around" by House of Pain, McDonald's). I averted my eyes.

Anyway, I'm on the train. Not great service.

Okay. Just know that I want to see you. Badly. I can meet you later tonight? Any chance you'll still be in Manhattan? Or I can come to you in Brooklyn? See your place? Meet the famous Chris Harrison? Before he leaves to shoot the next season of The Bachelor?

I do have some pretty old cashew yogurt and flat seltzer in my fridge. So, I'm definitely in good shape to host.

But do you have a desk? 'Cause that's really all that matters.

I could just see him smiling his adorable smile—that grammatical dimple.

All right. Stop texting me and get to work, so we have a chance of hanging later.

Sounds good. Keep me posted.

Will do. Wish me luck.

I wish you luck, Wren Pinkus.

I smiled again and almost looked up, but then remembered the man across the way and rearranged my face into a death glare. Sure enough, he was still leering at me. I fixed him with my meanest stare and didn't blink as he started to get uncomfortable, shifting in his seat. Finally, he stood and crossed to the subway car's doors long before they opened, opting to hold a pole and face out. He mumbled something—probably "dyke." I rolled my eyes. *Success!* A woman around my age across the way caught my eye and shook her head (old age, "Winter Song" by the Head and the Heart, meatloaf and mashed potatoes). #Solidarity.

Feeling pleased with myself, I checked my lipstick in my cell phone camera. Then, satisfied, I scrolled through my email, noticing one from Angeline, the administrator at the Collins Foundation. The subject was: Next Grant Cycle.

Huh. I hoped they weren't doing away with the grant for next quarter. That would be a huge issue for our organization. We relied on it so heavily. We'd have to seek out a whole bunch of new funding to compensate.

I clicked on the email.

Dear Wren,

We could not help but note the absence of an application from Operation Sewage for this grant cycle. As evidenced by our past awards, we have deep respect for the work your organization has done, supplying plumbing to underserved and struggling communities, and do hope that you'll submit paperwork for the next round, in three months.

Best,
Angeline

I almost passed out on the spot. There had to be some mistake. I hadn't missed the deadline—it was next week! Panic rose as bile in my chest. I had checked my spreadsheet only days ago. The deadline was next Friday! I scrolled for Angeline's previous email, opened it and clicked on the attached pdf titled "Application." Sure enough, the cover page listed an amended due date: yesterday. The application was due a week earlier than in previous years.

Oh God. My hands were shaking. As quickly as I could, I typed out a reply:

Angeline, thank you so much for reaching out. I am mortified. I'm afraid I've been grappling with a personal emergency and overlooked the fact that the deadline had changed this year. Of course we intended to apply! The Collins Foundation grant means the world to our organization. It allows us to continue to service these deserving communities, who are very much in need. In fact, Anton is currently in Panama, scouting our next project, a trip which your award helped us fund.

Is there any chance that I might submit an application today? I know that's out of the ordinary, but we have such a longstanding relationship. Perhaps you could forgive us this one error? Is there any way?

Best,
Wren

I stared at the subway ads for Fresh Direct and awaited a reply. I am not someone who prays, but I found myself repeating *please, please, please!* in my head, begging someone—I don't know who—for salvation. I had never made a mistake like this before, but this one was so egregious that I knew Anton would not be able to forgive it. On the train, the Wi-Fi service was going in and out as we rattled from station to station. *C'mon, c'mon, c'mon,* I begged.

Angeline would help me, right? We had worked together for years. She knew me! The editorial assistant's prompt response landed in my inbox as we pulled into the Rockefeller Center Station at 47–50th Street. Crowds bustled in and out, as I sat—away from the fray—and clicked it open without breathing:

Dear Wren,

We are terribly sorry about the mix-up. Yes, we were forced to switch the application deadline this year to accommodate our bi-annual board meeting, which happened a week earlier, as well. Unfortunately, our board has already assessed the applications submitted and has come to decisions about awards. It would be unethical, and also impossible, to add another application to the pile of contenders.

Please do submit for the next cycle though. Again, we have great respect for your organization and wish you all good things.

I'm sorry for any personal issues. We send our best to you and yours and hope that you're safe and well.

Best,
Angeline

That was it. No recourse. I dropped my head into my hands. I thought I might throw up. I tried to take a deep breath.

When I sat up and looked around, I noticed that both the scumbag and nice woman across the way had disappeared. But I wasn't surprised. Even though I hadn't seen them leave, I had felt their exits in my bones, the same way I knew that I was about to be out of a job.

CHAPTER 39

Stewart. Remember how I was the responsible one?

CHAPTER 40

Two stone gargoyles flanked the stairs up to the entrance of the Institute of Television Arts. As I started up, my phone vibrated—my mother trying me back. I pressed Decline. I had to try to hold it together.

Just inside the glass doors, under high ceilings, an imposing guard sat helping some new arrivals at a steel security desk (embolism, "Even Now" by Barry Manilow, Christmas ham). The predictably stark, white walls were hung with photos of TV legends: Lucille Ball, Bob Newhart, Carol Burnett, Burt Reynolds, James Gandolfini, Tina Fey.

I examined their familiar faces, as I worked to calm myself down. So I had no job. That's okay. I'd find something else, right? Someone would hire me despite the tremendous gaff? First, I had to get up the guts to tell Anton before the foundation publicly announced the grant recipients. I was flooded with dread.

The Collins Foundation award was yet another thing I had taken for granted. Obviously, my mind was on other things: Stewart, the vultures and, let's be honest, George. I knew I'd been slacking off. I was just having so much trouble focusing. If I'd been honest with myself, I could have told Anton that I was having a tough time and needed a week or two off. I could have passed the Collins grant off to a coworker, Beatrice or Mark. No one would have begrudged me that. But that ship had sailed.

The guard finished assisting the people in front of me and sent them on their way with an efficient wave. "Hello. How can I help you today, young lady?"

"Um. I'm here to . . . my friend . . . Stewart Beasley." I couldn't find the words to explain my presence. "I'm sorry. That was really inarticulate. I'm not myself today."

The man's brow crinkled in concern. I pictured him having daughters and multiple grandkids. "That's okay, dear. Are you here like the others? To preview the tribute gallery for the late Mr. Beasley?"

The late Mr. Beasley. Very distinguished. "Yes. Thank you."

The guard asked to see my ID, then handed me a green-and-white "Guest Pass" sticker. As I accepted it, pressing it to the outside of my jacket, he said, "You lost someone. Be easy on yourself. It's normal to feel out of sorts."

A lethal combination of self-loathing and self-pity threatened to overflow. "Thank you, sir," I managed. "That's very kind." I wanted to climb behind the desk and stay with this giant teddy bear of a man instead of heading into the gallery. I would tell him all about the career I fucked up and the friend I lost and how confused and alienated I felt. And he would understand.

But that was not to be. I nodded goodbye sadly.

As if the universe wished to demonstrate the diametric opposite of this wonderful human, Blair stood feet away in the lobby. She was frowning and jabbing at her phone like it had stolen her boyfriend. I tried to slip past, but got caught. "Wren!"

I pretended that I hadn't noticed her. "Oh. Blair. Hi. I was just heading to the gallery. I'm a little late. The trains—"

"Yeah," she huffed. "We've been waiting for you."

She grabbed me by the arm and pulled me toward an open doorway, off to the right. I would have shaken her off, but I was too stunned. Once inside, I saw everyone was milling around, unconcerned about the time. It didn't look like I'd been holding anything up. I yanked my arm free.

"Where is George?" Blair barked.

"He can't make it." I rubbed my skin where her hand had been.

"Right. Of course. Fantastic. He couldn't have let me know that or anything!"

"What's the difference?" Apparently, at least in Blair's mind, this event had become her show. She glared at me and was about to answer, maybe bite my head off, literally, but a middle-aged woman with short spiky gray hair and nerd glasses interrupted us. "Hi! I'm Fernanda. The curator for the gallery here. You are?" She extended her hand, revealing a silver cuff bracelet and some chunky rings. I liked this lady on sight. There was something familiar about her. (Dementia, "Black Bird" by the Beatles, knishes, cucumber salad, cookies, the works.)

I shook her hand. "Nice to meet you. I'm Wren."

"Ah. Very nice to meet you. I'm sorry for your loss."

"Thank you for organizing all of this on such short notice."

She waved that off. "I'm Brazilian *and* Jewish. I'm culturally conditioned to dive right into commemoration after death. Short timelines."

I thought maybe I'd add churrascaria meat to her funeral menu.

"I understand you're assigning the personal speaker," Fernanda continued. "Have you decided who will be participating? It would be great to have them come thirty minutes early tomorrow, so we can coordinate the order and let them get accustomed to the stage."

"That makes perfect sense." Why did I feel like I had failed at this too? Because I had. I ran a hand through my hair. "So, I was hoping that Stewart's sister Kate would be speaking, but she, well . . ." I stumbled.

"I understand. Sometimes it's just too upsetting for the family."

"So I need to determine who it will be instead."

"Just pick someone!" Blair snapped. "It's not that hard."

I spun around to face her. "What is your deal today? I will."

"My *deal* is that the event is tomorrow and you were asked to do one thing. And you're like lording it over everyone."

"Blair. I'm not your fucking assistant. Don't talk to me like that."

"Not to worry!" Fernanda raised her hands to stop us. "As long as we know who it's going to be thirty minutes beforehand and have the correct pronunciation of his or her name, we'll be good."

Blair was shooting daggers at me. I wanted to shout obscenities in her stupid cow face, but I decided to act like an actual human being instead. I was afraid of what I might say if I opened the floodgates anyway. "Thank you, Fernanda. For all your hard work. I'll make sure that happens."

"Great. So in the meantime, take a look around." She swept her arm through the air to indicate the rest of the space. "Make sure everything looks as it should to you. We think it's come together quite nicely, but you never know when we might have missed something—a detail that only Stewart's close friends and family would notice."

I took her up on the invitation, if only to get away from Blair, and stepped away. The gallery was comprised of one large square room with several glass cases on pedestals. Videos were playing in a dark adjoining enclave—maybe *Manic Mondays* episodes on a loop? It was clear that visitors were meant to travel left to right based on the wall text describing Stewart's background, but I decided to work backward. The story had a happier ending that way.

The first glass case held Stewart's Emmy, for one thing, as well as some *Manic Mondays* stills and the core elements of his costume—namely an ironic T-shirt that said "Slurpy's" in green letters. There were signature props, as well, from episodes that had won accolades—the fuzzy dice from his character's car, the fridge magnet that looked like a police officer and repeated, "STEP AWAY FROM THE REFRIGERATOR!" when the characters got too close. A cushion embroidered with the words, IT'S NOT ME. IT'S YOU, which had inspired a romantic arc on the show.

When I had first watched the *Manic Mondays* pilot during a small get-together at Stewart's New York apartment, I thought it was funny, but not different than other single-camera comedies about a bunch of messed up twentysomethings in delayed adolescence. But the show had caught on like wildfire. The cast was magic together; the writing was stellar. Right away, it had become a cultural cornerstone, attacking issues like gun control and sexual harassment without ever having that "Movie of the Week" feel. Mostly, it was very, very funny.

That night it premiered, Stewart and I wound up in the kitchen at the same time, refilling our drinks in those pretty etched glasses.

"So, do you think this is it?" I asked. "Everything you've dreamed of? The big break?"

And he said, "God, I hope not."

I was thrown. "Why?"

"Because. I want to keep searching forever. I don't ever want to find 'the thing.' That means you're done."

Now, I found myself trying to remember the exact look on his face in that moment. I was already having trouble recalling certain details about him—like his hands. What did they look like again? Were they nice? Ugly? Big? Small? I could barely recall. Maybe I'd find a picture of them here.

Slowly, I made my way around the room. Fernanda and her team had done a lovely job tracing his entire life's trajectory; I moved back through theater in New York to graduate school to high school productions of *Anne Frank* and, yes, *Grease*. (Keith made the wall as the nerd.) Video interviews played on a flat-screen in one corner. As I watched Stewart talk, I was entranced by his mannerisms, like that habit of pushing invisible glasses up the bridge of his nose. It was just so him. *Stewart. Gone. You are gone. This is a tribute to you.*

Madison hurried up beside me. "Oh, good! Wren!" She was stuffed into a dark-purple belted dress—something buttoned up and Anne Taylor–like—with a matching headband. I felt an unexpected wave of affection for her, a dolphin in a sea of sharks.

"Hi, Madison." I kissed her on the cheek. "How are you?"

"I'm okay!" She beamed as always. "This is amazing, but so sad!"

"It is." I allowed my eyes to scan the walls, relic to relic, photo to photo. "I can't believe he's gone. And I can't stop saying that. Still. I think I may never stop."

"I know." She frowned, looking like a doodle someone might draw to approximate sadness. "I'll let you look around. I'm sure you have people to greet."

I didn't bother mentioning that I was avoiding everyone.

"But before you go, I wanted to say thank you."

I looked at her in surprise. "Oh! Madison, for what?"

"Well," she lowered her voice and leaned in, "I was a little uncomfortable during that conversation with Keith. You know, about the artwork. I appreciated that you and George supported me." She smoothed her hair, obviously nervous about revealing any negative feelings about the group of friends.

"Not at all! Anytime. The artwork was going to the family. He should have respected that!"

"Yeah." She looked at the ground. "Only it didn't."

"Sorry?"

"The Elizabeth Peyton he wanted. Blair told Helen how much she admired it, so Helen told her to take it. You know, Helen just doesn't want to deal with any of it. She'll say yes to anything right now. I tried to convince her to wait on some of these bigger items, but she won't listen."

I shut my eyes. I don't know why I was surprised by anything anymore. Of course, Blair was as bad, if not worse, than the others. She had stolen that artwork right out from under Keith—no shame—and taken it for herself. "I didn't know that." I tried not to care. Let them tug-of-war over the stuff. It wouldn't bring Stewart back, I told myself. But a wave of anger had taken hold; I looked down at my hands and realized I was shaking.

"So I just wanted to say thank you." Madison looked up at me from underneath her bangs. "For not being—well, you know. Thank you for not making things harder."

"Of course. I really didn't do anything." I meant it. As she walked away, I tried to take a deep breath, let go, and just focus on the exhibition.

I figured I'd tackle that adjoining room last—after I made my way through childhood. Maybe I'd be ready for some *Manic Mondays*, after all.

Toward the end (or the beginning, depending on how you looked at the show), the walls were hung with adorable pictures of Kate and Stewart framed in black, looking goofy and young, limbs tangled around each other on Halloween. I was searching for that photo of me and Stewart post–*Robin Hood*, when I felt a tap on my shoulder. I turned around.

"I heard you don't have a speaker yet." Fucking Keith.

"Nope." *Dirt bag.* I would have loved to confront him about the article, but Fernanda was standing nearby and I didn't want her to think I was a problem. Instead, I ignored him, turning immediately back to the wall, scanning it for the photo.

"It's short notice, but I'll do it, if you need me."

When hell froze over. "Oh, I wouldn't want to put you out."

"It's fine. I can make the time."

I tore my eyes off the wall and looked at him. "Thanks for the offer. I'll keep it in mind. But I think you've already said your piece." *Dick.*

He looked surprised. I guess he'd expected me to say yes.

"But—"

I was about to turn back to the wall, when I heard something like a mumble off to my left. Keith and I both swiveled to find Brian and Mallory standing beside us like a two-headed monster. They were a foot too close. Brian was apparently saying something.

"What did he say?" Keith demanded.

"SPEAK UP, HONEY! HE SAID HE WOULD LIKE TO BE THE ONE TO SPEAK AT THE TRIBUTE."

Keith and I exchanged a confused look. For once, we were in agreement. I wanted to take Mallory and Brian's heads and slam them together.

"Do you think that's a good idea?"

"YES. WHY NOT, KEITH?"

"I don't really think public speaking is Brian's thing."

"HE'S ACTUALLY A BEAUTIFUL PUBLIC SPEAKER. YOU DON'T KNOW BECAUSE YOU DON'T EVER LISTEN TO ANYONE ELSE."

"Hey, don't attack me!"

They started to argue. I decided to tune them out as best I could. I was hanging on by a thread. I turned back to the wall, scanning again for the picture of me and my dead friend. I couldn't find it anywhere. I sighed. What choice did I have?

Blair was standing by the entry with a clipboard, who knows why. Maybe she thought it made her look important. I could see Stewart's ring glistening on her finger like a shiny *fuck you.* Her blond hair was militantly beach waved and shellacked, too uniform to evoke anything windblown. She was missing the point, as usual.

I walked up to her. "Hey."

"Sorry about before. I'm just stressed with organizing everything by myself."

I couldn't care less. No one asked her to take over. "Right. I just wanted to let you know that there's a photo missing. Maybe Fernanda and her people missed it?"

Blair crinkled her nose. "Which photo?"

"The one of me and Stewart—you know, after that school play? You took it that day when we first organized everything to put it in the exhibition pile?"

"Oh, that." She waved it—and me—away with her hand and looked back down at her clipboard, moving onto the next thing. "I never gave it to them."

"Wait, what? Excuse me?"

"Yeah. I felt like it wasn't that good a picture. It's probably in a stack somewhere at Helen's now."

My mouth dropped open in outrage, my face pulsing with white hot anger. "Are you fucking kidding me?"

She looked up at that. "Sorry?"

I knew my voice was raised; I was making a scene, but I didn't care anymore. "What gives you the right to make that call? That was important to me! It's a part of Stewart's history. You can't just erase it because it didn't have the right lighting! Or, more importantly, because *you* weren't in it. Let's be honest."

"Wren, control yourself. It's not personal. The photo just wasn't right."

"It's not personal? It's not fucking personal? What could be more personal than this? Stewart is dead! This is his tribute. You knew how much I wanted that picture. You kept it from the curatorial team and then didn't even bother to hold it for me! God forbid you acknowledge someone else's relationship with him!"

Blair rolled her eyes and pretended to be annoyed, but I could tell she was freaked by the way she kept blinking her stupid beady eyes. She wasn't used to being confronted. "Wren, it's not my job to—"

"No. You're right. It's not your job. None of this was your job! You swept in and took over, showing up where and when you were never supposed to be and acting as if you were doing us all some huge fucking favor. But really you just needed to feel significant. Well, guess what, Blair? Stomping around, ordering people to do things and disseminating Stewart's things like you have some special ownership doesn't change the fact that your relationship with him was surface. You know it, and I know it. We all know it. He tolerated you because you served a purpose."

Her eyes flooded—crocodile tears. "I was his best friend. I loved him."

"Please. Don't you dare play the victim. I'm sick of it."

"Wren, stop it!"

"You stop it, Blair! Are you proud of yourself? You've turned grieving for Stewart into a competitive sport! You've cheapened it and him!" I whipped around to face the vultures. "All of you disgust me! You should be ashamed of yourselves."

They looked at me like I was from another planet. Like I was the problem. Willow exhaled air from her mouth in what I could only imagine was an attempt to deflect my negative energy. I shook my head. I turned. And I left.

As I rushed outside, I passed Jimmy in the doorway. By the look on his face—half pride, half fear—he had seen the whole thing. He opened his mouth to say something, reaching out a hand to stop me, but I wasn't pausing for anything. He hadn't been around this whole time; he hadn't given us the space to remember Stewart together. He hadn't been there for me. It was too late to talk now.

CHAPTER 41

Stewart. Soooo, I might have freaked out a little.

Remember when Matthew Simonsson kissed Kim Yu and I found out and confronted them both in the lunchroom in front of our whole grade? Remember my reaction then?

This was worse.

CHAPTER 42

Outside, a fierce wind had started blowing. That can happen in New York City. One minute it's calm and the next it's a gale. I remember once being blown into the side of a parked van as a kid, trying to walk home from school. Now, napkins flew off a nearby hot dog cart. A woman crossing the street lost her red scarf and ran to rescue it from the gutter, where old Starbucks cups and cigarette butts danced as if choreographed by Balanchine. (Hit and run, "Vincent" by Don McLean, dim sum—'cause that's good finger food!)

I hurried down the street and out of view in case anyone came to look for me. I doubted they would. Willow was the best bet and even she had been staring at me with the kind of pity reserved for lunatics on the train—sympathy at a safe distance. The wind pounded my face and blew my hair back, as I fought against it. It rushed past my ears, obscuring the city's other sounds: horns, conversations, transactions, birds. I was wearing my leather motorcycle jacket instead of my warm Uniqlo puffer because I thought I was seeing George and wanted to look cute. I chided myself for making myself uncomfortable for some guy, as I crouched low and stuffed my hands in my pockets, throwing a shoulder to cut through the gusts.

Once around the corner, I stopped and backed my body up against a bodega storefront. You learn that trick as a kid growing up here. On the way to school, you wait for the light ten feet back against a building because they block the wind, especially off the Hudson on the Upper West

Side. Which, I suddenly remembered, was where I needed to be shortly to meet Belle Rose. First, I needed to catch my breath.

I found calm beyond the wind's reach. People milled past me holding briefcases and afternoon coffee cups; a man across the street wore a sandwich board advertising hoagies. I felt bad for him. That was a crappy job on a day like today. (Hypothermia, "Really Gonna Miss You" by Smoky Robinson, HOAGIES FOR ALL!)

What a mess! The hoagies, yes. But also my life. Had Blair deserved that level of ire or was I reactive coming off the screw-up with my job, Keith's interview and the eBay listings by Mallory and Brian? No doubt I was on edge, but the way she commanded ownership over this experience—like a child snatching the biggest piece of birthday cake only to lord it over the others as a symbol of her dominance—made everyone else's behavior worse. Keith was awful, but maybe he wouldn't have overcompensated as much if he hadn't been trying to impress her; she was leading him on. Mallory and Brian were inappropriate and opportunistic, but maybe they wouldn't have grabbed so much stuff if they hadn't felt it being pulled out from under them—like they had to make a mad dash for their share. If only they had felt like someone was truly looking out for their best interests, like someone cared about *their* history with Stewart and what he meant to them. Willow definitely would have been more mellow about her ceremonies and her fascistic positivity if she'd been permitted to enact them as she'd planned, without countless warnings and "suggestions." Jimmy had bailed on this whole experience. Maybe he wouldn't have felt such a strong desire to flee if Blair hadn't come at this grieving process like it was something to win, shoving us all out of the way. She had positioned herself as the gatekeeper to Stewart's memory. Now, everyone felt one step removed like they had to prove their significance in order to earn their sadness. We all just wanted permission to remember our version of him. We all just wanted to be seen. Blair wasn't allowing that to happen. Why did one person's mourning have to devalue another's?

Right or wrong, the inside of my head was chaos, a kind of existential aneurysm. I needed to talk to someone. And not the drunk, homeless man tripping toward me down the street, yelling at lampposts. (Cirrhosis, "My Way" by Elvis Presley, the city's finest soup kitchen.) I ducked inside the bodega to avoid a run-in with him.

The door's bell jingled as it swung back into place. The shop was warm, smelling of bacon and damp produce. A few tables were scattered in the back, glossy with grease. I walked toward the rear to draw less attention. Safely tucked by the salad bar, I stared at my phone and tried to figure out who I could call to help me screw my head back on straight.

Before I could decide, my phone rang. I was startled. I looked around like I was being watched.

Gretchen's name flashed on the screen like digital salvation. Maybe she and I had best friend ESP?

"G?" I heard my voice crack.

"Oh, thank God. I was afraid I wouldn't get you! Are you okay?"

"I've had better weeks."

"Ugh. I'm so sorry."

I picked an Honest Tea up off the shelf and pretended to examine the ingredients, buying time in the bodega. It would be too cold and windy outside to hear, even if the belligerent derelict had passed.

"I'm so glad you called," I wheezed. "I've been missing you so much lately and I'm all kinds of screwed up. I can't even think straight. So much has happened."

Gretchen laughed. I could picture her tossing her black curls back. "Well, it must have to make you lose it on Blair that way! Tell me exactly what you said! That witch had it coming."

I ran a hand through my hair—or tried to. The wind had tied it in knots. I was about to give Gretchen the play-by-play when I realized that something was awry.

"Wait. How do you know I lost it on Blair?"

There was a pause. It stretched for a good thirty seconds. I waited it out. Finally, she said, "That's kind of hard to explain."

"Gretchen. Did Jimmy tell you?"

"He might have," she mumbled.

Why hadn't I seen it before? It was so obvious! The way they'd both disappeared on me; the way she'd asked if Jimmy was definitely coming before every Stewart-related event.

"What the hell? Why didn't you guys tell me?"

"We thought it might make you feel alienated because of the timing. With Stu gone, we figured you might feel left out if you discovered that the two people you needed most were dating."

I almost threw the Honest Tea across the store in frustration. "So you both decided to abandon me entirely instead?"

"Wren, I'm so sorry. It was stupid." I could hear her futzing with something—maybe tapping a pen on her desk. "It seemed like a good idea at first, but then I realized I couldn't be anywhere with both of you because it would require lying to you."

"You did lie to me."

"Yes, but it was a lie of omission. I don't care what that romantic lit professor we had in college said: that's not as bad as straight out lying."

"If you say so."

Suddenly, I felt done with the conversation. The last thing I needed on top of everything else was to waste my time assuaging Gretchen's guilt. She was supposed to be my best friend. I needed her. Because my other best friend was dead. Plus, I needed to get uptown to meet Belle.

"Look, I have to go." I walked to the register. I had handled the Pomegranate Blue iced tea for long enough that it had become mine whether I wanted it or not. Kind of like the People's Choice Award.

"Are you so pissed at me?"

I tucked the phone between my ear and shoulder as I pulled my debit card from my wallet.

The man behind the counter (mugging, "Just a Dream" by Nelly, Mansaf lamb and rice) pointed to a handwritten sign that proclaimed a ten dollar minimum. Of course, I had no cash. I could either buy eight dollars' worth of artisanal chocolate or use the shady ATM machine in the corner. I didn't have it in me.

I grabbed a dark chocolate bar stuffed with salted cashew butter off a counter display and held it up. He nodded; that got me to the threshold. It was preposterous, but I couldn't have cared less in that moment. *Fine.*

"Wren?"

"I'm here. Yes, Gretchen, I'm a little mad. Because you lied to me and went AWOL."

"I know. I'm so sorry. Seriously. I suck. I love you."

I rolled my eyes—at no one. "I assume this has been going on since the funeral?"

"Um . . ."

"Don't even think about lying!"

"Okay, yeah. We hooked up and then, I don't know. Instead of going home and never speaking again, we just . . . it's hard to explain."

"Not really." I rubbed my eye with my sleeve, exhausted. "You like him. You've always liked him."

"Except when I hated him."

"Especially when you hated him." I didn't feel like talking through the ins and outs of Jimmy and Gretchen's whirlwind romance at the moment. "Look, I have to go."

"Okay. But you said you needed to talk. Do you want to call me back later?"

I shrugged. "Maybe tomorrow. I don't know." I hung up. She was halfway through saying goodbye. I wasn't even sure if I was angry or disappointed. I just felt alone.

I thought about calling George, but this seemed like a lot to pile on him. Maybe if nothing had happened between us, it would have felt okay to lean on him. But it seemed very heavy—and boyfriendy—in light of our recent nakedness. I was worried he'd experience it as pressure. Instead, I went back outside and called a Lyft.

My driver, Craig, arrived four minutes later. The interior of his green Hyundai Sonata was draped with a cloth covering, ostensibly to protect the car's upholstery. It seemed superfluous since the car was gross. He wore sunglasses, though it wasn't sunny, and the air smelled vaguely of pot. (Mysterious disappearance, "I'll Be Missing You" by Notorious B.I.G., Wendy's.) I buckled my seatbelt.

"Wren?"

"Yup."

"Cool." He pulled away from the curb, as I stuffed a whole row of chocolate into my mouth.

"How's your day?"

"Fantastic," I mumbled, cheeks full. "How's yours?"

I wasn't sure if he answered. I stared out the window as Midtown became Central Park South and then the Upper West Side. Big, nondescript buildings morphed into the landscape of my youth. It was so much. It hurt my heart.

CHAPTER 43

Stewart. Can this be over now, please? I want to be done. When are you coming back to life?

CHAPTER 44

I stood outside of City Diner, trying to get in the right headspace. I couldn't meet this girl, who also seemed unhinged, until I got ahold of myself. In the window's reflection, my eyes looked crazy even to me. I took three deep breaths. I would find another job, I could avoid Blair forever after tomorrow, I would give Gretchen and Jimmy the silent treatment, wrap my mind around them as a couple and eventually officiate their wedding. But not right now. None of that could come to fruition at the moment, so I needed to accept my current circumstances and deal with the issue at hand: Belle Rose.

Sit with the discomfort. Pain is inevitable. Suffering is a choice.

I wanted to tell Stewart to shut up, but he was in my own head.

I peered through the window. I could see Belle sitting at a red booth, light brown hair hanging in her face, oversized army jacket dwarfing her small frame. I thought about texting her and canceling, but I'd come all this way and convinced her to meet me. I had a feeling if I bailed, she wouldn't come again.

So I swept a fingertip under each eye to triage my smeared eyeliner. Then I exhaled, grabbed the metal door handle, and went inside. The air was chilly like the air-conditioning was on instead of the heat, despite the dropping temperatures outdoors. I felt grateful for my scarf, which I tucked closer around my face. Stalling, I stopped at their ATM to take out cash. I figured it would be good to have some, so I didn't end up in another card-limit situation. Then I crossed to the table. "Hi," I said. "I'm Wren."

Belle looked up, taking me in. Her expression didn't change. "Hey."

I was surprised by two things: first, the cavernous dark circles around her eyes; second, how young she was. She couldn't have been more than twenty-five. (Overdose, "Heaven Knows I'm Miserable Now" by the Smiths, coffee.)

I slid into the booth across from her. The leather was sticky and held together by silver duct tape. She was already sipping from one of those heavy mugs, a nondairy creamer tub and empty sugar packets littering the table in front of her. The way she was slumped over reminded me of an overflowing laundry bag. I hadn't done laundry in ages.

A waitress appeared on cue. Her hair was pulled back in a bun, a pencil sat behind her ear. She was not a day under sixty. (Emphysema, Barbara Streisand's "Memory," blintzes.) They don't employ out-of-work actors at legit New York diners, only career waiters. Old school. She barely glanced at me. "What can I get you?"

"Um. I think maybe just tea to start?" We both knew I wasn't ordering anything else.

"We've got English Breakfast, Earl Grey, and Chamomile."

"English Breakfast is great. Thanks."

"Should I leave a menu?" Her hand hovered over both, ready to take them away.

"Are you hungry?" I asked Belle. She shook her head. It seemed to require effort. "I think we're good."

The waitress grunted and left.

"So thanks for meeting me," I said. "It's crazy windy out."

Belle rubbed her eyes with her fists like a child and yawned. "No problem. It's good for me to get outside, I guess."

"Yeah. It sounds from your posts like maybe you've been having a tough time?"

She nodded. Then her eyes welled up. I felt pretty bad for her and like a terrible person for laughing at her Facebook messages to Stewart.

"It's so hard. I get it." I sat back in my booth. "So I don't know if Stewart ever really mentioned me, but our mothers became friends when they were pregnant. We were next door neighbors as small kids and they sent us to school together."

She nodded. "Yeah. I remember he mentioned you. He said you had a cat named Ryan Seacrest or Jeff Probst or something?"

Jesus Christ. For how long had Stewart been dining out on my pathetic cat lady life? "Close enough. How did you guys know each other?"

She wiped her eyes with a stained napkin. "We met in this group. They called it Temple."

"Like a synagogue? You're Jewish?"

"Yeah, actually. Rose is really Rosenberg. But this wasn't synagogue. Calling it 'Temple' was just a joke. It was named after Shirley Temple, I guess? I don't even know why. Maybe because she worked in the industry for so long and she got out?"

"It was a Hollywood group?"

"Kind of. It's hard to explain. It was like a support group for people who were too famous to go to support groups 'cause they'd be, like, recognized."

"A celebrity support group," I nodded. "Okay. To help them navigate the film business? Like for networking?"

"No. It was for people to be able to, like, talk about the difficulties in their lives."

The waitress returned with my hot water. A wedge of lemon and a bright-yellow Lipton teabag perched on the saucer. I waited until she was gone to continue. "So a place for celebrities to come and talk to each other about their struggles with fame?"

She nodded. "Basically. Except it wasn't just about being, like, famous. Some of them had addiction problems and stuff like that."

I hesitated, holding my breath. "Stewart?"

"No, no. Of course not. Stu was so structured and hardcore. He barely even let himself eat In-N-Out, except on special occasions. He kept the rest of us in line." She half-smiled, then resumed frowning. Her eyes flooded again.

It was true. Stewart was regimented: shirts ironed, diet strict, outlook positive. That was the directive. I wasn't sure how far I could push this, but I figured I had nothing to lose. I dunked my tea bag in the water. "Belle, I hope you don't mind me asking: Why were you there?"

She wagged her head back and forth, then seemed to land on the answer. I didn't think she was capable of lying—or even that she cared who knew. "I was having some drinking problems. Like overdoing it. Blacking out sometimes."

"And you're a . . . you were on TV or in movies?"

"No, no. I can't act. Or sing. I was just hardcore in the party and club scene for a while. I kind of, I don't know, people, like, just started to know me. I got an Insta following. Tabloids started to follow me; I dated a couple of musicians. I started a hat line. Whatever."

Ah. Famous for nothing. An influencer.

She seemed so tired. When did she do all that? When she was fourteen? I'd be tired too. "Anyway, the group still exists. I'm not really supposed to talk about it. But it was started by this director who I got to know and, when he saw me out one night and I was, like, shit-faced, he told me to call him if I ever got sober. So I did. And that's where I met Stu."

What a weird world: one in which fame entitles you to a VIP AA meeting. I bet there were people out there faking issues to gain access at this very moment.

"And you guys hit it off?"

"Yeah. I mean, at first I thought he was kind of a dick. He kept making snarky comments and stuff. But he was hilarious and then I realized what a sweet guy he was at heart." She came to life while talking about Stewart; her face brightened. "He was nothing like that character he played on TV—that guy was so obsessed with himself. Stu was the opposite. He made you feel like all your choices were okay, even the bad ones, as long as you did what you could to fight your demons." She dipped her spoon into her coffee cup and swirled it even though there was barely anything left. The metal spoon clinked against the sides like a wind chime.

I thought about what she said. She wasn't describing the Stewart I knew, or I should say, that wasn't who Stewart was for me. But I could see now how maybe he could have been someone different for someone different. I thought about what Willow said: maybe someone with whom he didn't "exchange judgment." Maybe someone with whom he had a pact—literally within a support group—of listening without criticism.

"Were you guys, like, together? Romantically?" I sounded so old.

Belle shook her head. "No, it wasn't like that. I mean, I don't know. Maybe I would have been open to that once we both felt better. Any girl would have been lucky."

Once we both felt better. So Stewart hadn't felt well. It was true. Everything that Willow suggested; everything that Morgan said; everything that this broken young woman was telling me now. He had struggled and he didn't feel he could tell me. I had thought I was his closest friend. What was our relationship really? Had I destroyed it that night when I refused to hear him out? Should I have listened no matter what he or I really felt? Did I turn things forever strained between us?

I think I love you.

You don't.

Or had I destroyed us long before that—as soon as I began to think of him in this one limited sellout way? When I refused to see the part of him that might have helped someone like this girl, just because?

"And Stewart was there because—?"

"Because he felt sad sometimes. He had, like, 'dark days.' That's what he called them. He said it was because he felt dark and everything went dark—meaning he couldn't do anything."

"Were there other people like that in the group?"

She considered the question. "Kind of. I mean, everyone had demons, for sure. But, like I said, a lot of people had addiction or something specific. A couple of women had gotten into drugs after being sexually assaulted. That came up a lot during the whole #MeToo thing. A few of the men were addicted to steroids. You know, like, for action movies. Pain killers. That kind of thing. But you could talk about anything that was upsetting you or that you were struggling with. I mean, like, you still can, but I haven't been since Stu—" Suddenly, tears gushed from her eyes. She started sobbing. I wasn't sure what to do.

I put my hand on her forearm, which rested on the table, and said, "It's okay, Belle. It's going to be okay." Was it though? I had already been vibrating from head to toe when I walked in. Now, with every passing second, a knowledge that I now realized I'd possessed ever since Stewart died was cementing in my head—becoming conscious. My relief about the aneurysm, my search for answers, the death in New York and not LA. The fact that he didn't call. I knew it like I knew my own name.

I didn't want to bail on this girl as she wept under a diner's fluorescent lights, but I needed to leave. I needed to act. I felt like if I didn't stand up, I would take off like a rocket into outer space.

"Belle, are you going to be okay?" I handed her my napkin. She was starting to calm down. She shrugged. *Not really.* "Do you have someone? Professional? To talk to?"

She nodded and wiped her nose with the sleeve of her jacket. "That's why I came back to New York. To stay with my parents and see my old therapist. She knows me."

Old therapist? Like she'd been around for a while? As far as I could tell, she was doing a bang-up job. Well, it was better than nothing. "Okay. I'm glad you're talking to someone. Do you know about the tribute tomorrow night?"

"I'll be there," she nodded. "Stu's mom emailed me the details."

Of course she did. Because Helen knew her. Helen knew everything. It was all I could do not to jump out of my skin. "Okay, Belle, I have to go. I'm so sorry to run out on you when you're feeling so sad."

She looked up at me, impassive. "I'm always sad."

"I'm really, truly sorry to hear that."

I took money out of my wallet—I don't know how much—and left it on the table. I didn't have it in me to deal with taking our ticket to the register. Minutes before, my scarf had been a comfort against the cold, but now it felt like it was strangling me, along with the stench of burgers and Greek salads. I needed answers. All of them. Now.

I left. Outside, the wind was still whipping. It was bitter cold. I hailed a cab. I wasn't messing with any trains right now. I gave the driver the address—at least I must have, though I barely remembered it later. I was vaguely aware of repeating, "Oh my God," over and over again. It was like finding out about Stewart's death for the first time—again.

I texted George:

Hey. It's a long story, but I just had coffee with this girl Belle who was a friend of Stewart's from this support group in LA. It's too intense to explain over text, but I finally realized what I've been searching to find out this whole time. I'm going to the Beasleys' to talk to Helen.

He didn't respond until my taxi was pulling up to the near corner on Central Park West.

Wren, wait. What do you mean? Did you call Helen? Don't go there. Call me first. Let's talk. We'll go together.

No, I'm already here. I'm going up.

Wren, seriously. Wait for me. Are you okay? I'm leaving now. I'm getting into a cab. I'll be there in twenty minutes.

I can't wait. I'll call you afterward.

I stepped out of the taxi; the wind almost knocked me over. The light outside was dimming. The trees in the park looked ominous instead of scenic, like something out of *The Wizard of Oz*.

The doorman was that same guy, Bill, but he didn't look askance at me this time. Maybe he recognized my face.

That made one of us: When I looked at my reflection in the mirror, someone pale and drawn peered back at me. My hair was a rat's nest and my scarf was falling half off. My appearance was the embodiment of my inner life. I yanked at one end of my scarf, pulling it off entirely and bunching it in my hands. For once, I didn't care what Helen thought.

"I'm here to see the Beasleys."

"Name please?"

"Wren."

He picked up the phone in his white gloved hand and punched in some numbers. He waited for what felt like an eternity to me—like a hungry kid on Yom Kippur—and then finally, he said, "Good evening. I have Wren here to see you." He nodded, then hung up. "Fourth floor."

My need for the truth had eclipsed my nerves. When the elevator doors opened upstairs, I walked into the apartment without a shred of doubt.

"Hello, Wren." I whipped around. Helen was standing at the entrance to the living room, her white hair in its coiffed bob, large diamond studs sparkling in her ears. "I startled you."

"No, I was just expecting Madison."

"Ah. No, she left early today. She's been working long hours and I'll need her tomorrow night at the tribute. I figured she could use a bit of—whatever they call it—'me time.' Ted is here. He's just lying down in the bedroom."

I nodded. "I'm sorry to barge in."

"It's all right. I guess you could say I've been expecting you." She gestured toward the stark living room furniture. "Shall we?"

She sat in a calfskin Le Corbusier chair across from me, as I settled onto the angular couch—no give beneath me. An orchid stood between us on the low coffee table, fragile and haughty.

"So what can I do for you?"

I cleared my throat. I hadn't figured out exactly how to phrase this. "I just had coffee with Belle Rose."

"I see. She's a bit of a mess that girl, but Stewart was fond of her. She's sweet, I suppose, and he loved an injured bird."

"The thing is, since Stewart . . . since he's been gone, I've been on this search. I thought it was about resolving our relationship in my head; I thought that I needed proof that we'd been as close as I believed. There are so many people walking around feeling as if they can't live without him. I thought I needed confirmation that our friendship was real."

Helen regarded me with those sharp blue eyes. "Of course it was, dear. He adored you." I could feel the *Who knows why?* hanging in the air. But she surprised me and added, "You were a very dear friend to him, Wren."

"Thank you. I loved him."

"I know you did."

I had to get this out. I had to ask the question, get the real answer, and there was no use in stalling. I looked at the rug, but I soldiered on. "The thing is, it turns out that I wasn't only searching for proof of our closeness. I also had this feeling, however unconsciously, that I was missing some part of the story—Stewart's story." I raised my head and looked her in the eye. I felt I owed us both that directness. "And I was, wasn't I? Missing something?"

After a pause, Helen nodded. I knew it was the truth, but the confirmation winded me yet again. I closed my eyes to collect myself. And I waited.

Finally, she brushed an imaginary hair from her forehead. "Belle doesn't know, by the way. She knows about the depression. But she doesn't know how it ended. None of Stewart's friends know. So I would ask for your discretion."

"Of course." I took a deep breath and readied myself. I thought about all the times I imagined Helen getting the call, finding out that her son was gone. All those scenarios were wrong. It had been much worse than I could have imagined.

"Stewart battled depression his whole life. Surely you realize now that you saw signs of it—from childhood, when we had to pull him out of school, to later in life. I'm not sure how much he shared with you. My instinct from the beginning was to hide it from the world. I didn't want him to suffer for other peoples' perceptions or stigmas. Maybe that was a mistake. Kate certainly thinks so."

Right. *Kate.* This explained why she wouldn't interact with her mother—the details of which she said I deserved to know—why she wouldn't deliver a eulogy at the tribute. How could she speak when she couldn't tell the truth? Poor Kate. Poor everyone. I felt horrible for having judged her.

"Anyway, Stewart had been having a particularly hard time lately. He had had many very good years, but it started getting difficult again in the last two, especially in the past couple of months. The network very quietly agreed to postpone their shoot schedule while he got himself together. It's Hollywood. Probably everybody assumed he was addicted to pills or cocaine." She rolled her eyes.

"Nothing seemed to be working. In the past, he had tried different combinations of medications, different outpatient programs. Something always made him feel better eventually. But, this time, he couldn't climb out of the funk. And, you know Stewart, it felt like failing to him."

I did know Stewart. I could only imagine his frustration and anger.

Helen crossed and recrossed her ankles. We were getting to the most difficult part. I was afraid to breathe. "I didn't know he was in New York to be honest. If I had, I would have made him stay here at the apartment with me. I had already bought a ticket out to LA for the next day; I could tell things were dire. But I guess he flew into the city. He had saved up enough pills over the last months. And, that evening, he took a cab home to that apartment on Crosby and he lay down in the den and—he took them. All."

She looked me dead in the face. Like I was the facts. Like she could not look away. Those blue eyes welled. She was silent. I felt like a thousand pounds rested on my chest. Who knew devastation weighed so much? I thought it might crush me. How would I ever get up off that couch? How was Helen living and breathing?

"That was it. His neighbor came in the next morning and found him. The rest you know."

"I'm sorry," I managed. And I was—for her, for Kate, for me, most of all, for Stewart. I felt like my heart was cracking in two. So much pain, so senseless. "He never told me."

"I'm surprised actually. I thought he told you everything. But I'm sure that's my fault: I trained him to keep it to himself. A WASP to the end, I suppose. The thing is, it always worked for Ted."

"Ted?"

"Oh, yes. Stewart's father struggles with the same issues. You might have noticed that he sometimes makes himself scarce? He requires a lot of space. To manage the situation."

All these years, I thought that Ted Beasley was just a workaholic without much interest in his kids. And perhaps that was true—but with many more layers. People are complicated. And I'd made a lot of assumptions.

Poor Stewart. Poor sad Stewart. If only I had known.

"There was nothing anyone could have done," Helen said, reading my mind. "Of course, I've gone over it a million times in my head and will a million more. Stewart had tried everything. He was a grown man—although he will always be that little boy to me. He had considered this . . . resolution . . . for a long time. As you know, he even got some of his papers in order. Of course, he didn't say it was imminent because George would have been alarmed and tried to stop him, but he made sure he was prepared. You can imagine how shocked George felt when I called to tell him what had happened. He felt responsible."

When I called to tell him what had happened. My mouth dropped open. "Sorry. George knows? The truth?"

"Well, yes. Stewart had left me a letter with certain instructions, the first of which was to call George. I had to tell him the truth. He couldn't manage the estate issues and help deal with the insurance company without knowing what really happened."

George knew the truth. George knew and he didn't tell me. He let me run around like an idiot playing Nancy Drew. He let me obsess over aneurysms and brain implosions. All this time, I thought we were a team—

Not them, Wren. They didn't steal him. It was his own body. His own brain.

George lied.

At that moment, as if by clockwork, the elevator door opened and in walked the man himself. Of course, the doorman loved him and would never make him call up. He was frazzled, having run up here to stop me. He hadn't wanted me to find out this way. His hair was sticking up; his jacket hung open. Was he hoping to stop me from learning the truth? Or had he wanted to tell me himself before I found out? Too little too late, regardless.

I watched his eyes dart around the entryway, then land on us in the living room. He made eye contact with me, watched my mouth tighten. Then he parted his lips to explain, but what could he say? Especially with Helen sitting there?

"Sorry to interrupt. I came . . . I just thought, maybe I could . . . help."

I stood. "I was just leaving. I've taken up enough of Helen's time." I turned to her, a new understanding between us. "Thank you. For being candid."

She nodded. I couldn't blame her for protecting her son. I thought she'd made a giant mistake, encouraging him to keep his pain a secret. But she did her best. That's all any of us can do. George, on the other hand—I could blame him.

"Okay," he said. "I'll go too."

"That's okay," I said. "I'd like to be alone."

I crossed to the elevator and pushed the button. He was standing a couple feet away; it might as well have been miles for the detachment I felt. He lowered his voice, "Let me talk to you."

I shook my head.

Helen said, "George. It's actually good fortune that you're here. I've just received some paperwork that I don't understand. I could use your expertise."

He looked from me to her.

"Of course," he said, still staring at me with pleading eyes. "I can help you with that, Helen. I'll just wait for the elevator with Wren, to see her out, and be right in."

Helen nodded and started back toward her office, with a wave.

"Wren. Are you okay?"

I refused to look at him. "Never better."

He took a step toward me, so he was only a foot away. "Look, I can explain—"

I snapped my head up and glared at him, "You can explain what, George? That you knew that Stewart killed himself? And lied to my face?"

He closed his eyes and exhaled. "Look, of course you're deeply upset. I understand that you're angry—"

"Well, congratulations! You get a hundred percent on the emotional IQ test. And a failing grade at everything else." My head was throbbing. Now that I knew that Stewart hadn't had an aneurysm, it occurred to me that I was free to have one—the odds had gone up.

"Wren, I did the best I could. You have to believe that! Helen asked me to keep the details private."

"Private from me? Even after everything?"

He looked at the ground. "I know, I know. It's so complicated. But, please believe me: one thing had nothing to do with the other!"

The rage that rose in me in that moment was its own entity. If we were anywhere else, I'm sure I would have shouted in his face—or maybe transformed into a wild beast and ripped him limb from limb, but I couldn't do that here. Instead, I took a step toward him and said quietly, "How fucking dare you. You don't get to decide what's connected to what. That night, you told me that his brain stole him. You said it was a 'mechanical malfunction'! 'Bad luck'!"

"It was, Wren! I stand by that. Maybe it wasn't an aneurysm, but it was dumb, bad luck. It was a stupid chemical anomaly in the way he was built. The depression was as much a twist of fate as anything else! Just as out of his control!"

"That's bullshit," I growled. "The fact remains: You knew that my best friend committed suicide and you didn't tell me. You let me go on and on about the pills he was prescribed and his bout with mono and the whole time, you knew. You acted like we were in this together, but you let me be the idiot."

"Wren, I never thought you were an idiot. Well, maybe when you couldn't work the bathroom lights in my hotel room."

"Don't you fucking dare be clever right now."

"The truth is, on some level, I felt that you knew. You seemed to have all the facts. I felt like maybe you didn't see what was taking shape in front of you because you didn't want to know."

"You don't get to decide that! I knew I should never have trusted you. I don't know what I was thinking!"

The elevator *pinged* and opened. I stepped inside, dizzied by the overhead lights.

"Wren. Please understand. Let me talk to you. I want to make sure you're okay. This is a lot to absorb by yourself."

"I'm not okay, George." I crossed my arms over my chest, which was rising and falling at an alarming rate. "But it's not your problem."

As the doors began to close, he opened his mouth to speak, but nothing came out.

CHAPTER 45

CHAPTER 46

The ride home passed like it never happened. Ostensibly, people boarded the train, settled in across and beside me with newspapers and books, hovered above me scrolling through their emails and Instagram feeds, but I was unconscious of it all.

I was angry at myself, but, more than that, I was stunned by the human brain's capacity to pick and choose what it sees. However angry I was at George, he had a point about the reality that I'd refused to see.

I was so consumed with my own martyrdom—so invested in the narrative I was creating—that I'd missed an obvious trail of breadcrumbs: the ring Stewart had taken off and placed in his drawer, the secret trip to New York during which he hadn't reached out to a single soul. (It wasn't just me he'd avoided, but I'd been too busy with my own hurt feelings to notice.)

I thought about our last phone call, the tension in his voice, his concern about what would happen to me if he wasn't around. (Had he said "if" or had he said "when"?) He had gotten paperwork in order; he'd named me as a planner for the arrangements of his death. That's not something he would have done thinking fifty years down the line. He knew I wouldn't go first because he knew when he was going to die.

The messages might as well have been written in fluorescents. But, if you close your eyes against the light, you're still in the dark.

Or had I actually known? Some small part of me? I thought about the moment that Gretchen told me—I had felt relief. I had! For an instant, before the shock set in and I began to frame the news, close my hands around it and mold it to my specifications, I had felt relief! If I searched my soul, I had felt Stewart's unctuous unhappiness during our last conversation, had sensed nervously a depth of sadness that I could not plumb. I had sensed the black hole. Maybe that's why I hadn't wanted to tell anyone about it.

Once home, sitting on the couch in the dark in my apartment with my hands limp at my sides, unclear on how I'd gotten there, I recalled the last conversation Stewart and I had had in person.

He sat next to me in a cab. It was the end of the night and he'd offered to pay for a fancy Uber to take him home and then me all the way to Brooklyn. That's just what he was like. It wasn't showing off; it was just no big deal. He came from money, he earned a ton of money. Money wasn't a factor—even though, in some ways, it was the only factor.

The car was giant and black with silver gleaming from its edges. Maybe an Escalade. The interior was smooth leather and looked new, but it reeked of old socks. I remember wondering whether we were smelling the passengers before us and then feeling uncomfortable in my seat.

We were talking about something—someone famous had died. There was that rash of celebrity deaths and suicides around that time. So maybe that was it. We were discussing how sad it was for the children. It was a conversation I could have had with anyone. Surface. And then he said, "Sometimes I think it wouldn't matter that much if I died."

I was caught off guard. It was the first time I had seen him in a while. We were always close, of course, but it took us a minute to warm back up after a long absence. That's normal, I guess. I was still feeling clumsy, trying to claw back to our regular level of intimacy. All night, I'd felt I couldn't quite penetrate his shell. I kept reaching for the real Stewart and coming back with a well-behaved approximation. Now he was serving this doozy up. It was a lot at once.

So I said, "Stewart. What does that mean? Do I need to worry about you?"

It wasn't as heartfelt as it sounds. I thought he was fishing, like he wanted me to tell him how much I cared. And I wasn't in the mood. I thought he was being dramatic. Stewart was dramatic, after all.

There was a part of me that always resisted giving him what he wanted, maybe because I felt I was the only one who did.

He shrugged. His forehead had a sheen of sweat; it was hot for May. I noticed he was wearing glasses for the first time in years, so he had something concrete to push back up onto his face. He said, "I mean, my fans would care for a second—people who like the show and would be disappointed that 'Drake Glover' was lost to them."

"You literally have a fan club."

He grunted, forced a half smile. "Yeah. I guess I do."

"I think people would care more if you died than if most people did—sadly."

"Sadly?"

"No, I'm teasing. I just mean that people know who you are. You would be missed—by friends and strangers."

"But, I mean, I don't have kids or a partner. Everyone would be fine. Don't you think? If one day I disappeared?"

"Stewart. Please." I was impatient. "That's just silly." I rested my hand on the door handle; I guess I wanted out.

That's just silly.

I hadn't wanted to indulge his neediness. Too much pride. Too much awkwardness. Too much distance where I wanted to pretend there was none. I shut him down.

He tried to tell me.

That's just silly.

He changed the subject then.

I closed my eyes against the memory, like I could make myself invisible, make the truth vanish like he disappeared himself. My whole body ached. This was it: the real grief, the guilt, if I let it come. I was subsumed by an all-encompassing ache. It took over my insides like the vibration of heavy bass until I stopped being able to tell where the sensation ended and I began. Then the scales tipped; I became more pain than me.

Why didn't I reach over and squeeze his hand? Why didn't I give him what he was asking for? Did he want me to stop him or was he looking for permission to leave?

I would not be fine if you disappeared, Stewart. I need you. I love you. You are a part of me and losing you is losing me. Stewart, you are important. You are essential. You are the globe, Stewart. My globe. I care. I would not be fine.

CHAPTER 47

Dear Stewart, I am not fine.

CHAPTER 48

I called my mother. It was time. In my bones, I knew I'd reach her. Besides, I needed to talk to someone and there was no one else left.

It happened as I'd imagined it would. I guess I'd known that all along too: The phone rang, one and a half times.

"Hello? Wren? Is it really you? We were beginning to think you'd joined a cult. But then you've never really liked structure. Or people who don't bathe." She laughed.

"Hi, Mom."

"Wren, honey," she said, her tone more urgent. "Are you okay?"

I parted my lips to answer her, but found that I couldn't. My mouth felt dry.

"Wren? Are you okay?"

I opened my mouth two more times before I finally managed to make words come out. "Mom," I said, my voice cracking. "I'm really sad."

And that was it. The first tear escaped my eye like a dam breaking. Once they started coming, they wouldn't stop until I was struggling to catch my breath like a child thrown from a seesaw.

"It's okay, sweetie," my mother coaxed. "Oh, baby. Of course you're so sad. I wish I was there. I wish I could give you a hug. It's going to be okay. You're going to be okay."

When I finally calmed down enough to talk, between hiccups, I told her everything: about my job, the vultures, Gretchen, George (minus certain choice details) and, of course, the truth about Stewart.

A kind of moan escaped her lips when I revealed that part. "Oh, no. That poor boy. What a terrible, tragic waste. Poor Helen. God. I can't imagine."

"I know! And I just can't understand why he didn't confide in me. Other people knew about his 'dark days'! Why didn't he tell me? Why didn't he trust me? I think maybe he tried to and I blew him off."

"You said you knew he was depressed sometimes?"

"Yes. Sure! A little blue maybe. Not Sylvia Plath, Vincent Van Gogh, Elliott Smith despondent!"

"Sweetie, there's nothing you could have—"

"I know! I know! I'm not arrogant enough to think otherwise. But I'm surrounded by people who at least claim to be so confident in their relationships with him. I would have said that we were closer than any of them before, but now I'm doubting it all!"

"Oh, Wren." My mother sighed. I could practically hear her rotating her wedding ring while she thought, her perpetual habit. "Baby. It doesn't matter who was closest with him. Comparing your relationship isn't going to land you anywhere good. There is no winning in the race for Stewart's affection—because he's gone."

Stewart. Gone.

I started crying quietly again. Because I missed him, because I couldn't bring him back, because I finally felt his loss like it was real, because—in that moment—I realized I'd been complicit in turning his death into a competition.

"You can honor him by remembering the individuality of your relationship—what you meant to each other all this time. How he shaped you. That's all that matters. Not what anyone else had with him." I could picture my mother leaning over the kitchen counter—lined with my grandmother's antique Mason jars of sugar and flour—head resting on her right hand, eyes narrowed in concern. Then she said, "Did I ever tell you about when you and Stewart learned to climb stairs for the first time?"

"I don't think so." Catching my breath, I stood and walked over to Stewart's People's Choice Award, picking it up. It didn't seem grotesque, creepy, or funny to have it anymore. It just seemed like a meaningless hunk of glass. "We learned to walk up the stairs together?"

"Sort of. At around fifteen months, Stewart started charging the five or so steps in the lobby that led up to the mailboxes."

I could picture them instantly: they were white marble with a bronze railing. I had probably jogged up and down them a thousand times in my life.

"Well, he just started trying to run up them. No matter how Helen tried to dissuade him or hold him back, he was consumed with besting them. He tried every day for several weeks, always falling down and hurting himself. And you would just watch him. You never took a step in that direction."

"That sounds right." I put the award down, unsure of what to do next.

"Yes. But then one day, he just stopped. He gave up trying. That's when you started to try. See, you had been studying the whole time—only you had a different strategy. So you approached those steps, and you carefully took just one on that first day. The next day, you tried two, and so on. By the end of the week, you had the steps down. And he would stand at the bottom and watch you."

"Helen must have loved that." I stared out my back window onto other people's roof decks, decorated with plants and plastic lounge chairs.

"Well, yes. You can imagine. She insisted that he'd grown bored and that you were finally getting around to what he was already over. She always needed to believe that he excelled beyond every other child."

"He did eventually figure out how to walk up the stairs."

"Yes, I believe so. But you always had different ways of approaching the world. Stewart was trying to best something—go big or go home. You were just trying to make a place for yourself. I think that's part of why you valued each other so much. Seems to me like Stewart tried really hard to best this depression by living life as big as could be and, ultimately, didn't have it in him. It seems like you've been watching and waiting for long enough. Maybe it's time to attack some stairs. In his honor."

I dropped my face into my free hand and rubbed my eyes. "Mom, I don't know where to begin."

"Well, you can start by resolving this issue with Operation Sewage."

"By apologizing and begging Anton to let me keep my job?"

"What? No! Have you been listening at all?" She groaned. "You obviously feel ambivalent about the work. Apologize to Anton, offer to do whatever you can to fix things and then go find another career, honey. You're understimulated."

If I was honest, I had experienced a kind of relief even in the panic of realizing my gargantuan error—an untethered, terrifying relief. I said, "I thought you were happy that I picked something stable?"

"Sure. I'm your mother and I want you to have health insurance. But it's obvious that you're ready for the next thing. I think you need to live life a little bit less carefully. Also, really, Operation Sewage is the worst name."

I scrunched up my nose. "It really is." I felt myself smile, then we both started to laugh.

Deeming the situation diffused and safe, Chris Harrison sidled up beside me, purring and bumping his nose against my calf. I bent down and pet his soft fur.

"What about George? He lied to me."

"Well, there are lies—and then there are lies. Ideally, he would have confided in you. But that would have meant betraying Helen. What would you have had him do?"

I sighed. "I'm not sure."

"Either way, don't you think it's positive that you liked someone like him? Someone different? Who isn't developing a for-profit T-shirt app with a 0.001 percent, supposedly to benefit women in third world nations?"

I grunted noncommittally, flopping down on the hexagonal rug next to Chris Harrison. "And the rest? Gretchen? The vultures? Was I wrong?"

"Well, that's your call, baby. Maybe you need to think about what these relationships mean to you—and what's worth saving. Or forget them all, come move back in with us up here and find new friends. We miss you! *I* miss you! Your father refuses to watch *The Crown* with me."

When I hung up with my mother, I felt like a wrung-out rag, but also calmer and clearer than I had since losing my friend. I picked up Chris Harrison and plopped him onto my chest. Out of pity, he stayed. I stared at a crack running the length of my painted tin ceiling.

Whether I liked it or not, my life had changed. Stewart had died and taken the old me with him.

That's when I noticed it: my Operation Sewage canvas tote, slumped behind my white leather pouf. At first, I groaned at the reminder of my nonexistent career, but then I remembered what waited inside it. I sat up. Chris Harrison leapt off me and stalked away, our moment of peace interrupted. *Ingrate.*

I dragged the bag toward me, heavy with its contents, and dug inside, pulling out *Unearthing the Answer: Manifesting Your Authentic Self.* I stared at the celestial cover for a good long time before cracking it open. What I found inside stole my breath: There were notes all over the margins in Stewart's handwriting. As I flipped through the pages, I saw that he had marked up the whole book, underlining and highlighting. Words like *heal, joy, process,* and *journey* leapt out at me.

My heart broke. I hung my head. *Destroyed.*

Stewart hadn't bought this book as part of some silly trend; he was desperate for a solution. He was working to help himself and (now that I'd met Belle, I understood) other people in pain, as well. He had tried so hard. All this time, I thought he'd been deep into this superficial world. In fact, he was looking for distraction, for a life fantastic enough to keep him going, for eyes on him so he couldn't fade away.

As I finished leafing through the pages, my thumb rested on the edge of the back cover, so that its inside flap was visible. On cardboard arched from use, Stewart had written a list of things to do. His last line item was written in all caps: *GET BETTER.*

CHAPTER 49

Stewart, I looked up what happens in your brain when you're depressed.

Basically, when you're really stressed out or have a chemical imbalance, your brain produces too much cortisol—and that wreaks havoc. It slows the production of new neurons and shrinks existing ones. And it can shrink the prefrontal cortex, which is the part of your brain that regulates your emotions and helps you make decisions.

It's just like you to overproduce something—to go too big.

That's all to say that I forgive you for yelling at me in high school about Kurt Cobain and my desire for a stable career. (I know now that you were fighting against what he—and you—both eventually succumbed to.) And maybe it's not your fault that you picked that super ugly floral shirt for prom (about which I enjoyed torturing you for years) because your decision-making skills were impaired. Although, the research on depression doesn't say anything about bad taste.

I wish you had told me. Not because I could have helped, but because I could have tried. I could have let you off the hook more. I could have appreciated you.

Mostly, though, I want to say: I am impressed by you. You had all this going on and you still managed to be one of the best people in the entire world. What an exceptional person to be.

CHAPTER 50

I was standing in front of the bodega, around the corner from the Institute of Television Arts. That same sad sack was across the street wearing his hoagie sandwich board.

This time, I had at least tried to dress appropriately for Stewart's tribute, but no woman has ever been sufficiently warm in a dress and stockings. I shivered, arms crossed.

"You look freezing."

I turned to find George standing behind me in a suit with a black overcoat, dapper as hell. His hair was still damp from the shower. I felt a fluttering in my stomach and, despite my resolution, an urge to brush the rogue strands from his forehead. He bit his lip, awaiting my reply. Was he nervous?

Last night, after a heart-to-heart with cat Chris Harrison, I'd decided how I would play things with George: I'd be cordial and that's it. He lived three thousand miles away in LA. I understood now that the truth about Stewart has not been his to share. He barely knew me. Why should he have betrayed Helen, and his professional oath, to tell me anything?

But I took one look at George now and I knew that I was in deeper trouble than I'd let myself believe. It was embarrassing really. The intensity of my attachment was so disproportionate to our single week of knowing each other, however significant this particular chunk of time. This wasn't *The Bachelor*! This was real life. And yet, somehow, I'd lost the thread of where Stewart's loss ended and my affection for this new man began. What I was feeling had to be some kind of . . . what was the word that

Gretchen always used? *Transference.* That's what this was. Either that or George's eyes were that amazing.

"That's because I am," I finally managed, stuffing my hands in my pockets. "Freezing."

"Should we talk inside the deli?"

I gave him the side-eye. "This, my dear, is a bodega. No respectable New Yorker would call it a deli."

"Who said I was respectable? Or a New Yorker?"

He opened the door. I led him, out of habit now, to my spot by the beverages in the back. It was basically my new office. I did my best to make my expression impassive and looked up at him. "So what's up? You said you needed to talk about something Stewart-related."

"Yes. This meeting was not personally motivated." He bobbled his head from side to side. "Okay, maybe it was a little personally motivated."

"It's okay," I sighed. "I'm over it. I'm not that mad anymore."

"Well, good," he exhaled. "That's a giant relief. But I still want to apologize. Wren, I wanted to tell you so badly. It was torture to keep it to myself. I felt you deserved to know. Of course I did. But I had promised a grieving mother and we had attorney-client privilege and . . . basically, I convinced myself that, ultimately, how we lost Stu wasn't as important as just supporting each other because we did."

I weighed that in my head. "In some ways maybe that's true; in some ways, maybe not."

"Also, I didn't want to make you responsible for keeping that secret from the rest of the group." He rubbed at the back of his neck. "It's not a small stress, hiding the truth."

"I believe it." I thought about how anxious he'd looked when I met him outside of the Beasleys' that time. No wonder! I'd been so wrapped up in my own sense of injustice that I'd assumed his discomfort was about my tension with Helen. "Look, I wish you hadn't lied, but you were also in an impossible position and you don't owe me anything." I fiddled with the button on the cuff of my coat. "You have to understand, finding out the truth, especially that way, was like discovering that Stewart was gone all over again. It was shocking."

George looked at the ground, then back up at me. I could see tears in his eyes. He took my hand; his was much warmer than mine. Electricity shot up my arm like static shock. "Wren. I'm so sorry. Please know that. I hate that I made this worse for you. When I found out, I felt so responsible. I would hate for you to feel that way too."

Honestly, I would have forgiven George anything in that moment. I didn't want to be mad; I wanted to kiss him. But I wouldn't.

The man behind the counter was looking at us warily. I pulled George into the chip aisle and out of view, then turned to face him. "I do know that. I promise. And I know you probably feel extra pressure because of what happened between us the other night, but you don't owe me—"

"Wait, stop." He held up his hands as if for a double high-five. "Why do you keep saying I don't owe you anything? Tell me you're not about to apologize for the other night."

"Well, not apologize." I put a hand on my hip. "I mean, like, you're welcome, but—"

"Tell me you're not about to give me some prepared speech about how it was a mistake and I'm off the hook."

That's precisely what I was about to do. "Um. I just don't want you to feel pressure because you live in LA and I get that. I'm not—"

George dragged his hands down his face, then rested a palm on each of my shoulders. "Wren, no. Please. Stop. It wasn't a mistake. Not for me. I haven't felt this way about someone in . . . maybe ever. The distance is an issue, but we'll figure it out. If you feel the same way?"

"Really?" I was taken aback. "You want to figure it out? Like, *us*?"

"You don't?"

"No, I do, but I thought I was being irrational. Maybe because of the grief—"

"Well, you are irrational sometimes. And impossible and maddening and challenging and cannot take a joke, but also smart and beautiful and fascinating and grounded and kind and very, very decent. Also, sometimes indecent—at the right moments."

"I *can* take a joke. When it's funny. And well-timed."

"Of course that's your one takeaway from everything I just said!"

I felt a surge of happiness about which I felt instant guilt. "But isn't this so weird? Considering that Stewart just died and that's how we met and—"

"It is weird," he nodded. "But I think, so far, we do weird well."

Are things going to be weird?

I hope so.

Oh, Stewart. How is it that you've only been gone a week? Will you live forever in my mind?

"I guess weird is where I live."

"I like you and your weirdness," George said, stepping toward me, so that we were only inches apart. "You're pretty cool—for a last resort."

I shoved him. He leaned in and kissed me then, in an inappropriate place at an inappropriate time. I felt my head fall against a Smart Food popcorn bag, like a crinkly pillow, as he pressed me into the shelving behind us. A warmth coursed through me. I was delighted, I was enamored, I was falling backward as the unstable shelves shifted with a squeal.

We righted ourselves, laughing. "We really know how to pick a spot."

George let me go and began digging in his coat pocket. "Look, I know this is all jumbled and messed up and, my God, it is definitely unorthodox. I'm the lawyer; I was his friend. It's all confused. But maybe this is a good time to tell you the other reason why we're here. I mean, aside from my groveling."

"Oh. This wasn't just a ploy to get me here?" I pulled the shelving back into place. We were spending so much time in here, we really needed to buy something. That chocolate had been astronomical, but delicious. Or maybe some Popchips? I looked back at George. He was holding out an envelope. "What's that?"

"It's a letter. From Stewart."

I inhaled sharply. "Seriously?"

He nodded.

I stared at the white rectangle stiff in his fingers for a long moment before I reached out my hand to take it. It felt too valuable to have out in the air. I took it and pressed it safe against my chest. "A suicide note?"

"More like a directive."

"For me?"

George nodded. "For you."

"Why now and not before?"

"His instructions: apparently, these were inside a larger envelope reserved only for his mother. You know how the sense of drama would have appealed to him."

"So I would have found out either way then? The truth about what happened?"

"At some point. Yes. I think Helen would have waited as long as she could to tell you, but she would have had to honor his wishes in the end." George bit his lip. The fluorescents above us flickered. He braced himself, his fingers closing around the sharp edge of a shelf. "But Wren, mostly likely, everyone is going to find out eventually. In this day and age, stories like this—about celebrities—don't stay private. Helen is just buying time, trying to gather her strength and take a beat before the secret comes out. Stu was a public figure. For better or worse, we don't own his story. I need you to prepare yourself for that too."

I took a moment to digest that, dizzied by the indignity. Of course. Someone would dig up the truth. They would all know: the vultures, the press, the counter guy with the shiny face at Stewart's corner bagel shop. And they would be giddy with it—a whole other kind of loss to own. *The price of fame.*

Poor Stewart. My Stewart. Their Stewart.

My hands were shaking. "I can read it now though? The letter?"

"Of course. Just suffice it to say that Stu would have approved . . . of us."

"You read it?"

"No. No one is meant to read it but you. But I got my own this morning. I didn't know about it until today when Helen gave it to me. Promise." He crossed his heart, then leaned over and kissed my cheek, sweetly, and turned to leave.

"Wait! Where are you going?"

"To wait at the Institute. I don't want to crowd you while you read. I figured you might want privacy."

"Please don't leave!" I yelped before I could stop myself. I looked down at my shoes, up at the wall of snacks. Then, I said to the ceiling, "I think I'm scared to read it alone."

I lowered my gaze to George's face. He watched me for a minute and then slid an arm around my shoulder. "Okay. Then, I'm not going anywhere."

He bought us a cashew butter chocolate bar and we sat down at one of the dinky metal tables. My name was written on the outside of the envelope. Just seeing Stewart's handwriting tugged hard at my heart. I opened the seal.

I had written him so many letters, it was strange to have one go the other way. Like somebody flipped the universe.

CHAPTER 51

Dear Wren,

I'm going to make this short and sweet because I've got some-where to be. That's a joke, in case you still have a sense of humor after all this happens.

I'm sure you're going to be upset as fuck. I'm not feeling too amazing myself, although having finally made this decision is bring-ing me some relief. So I'll say two things up front so you know: I love you very much and it's not your fault. I'm just done. I've been battling this thing for a long while and I'm tired. I used to be afraid sometimes of what I might do to myself. Now, my fatigue outweighs my trepidation. I'm sorry I wasn't able to explain it better. Ask Kate about the details. She'll be willing to share more than my mother.

I'm doing a few things in preparation and I'm sure you'll object to all of them: First, by now you know that I've asked you to handle some funeral arrangements and such. You may have been surprised, since I hardly think of you as my ideal party planner. It's mostly a ploy to get you to spend time with my friend, George. Maybe it's a match made it hell; I don't know. But you have always reminded me of each other. I think maybe that's why I never introduced you in life. I was afraid you'd get along better than either of you do with me and leave me all alone. You both need to let loose; you're both better humans than me; you both really like Aaron Sorkin shows. Either way, the thought of you knowing George makes me feel a little better about leaving you solo—even if you only hangout for a few days.

The other part, about which you're only learning now, is that I'm leaving you some money—a bunch actually. You can't object or wave me off because I'm already dead, so just accept it. It's selfish, in truth. I'm getting the last word in our lifelong argument about your goals and potential.

The money represents two things: stability and freedom. I never appreciated your characterization of me as an overprivileged ass, but I do think there's truth to it being different to explore the world without worry. (Of course, money can't buy all peace of mind, as evidenced by my current state.)

This way, for at least a short while, you can live your life as if you don't have to worry about health insurance and salaries and gainful employment. Anyway, I can't force you to use it as I would like, but I hope you'll allow yourself at least an adventure or two—or some time off from being so damn responsible. Maybe consider the idea that there are countless ways of seeing things. What would life look like without fear?

You are one very bright spot in this world, Wren. I hope I was for you too. As much as you can, please love yourself as I have loved you. Please don't be too disappointed.

Yours Forever,
Stewart

CHAPTER 52

I read the letter three times, then buried my damp face in George's soft cashmere coat for a long time. Eventually, it was time to walk to the Institute.

George seemed to understand that I didn't want to talk. I needed a moment—before bursting into that tribute and facing all those people with my puffy red eyes—to absorb what I'd learned.

Poor Stewart. He fought so hard against this. For his whole life.

How despondent did someone have to be to make a decision like this with so much planning and clarity?

Outside, George and I paused at the bottom of the stairs, those gargoyles leering above us.

I wrung my hands. "I think I'm nervous."

"Why?"

"I know this sounds silly considering all my complaining, but what happens after this? We say this official goodbye and then what? We're just meant to resume our lives and grieve on our own? Move on?"

"Yeah. I guess so—unless you'd like to make an annual date with Blair."

I recoiled.

He laughed. "Yeah. That's what I thought."

CHAPTER 53

Stewart. I think you rendered a happy ending impossible. I hope you're happier at least. Or in less pain.

Some days, I think the worst part of your loss for me is the number of years I will have to exist on this planet without your jokes—without my partner in crime.

On other days, I am devastated by what a young Stewart would have thought of this ending: how disappointed you would have been as that third grade kid—champing at the bit to play basketball instead of learn grammar—to know that this is how your life would resolve itself. I keep thinking there must be some way to alter this outcome. But there's not. Death is as final as things get. There are no do-overs.

I choke on sadness at unexpected moments: doing the laundry, when the wrong song blasts from Alexa's speakers, walking down the street when I believe, for a moment, I've caught a glimpse of you. My eyes deceive me.

You made the world Technicolor. It will always be grayer now.

As my mother says, death is "fundamentally unacceptable." But you are gone nonetheless.

CHAPTER 54

At front, a poster was displayed on an easel welcoming guests to "A TRIBUTE CELEBRATING THE LIFE AND WORK OF ACTOR STEWART BEASLEY: BENEFITTING THE BRAIN ANEURYSM FOUNDATION." I felt strange about having roped the charity in when that wasn't Stewart's real cause of death, but I suppose it benefitted a good cause.

The sign bore the charity's logo and a picture of Stewart as Drake in that damn kitschy T-shirt. He looked happy and like he was keeping a secret. For a moment, I felt surprised that he wouldn't be here for this. Then I remembered why and righted myself. When would that understanding become the new normal? I both anticipated and dreaded it.

Inside, a crowd of people had begun to assemble—the early birds. They milled from the lobby into the gallery space, chatting quietly and sipping white wine from clear plastic cups. Many of them were strangers to me; the Institute had invited their members and the public to the event. The gallery exhibition would be up for two months, so that anyone interested could come peruse. Stewart was a celebrity. They would share him with the world.

Helen and Ted, looking a bit dazed, stood off to one side greeting people. Kate stood nearby. The family wasn't speaking to or looking at each other, but I guess, in their way, they were supporting each other by being there. Kate held Meryl's hand. She caught me looking their way, smiled, and mouthed "thank you." I wasn't totally sure for what. I smiled back. I would definitely call her to talk once the dust had settled a bit, now that I knew the truth and we could have an honest conversation.

Belle was leaning against a far wall. As far as I could tell, she still hadn't changed her clothes—same army jacket. Keith was talking at her, his hand planted on the wall above her head, but she wasn't making eye contact as she answered him. Smart girl. She looked in my direction and we nodded at each other.

I noticed Morgan Tobler and a man I recognized as her husband from Instagram pictures, as they lifted cups of wine from a passing waiter's tray. I made a mental note to find her later and say hello.

In the meantime, George and I made our way over to Helen, waiting patiently for her to finish talking to an overstuffed older couple—he with a comb-over, her with a new face. (Plastic surgery mishap, something by a symphony, catering from Café Boulud.) I was no longer nervous to face Helen. After the evening before, there was no pretense left. She was just a human being, doing her best to stay standing.

As the couple moved away toward the gallery, Helen's eyes rested on me and then George, then on our clasped hands. A small tightening of the lips was the only indication that she'd noticed anything. Was it a smile or a frown? How much did she know about Stewart's designs? "Hello, dears." We dropped hands, as she gave us each a kiss on the cheek. "The exhibition looks lovely."

"They did a beautiful job," I agreed. "I'm looking forward to checking it out with more time now."

George nodded. "I can't wait to see it."

Helen tipped her head in the gallery's direction. "Go look." We started to move away, but then she put a hand on each of our shoulders and we turned back to face her. "Thank you both. For everything. Please don't be strangers." She tried to smile, but her eyes were flooding.

"Thank *you*," I said. "For creating the most spectacular human being." I meant it.

She held my gaze until the last moment, as she turned to greet another attendee. George and I walked away toward the exhibition.

"Yo! Georgie!"

Some spray-tanned bro in a boxy suit was motioning George over. He waved and smiled, then gritted his teeth in apology to me. "Benny. From my office. He's the absolute worst. Total dick. All the stripper stories. I'm happy to introduce you, but I don't recommend it."

"Thanks for the warning." I was definitely not in the mood. "I'll be in the gallery."

I made my way through the crowd and into the show. People were examining the photos and relics, discussing them. It was like a gallery at the Museum of Natural History, only instead of "Primitive Man," we were learning about Stewart. It occurred to me that people might have liked to see the People's Choice Award, after all. *Oh well.*

I went in chronological order this time, starting with the wall text: "STEWART BEASLEY WAS BORN IN 1984 IN NEW YORK CITY TO HELEN AND THEODORE . . ."

When I got to the childhood display, I was surprised to find my photo—the one of me and Stewart after *Robin Hood*—mounted and prominently featured. Well, I wasn't exactly proud of my outburst the day before, but it seemed I'd been heard.

"Madison was able to find the photograph at Helen's this morning." I turned to find Blair standing beside me, ever orderly in a short, dark floral shift dress and heels. Her hair was, per usual, styled into symmetrical waves. The amount of money she spent at Dry Bar could fund a small country. She smelled like too many flowers. "Fernanda agreed that it deserved prominence whatever the quality, being the first example of Stewart's love of the theater."

I wasn't sure what to say. I wasn't sorry for the day before, even though I'd lost my temper. I couldn't let go of the way she'd behaved throughout this whole process, and I still had no doubt of why the photo had initially been omitted—even if she couldn't admit the truth to herself. "I'm glad," I finally replied. "It means a lot to me to have it here."

We both remained there, looking straight ahead, as people bustled past us, murmuring and remembering. She said, "There's no proof of our relationship."

"Sorry?"

"You have photos and yearbooks and trips and whatever to point to. On record, I just seem like Stu's publicist."

I turned to face Blair in surprise. She was looking at me too. "But that's not the truth. Our relationship wasn't 'surface.'"

"Okay."

"You look down on us. You think you're above it all. But we haven't done anything wrong. We're just doing our best to mourn him."

I shrugged. "Okay."

"We *all* miss him. We *all* relied on him."

Before I could censor myself, I snorted, "For what? VIP access to parties?"

Blair narrowed her eyes. "I can get that myself, thank you." She cocked her head as if trying to decide if I was worth the oxygen. Then she took a step toward me, leaning in. "You probably don't know the details and probably don't care, but deciding I wouldn't be an actor was rough on me," she said quietly. "I was in terrible shape—depressed, sad. I was threatening to move home to Minnesota to live in my parent's basement. And it's not even a finished basement."

"But is there a Ping-Pong table? Because I feel like that's really the determining factor."

She was undeterred. "It was Stu's idea that I try my hand at publicity and—despite the fact that I had literally no experience and he was taking a big risk—he put his career in my hands."

"Okay. So?"

She raised a hand to silence me; I felt like it silenced the chatter around us too. "And when, during college, Brian couldn't move back home after graduation as planned because his mother had remarried this horrible, abusive man, Stu offered him a bedroom for as long as he needed. He stayed for almost a year."

I had forgotten that. "That's true, I guess, I didn't remember—"

"And when Mal wanted desperately to go to grad school for costume design, but didn't feel confident enough to apply, Stu walked her through the application process from start to finish because he'd done it for his MFA. And, when she didn't get enough financial aid, he helped her get a part-time costume assistant job on a soap in New York—no strings. And he continued to help Brian and Mal financially from time to time because neither one of them has family support or comes from money. That's probably why they're panicking and selling his stuff on eBay."

I rocked on my feet, shifting my weight. I hadn't known that. "You think anyone makes time for Keith?" Blair continued, her voice sharpening. "Could stand listening to his god-awful bullshit? But Stu did! And he even tried to help him get cast, lord help him. That's why Keith was ever 'out in LA for pilot season.' Stu called in favors and hooked him up with a junior agent. That's why!"

Blair crossed her sinewy arms and stared at me—like it was a dare. Like she'd dropped the mic.

"So what's your point?" I shrugged and crossed my arms too. "Stewart did favors for all of you? And you'll miss the perks?"

"You don't get it, Wren," she hissed. "And, sorry, but I kind of feel like you never have. We didn't just rely on him for those acts of kindness. We relied on him to *believe* in us. When no one else did. That was his true gift. And he believed in you, too, Wren. The only difference is, you didn't believe him when he did. And now I think you're pissed that you missed out."

I felt the weight of that like an anvil to the chest.

I was struggling to find higher ground and failing. I felt like a sanctimonious ass. All I could think was, *I am a vulture too*—and maybe the worst kind. I didn't hoard his stuff or assume control of his death, but I stole away with the parts of Stewart that I wanted to own and refused to admit that anyone else had a right to his memory—or a different memory. Of course, these people had every right to claim Stewart as their loss; he had offered them so much. And, unlike me, they had allowed him to play the hero and help the underdog, something that I now realized made life meaningful for him. They allowed him to feel like something other than an empty vessel.

Maybe their mourning wasn't just about his fame. For them, he was this great beacon of hope. And they were trying desperately to hold on. I couldn't excuse all their behavior and I didn't want to, but I couldn't excuse my own either. I exhaled. "Okay."

"Okay?"

"Yes. I hear you."

She seemed to relax, her shoulders dropping from up under her ears. She adjusted her dress. We were silent for a minute.

I'd been so busy judging Stewart—and feeling pissed at him for choosing these people who seemed so despicable—that I'd missed the obvious. It wasn't fragile ego that drove him to keep the vultures around; it was tolerance. He could see their gaping weaknesses and he felt for them. Because he had what he saw as shortcomings too. Also, narcissists are good friends to choose when you don't want anyone looking too closely at you.

I figured maybe I should try to show some tolerance too. *This one's for you, Stewart.* "And Blair," I said finally. "For what it's worth, if there's anything I've realized over the course of the last week or two, it's that it really doesn't matter what other people think. It's only about what you know. The rest you can't control. We're each grieving the Stewart we knew at our most seminal points with him—not the one from last week. We're grieving who he made us."

She flushed, then looked up as if gathering strength. "But that's just the thing: I don't know anything," she said to the ceiling. "I can't remember one conversation we had really. It's like my mind has just gone blank. I'm starting to feel like maybe I invented our whole friendship!"

It was the most honest thing Blair had ever said to me. I even felt a modicum of empathy for her. Despite the painting; despite everything. I realized this must have been how Stewart saw her—vulnerable. Now, she wanted anything that the rest of us deemed important, so she could simulate closeness to him. "Blair. Stewart loved you. The truth is, he loved all of you." I had no idea how or why, but he had. I didn't say that part out loud. "He always said you would do anything for him."

I saw her absorb that. "I would have."

"He knew. And that's all that matters."

"I just feel so empty."

Me too. I exhaled a rattled breath. "I think that's loss," I said, realizing only as the words spilled from my mouth. "It's not the crying or the sadness or the organizing of funerals and tributes or the stuff you keep; it's the time in between when you miss the person and wish you could have them back. It's the absence of someone you love—the times you wish you could give them a call and then realize . . . you can't." *It's the black hole.* I missed my friend so much in that moment; I stared at that photo of him—those buck teeth. "I think we're all just trying to feel close to him in the best way we know how. Mallory and Brian do it by hoarding his stuff; Willow forces us into her ceremonies; and Keith—" That stumped me.

Blair frowned. "I'm pretty sure there's nothing redeemable about Keith."

I giggled; she did too. "I'm glad you saw that. I was worried you guys might be . . . you know . . . hanging out."

"Oh, God no! I'd rather be alone forever. He was just an available shoulder to cry on, but he pretty much moved on when I told him I couldn't represent him. I mean, he would have to actually be *in* something for me to do PR, you know? That's why I made sure he didn't get that People's Choice Award. The idea of it creeped me out, like he'd sleep with it at night or something."

We watched Keith from afar, still trying to win Belle's attention.

"I can't believe Stu is gone forever."

"It's unfathomable."

A couple of Stewart's costars from *Manic Mondays* walked through the entrance to the gallery then. They waved to Blair and she snapped back to attention, waving back. "I should go. Duty calls. I'm back to LA tomorrow, but I'm in and out of New York all the time. We should go get a gel mani or something sometime."

There was no way in hell, no matter how deep we buried the hatchet.

"You know, Wren, you and I are actually a lot alike," Blair said, flipping her hair over her bony shoulder. "However hard it was, we're not like the others; we handled this with class. I think that's why Stu loved us best."

Before I could disagree, Blair was pushing her way through the crowd toward Stewart's celebrity friends. I sighed, then remembered that I was here for a reason. I needed to find Fernanda to give her the speaker information.

Back in the now crowded lobby, the hum of conversation had amped up. I noticed Mallory and Brian standing in a corner, dwarfed by the bedlam, small and unsure, clutching each other's hands like life rafts. Now, I saw them through Stewart's eyes: insecure, alone, wounded birds. His acceptance meant everything to them; it made them feel *acceptable*. He didn't keep the vultures around to make himself feel good. He helped them because he could—because in their relationships, he could be the strong one. The one who had it together. The straight man.

I was so busy seeing them as if for the first time that I barely noticed a tall woman in a tweed trench nudging past me. "Wren!" Gretchen grabbed my hand. Jimmy stood beside her; he winked at me sheepishly.

"Gretch! I can't stop now. I just realized the time. I need to find the organizers!"

She leaned in so I could hear her above the din. "Okay. But are you still mad at us?"

Us. It made me smile, despite myself. "No! Go forth and be . . . whatever you guys are!"

Jimmy snorted. "See? She's fine!"

Gretchen ignored him. "Are you looking for George?"

"No! Why?"

"Because your parents just got here and your mother asked me which one was George and, first of all, I don't even know! And Jimmy is useless with faces. But, second of all, more importantly, why does your mother even know about him? What happened to not using your friend's death 'as an excuse for a fling'?"

I raised an eyebrow. "It's not a fling."

"Ooh," She pursed her lips. "Now, I'm really intrigued."

So much had happened; it had been days and a millennia at the same time. "Long story. For later."

Gretchen mock pouted. "Fine. Go mourn your friend and whatever. But I want the details ASAP! I'm your best friend too, you know. And I have the benefit of still being alive."

"Shhhhh." Jimmy shook his head, covering his eyes with his hand and suppressing a grin. "Dude. That's so inappropriate. You're worse than I am."

She flipped her hair over her shoulder. "What? It's a joke. Levity in times of sadness, right?"

I left them happily bickering and wove toward the entrance to the auditorium. As I'd hoped, Fernanda was standing by the closed doors. She was wearing something asymmetrical and Japanese, like she was wrapped in gray origami.

"Ah, Wren! Thank goodness!"

"I'm so sorry. There are so many people here. I couldn't find you!"

"The turnout is impressive." She surveyed the crowd. "I hope you're pleased."

"Very. Stewart would have been too."

"So I just need the name of the person who will be speaking on Stewart's behalf today." She popped the cap off her pen and readied to write on an index card.

"Right. Wren Pinkus."

She looked up at me. "That's you."

"It is."

"Okay, then. Fair enough. I'll tell them to open the doors. I look forward to hearing your words."

I found George waiting patiently at the back as everyone began to file into the auditorium. He shook his head. Apparently, I'd dodged a bullet by avoiding his coworker.

"Nightmare?"

"That guy is the worst."

"That's a distinction in this crowd. Myself included." I leaned my head against his chest and sighed. "Hey, can I ask you a question?"

"Sure."

"Is it enough money—what Stewart left me—to travel a little? Like he suggested?"

George nodded. "Is that what you want to do with it?"

I was on the fence. My immediate impulse upon reading Stewart's letter was to give the money away, donate it (and I knew I probably would). I didn't want to benefit from his death. But, as much as I hated to admit it, what Blair said had resonated. I hadn't let Stewart help and inspire me like he'd wanted to when he was alive. His letter said it was his last chance to fight for my bigger dream. The money aside, maybe it was time to pursue something larger. Travel. Try for grad school again. *Make a run at the stairs.* "Well, since I don't have a job anymore . . ."

George opened his eyes wide. "Wait, what?"

"You know how we kept wondering how everyone was keeping their jobs despite spending so much time obsessing over Stewart's death? Well, I may have overlooked a major detail and lost mine."

"Are you serious?" His forehead crinkled in concern. Maybe Stewart was right about George needing to loosen up a little. I could already see him strategizing, questions forming in his mind: Was there legal recourse for keeping the job? What were the grounds for the firing?

"Yup. But my boss was pretty cool about it, considering the enormity of the error. He said he'd been thinking I was ambivalent about the work lately and this seemed like proof. I agreed. So I'm tying up loose ends and then I'm done in four weeks."

"So what will you do?"

I shrugged. "I'm not sure, but I think first I might take Stewart's advice, crazy as that seems. He was right about you, after all. I think? Well, the jury is still out, but you know."

George smirked, then wrapped his arms around me and pulled me close. I didn't care who saw us anymore. Let them think what they would. Falling for George wasn't my worst transgression during this whole thing.

"You know, LA is nice this time of year. Maybe you should travel there? And stay." He raised his eyebrows.

I titled my head up toward his, resting my chin on his chest. "Hmm. Maybe en route to Asia. Although that seems a little roundabout since I think I'll start in Turkey. Stewart said that it was amazing in Istanbul, and I haven't been since I was a kid."

"Huh. Want a companion for part of the trip?"

"Sure! But who?"

George shook his head at my bad joke and mussed my hair. Around us, a smattering of strangers still milled.

It occurred to me in that moment that George's funeral was the only one I hadn't planned throughout this whole process. I couldn't get it right. Maybe because, even from the beginning, I didn't want to entertain its possibility.

I hadn't planned my own either.

CAUSE OF DEATH: Painless old age with all faculties intact. Obviously.

AFTER-DEATH RITUAL: I would rather not think about it, but let's just say I'm not a fan of the idea of living in a box for all eternity.

SERVICE: Large and festive.

PROCESSIONAL MUSIC: "Landslide" by Fleetwood Mac. No-brainer.

MEMORIAL BUFFET: Sushi. And that cashew butter chocolate. It's my funeral, after all. Spare no expense!

CHAPTER 55

I stood at the podium, microphone at the ready, staring into a kind of mobile darkness. The spotlights on me had rendered the audience invisible, but I could hear their movements, see flickers in the blackness. That was okay. Sometimes you don't need to see people to know they're there.

I took a deep breath and then I began:

"Hi. I'm Wren. I'm one of Stewart's oldest friends, for those of you who don't know. Since losing Stewart, I—like many of you—have found myself feeling, in my sadness, like the one person I'd like most to confide in is gone. It's started me wondering, how can we keep him with us? How can we continue to make him known to the world now that he's gone? What is his story?" I heard my voice waiver; I would insist on its strength.

"So here goes:

"What would I tell them about you? The ones who only knew your contours? You, as a paper doll on which to pin a picture?

"What would I tell the ones who shared excited whispers over green juices the morning after? Who posted the news online with frowny faces and then moved on with their days?

"What was the story I'd want them to know?

"Was it of a little kid, spastic and unchecked, bouncing off walls? Was it of a teenage you, first gawky, then too cool?

"Was it of us falling against each other during those struggling years? You, sitting next to me, wrapped in a comforter, sleep and cigarettes on your breath? For sure, it was not the story we'd all like to forget: You, alone. In those last moments.

"Would I tell them you were funny? Because you were. To me, one of the funniest people in the world. Would I tell them about your talent? Because it was boundless. But what good is something that loses all value in the dark? Would I tell them that you were adorable? Because you were. Some of the time to me, a lot of the time to others. Would I tell them that you were selfish but sweet? You had a soft spot for kindness in others but didn't require it of yourself.

"I would not tell them that you loved me, although I know now that you did. In a way that was at once simple and complicated as hell. Like a sibling. Like a best friend. Like an object. Like an idea. Like a competitor. Like a book that you once loved and still carry from apartment to apartment when you move—formative, but no longer top of mind.

"What hole did you leave in the world—aside, of course, from the one in my heart? What would I tell those strangers—even the ones who considered themselves your friends?

"What was the story of you?

"What I've realized since you've been gone is that, you, Stewart, were a man of many stories. I knew you as a dreamer—with a deep sense of irony, but also passion—who went full-throttle at everything you wanted. Others knew you as a caretaker, kind and supportive without judgment or criticism. The world knew you as charming and talented, a genteel, gracious success. There are no doubt infinite incarnations of you.

"We all knew different versions—all of them unique and vibrant—which we'll carry with us as we move about our lives, missing you, but also holding you close.

"Whoever you were, I loved you, Stewart—dimensionally and unconditionally. And I always will."

CHAPTER 56

Stewart, when I stepped down from the podium, your funeral song began to play. It was Judy Collin's "Amazing Grace." You know, the version that starts out a capella?

Amazing Grace! How sweet the sound
That saved a wretch like me.
I once was lost, but now I'm found,
Was blind, but now I see

It wasn't the song I would have picked for you in my funeral plan. Not based on the you who I knew. You probably wouldn't have picked it either.
But you know what? That didn't matter. It was beautiful.

ACKNOWLEDGMENTS

For me, as for many others, 2017 was a watershed year. The country changed hands. I had my second baby. I experienced loss on a scale I never had before: my uncle, a college friend, one of my closest friends since childhood. I started writing this book. I guess it's only fitting that I'd end up editing the manuscript during a pandemic.

Perhaps more than any other story I've written, it has been so important to me that *Competitive Grieving* "see the light of day" as a kind of tribute. (That's how I keep finding myself expressing it; read in what you will.)

Many people are to thank for making that possible: First, a huge thank you to my agent and fellow Brooklyn mom, Faye Bender of the Book Group. Your supportive and direct approach has inspired complete confidence from moment one. I'm so grateful to have you in my court.

Thank you to Addi Black at Blackstone Publishing for falling for and championing this story, to Holly Rubino and Ember Hood for your exacting eyes, and to the rest of the team for your support.

Thank you to Nicola Wheir, my literary-world Sherpa, for your boundless generosity and humor, insightful notes, and unparalleled hostess skills. Thank you to Peter Harris for your perpetual and contagious enthusiasm and for the long talks as we sorted through the rubble. Thank you to Morgan Arenson for giving me the inside scoop on grant writing. And thank you to my writing group ladies, Emily Barth Isler, Hanna

Neier, and Katie Schorr, for your invaluable feedback and for that one extraordinary trip. You know the one.

Thank you to my father, Paul, for teaching me the value of humor, especially in dark times, and to my mother, Lynn, for showing me what a strong woman (and editor) looks like. Thank you to my big sister, Claudia, for reading early drafts, answering countless texts about wording, and supplying baked goods when needed (which is always). Thank you to my in-laws, Hal and Marilyn Weiner, a dream team of negotiation coaches and cheerleaders.

Thank you to my husband and plot guru, Andrew, for believing in me more than anyone else in the world does (and probably more than I merit). Thank you to my "combo shombo" potatoes, Estella and Levi, whose hugs got me through my moments of sadness and whose laughter gets me through everything else.

Thank you to Megan Wahtera and Rachel Leonard for showing me daily what true friendship—and sisterhood—means. Thank you to Tova Weinberg for so eloquently, openly, and empathically talking me through what it means to both struggle and grieve.

Finally, Nick Zarin-Ackerman, this book goes out to you and your loving, warm family (who is fortunately nothing like the one in this book). This is not your story, but you were with me as I wrote it.

Nick, I would not be the person I am without you. You are a part of me. I miss you every single day.